Oswald Seidensticker

The first Century of German Printing in America

1728 - 1830

Oswald Seidensticker

The first Century of German Printing in America
1728 - 1830

ISBN/EAN: 9783741124112

Manufactured in Europe, USA, Canada, Australia, Japa

Cover: Foto ©Andreas Hilbeck / pixelio.de

Manufactured and distributed by brebook publishing software
(www.brebook.com)

Oswald Seidensticker

The first Century of German Printing in America

GÖTTLICHE

Liebes und Lobes gethöne

Welche in den hertzen der kinder
der weißheit zusammen ein.

Und von da wieder aufzgeflossen

ZUM LOB GOTTES,

Und nun denen schülern der himlischen
weißheit zur erweckung und auf-
munterung in ihrem Creutz und
leiden aus hertzlicher liebe mitgetheilet.

D A N N

Mit lieb erfüllet sein, brin'gt Gott den besten Preiß.
Und giebt zum singen uns, die allerschönste weiß:

++

Zu *Philadelphia:* Gedruckt bey *Benjamin
Franklin* in der *Marck-straß.* 1730,

·THE

FIRST CENTURY

OF

GERMAN PRINTING

IN AMERICA

1728 – 1830

PRECEDED BY A NOTICE OF THE LITERARY WORK
OF F. D. PASTORIUS,

BY

OSWALD SEIDENSTICKER.

PUBLISHED BY THE
GERMAN PIONIER-VEREIN OF PHILADELPHIA.

PHILADELPHIA: SCHAEFER & KORADI.
1893.
E.V.
E.M.

PREFACE.

Bibliography is the handmaid of history and in this capacity, it is hoped, the present publication will be of some service. Attention may be called particularly to the books and pamphlets, linked in some way with the German churches and sects of Pennsylvania and adjoining states. Nor are political events and party struggles without their bibliographical echo in German. Furthermore it is evident, that the successive planting of the printing press in new localities is a significant fact, marking an advance in the pioneer life of the spreading population and, hence, not to be overlooked by the historian. The kind of printing matter demanded by the people will also throw some light upon their spiritual needs and leanings, but it must be born in mind, that, in addition to the domestic supply, imported books were, even at an early period, to be had, as we see by the published lists and catalogues of Christopher Saur, Henry Miller, Franz Hasenclever, Andrew Geyer, Jacob Lahn, Christian J. Hütter and others.

An attempt at a bibliographical survey of German books, printed in America during the last century, was made by the writer in a series of articles, contributed in 1876—1878 to the *Deutsche Pionier*, a German Monthly published in Cincinnati. Newspapers and almanacs were not included, but separately treated in later publications. The present record has been extended to 1830, thus rounding a full century. New material which has since turned up could be embodied; the German papers, periodicals and almanacs have been duly registered. The latter have, without an exception, the quarto form favored by the Germans, run from 36 to 48 pages and contain reading material both instructive and entertaining. Nearly all of them have on the coverleaf a woodcut or copperplate print, representing a scene or scenery which combines realistic and emblematical elements.

Some features of the German book record are invested with special interest. As in the history of immigration, so in the history of printing the sects take the lead. Devotees to mystic transcendentalism, Inspirationists and Dunkers were the first to avail themselves of Gutenberg's art. The Ephrata publications will always belong to the curiosities of literature, but it is not generally known, that even before the founding of the Ephrata convent mystic utterances of Conrad Beissel and his friends were brought out in print by Benjamin Franklin and Andrew Bradford. Mysticism seems to have hovered over Ephrata like a *genius loci*, for, long after the cloister press had become silent, Joseph Bauman continued with the publication of theosophic and other abstruse writings.

A good deal of mystic leaven pervades also the *Kleine Davidische Psalterspiel*, which was the favorite hymnbook of the "Inspired" in Germany. In Pennsylvania it was reprinted up to 1830 at least ten times (1744, 1760, 1764, 1777, 1781, 1795, 1797, 1817, 1830) and in Baltimore once (1797), showing how popular it was with the sects. Many of its hymns were admitted in the *Weyrauchshügel* of 1739, which was compiled for the Ephrata brethren and is the first American book printed in German type.

Quite notable among the German publications are the three Germantown editions of the Bible, respectively of 1743, 1763 and 1776, all of quarto size and well printed on good Rittenhouse paper. The first English Bible printed in America, appeared in Philadelphia 1782 and was a duodecimo edition. The German Somerset Bible of 1813 is the first Bible printed west of the Alleghanies and the folio edition, published by J. Bär in Lancaster 1817, was the largest book printed in Pennsylvania up to that time.

Another famous book, of which the German edition preceded the English on American soil, is *Bunyan's Pilgrim's Progress*. Christopher Saur printed it in 1754.

It is, also, worthy of notice that the first religious magazine of Pennsylvania was the *Geistliche Magazien*, published by C. Saur in 1764 and the following years.

For the different religious denominations and sects different hymnbooks and catechisms were required. Notes accompanying the titles show for what religious bodies they were intended. Perhaps the most curious of all is the *Ausbund* (1742, 1751, 1767, 1785 and 1815) with its historical hymns in praise of persecuted Christians, mostly Baptists of Switzerland and Germany. It was in great favor with the Mennonites.

The Lutherans used in their churches a reprint of the *Marburger Gesangbuch* (1759, 1762, 1770, 1774, 1777), till in 1786 an authorized collection adapted to American churches was published. The Reformed congregations did the same, reprints of German collections appeared in 1752, 1753, 1763 and 1772 ; they were superseded by an American hymnbook (*Neu Eingerichtetes Gesangbuch*), of which the first edition came out in 1797. A fusion hymnbook for Lutherans and Reformed does not seem to have been in use till 1827.

Some years have their distinctive literature responsive to the complexion of the times. In 1742 a turbulent wave of religious controversy arose around the towering figure of Count Zinzendorf. In 1748 and still more in 1764 political dissensions led to an animated pamphlet warfare, in which the Germans heartily participated. The Revolution, also, is reflected in several German publications, the most important of which is the pamphlet of 1775, authorized by the German churches and the German Society, in favor of armed resistance.

It will be readily observed that the period after the revolution had different characteristics from that preceding it. As German printing began to spread over a larger area, its vitality appears to have receded from the old centres, Philadelphia, Germantown and Ephrata ; the successors of Saur, Miller, Steiner, Cist and the Ephrata Brotherhood were small men, who did not rise to distinction. In Philadelphia the German newspaper, which in the last century, had attained a vigorous growth, shriveled away ; no trace of it can be discovered between 1815 and 1825. On the other hand, Lancaster, Reading, Allentown, Lebanon and many other towns became quite active in German printing and several of them supported more than one paper. Lancaster could in 1817 boast of the largest book till then printed in Pennsylvania, the splendid folio edition of the German bible, published by Johann Bär, just as the *Blutige Schauplatz*, printed at Ephrata in 1748, had been the largest book of the colonial period.

The reason why German printing in Philadelphia declined is easily accounted for. German immigration received a check through the American Revolution and remained sluggish till the end of the Napoleonic era. The full effect of this shortage became the more apparent in Philadelphia as the old immigrant element gradually died away without being replaced by a sufficiency of fresh recruits. This accounts also for the difficulty of keeping up the German language in the Lutheran and Reformed churches. In the country the conditions were different. The German language had there gained a firm foothold and become hereditary from generation to generation. The German press was not exclusively dependent on the continuance of immigration. It is, perhaps, not useless to remark that the German country papers were *not* written in Pennsylvania dialect.

The whole number of places where German printing was carried on during the first century of its existence amounts to 47. Of these 31 are in Pennsylvania, 3 in Maryland, 4 in Ohio, 5 in Virginia, 1 in Massachusetts, 1 in New York, 1 in New Jersey, 1 in Nova Scotia. But the proportion in favor of Pennsylvania will be much greater, in fact, overwhelmingly greater, if the number of publishers or publications be counted. Outside of Pennsylvania only Maryland and, perhaps, Ohio and Virginia can fairly claim a German printing press prior to 1830. The only German publication of New Jersey is a Testament printed from plates that were made in Philadelphia, the only one in Massachusetts a German Reader to be used in Harvard College, and New York is represented only by a futile attempt to establish in 1819 a German paper in the city of New York. Strange as it may appear, the launch of the New York *Staatszeitung* on Dec. 24, 1834 was also the starting point of German printing in New York, an event not beyond the reach of memory of persons yet living.

Of the sources which have been drawn upon for the following compilation, collections of the books themselves were the principal ones, as they are the most satisfactory. Philadelphia harbors three of considerable extent, that of the Historical Society consisting chiefly of the Cassel Library of German Americana, that of the German Society and that of Judge Pennypacker. In addition to these, some other libraries in Philadelphia, the State Library

in Harrisburg, the Lenox Library in New York and the very fine
collection of Mr. H. Heilman in Lebanon have been consulted.
Many titles were obtained from old German newspapers, such as
Saur's Germantown paper, (Hist. Soc. of Penna.); Miller's Staats-
bote, (Hist. Soc., Phila. Library, German Soc.); Steiner's Cor-
respondenz, (Hist. Soc.); Lancaster Zeitung, Americanischer
Staatsbote and Lancaster Correspondent, (Mechanics Library in
Lancaster); Volksfreund, (Baer's Publishing House in Lancaster);
Reading Adler, (Adler Office in Reading); Morgenröthe, (State
Library in Harrisburg). Circumstances prevented the examin-
ation of the Friedensbote, of which there is a complete file in
Allentown, beginning with the year 1812. Some titles, not found
elsewhere have been copied from sales catalogues, e. g. those of
Mr. Zahm in Lancaster. For information on newspapers, county
histories were in some instances found quite useful, in others
disappointing and unreliable. Of very much service has been the
excellent work of Mr. Charles R. Hildeburn, *The Issues of the
Press of Pennsylvania, from 1685—1784*, Philadelphia 1886, and
this indebtedness has been increased by the author's kindness in
furnishing some titles of books since discovered, Correspondence
with several gentlemen outside of Philadelphia has, likewise,
resulted in useful information.

In spite of these efforts to make the record as complete as
possible, the writer is quite aware that there must be gaps and
inaccuracies. This is particularly felt to be the case in the period
from 1800—1830 in consequence of two adverse circumstances.
While the older publications have found a safe refuge in the
libraries of societies and collectors, those of more recent date are
doomed to the waste basket or lost sight of as devoid of value
and interest. And secondly, the diffusion of German printing
over a large number of towns, some of them quite small, increases
the difficulty of tracking prints older than sixty years.

A few remarks on particular points may not be amiss. There
was formerly no distinction between the printer and publisher of a
book or paper, both were combined in the same person. Some
exceptions, however, occur. G. Keating in Baltimore was
presumably only the publisher, and Samuel Saur the printer of
the book noticed under 1796; it is not believed that Jacob D.
Dietrichs of Winchester printed in 1805 the almanac, that bears

his name on the title page, it was a Hagerstown print. A few other instances of the same kind have been mentioned in the text.

Books printed abroad with the false imprint "Philadelphia", "Germantown" or "Boston" have been excluded from the following pages. Emil Weller's book on *Falsche und fingirte Druckorte*, Leipzig 1864, can, however, not be considered a safe guide, so far, at least, as America is concerned. He has put on his black list a number of German-American books the imprint of which is, unquestionably, genuine.

Titles in Roman type indicate that the whole book was thus printed.

The English publications of the older German printers have been included, as it seemed to be a matter of some interest to make a full exhibit of their printing record. It would have been impracticable to pursue the same plan with those of later times. In the case of older and rarer books the libraries have been indicated where they may be found. But the mention of one place does not imply that it is the only one. H. S. stands for Historical Society of Pennsylvania, G. S. for German Society and S. W. P. for the collection of Hon. S. W. Pennypacker. Mr. C. H. Hildeburn's name has been placed under the titles taken from his *Issues of the Press of Pennsylvania*, and those furnished personally.

The pleasant duty remains to express cordial thanks to all who in any way have rendered assistance to the writer. In examining collections of books and files of papers he has been materially aided by the courtesies of Mr. Frederick D. Stone and Mr. John W. Jordan, Hist. Soc. of Penna., Hon. S. W. Pennypacker, Phila., Dr. Wm. H. Egle, State Librarian at Harrisburg, Mr. Wilberforce Eames, Librarian of the Lenox Library, N. Y., Mr. H. Heilman in Lebanon, Mr. Wm. S. Ritter in Reading, Messrs. Reuben A. and Christian R. Baer in Lancaster. For valuable information he is much indebted to Mr. H. A. Rattermann, Cincinnati, Mr. Abraham H. Cassel, Harleysville, Pa., Mr. E. A. Weaver, Phila., H. L. Fisher, Esq., York, Mr. Charles R. Hildeburn, Phila., Rev. Dr. John G. Morris and Rev. F. Ph. Hennighausen of Baltimore. For the photographic copy of the title of the Franklin print of 1730 thanks are due to Mr. Julius F. Sachse of Philadelphia.

The Writings of Franz Daniel Pastorius.

While F. D. Pastorius plied his industrious pen on a great variety of subjects, only few of his writings were brought out in print and the couple of German books, of which he is the author, were published abroad. His literary work, therefore, does not strictly fall within the lines of a bibliography concerned with the issues of the German-American press. But considering the eminent place he occupies at the head of German immigration and the interest taken in all his doings, an exception in his favor may be allowed, especially as so little is known of his occupation as a writer.

The manuscripts which Pastorius left have been scattered and nearly all lost. But a list of their titles in his own handwriting is found in the "Beehive," the folio spoken of below and also in a little manuscript volume, "Res propriae F. D. Pastorii", in possession of the Historical Society of Pennsylvania.

I.

WRITINGS OF PASTORIUS IN PRINT.

1. Disputatio inauguralis de Rasura Documentorum. — pro Licentia Summos in utroque jure Honores ac Privilegia Doctoralia more Majorum rite capessendi d. 23, Nov. 1676. Altorffi.

> This is the thesis Pastorius submitted for obtaining the degree of J. U. L. (Juris Utriusque Licentiatus.) The only copy known is in possession of Hon. S. W. Pennypacker.

2. Vier kleine doch ungemeine und sehr nützliche Tractätlein: 1, De omnium Sanctorum vitis. 2, De omnium Pontificum statutis. 3, De Conciliorum Decisionibus. 4, De Episcopis et Patriarchis Constantinopolitanis. Das ist: 1, Von Aller Heiligen Lebens-Uebung. 2, Von Aller Päbste Gesetz-Ausführung. 3, Von der Concilien Stritt-Sopirung. 4, Von denen Bischöffen und Patriarchen zu Constantinopel. Durch Franciscum Daniel Pastorium, J. U. L.

> The dedication to Tobias Schumberg in Windsheim, former teacher of Pastorius, closes: Aus der in Pennsylvania neulichst von mir in Grund angelegten Stadt Germanopoli. A. C. 1690.

3. Ein Send-Brieff Offenhertziger Liebsbezeugung an die sogenannten Pietisten in Hoch-Teutschland. Zu Amsterdam. Gedruckt von Jacob Claus, Buchhändler. 1697.

> At the close of page 15: Von Eurem liebgeneigten Freund Frantz Daniel Pastorius. Germantown in Pennsylvania, den letzten December 1696.

4. Henry Bernhard Koster, William Davis,. Thomas Rutter and Thomas Bowyer, four boasting Disputers of this World briefly rebuked. Printed and sold by Wm. Bradford, of the Bible in New York 1697.—The writer, Francis Daniel Pastorius, has signed his name on page 15.

5. Umständige Geographische Beschreibung der zu allerletzt erfundenen Provintz Pennsylvaniae, in denen Endgräntzen Americae, in der West-Welt gelegen, durch Franciscum Danielem Pastorium. Frankfurt und Leipzig. 1700. 12 und 140 S.

> The book was edited by Melchior Adam Pastorius, the father of the writer. A new edition without any textual changes or additions appeared in 1704. There was also an earlier edition, a copy of which is owned by the Hist. Soc. of Penna., probably printed in 1692, as it is attached to a Description of Windsheim (Pastorius' native city) written by Melchior Adam Pastorius and printed at Nurnberg in 1692. It fills only 32 pages, the revised contents of which have been expanded in the edition of 1700 to 45 pages and supplemented by new material covering 95 pages.

6. Pastorius' Primer, published in Philadelphia about the year 1700.

> The existence of this book, of which no copy has been discovered, is attested by entries into the minutes of the Friends' Quarterly Meeting and by Pastorius' Cash Book. It is very likely the first school-book printed in Pennsylvania and a copy of it, if found, would be a treasure.

II.

MANUSCRIPT BOOKS OF PASTORIUS.

a. *Folio.*

Francis Daniel Pastorius his Hive, Beestock, Melliotrophium Alvear or Rusca Apium. Begun Anno Domini or in the year of Christian Acc't 1676.

This large folio written in a very close but neat and legible hand was compiled for Pastorius' children and is a sort of cyclopedia of knowledge, mainly covering history, biography, religion, ethics and language. It, also, contains extensive collections of inscriptions, epitaphs, proverbs, poetry, (original and selected), pithy sayings, acrostics etc. He himself remarks that his Hive contained in 1676 about two thousand little honey-combs and was continued for the use of his children.

The book is preserved and the property of Mrs. Washington Pastorius Germantown.

b. *Quartos.*

1. Acabemiſche Sparſtunben.

2. Miscellanea Theologica et Moralia.

3. Formulae Solennes or Several Forms of such Writings as are vulgarly in use, whereunto an Epistolography is annexed.

4. Confusanea Geometriae ober Einfältiger Unterricht vom Lanbmeſſen.

5. A breviary of Arithmetick and Arithmetical Hotch-Potch.

6. Lingua Anglicana or some miscellaneous Remarks concerning the English tongue.

7. Lingua Latina or Grammatical Rudiments.

8. Emblematical Recreations.

Transcribed into the Bee Hive.

9. Semel insanivimus omnes ober Poetiſche Einfälle.

(Original poetry in German, transcribed into the Bee Hive.)

10. Collection of some English Manuscripts.

11. Collection of English Rhymes, alphabetically digested.

Probably identical with the extensive series of couplets arranged in alphabetical order in the Bee Hive.

12. The Young Country Clerk.

13. Pennſylvaniſche Geſetze.   Item Germantown Statutes.

14. Deliciae Hortenses or Garden-Recreations.—Voluptates Api-
anae : Nectar et Ambrosia.

> English and German poems on gardening and bee rearing.   The original
> MS. is in possession of the German Society.

15. Good Counsel for bad Lawyers and Attorneys.

16. Vaticinium de Reditu Guliclmi Penni.

   c.   Octavos.

1. Itinerarium ober Reiſebeſchreibung.

2. Liber Epitaphiorum.

3. Phrasiologia Linguae Germanicae.   Krafft unb Safft ber Teut=
ſchen Helbenſprach.

> A stout volume of German synonyms, phrases etc.   Was in possession of
> the late Horatio Gates Jones, Esq.

4. Miscellanea Prima ober Acabemiſcher Sparſtunben Vorläufer.

5. Medicus dilectus ober Artzney=Büchlein.   Talia qualia Medicinalia
et Artificialia.

> A volume of 270 closely written pages, in possession of the Hist. Soc. of
> Penna.   Its first Title begins: *"Artzney und Kunst ist all umsunst ohne Gottes
> Gunst"* and is dated 1695.   The book consists of two parts; the first enum-
> erating the diseases of man and beasts with the remedies to be applied;
> the second is a list of drugs, mainly herbs, with their medical properties.

6. Oeconomia ober Kurtzer Begriff einer Wohlbeſtellten Haußhaltung.

7. Theologia Anglicana.

8. Melligo Sententiarum.

9. Calendarium Calendariorum or a Perpetual Almanack.

10. Onamastical considerations.

> A book on names, probably identical with a chapter in the Bee Hive on
> the same subject.

11. Vademecum or the Christian Scholar's Pocket book.

12. Nec tutus piscis ab Anglo, sive a few observations concerning
Angling with several tracts on husbandry.

13. Mecum Liber ibis ad Illos, quos doceo Numeros, Scribere quos doceo. Or The Widow's double Mite. To Cypher and to Write. Containing first exemplified Rules of Arithmetick and secondly Rythmical and Proverbial Copies.

14. The Good Order and Discipline of the Church of Christ.

15. The monthly Monitor, Or my First Born Son of Husbanderia.

16. Bernh. Pet. Karl's Catechism. Englished by me.

17. Apiarium oder Bienenbüchlein.

18. William Penn's Früchte der Einsamkeit von mir verteutscht.

19. English Rhymes.

20. Alvearialia.

> It appears by a communication in the Public Ledger that this manuscript is owned by a gentleman in Philadelphia, whose name is not given. It is a volume of 359 closely written pages and contains material intended to be transferred to the Bee Hive.

21. Private Annotations.

22. A Fascicle of several manuscripts.

d. Duodecimos.

1. Lingua Gallica, sive Additamenta quaedam ad Institutionem Francisci de Fenne.

2. Lingua Italica, sive Additamenta nonnulla ad directionem Caroli Caffae.

3. Anglia sic scribit sic loquitur, or True and Good English.

4. Latinae Primordia Linguae.

5. Law Terms added to the Compleat Justice.

6. Anhang zu Rolbs Gartenbüchlein.

> Some of these books were evidently compiled for use in the school which Pastorius kept in Germantown from 1702 till 1719. Two manuscripts of an entirely personal nature and not included in the list are still in existence, viz:
> Res propriae, an inventory of Pastorius' effects, owned by the Historical Society of Pennsylvania, and his Account Book from 1701 — 1719, the property of Mr. George M. Wagner in Germantown.

German-American Bibliography.

1728 — 1830.

1728.

(Philadelphia. *Andrew Bradford ?*)

Beissel, Conrad. Das Büchlein vom Sabbath.

It is a strange and remarkable fact, that German printing in America was ushered in by those religious visionaries, who, headed by Conrad Beissel, aspired to inaugurate a new era of Christianity and who,s ubsequently, became noted as the Ephrata brethren. They separated from the Dunkers on various grounds, Sabbatarianism, preference of celibacy and a system of mystic theology. Prior to the establishment of the Ephrata cloister (1735) they dwelled near the Conestoga river in Lancaster County, Beissel occupying a house on Rudolph Nägely's farm. During this time of preparation, the leader wrote and published three doctrinal tracts, which are the first outlines of the ascetic and mystic views which were fully developed in the Ephrata community.

The only knowledge we have of these books is derived from the *Chronicon Ephratense* (p. 35, English translation p. 43 and 44). It is very probable that Andrew Bradford in Philadelphia printed them, using Roman type. On the *Büchlein vom Sabbath* the *Chronicon* remarks: "It led to the public adoption of the seventh day for divine service. Before this the meetings of the brethren had been held on Sunday, and the Sabbath was quietly kept."

(Philadelphia. *Andrew Bradford ?*)

Beissel, Conrad. Neun und neunzig mystische Sprüche.

See the remarks on the foregoing book. The mystic utterances of this publication probably resembled the *Theosophische Sprüche* contained in the *Theosophische Lectionen* printed at Ephrata in 1752.

1729.

Philadelphia. *Andrew Bradford.*

Weiss, Georg Michael. V. D. M. Da. in der Americanischen Wildnusz unter Menschen von verschiedenen Nationen und Religionen hin und wieder herum gewandeldte und verschiedentlich Angefochtene Prediger, Abgemahlet und vorgestellet in einem Gespräch mit einem Politico und Neugeborenen Verschiedene Stuck insonderheit die Neugeburt betreffende,

Verfertigt und zu Beförderung der Ehr Jesu selbst aus eigener Erfahrung an das Licht gebracht. 8vo. Title and Hymn
III—V. Text 1—29 pp.

Title furnished by Mr. R. Hildeburn. Rev. G. M. Weiss was born at
Stebbeck in the Palatinate in 1700, came to America in 1725 and died at
New Goschenhoppen, Pa. in 1763. He was the earliest Reformed minister
in Pennsylvania.— There existed at the time when the pamphlet was written a sect in Pennsylvania, who called themselves the *New-born* and claimed
to be without sin or "impeccable".

1730.

Philadelphia. *Benjamin Franklin.*

Beissel, Conrad. Die Ehe das Zuchthaus fleischlicher Menschen.

The book and the time of its publication are mentioned on p. 47 (transl.
p. 58) of the *Chronicon Ephratense*, which remarks, that the "Ehebüchlein"
declares matrimony to be the penitentiary of carnal men. The title and the
imprint are given on the authority of Mr. J. F. Sachse.

Philadelphia. *Benjamin Franklin.*

GÖTTLICHE *Liebes und Lobesgethöne*, Welche in den hertzen
der Kinder der Weiszheit zusammen ein und von da wieder
aussgeflossen ZUM LOB GOTTES und nun von denen
schülern der himmlischen weiszheit zur erweckung und auf-
munterung in ihrem Creutz und leiden aus hertzlicher liebe
mitgetheilt. DANN
  Mit lieb erfüllet sein, bringt Gott den besten Preisz
  Und giebt zum singen uns die allerschoenste weisz.
Zu Philadelphia: Gedruckt bey Benjamin Franklin in der
Marckstrass. 1730. 12mo. 96 pp.

Copies of this extremely rare book are in the collections of the Historical
Society of Penna. and Hon. S. W. Pennypacker. It contains 62 hymns, all
of which appear to be original compositions written by Conrad Beissel (who
contributed 31) and his associates, during their sojourn near the Conestoga river. Mystic exaltation revels in rythmic measures and free use is
made of the vocabulary of sensual love to symbolize religious ecstacy. The
same holds true of all other hymnbooks issued by the Ephrata brethren.
They followed in the wake of men like F. Spee, J. Scheffler and G. Arnold,
who took the Song of Solomon to be a sacred pattern and unexceptionable
warrant of their style.

1730.

Philadelphia. *Andreas Bradford.*

Der Teutsche Pilgrim, mitbringende seinen sitten Calender. Auf
das Jahr nach der Gnadenreichen geburt unsers Herrn
und Heylandes Jesu Christi MDCXXXI. (welches ein gemein Jahr von 365 Tagen ist). Auf den Pennsylvanischen
Meridianum gerichtet, jedoch in denen beyliegenden Orten,

ja von Newfoundland an biss Carolina ohne merklichen
Unterschied gar wohl zu gebrauchen.   Zum ersten mahl
herausgegeben.

This is the first German almanac published in America.   No copy is at
hand to verify the title, which is taken from the Penna. Magazine of
History and Biography, vol. VI., p. 370, and evidently not quite correct.
The type used was unquestionably Roman.   Andrew Bradford, a son of
William B., the first Pennsylvania printer, established himself in Philadelphia 1712, founded the Weekly Mercury and printed a number of books
and almanacs.

1731.

Philadelphia.   *Andreas Bradford.*

Der Teutsche Pilgrim.— Calender auf das Jahr 1732.

See 1730.

1732.

Philadelphia.   *Benjamin Franklin.*

VORSPIEL DER NEUEN WELT. Welches sich in der
letzten Abendröthe als ein paradisischer Lichtesglantz unter
den Kindern Gottes hervor gethan. IN LIEBES, LOBES,
LEIDENS, KRAFFT und Erfahrungsliedern abgebildet,
die gedrückte, gebückte und Creutz-tragende Kirche auf
Erden. Und wie inzwischen sich die obere und Triumphi-
rende Kirche als eine Paradiesische vorkost hervor thut und
offenbahret. Und daneben, als ernstliche und zuruffende
wächterstimmen an alle annoch zerstreuete Kinder Gottes,
das sie sich sammlen und bereit machen auf den baldigen:
Ja bald hereinbrechenden Hochzeittag der braut des Lamms.
Zu Philadelphia: Gedruckt bey Benjamin Francklin, in der
Marckstrass. 1732. (Sm. 8vo. 200 pp.)   H. S.

This book, of which only a few Copies have been found, contains all the
hymns of the *Göttliche Liebes* and *Lobesthöne* (1730) with the addition of 55
new ones of which 24 were written by C. Beissel, the rest by Michael
Wohlfahrt, Martin Bremer and others.

Philadelphia.   *Andreas Bradford.*

Der Teutsche Pilgrim.— Calender auf das Jahr 1733.

The Pennsylvania Magazine of History and Biography (vol. VI. p. 370)
notices of Bradford's German almanacs only those for 1731, 1732 and 1733.
Whether more were issued is not known.

Philadelphia.   *Benjamin Franklin.*

* Philadelphische Zeitung.

We know of this paper only through an advertisement in Franklin's
Pennsylvania Gazette, of June 11, 1732, to which Mr. R. Hildeburn first
called attention. It reads as follows:

The Gazette will come out again on *Monday* and continue to be published on *Mondays*. And on Saturday following will be published *Philadelphische Zeitung*, or a Newspaper in High Dutch which will continue to be published on Saturdays once a Fortnight, ready to be delivered at Ten a Clock to Country Subscribers. Advertisements will be taken in by the Printer hereof and by Mr. Louis Timothee, Language Master, who translates them.

1733.

German advertisements begin to appear in the Philadelphia Weekly Mercury.

1736.

Philadelphia, *Benjamin Franklin.*

JACOBS Kampff- und Ritter-Platz, Allwo der nach seinem ursprung sich sehnende geist der in Sophiam verliebten seele mit Gott um den neuen namen gerungen, und den Sieg davon getragen. Entworffen in Unterschidlichen Glaubens- und leidens-liedern, und erfahrungsvollen austruckungen des gemuths, darinnen sich darstellet, so wol auff seiten Gottes seine unermuedete arbeit zur reinigung solcher seelen, die sich seiner fuerung anvertraut. Als auch auff seiten des Menschen der ernst des geistes im aushalten unter dem process der läuterung und abschmelzung des Menschen der Sünden samt dem daraus entspringenden lobesgethön. Zur gemüthlichen erweckung derer die das heil Jerusalems lieb haben. Verleget *Von einem Liebhaber der wahrheit die im Verborgenen wohnt.* Zu *Philadelphia,* gedruckt bey B. F. 1736. (12mo. 52 pp.)   H. S.

This volume, in typography and general appearance quite similar to the previous German issues of the Franklin press and as rare, contains another instalment of mystic hymns numbering 32, of which 28 were written by Conrad Beissel. The back of the title page has these words: *"Gott gibt dem Geist nicht nach dem maass, das geheimniss ist gross, die vernunfft kans nicht messen."* The very abstruse preface is dated: *Ephratha in der gegend Canestoges, den 27. April 1736.* The first of the conventual buildings at Ephrata was erected in 1735. The above appears to be the earliest public mention of the name.

1737.

Philadelphia, *Benjamin Franklin.*

Wohlfahrt, Michael. Die Weissheit Gottes schreyende und ruffende den Söhnen und Töchtern des Menschen zur Busse, seynde das Wort des Herrn, das Michael Wohlfahrt verkündiget hat dem Volck. In Philadelphia gedruckt und zu verkauffen bey Benjamin Franklin und Johannes Wüster in der Marckt-strass.

Advertised in the Pennsylvania Gazette, Jan. 13, 1737.

Hildeburn.

Wellfare, M. The Wisdom of God crying and calling to the Sons and Daughters of Men for Repentance. Being the Testimony delivered to the People in Philadelphia Market Sept. 1734 by Michael Wellfare; Together with some Additional Remarks on the Present State of Christianity in Pennsylvania.

Hildeburn.

This is a translation of the foregoing.

Michael Wohlfahrt, born at Memel, Prussia, 1684, was associated in early life with mystic sects, joined Conrad Beissel, 1724 at Swedes Spring, Lancaster County, and assumed in the Ephrata Cloister the name brother Agonius. He was one of the hymnwriters. Died 1741. The above pamphlet contains the substance of an address delivered in the Market at Philadelphia, September 1734, when, clothed in the garb of a pilgrim and calling himself the messenger of the Lord, he denounced the iniquities of the people and exhorted them to repent. On a previous occasion, October 14, 1729, he forced himself upon a Quaker meeting and entered into a discussion. The *Chronicon Ephratense* (p. 35, transl. p. 43,) remarks of the incident: The speeches and replies are in print, but too lengthy to reproduce them. Of these ealier publications no copy has hitherto been found.

1738.

Germantown. (Germanton.) Christoph Saur.

Der Hoch=Deutsch Americanische Calender. Auf das Jahr nach der Gnadenreichen Geburth unseres Herrn und Heylandes Jesu Christi 1739. In sich haltende: Die Wochen=Tage; Den Tag des Mo= naths; Tage welche bemerckt werden; Des Monds Auf= und Unter= gang; Des Monds Zeichen und Grad: Voll= und Neu=Licht; erst und letzt Viertel: Aspecten der Planeten samt der Witterung; Der 7 Sternen Aufgang, Süd=Platz und Untergang; Der Sonnen Auf= und Untergang; Nebst einem Bericht, woher viele im Calender vorkommende Dinge herstammen; Erklärung der Zeichen, Aderlaß= Täfflein, Anzeigung der Finsternüsse, Courten, Fären u. s. w. Eingerichtet vor die Sonnen=Höhe von Pennsylvanien: Jedoch in denen angrenzenden Landen ohne mercklichen Unterschied zu gebrauchen Zum Ersten mal herausgegeben.

Saur's almanacs were published with same title, in the same style and size and with the same wood cut on the front page, representing a landing scene, for forty years and were then continued by other firms. The Historical Society of Penna. has a complete set, (part of the Cassel Library); the German Society and Judge Pennypacker have also many of these almanacs, though no full sets. Christoph Saur made his almanacs a vehicle for disseminating religious principles and useful information. He was born at Laasphe, Westphalia, in 1693, came to Pennsylvania in 1724 and established his famous printing house in Germantown 1738. He was the first printer who used German type.

In an interesting letter written by him Nov. 17, 1738, and published in the *Geistliche Fama*, No. 25, p. 85, he mentions his recently founded establishment. Speaking of his gratitude for all the blessings bestowed upon him by God and his desire to serve and glorify the Almighty, he continues: "Therefore I have been anxious to set up in this country a German printing press, which N. bought for me and has forwarded to this place. Now I could find no more convenient device, to make it known throughout the land than to print an almanac, the title of which I send herewith, together with a copy of a translation from the English." By the latter, undoubtedly, is meant the following print.

Padlin, B. Eine Ernſtliche Ermahnung an Junge und Alte: Zu einer Ungeheuchelten Prüfung Jhres Herßens und Zuſtandes. Kürßlich aus Engeland nach Amerifa geſandt, und wegen ſeiner Wichtigfeit aus dem Engliſchen ins Deutſche treulich überſeßt: Von einem Lieb=haber der Wahrheit. Fol. 1 S.

Only two copies of this broadside are known to exist, one in the collection of the Historical Society of Penna., the other in that of Judge Pennypacker, Christopher Saur here spells his name Sauer, as he occasionally does in other prints of the earlier period.

1739.

Germantown. Chriſtoph Sauer.

Zionitiſcher Weyrauchs=Hügel Oder: Myrrhenberg, Worinnen allerley liebliches und wohl riechendes nach Apothefer=Kunſt zuberei=tetes Rauch=Wercf zu finden. Beſtehend in allerley Liebes=Wür=cfungen der in GOTT geheiligten Seelen, welche ſich in vielen und mancherley geiſtlichen und lieblichen Liedern aus gebildet. Als darinnen der leßte Ruff zu dem Abendmahl des groſſen Gottes auf unterſchiedliche Weiſe trefflich aus gedrucfet iſt; Zum Dienſt der in dem Abend=Ländiſchen Welt=Theil als bey dem Untergang der Sonnen erwecften Kirche Gottes, und in ihrer Ermunterung auf die Mitter=nächtige Zufunfft des Bräutigams ans Licht gegeben. 12mo. Vorrede 10 S. Text 792 S. Regiſter. G. S.—H. S.—P.

The Weyrauchs Hügel is a large hymn book, which C. Saur printed for the Ephrata brethren and the first American book in German type. The preface is dated: Ephrata, den 14. des 4ten Monats 1739. The work contains 654 hymns in 33 divisions, each inscribed with a heading as funtastic as the general title. After page 744 follows an appendix of 38 hymns with the separate title: Die Ehmals verdorrete, Nun aber wieder grünende und Frucht=bringende Ruthe Aarons.

The epithet *Zionitische* was probably suggested by the fact that a new monastic building was erected for the brethern in 1738 on the hill called Zion. The Weyrauchs Hügel includes nearly all hymns contained in the three Franklin prints of 1730, 1732 and 1736 with a few new ones composed by C, Beissel and his friends. But the large bulk of the text consists of material obtained elsewhere, mainly from the *Kleine Davidische Psalterspiel der Kinder Zions*, a collection of hymns used by the "Inspired" in Germany and for the first time reprinted in America by Christoph Saur in 1744.

Saur, Christoph. Ein abgenöthigter Bericht: oder zum öfftern begehrte Antwort denen darnach fragenden dargelegt; Jn ſich haltende: zwey Brieffe und deren Urſach. Dem noch angehänget worden eine Hiſtorie

von Doctor Schotte und einige Brieffe von demselben zu unseren
Zeiten nöthig zu erwegen.

The only copy known of this print is in possession of Hon. S. W. Pennypacker. It furnishes authentic and interesting details of the quarrel between
Ch. Saur and C. Beissel, of which the Chronicon Ephratense gives some
account. While the Zionitische Weyrauchshügel was being printed, Saur's
attention was called by the proof reader to the peculiar style of some of the
original hymns, one of which (No. 400) appeared to be a fulsome and
almost idolatrous glorification of Conrad Beissel. Much exercised in mind
he remonstrated with the latter and suggested the omission of the objection-
able hymn. Beissel answered with haughty insolence and Saur's retort was
a dose of sarcasm. These shots of the two saints constitute the main portion
of the pamphlet. For a translation of the incriminated hymn and the spicy
correspondence, by Judge Pennypacker, see Pennsylvania Magazine vol. XII.
p. 76—90.

Ein A. B. C. und Buchstabierbuch, bey allen Religionen ohne billigen
Anstoß zu gebrauchen.

Whether published in 1738 or 1739 cannot be determined. The book is
advertised in the almanac for 1740.

Der Hoch=Deutsch Americanische Calender. Auf das Jahr 1740 u. f. w.
Zum zweyten mal herausgegeben. 4to. 24 S.

Contains the announcement of Saur's paper, "Der Hoch-Deutsch Pennsylvanische Geschichtsschreiber," the first number of which was distributed
with the almanac.

* Der Hoch=Deutsch Pensylvanische Geschicht=Schreiber, Oder: Samm=
lung wichtiger Nachrichten, aus dem Natur uud Kirchen=Reich.
Erstes Stück. August 20. 1739. (9½ x 7 i.)

Considering that B. Franklin's Philadelphische Zeitung (1732), if published
at all, could have been only of very short duration, Ch. Saur's paper really
marks the beginning of the German newspaper of America. The publisher
at first thought, that it would do to issue a number once every three months,
but the paper appears to have come out once a month (the 16th) at the
outset. From October 1st 1756 it appeared twice a month and from January
1, 1775 every week. At first it was of small 4to. size, about 1752 it became
a folio. All the time the original subscription, 3 shillings a year, remained
the same. In 1745, 1746 and 1768 the name of the paper underwent changes,
it was at last called simply Germantauner Zeitung. In its flourishing period
it had about 4000 subscribers. Thanks to the efforts of Mr. Abraham H.
Cassel portions of the file have been saved and are now in possession of the
Historical Society of Penna., viz. from April 16, 1743 to November 1, 1751,
and from January 16, 1754 to December 1761.

1740.

Germantown. (Germanton.) Christoph Saur.

Georg Weitfields Predigten. Aus dem Englischen ins Hochdeutsche über=
setzt. Drei Theile. Erster Theil 8vo. 18 S. Zweiter Theil 16vo.
76 S.   H. S.

George Whitefield's sermons which at that time made a wonderful impression were printed in 1740 by Benjamin Franklin.

Tennent, Gilbert. Die Gefahr bey unbekehrten Predigern, vorgestellt
in einer Sermon über Marcus am VI. v. 34. Geprebigt zu Notting=
ham in Pennsylvania, den 8. März 1740. Aus bem Englischen ins
Deutsche übersetzt. 16mo. 45 S.   H. S.

Gewissenhafte Vorstellung vom Mangel rechter Kinder=Zucht und zugleich
wie solche zu verbessern wäre. Freunden und Feinden zum Nachbenken.
Gebruckt im Jahre 1740. 16mo. 32 S.   H. S.

Probably printed by Christ. Saur.

Der Hoch=Deutsch Amerikanische Calender. Auf bas Jahr . . 1741,
u. s. w. 4to. 24 S.

The copy of the Historical Society is printed in black and red. Very
likely two editions were printed, one in black, the other in two colors.

* Der Hoch=Deutsch Pensylvanische=Geschicht Schreiber, Ober: Sammlung
Wichtiger Nachrichten aus bem Natur und Kirchen=Reich.

1741.

Germantown. (Germanton.) Cristoph Saur.

Bekanntmachung. 4v. 2 S.   H. S.

Under this heading Ch. Saur published the prospectus of his Quarto Bible
which appeared in 1743. On one page the reasons are stated that induced
him to undertake the work, with some details on typography, terms of
subscription, price etc., the other is a specimen page of the print.— A similar announcement appeared in Franklin's Pennsylvania Gazette of March
31, 1742.

(Gruber, Johann Abam.) Einfältige Warnungs= und Wächter=
Stimme an bie gerufene Seelen dieser Zeit. Verfaßt im Jahr 1741.
Von einem Geringen. Psalm 74, 21. 4to. 1 S.   H. S.

A rhymed exhortation in 11 verses of 6 lines each.

Johann Adam Gruber was the son of Eberhard Ludwig Gruber (1665—
1728), a learned clergyman, who for his leaning to mysticism was dismissed
from the pulpit and became the leader of the Inspiration Separatists in
Southwestern Germany. The son joined and worked for the same sect but
in 1726 emigrated with some fellow believers (Mackinet, Gleim) to Pennsylvania and settled in Germantown. He was a ready writer in prose and
ryhme, using the pseudonym *Ein Geringer*. He resisted the solicitations of
Count Zinzendorf and probably wrote for Fresenius Nachrichten, vol. III,
Frankfurt and Leipzig 1748, the adverse account on Moravian affairs in
Pennsylvania, accompanied by an extensive array of documentary material.

Law, Wm. Die Gründe und Ursachen der Christlichen Wiedergeburth,
Ober bie Neue Geburth durch Christum. Aus bem Englischen ins
Deutsche übersetzt.

Hildeburn.

Eine Betrachtung des Lasters der Trunkenheit, welche zu einer nothwendigen und wohlgemeinten Warnung vor dem übermäßigen Trinken mitgetheilet wird. 16mo. 55 S.

Der Hoch-Deutsch Americanische Calender. Auf das Jahr . . 1742 u. s. w. Zum Vierten mal herausgegeben. 4to. 24. S.   H. S.

* Der Hoch-Deutsch Pensylvanische Geschicht-Schreiber, Oder: Sammlung Wichtiger Nachrichten aus dem Natur- und Kirchen-Reich.

Philadelphia. *Benjamin Franklin.*

Weiser, Conrad. Ein Wohlgemeindter und Ernstlicher Rath an unsere Lands-Leute die Teutschen. Fol. 2 pp.   H. S.

An election circular. Conrad Weiser, then living in Tulpehocken, advises his countrymen, not to vote for the Quakers who opposed the levying of taxes for all kinds of warfare, even defensive, but for the Government candidates. He calls attention to the dangers threatening from a league of the French in Canada and on the Ohio with the Indians.

1742.

The bibliographical record for the year 1742 owes its fullness and interest chiefly to the presence of Count Zinzendorf in Pennsylvania. Soon after his arrival in Philadelphia (Nov. 24, 1741) he arranged a series of conferences with the object of drawing the godly-minded of all German denominations and sects into a spiritual brotherhood without destroying their allegiance to their several creeds. In this he failed. The delegates from other religious bodies withdrew and left the field to the Moravians. Zinzendorf made, however, an impression on a number of Lutheran and Reformed congregations and induced them to accept ministers ordained by him or his coadjutors. The result was dissension and bitter controversy, which was spread before the public in print. Zinzendorf and his friends had their printing done mainly by B. Franklin. In the following list of the Franklin prints the reports on the Conferences are placed first. They have separate titles but continuous paging.

Germantown. Christoph Saur.

Ausbund. Das ist: Etliche schöne Christliche Lieder Wie sie in dem Gefängnüs zu Bassau in dem Schloß von den Schweitzer-Brüdern und von anderen rechtgläubigen Christen hin und her gedichtet worden. Allen und jeden Christen, welcher Religion sie seyen unpartheyisch fast nützlich. 12mo. Vorrede 10 S. Text 812 S.; Angebunden: Confessio oder Bekanntnüß von Thomas von Jmbroich. 20 S. Ein wahrhafftiger Bericht von den Brüdern in Schweitzerland. 46 S.

A large song book, highly esteemed by Mennonites. It was originally published in 1583 and printed in Basel as late as 1838, Germantown editions appeared in 1742, 1751, 1767 and 1785. It contains songs on martyred Christians, especially Baptists, persecuted, tortured and killed by other Christians. Some of the airs, such as: *Es ging ein Fräulein mit dem Krug*, and *Ich sah den Herrn von Falkenstein*, are in strange contrast with the lurid contents of the songs. Many of these give biographical details of the martyrs.

Bekanntmachung.

(Unterzeichnet.) Friedrichs Township in Philadelphia County, den 15. September 1742. Heinrich Antes. 1 Blatt. H. S.

Those desiring to hear Count Zinzendorf preach after his return from his missionary tour among the Indians were requested to come forward with their application. In *Fresenius Nachrichten*, vol. III. p. 715—717, the paper is reprinted and attributed to Pyrlaeus, a Moravian minister and close friend of Zinzendorf.

Gruber, J. A. Ein Zeugniß eines Betrübten, der seine Klage aus= schüttet über die unzeitige, eigenmächtige, übereilte Zusammen=Beru= fung und Sammlung verschiedener Partheyen und erweckten Seelen, so unter dem Namen Jmanuels vorgegeben wird. 12mo. 8 S. H. S.

Five pages in prose and three in verse. The little pamphlet appears to be aimed against Count Zinzendorf though his name is not mentioned.

Hirten=Lieder von Bethlehem enthaltend eine kleine Sammlung evangeli= scher Lieder zum Gebrauch vor Alles was arm ist, was klein und gering ist. 12mo. 128 S. Register 10 S. S. W. P.

A collection of 369 hymns of older and later dates, which Count Zinzen- dorf had printed by Ch. Saur soon after his arrival. According to *Fresenius Nachrichten*, vol. III, p. 138, another altered edition in Roman type subse- quently appeared.

Kempis. Das Kleine A. B. C. in der Schule Christi. Aus denen Werklein des gottseligen Thomas A. Kempis in Reimen verfasset und mit der H. Schrifft concordiret. Fol. 1 S. H. S.—S. W.

(Zinzendorf. Vorschlag zur Errichtung einer Deutschen Schule.)

A handbill dated Germantown, March 22, 1742, without signature. Parents wishing their children to attend German School are requested to make application April 6, 1742. The paper is reprinted in *Fresenius Nachrichten* vol. III. p. 740, and in *Büdinger Sammlungen*, vol. II, p 845, followed by another signed by Joh. Bechtel, which proposes a convention of country delegates in Bethlehem for the discussion of the school question.

Der Hoch=Deutsch Americanische Calender. Auf das Jahr . . 1743 u. s. w. Zum Fünften mal herausgegeben. 4to. 24 S. H. S.

* Der Hoch=Deutsch Pensylvanische Geschicht=Schreiber, Oder: Sammlung
Wichtiger Nachrichten aus dem Natur= und Kirchen=Reich.   H. S.

Philadelphia. *A. Bradford.*

Boehm, J. P. Getreuer Warnungs Brief an die Hochteutsche
Evangelish Reformirten Gemeinden und alle deren Glieder,
in Pennsylvanien, Zur getreuen Warschauung, vor denen
Leuthen, welche unter dem nahmen von Herrn-huther
bekandt seyn. Umb sich vor deren Seelverderblichen und
Gewissen-verwüstenden Lehre zu hüthen und wohl vorzu-
sehen, damit sie nicht durch den schein ihres euserlichen
scheinheiligen Wesens, und selbst eingebildeten Gerichtigkeit
und Heiligkeit, zu ihrer Seelen ewigen schaden, mögen ver-
führt werden. Nach dem Exempel eines Ehrwürdigen Kir-
chen-Raths von Amsterdam in Holland. Und nun vor dem
allmachtigen Gotttragender Pflicht und Schuldigkeit halben,
geschrieben von mir, Joh: Ph: Böhm, Hochteutschen Reform:
Prediger, der mir anvertrauten Gemeinden in Pensylvanien.
Zu Philadelphia: Gedruckt bey A: Bradford 1742. 8vo.
iv, 96 pp.

(Hildeburn.)

John Philip Boehm arrived in America not later than 1720 and after
ministering for several years to reformed congregations in Falkner Swamp,
Skippack and Whitemarsh was ordained in 1729. He then took his
residence at Whitepain township, Montgomery County, where "Boehm's
Church" still keeps his memory alive. He preached to the Reformed
congregation in Philadelphia when Count Zinzendorf arrived, whose
advances he repelled. The severe strictures of the *Getreue Wurnungsbrief*
were as sharply answered in Neisser's *Aufrichtige Nachricht.*

Philadelphia. *Benjamin Franklin.*

Authentische Relation von dem Anlass, Fortgang und Schlusse
der am 1sten und 2ten Januarii anno 174½ in German=
town gehaltenen Versammlung einiger Arbeiter derer meis
ten Christlichen Religionen und vieler vor sich selbst Gott-
dienenden Christen-Menschen in Pennsylvania. 4to. 15 S.

H. S.

Authentische Nachricht von der Verhandlung und dem Ver-
lass der am 14den und 15den Januarii Anno 174½ im
sogenannten Falckner-Schwamm an Georg Hübners Hause
gehaltenen Zweyten Versammlung sowol einiger Teutschen
Arbeiter der Evangelischen Religionen als Verschiedener
einzelen treuen Gezeugen und Gottsfürchtiger Nachbarn.
Nebst einigen Beylagen. 4to. 17—40 S.

H. S. — G. S.

The "Beylagen" (appendices) are:

1. Heinrich Antes Circular-schreiben vom 15. December 1741.

2. Extract eines Schreibens aus Manhatawny vom 11. Januar 1742.

3. [*Gruber, J. A.*] Einfältige Warnungs- und Wächterstimme an die geruffene Seelen dieser Zeit. Verfasst im Jahr MDCCXLI von einem Geringen.

4. [*Zinzendorf.*] Liebes-Echo einiger versammelten Seelen die geruffen sind und die kommen wollen auf die gehörte Warnungs- und Wächter-Stimme des Geringen.

Zuverlässige Beschreibung der Dritten Conferenz der Evangelischen Religionen Teutscher Nation in Pennsylvania, welche am 9., 10. und 11. Februarii 174½ in Oley an Johann de Türck's Hause gehalten worden; samt denen dieses mahl verfassten Gemein-Schlüssen. 4to. 41—58 S. G. S.—H. S.

Vierte General Versammlung der Kirche Gottes aus allen Evangelischen Religionen in Pennsylvania, Teutscher Nation; Gehalten zu Germantown am 10. 11. 12 Martii im Jahr 174½. An Mr. Ashmeads Hause. 4to. 59—76 S. G. S.—H. S.

Gruber, Johann Adam. Gründliche An- und aufforderung an die ehmahlig erweckte hier und dar zerstreuete Seelen dieses Landes, in oder ausser Partheyen, zur neuen Umfassung gliedlicher Vereinigung, und Gebets-Gemeinschaft; Dargelegt aus dringendem Hertzen eines um Heilung der Brüche Zions ängstlich bekümmerten Gemüths im Jahr 1736. 4to. 1—14 S.　　　　　　　　　　　　　　　　H. S.

This is an inexact print of a paper which Gruber had written though not published in 1736. The author, whose consent for printing it had not been asked, felt aggrieved at the liberty taken with his manuscript, a number of words and passages having been left out, altered and inserted. See *Fresenius Nachrichten* vol. III, p. 351 and 352. The 14 pages of Gruber's pamphlet, it will be observed, fill the gap of pages between the preceding and the following papers.

Extract aus unsers Conferenz-Schreibers Johann Jacob Müllers Geführten Protocoll bey der Fünften Versammlung der Gemeine Gottes im Geist, gehalten in Germantown 1742, den 6ten April und folgende Tage. Nebst einer Vorrede an die Ehrwürdige Conferenz aller Arbeiter bey der Kirche Jesu Christi in Pennsylvania. 4to. 93—102 S.　　　　H. S.

Extract aus des Conferenz-Schreibers Johann Jacob Müllers Registratur von der Sechsten Versammlung der Evangelischen Arbeiter in Pennsylvania und der Gemeine Gottes im Geist Siebender General-Synodus. Zu Philadelphia am 2. und 3ten Junii 1742. st. v. 4to. 105—120 S.   H. S.

Bechtel, J. Kurzer Catechismus vor etliche Gemeinen Jesu aus der Reformirten Religion in Pennsylvania, die sich zum alten Berner Synodo halten, herausgegeben von Johannes Bechteln, Diener des Worts Gottes. 12mo. 42 S.   H. S.—G. S.

> Johannes Bechtel (b. 1690, d. 1777) had been preaching to the Ref. congregation in Germantown since 1726. In 1742 he was drawn over to Count Zinzendorf's "Congregation of God in the Spirit" and prepared for its Reformed fraction a catechism founded on the decrees of the Synod of Berne, which was to supplant the Heidelberg Catechism. The book was reprinted in Germany verbatim in German type, even the imprint "Philadelphia. Gedruckt bey Benjamin Francklin" being reproduced.

Die Confusion von Tulpehocken. 4to. 8 S.   H. S.

> Moravian account of a quarrel about the pastorate of a Lutheran church near Stouchsburg, Berks Co. Pa, the respective parties being Caspar Stoever (here called Stiever), a Lutheran and Gottlieb Büttner, a Moravian. See also Hallische Nachrichten. N. Ed. vol. I, p. 191 and 192.

Neisser, G. Aufrichtige Nachricht ans Publicum, über eine von dem Holländischen Pfarrer Joh. Phil. Böhmen bei Mr. Andr. Bradford edirte Lästerschrift gegen die so genannten Herrnhuter, das ist, Die Evangelischen Brüder aus Böhmen, Mähren u. s. f., Welche jetzo in den Forks von Delaware wohnen. Herausgegeben von Georg Neisser, aus Sehlen in Mähren, Schulmeister zu Bethlehem. Cum approbatione Superiorum. 4to. 18 S.   H. S.

[*Zinzendorf.*] Etliche zu dieser Zeit nicht unnütze Fragen über einige Schrift-Stellen welche von den Liebhabern der lautern Wahrheit deutlich erörtert zu werden gewünschet hat.ein Wahrheit-forschender in America im Jahre 1742: So deutlich und einfältig erörtert als es ihm möglich gewesen ist Von einem Knecht Jesu Christi. 4to. 14 S.   H. S.

> Zinzendorf's answer to J. A. Gruber's 32 questions. Printed also in Büdinger Sammlungen vol. II, p. 868, and Fresenius Nachrichten vol. III, p. 329.

[*Zinzendorf.*] B. Ludewigs Wahrer Bericht de dato Germantown den 20sten Febr. 174½. An seine liebe Teutsche und wem es sonst nützlich zu wissen ist, wegen sein und seiner Brüder Zusammenhanges mit Pennsylvania. 4to. 26 S.   H. S.

[*Zinzendorf.*] Letzte Privat-Erklärung für Pennsylvania, über Jemands Bericht, der sich nicht nur über eine unter seinem Namen, ohne sein Wissen und Willen und noch dazu unganz gedruckte Schrift beschweret, sondern auch über die Gemeine des Herrn das Urtheil spricht. 4to. 12 S.   H. S.

> A reply to J. A. Gruber's complaint about the unauthorized and incorrect publication of his pamphlet.

[*Zinzendorf.*] Ludovici a Thürenstein in antiquissima fratrum ecclesin Ad taxin kai euschemosynen diaconi constituti et h. t. ecclesiae quae Christo Philadelphiae inter Lutheranos colligitur, Pastoris, Ad Cogitatus Ingenuos Pium desiderium, h. e. Epistola ad bonos Pensylvaniae Cives Christo non Inimicos . . . conscripta. Philadelphiae ex Officina Frankliniana. 4to. 8 pp.   H. S.

> Count Nicolas Ludwig von Zinzendorf, who called himself also von Thürnstein, had received from a part of the Lutheran congregation in Philadelphia a call to the ministry and hence considered himself its pastor and inspector of the Lutheran church in Philadelphia. On his collision with the Rev. Heinrich Melchior Muhlenberg see Autobiography of the latter, published at Allentown 1881. p. 142—150.

Philadelphia. *Isaias Warner.*

[*Zinzendorf.*] Diejenigen Anmerkungen, welche der Herr Autor des Kurzen Extracts etc. von dem Herren v. Thurnstein, d. z. Pastore der Evangel. Luth. Gemeine Jesu Christi zu Philadelphia in der Vorrede seiner Schrift freundlich begehret hat. 4to. 24 S.

(Hildeburn.)

> An English translation of this pamphlet was printed by B. Franklin. No copy of the *Kurze Extract* has been found. An English translation (*Compendious extract*) was printed by A. Bradford.

Printer not known, probably *Chr. Saur.*

Gruber, J. A. Kurzer doch nöthiger Bericht wegen der vor sechs Jahren verfaßten und nun ohne mein Wissen, Befragen und Willen (und das mit Beysetzung meines Namens, wie auch sonst unganz) von andern herausgegebenen Schrift: Aufforderung zur gliedlichen Gemeinschaft genant.

> Reprinted in *Fresenius Nachrichten* vol. III, p. 381—391. Zinzendorf replied in his *Letzte Privat-Erklärung.*

Philadelphia. (Printer not known.)

A Protestation of the several Members of the Lutherian and Reformed Religions in the City of Philadelphia jointly concerned in Lease of their Meeting House in Arch Street about the late Commotion which happened on Sunday the 18th of July 1742. 1 leaf.

Against Count Zinzendorf and his party.

1743.

Germantown. Chriſtoph Saur.

Biblia, Das iſt: Die Heilige Schrift Altes und Neues Teſtaments, Nach der Deutſchen Ueberſetzung D. Martin Luthers, Mit jedes Capitels kurtzen Summarien, auch beygefügten vielen und richtigen Parallelen; Nebſt dem gewöhnlichen Anhang des britten und bierten Buchs Esrä und des britten Buchs der Maccabäer. Germantown: Gedruckt bey Chriſtoph Saur, 1743. 4to. 995 u. 277 S. Reg. 3 S. Kurtzer Begriff von der Heil. Schrifft 4 S.   G. S.—H. S.—S. W. P.

First Bibel printed in America in a European language. It reproduces the text of the 32nd Halle edition and the charge of Saur's enemies that *his* Bible was not the genuine article had no foundation. The type was obtained from Heinrich Ehrenfried Luther in Frankfurt, to whom Saur made a present of 12 copies, some of which were given to distinguished persons.

Gruber, Johann Adam. Eines Geringen Bericht, was ſich zwiſchen ihm und Herrn Ludwig (Graf Zinzendorf), und andern ſeiner Zugehörigen, in der Herrnhuter Sache in Jahr und Tag begeben 1743, ſamt denen nöthigen Belegen.

Title from the reprint in *Fresenius Nachrichten* vol. III, p. 262. The original was probably printed by Christopher Saur. The book is a review of Count Zinzendorf's dealings with J. A. Gruber.

Gülbins, Samuel, geweſenen Predigers in den Drey Haupt=Kirchen zu Bern in der Schweitz ſein unpartheyiſches Zeugnüß über die Neue Vereinigung aller Religions=Partheyen in Pens Sylvanien. Wie auch von andern nöthigen Puncten. 1 Theil. 16mo. 127 S.

S. W. P.

Directed against Count Zinzendorf's scheme.

Hilbebrand, Johannes. Wohlgegründetes Bedenken der Chriſtlichen Gemeine in und bey Ephrata Von dem Weg des Heiligung. Wie derſelbe nicht allein in der Verſöhnung Chriſti, ſondern hauptſächlich in ſeiner Nachfolge zu ſuchen. Ingleichen Von der Verführung, da Fleiſch und Blut ſich zur Ungebühr des Verſöhn=Opfers Jeſu Chriſti anmaßt. Auf Begehren etlicher Freunde ans Licht gebracht durch Johannes Hilbebrand. Bey Veranlaſſung eines von der ſog. Herrenhutiſchen Gemeine erhaltenen Briefes. 45 S.   H. S.

Johannes Hildebrand (1679-1765) was one of the prominent men in Ephrata. He was looked upon as an adept in Jacob Boehme's theosophy. As a delegate to several of Count Zinzendorf's conferences he upheld the superiority of virgin life. After the third conference Hildebrand and his Ephrata colleagues withdrew from further attendance. He then took an active part in the literary warfare against Zinzendorf and the Moravians, about which see *Chronicon Ephratense*, transl. p. 152.

Hilbebranb, Johannes. Mistisches unb Kirchliches Zeugnüß der Brüderschaft in Zion, von den wichtigsten Puncten des Christenthums, nebst einem Anhang, darinnen dieselbe ihr unpartheyisches Bedencken an Tag gibt von dem Bekehrungs=Werk der sogenanten Herrenhutischen Gemeine in Pennsylvanien, unb warum man ihnen keine Kirche zustehen könne. 16mo. 44 S.   G. S.

Hilbebranb, Johanues. Schrifftmäßiges Zeugnüß von dem Himm= lischen unb Jungfräulichen Gebährungs=Werck, Wie es an dem ersten Abam ist mit Fleisch zugeschlossen, aber an dem zweyten Abam bey seiner Creußigung burch einen Speer wiederum geöffnet worden. Entgegen gesetzt dem gantz ungegründeten Vorgeben der Herrnhutischen Gemeine von einem heiligen Eheftanb, baraus sie das Ebenbilb Gottes auszugebähren vorgeben. 16mo. 20 S.   S. W. P.

Hochmann von Hochenau, Ernst Christoph. Glaubens=Bekennt= niß, geschrieben aus seinem Arrest auff bem Hoch=Gräfl. Lippisch. Schloß Detmolb, samt einer an die Juden gehaltenen Rebe. 24mo. 24 S.   H. S.

Hochmann (b. 1661), was a stirring, much persecuted teacher of mystic religion, whose views made a deep impression on Christopher Saur. His Profession of Faith was first published in 1702.

Lischy, J. Jacob Lischys Reformirten Prebigers Declaration seines Sinnes. An seine Reformirten Religions=Genossen in Pennsylvanien. 8vo. 8 S.

Jacob Lischy, a Swiss, favored Zinzendorf's "Church of Christ in the Spirit" without wishing to cut adrift from his Reformed faith. After defend- ing his straddling attitude before several conferences he, after all, abandoned his connection with the Moravians about 1748 and wrote against them. See Harbaugh's Fathers of the Ref. Church, Vol. I, p. 339—374.

Der Neue Charter. Ober Schriftliche Versicherung der Freyheiten, welche William Penn, Esq. den Einwohnern von Pennsylvanien unb bessen Territorien gegeben. Aus bem Englischen Original übersetzt. 4to. 55 S.   H. S.

Given away to all subscribers of Saur's paper.

Der Balsam von Gileab ober wie aller Partheyen Schaden zu heilen, auch von den falschen Propheten unb rechten Lehrern.

Advertised in Saur's paper Oct. 16, 1743.

Ein Kurßer Bericht von den Ursachen, warum die Gemeinschaft in Ephrata sich mit bem Grafen Zinzendorf uub seinen Leuten eingelassen. Unb wie sich eine so grose Ungleichheit im Ausgang der Sachen auf beyden Seiten befunden.

Reprinted in *Fresenius Nachrichten* III, pp. 462—474. No original copy known. It is a vindication of Ephrata against Count Zinzendorf and perhaps written by the Prior Israel Eckerlin. See *Chron. Eph.*, translation p. 154.

Ein Schreiben der herrnhutischen Gemeine aus ihrer Conferenz an Mstr Johann Hildebrand in Ephrata. Gegeben aus unserem Synodo in Philabelphia, d. 11 (22) Märtz 174⅜.   S. W. P.

It is uncertain who printed the last two publications, probably C. Saur.

Der Hoch=Deutsch Americanische Calender. Auf das Jahr . . 1744 u. s. w. Zum Sechsten mal herausgegeben. 4to. 32 S.   H. S.

* Der Hoch=Deutsch Pensylvanische Geschicht=Schreiber, Oder: Sammlung Wichtiger Nachrichten aus dem Natur= und Kirchen=Reich.   H. S.

Philadelphia. *Joseph Crellius.*

Ein Extract von der Registratur der Suprem Curt mit dem Nahmen-Register der letzthin Naturalisirten u. die Eyde mit dem Quäcker Attest.

Joseph Crellius advertises in Saur's paper of August 16, 1743 that this print is to be had at his office in Arch St. next door to the Blue Bells. The presumption is that he printed it.

* Das Hochdeutsche Pennsylvanische Journal.

From an advertisement in the Pennsylvania Gazette of Nov. 3, 1743 we learn, that Crellius started his paper in May of that year, and from a notice in Saur's *Geschicht-Schreiber* (June 13, 1743), that it was printed with English type, a supply of German type being expected.—The name of the paper is given on the authority of Thomas' History of Printing. Its publication was interrupted by sickness but resumed in November, after the printing office had been removed from Market Street to Arch Street, next door to the sign of the Blue Bells. How long the paper kept afloat we do not know. In November 1743 Crellius gave notice that he would open a German evening school. In 1746 he kept a store in Second Street and translated Benj. Franklin's *Plain Truth*. In the same year he returned to Germany, where he acted as commissioner of Emigration for New England. See Rattermann *Das Deutsche Element in Maine* in Deutsche Pionier, vol. 14, p. 142, and vol. 15, p. 78.

Philadelphia. *Isaiah Warner and Cornelia Bradford.*

Böhm, Johann Philipp. Abermahlige treue Warnung und Vermahnung an meine sehr werthe und theuer geschätzte Reformirte Glaubensverwandte wie auch alle andere, die den Herrn Jesum lieb haben, sein Heil. Evangelium und seine Heil. Sacramenten in höchstem werth halten. Fol. 4 S.   H. S.

A second warning against the Moravians. The writer signs himself: Joh. Ph. Böhm. Hocht. (eutscher) Ref. Prediger in Pensylvanien.

Bekanntmachung. Fol. 1 S.   H. S.

This is a public declaration by Vestrymen und Elders of the Reformed churches in Pennsylvania endorsing the character and doctrinal correctness of Johann Lischy. It is dated Heidelberg (Berks Co.) 29th of August 1743, and signed by nine delegates.

1744.

Germantown. Christoph Saur.

Anhang ober Appendix zu bem Charter von Verorbnungen.

Hans Engelbrecht's Göttliche Offenbahrungen sammt einer Erzählung seines wunderbahren Lebens.

Johann Engelbrecht, born at Brunswick, Germany in 1599, saw in his trances heaven and hell. An account of his visions, first published in 1640 at Hamburg, found many believers among the "awakened."

[Funck, Heinrich.] Ein Spiegel ber Tauffe mit Geist, mit Wasser unb mit Blut. Verfasset in neun Theilen. Germantown, Gebruckt im Jahr 1744. 12mo. 94 S.   G. S.

A Mennonite publication. Christopher Saur, not altogether approving of its doctrines, withheld his name from the imprint.

Luther. Der kleine Catechismus D. Martin Luthers. Mit Erläuterungen herausgegeben zum Gebrauch der lutherischen Gemeinen in Pennsylvanien. 16 unb 83 S.   G. S.

This catechism was edited, prefaced and annotated by Count Zinzendorf

Das Kleine Davidische Psalterspiel der Kinder Zions. Von Alten unb Neuen auserlesenen Geistes=Gesängen; Allen wahren Heyls=begierigen Säuglingen der Weisheit, Insonberheit aber benen Gemeinben des Herrn, zum Dienst unb Gebrauch mit Fleiß zusammen getragen, unb in gegenwärtig=beliebiger Form unb Ordnung, nebst einem boppelten barzu nützlichen unb ber Materien halben nöthigen Register, ans Licht gegeben. 12mo. iv, 530 u. Register.   G. S.

The larger *Psalterspiel*, of which the second edition appeared 1729 in Schaffhausen, contained 1047 hymns on 849 pages. Of these a selection was published as the small *Psalterspiel*, mainly for the use of the "Inspired," a sect, in which C. F. Rock, Dr. Carl and E. L. Gruber were prominent leaders. The American reprint became quite popular with some sects, Dunkers, Mennonites etc. as is evidenced by the numerous editions of the book (1744, 1760, 1764, 1777, 1781, 1795, 1797, 1813, 1829.) Many of the hymns have the mystic coloring, sentimental style and bold allegorism, favored in Ephrata.

[Tersteegen, Gerharb.] Der Frommen Lotterie, ober Geistliches Schatzkästlein.   S. W. P.

A collection of 381 tickets on which pious lines of Tersteegen and scripture passages were printed, enclosed in a neat leather case or wooden box. Good pious souls would find enjoyment and edification in drawing these cards, thus turning even play into a means of spiritual comfort.

Tractätgen von der Geringschätzung und Nichtigkeit unseres natürlichen und zeitlichen Lebens und wie wichtig und nothwendig es ist, daß man sich zu der unendlichen Glückseligkeit und ewigen Leben zubereiten lasse in der wahren Wiedergeburt. (Aus dem Englischen übersetzt.)

Verschiedene alte und neuere Geschichten von Erscheinungen der Geister, und etwas von dem Zustande der Seelen nach dem Tode. Nebst verschiedenen Gesichtern solcher die auch jetzo noch am Leben sind.

Glimpses at the world of spirits and tales of ghosts. The book went through several editions. (1748, 1755, 1792.)

Der Hoch=Deutsch Americanische Calender. Auf das Jahr . . 1745 u. s. w. Zum Siebenden mal herausgegeben. 4to. 32 S.

* Der Hoch=Deutsch Pensylvanische Geschicht=Schreiber, Oder: Sammlung Wichtiger Nachrichten aus dem Natur= und Kirchen=Reich.

Philadelphia. *Joseph Crellius.*

* Das Hochdeutsche Pennsylvanische Journal. See 1743.

1745.

Ephrata. Brüderschaft.

(Beissel, Conrad.) Urständliche und Erfahrungsvolle Hohe Zeugnüße Wie man zum Geistlichen Leben und dessen Vollkommenheit gelangen möge. Welche Ein Hoch=Erleuchteter und Gott=Ergebener Zeuge Jesu Christi, in seinem Geistlichen Tage=Werk erlernet; Und dieselbe, bey unterschiedenen Umständen, an Seine Geistliche Kinder, und Anverwandte, eröffnet; Von denselben aber um ihrer Vortrefflichkeit willen, gesammlet, und, zum Unterricht Anderer, ans Licht gegeben. 4to. 294 S. G. S. — H. S.

This work, Beissel's great effort in mystic theology and full of abstruse oddities, consists of two parts, viz. 37 Meditations and 73 Theosophic Epistles. The latter have a separate title: *Mystische und Erfahrungsvolle Episteln, in sich enthaltend, wie man zum Geistlichen Leben und dessen Vollkommenheit gelangen möge.* An earlier edition of the book published in the same year (1745) had different titles and another preface. They were removed and burned by order of Beissel, as they had been written by Israel Echerlin, against whom Beissel conceived a dislike. The new edition contains also six Epistles more than the first one. The original title, upon which Beissel is designated as "*Irenicus Theodicaeus*," i. e. Friedsam Gottrecht, reads as follows:

Zionitischen Stiffts I. Theil, Oder eine Wolriechende Narbe, die nach einer langen Nacht in der herrlichen Morgen=Röthe ist aufgegangen auf dem Gefilde Libanons, und hat unter den Kindern der Weißheit einen balsamischen Geruch von sich gegeben. Des von Gott hoch begna=

bigten unb beabelten fürtrefflichen Theologi ber Mystischen
Gottes=Gelahrtheit Irenici Theodicaei, Als welcher burch bie
Stimme bes Bräutigams bie Gefanbschaft bes aller=reinsten Geistes
ber Himlischen Sophia empfangen zur Offenbarung ber Parabisischen
Jungfrauschaft: unb ist gesalbet worben zum Priesterlichen Amt ber
Versöhnung in seiner Ihme von Gott anvertrauten Gemeine.   Beste=
henb in einer Sammlung geistlicher Gemüths=Bewegungen unb
Erfahrungs=voller Theosophisher Senbschreiben, welche von bem=
selben an seine vertraute Freunbe unb geistliche Kinber sinb gestellet
unb zu einem geistlichen Unterricht gesammlet unb ans Licht gegeben
worben.   283 S.

We have no Ephrata prints of older date than 1745.   It is likely, however,
that the strained relations between Conrad Beissel and Christoph Saur
which existed since 1739, led to the establishment of a printing press in
Ephrata, somewhat earlier than 1745.   The *Chronicon*, after discussing the
events of 1742, continues (p. 129, translation p. 152): "Soon after a printing
press was put up in the settlement." An advertisement in Saur's paper,
(Nov. 1743.) shows that a bindery was at that time in operation in the
cloister, hence it is likely that printing also was done.

Beissel, C.   Mystische Abhanblung über bie Schöpfung unb von bes
Menschen Fall unb Wieberbringung burch bes Weibes Samen.

Title in Hildebourn's Issues of the Pennsylvania Press upon Mr. Abraham H. Cassel's authority.

Eckerlin, Israel.   Die Richtschnur unb Regel eines Schreibers Jesu
Christi, welcher in bie ewigen Schätze ber Weißheit verliebet ist.
                                                                    H. S.

Burnt by order of Conrad Beissel after Eckerlin's withdrawal from the
cloister.

Eckerlin, Israel.   Der Wanbel eines Einsamen.

Burnt like the preceding print.   Title from the *Chronicon*.

Die Ernsthaffte Christen=Pflicht, barinnen schöne geistreiche Gebetter,
barmit sich fromme Christen=Herzen zu allen Zeiten unb in allen
Nöthten trösten können.   Nebst einem Anhang einer aus bem blutigen
Schau=Spiel übersetzten Geschichte zweher Blutzeugen ber Wahrheit,
Hans von Oberbam u. Valerius bes Schulmeisters.   24mo. 166 S.

Das Anbenken einiger heiligen Martyrer.   Ober bie Geschichten etlicher
Blut=Zeugen ber Wahrheit.   Nebst ihren Briefen welche sie kurtz
vor unb in ber Gefangenschafft geschrieben.   Wie solches in bem
blutigen Tooneel zu finben.   Aus bem Hollänbischen grünblich unb
treulich übersetzt burch Theophilum.   24mo. 120 S.   H. S.

A portion of T. J. Von Braht's *Het bloedig Tooneel*, of which a complete
German translation was made and printed in Ephrata in 1748.

Ernſtliche Erweckungs Stimm, in ein Lied verfaſſet über dem ſo lang
geſtandenen unb groſſen Cometen, welcher ſich im 10. Monat des
Jahres 1743 bas erſte mal ſehen ließ unb 10 Wochen lang geſtanden.
Von einem Freunb eingeſanbt unb auf beſſen Begehren zum Druck
beförbert.

Gülbene Aepfel in Silbern Schalen. Ober: Schöne unb nützliche Worte
unb Warheiten zur Gottſeligkeit. Enthalten in ſieben Haupt=Theilen.
Eſrata. Im Jahre bes Heils 1745, verlegt burch etliche Mitglieber
ber Mennoniſten=Gemeine. 12mo. 519 S. u. Regiſter.   G. S.

Hildebrand, Eckerlin etc.   An English translation of a tract against
the Moravian view on marriage.—It may have been printed
before 1745.

> The Chronicon says, (p. 129, transl. p. 152): "Soon after a printing press
> was set up in the settlement and there by the Prior's orders the same writing
> had also to be printed in the English language; but because he had done
> this arbitrarily and soon after left the Order, all his acts were annulled and
> also the English print condemned to the flames."

Germantown.   Chriſtoph Saur.

Eine Beſchreibung ber wahren Kirche, was unb wo ſie ſey.

Freymüthige unb unpartheyiſche Gebanken von ber Religion, Kirche unb
Glückſeligkeit ber Engliſchen Nation unter ber gegenwärtigen Regierung.
(Aus bem Engliſchen überſetzt).

Das Neue Teſtament unſeres Herren unb Heylanbes Jeſu Chriſti.   Ver=
teutſcht von D. Martin Luther.   Mit jebes Capitels kurtzen Summa=
rien.   Auch beygefügten richtigen Parallclen. 12mo. 592 S.

> Title in black and red.   First edition of the New Testament printed by
> Saur.

Der Hoch=Deutſch Americaniſche Calenber, Auf bas Jahr . . 1746
u. ſ. w.   4to. 24 S.   Zum achten mal herausgegeben.   H. S.

* Der Hoch=Deutſch Penſylvaniſche Geſchicht=Schreiber, Ober: Sammlung
Wichtiger Nachrichten aus bem Natur= unb Kirchen=Reich.   H. S.

> In October the title was changed into: Hoch-Deutſche Penſylvaniſche Berichte,
> Ober: Sammlung u. ſ. w.

1746.
Germantown.   *Christoph Saur.*

Die merkwürbige Geſchichte ober Bekehrung von Jacob Friebrich Duß,
ein Bäcker in Würtemberg.   Zwei Bogen.

Advertisement.

Der Pfalter des Königs und Propheten Davids. Verteutſcht von D. Martin Luther. 16mo. 251 S.   H. S.

Die umgewendete Bibel. Ein Tractätlein.

Advertisement.

Unterricht von der Einſammlung des Willens der Seelen. Ein ſtilles Herzensgeſpräch. 5½ Bogen.

Advertisement.

Vom Cometen.

Advertisement.

[Zubly, J. J.] Leichenprebigt, welche ein Reformirter Prediger in Savannah in Georgia einem alten lutheriſchen Prediger gehalten.
Advertisement in Saur's paper.
Rev. J. Chr. Gronau, pastor of the Salzburg Lutheran emigrants at Ebenezer near Savannah, died Jan. 11, 1745. John Joachim Zubly who preached the funeral sermon was born in St. Gallen 1724, came with his father to America in 1725, was sent to Halle to study divinity and after being ordained returned to America, where he became a prominent Reformed minister.

Der Hoch=Deutſch Americaniſche Calender. Auf das Jahr . . 1747 u. ſ. w. 4to. 32 S.   H. S.—G. S.

*Hoch=Deutſche Penſylvaniſche Berichte, Oder: Sammlung Wichtiger Nachrichten aus dem Natur und Kirchen=Reich.   H. S.
After the May number the word Hoch=Deutſche was dropped.

1747.
Ephrata. Druck der Brüderſchaft.

Das Geſäng der einſamen und verlaſſenen Turtel=Taube, Nemlich der Chriſtlichen Kirche. Oder geiſtliche u. Erfahrungs=volle Leidens= u. Liebes=Gethöne. Als darinnen beybes bie Vorkoſt der neuen Welt als auch bie barzwiſchen vorkommende Creutzes= und Leidens=Wege nach ihrer Würde bargeſtellt, und in geiſtliche Reimen gebracht von einem Friedſamen nach ber ſtillen Ewigkeit wallenben Pilger. Und nun zum Gebrauch ber Einſamen und Verlaſſenen zu Zion geſammlet und ans Licht gegeben. 4to. Vorbericht 5 S. Vorrede 14 S. Text 495 S. Regiſter 7 S.
Some copies have additional pages not numbered.
The first hymnbook printed in Ephrata. It contains only original material, consisting of 378 hymns inclusive of those already in the Franklin books of 1730, 1732 and 1736. Of the whole number about two-thirds were contributed by Conrad Beissel, showing his aptitude in this kind of composition. The rest were written by about 25 brethren and sisters in Ephrata, among whom Ludwig Höcker, Peter Miller and Michael

Wohlfahrt were the most prominent. The whole collection is divided into five parts, viz. *Der geistliche Brautschmuck der heiligen Jungfrauen, Das Kirren der einsamen und verlassenen Turteltauben, Abendländische Morgenröthe, Gülfende Herzensbewegung n der unter den Fittigen der verlassenen Turteltaube gesammleten Einsamen, Die zerfallene Hütte Davids.*

What is called *Vorrede von der Singarbeit* is really a Treatise on Harmony written by Conrad Beissel, which, in view of the charming effect of the Ephrata choral music, deserves attention.

There are several editions of the *Turteltaube* without change of date, but differing in extent and arrangement.

Germantown. (Germanton.) Chriſtoph Saur.

Ein Geringer Schein des Verachteten Lichtleins der Warheit, die in Chriſto iſt. . . Herausgegeben von einem Liebhaber der Wahrheit, auf Gutſinden und Koſten der Brüderſchafft, die ſolches Zeugnus träget. 16mo. iv, 28 S.

[Hildebrand, Joh.] Eine ruffende Wächterſtimme an alle Seelen die nach Gott und ſeinem Reich hungernd ſind. Oder eine Vorſtellung, wie der arme Menſch im göttlichen Leben erſtorben und im 4 elementiſchen Leben aufgewacht. Aus Erfahrung geſchrieben von einem nach Gott und ſeinem Reich ſehnenden Herzen. 12mo. 159 S.   H. S.

Holme, Benjamin. Ein Ernſtlicher Ruff in Chriſtlicher Liebe an alles Volck, ſich zu dem Geiſt Chriſti in ihnen zu bekehren. In Engliſcher Sprache herausgegeben von Benjamin Holme und ins Teutſche überſetzt 1744. Und noch einmal gedruckt zu Germanton 1747. Auf Koſten der Freunde. 12mo. 77 S.   H. S.

The first edition of Holme's, "A serious call in Christian love to all people", a Quaker book, appeared in London 1725.

Klare und Gewiſſe Wahrheit [Pſalmen 119, v. 160, Titum 1, v. 7.) Betreffend den eigenblichen Zuſtand ſo wohl der Wahren Friedliebenden Chriſten und Gottesfürchtigen als auch der verfallenen Streit= oder Kriegs=Süchtigen, zuſammt ihrer beyder Hoffnung und Ausgang. Schrifftmäſſig dargelegt von einem Teutſchen Geringen Handwerks-Mann. 8vo. 15 S.

A reply to "Plain Truth" upon religious grounds. Christopher Saur strongly opposed warfare of any kind.

Noch mehr Zeugnüſſe der Wahrheit, von einem Bauersmann im Buſch. Similar to the preceding.

(Terſteegen.) Geiſtliches Blumen=Gärtlein Inniger Seelen; Oder kurtze Schluß=Reimen, Betrachtungen und Lieder über allerhand Wahrheiten des Inwendigen Chriſtenthums; Zur Erweckung, Stär=kung und Erquickung in dem Verborgenen Leben mit Chriſto in Gott. Nebſt der Frommen Lotteri. In Teutſchland zum 4ten Mahl gedruckt und nun in America das erſte Mahl. 16mo. 486 S.   G. S.

Terſteegen, G. Glückliche Genügſamkeit der Stillen im Lande.
Brüderlich Lehr= Troſt= und Vermahnungsſchreiben von Gerhard
Terſteegen.

Eine Teutſch und Engliſche Grammatic, beſonders geeignet vor Teutſche
die Engliſch lernen wollen. Germanton Gedruckt bey Chr. Saur.
Advertisement.

Der Hoch=Deutſch Americaniſche Calender. Auf das Jahr . . 1748
u. ſ. w. 4to. 32 S. H. S.—G. S.

Penſylvaniſche Berichte, Oder: Sammlung Wichtiger Nachrichten aus
dem Natur= und Kirchen=Reich. H. S.

Philadelphia. Gotthard Armbrüſter.

[Franklin B.] Die Lautere Wahrheit, Oder Ernſtliche Betrachtung
des gegenwärtigen Zuſtandes der Stadt Philadelphia und der Provinz
Pennſylvanien. Von einem Handwercksmann in Philadelphia. Aus
dem Engliſchen überſetzt durch J. Crell. 12mo. 20 S. H. S.

A translation of Benjamin Franklin's famous pamphlet "Plain Truth"
which advocated vigorous measures for the defence of the frontiers of
Pennsylvania. The Quakers and the German non-resistant sects (Mennonites, Dunkers etc.) deprecated resort to arms and hence arose an animated
controversy in which the Germans took an active part. The following
passage, which occurs in Plain Truth p. 20, gives Franklin's opinion on the
Germans:

"Nor are there wanting, amongst us, Thousands of that *Warlike Nation*,
whose sons have ever since the time of Caesar maintained the character he
gave their fathers, of joining the most *obstinate courage* to all the other
military virtues. I mean the *brave* and *steady Germans*. Numbers of whom
have actually borne arms in the service of their respective princes; and
if they fought well for these tyrants and oppressors, would they refuse to
unite with us in defence of their newly acquired and most precious Liberty
and property?"

Deutſche Schrift gegen Chriſt. Saur.

A pamphlet, no copy of which has been found, censured Ch. Saur for the
stand he took on the war controversy. The latter makes in his paper the
following remark:

Und iſt in Philadelphia ein Büchlein gedruckt, nur allein, um den Saur recht
zu ſchänden, ſchmähen, läſtern mit allen erſinnlichen Scheltworten als Fantaſt,
Sophiſt, dummer Eſel, Maulchriſt, Hund, Narr, u. ſ. w., womit der Schreiber
beweiſen will, daß er ein guter Chriſt ſey.

Neu=eingerichteter Americaniſcher Geſchichts=Calender, auf das Jahr nach
der Gnadenreichen Geburt unſers Herrn und Heylands Jeſu Chriſti
1748, u. ſ. w.

This almanac, with slightly changed title, always fronted with the same
wood cut was printed by different publishers about twenty years. There
can hardly be any doubt that Gotthard Armbrüster, formerly an apprentice
and journeyman of Chr. Saur, printed its first issue. He located in Phila-

delphia as a printer about the time when Crellius left and perhaps took the same office in Arch Street, which the latter had occupied.

1748.

Ephrata. Brüderſchaft.

Braght, Tieleman Jans. Der Blutige Schau=Platz oder Mär=
tyrer=Spiegel der Tauffs=Gesinnten oder Wehrlosen Christen, die
um das Zeugnus Jesu ihres Seligmachers willen gelitten haben und
seynd getödtet worden von Christi Zeit an bis auf das Jahr 1660.
Vormals aus unterschiedlichen Chroniken, Nachrichten und Zeugnüssen
gesammlet und in Holländischer Sprach heraus gegeben von T. J. V.
Braght. Nun aber sorgfältigst ins Hochteutsche übersetzt und zum
ersten mal ans Licht gebracht. [Vignette einen Arbeiter mit Grab=
scheit vorstellend. Umschrift: Arbeite und hoffe.] Ephrata in
Pensylvanien, Drucks und Verlags der Brüderschafft. Anno
MDCCXLVIII. Fol. 2 Theile, Erster Theil: Vorrede 56 S.
Text 478 S. Register 6 S. Zweiter Theil: Vorrede 14 S. Text
950 S. Register 8 S. G. S.—H. S.—S. W. P.

This splendid folio is the largest and, in some respects, most remarkable
book of the colonial period. Pennsylvania Mennonites requested their
brethren in Holland in 1745 to have Tieleman van Braght's great work,
Het bloedig Toneel of Martelaars Spiegel der Doopgezinde, of weerelose Christenen
translated into German, but were not gratified. The Ephrata brethren
undertook the laborious task, making the translation, manufacturing the
paper and doing the printing and binding. Fifteen men were kept at work
on it during three years, though not without interruption, as the supply of
paper sometimes gave out. The copperplate for the print facing the title,
representing the army of martyrs marching towards heaven, was probably
executed in Holland.

Ephrata. M. M.

Die Beschreibung des Evangeliums Nicodemi. Von dem leyden unseres
Herren Jesu Christi, u. ſ. w. 16mo. 88 S. H. S.

Germantown. Chriſt. Saur.

Crisp, Stephan. Eine Kurtze Beschreibung einer langen Reise aus
Babylon nach Bethel. Aus dem 5ten Druck ins Teutsche übersetzt
1748. 16mo. 38 S.

Erscheinungen der Geister u. ſ. w. Zweyte Auflage.
See 1744.

Frell, Georg, von Chur in Graubündner Land. Von dem wahren,
ewigen Friedsamen Reiche Christi u. ſ. w. Allen Chatholisch=Evan=
gelisch=Friedfertigen Gutherzigen Christen zu weiterer Nachtrachtung
und Ermahnung u. ſ. w. 12mo. 15 S. G. S.

A plea for peace, gratuitously distributed. Frell lived at the time of the
Reformation.

Frey, A. Andreas Freyen seine Declaration oder: Erklärung auf welche Weise und wie er unter die sogenannte Herrnhuter Gemeine gekommen; und warum er wieder davon abgegangen. Nebst der Beweg=Ursache, warum ers publicirt. 16mo. 88 S.   H. S.

Two years later A. Frey published a notice in Saur's paper, that he had not revoked nor would revoke his declaration against the Moravians.

Eine Gründliche Anweisung zu einem Heiligen Leben zu gelangen. Ueber= setzt 1747. 1 Blatt.

Ein Gründliches Zeugnüß gegen das kürzlich herausgegebene Büchlein, genandt Plain Truth oder Lautere Wahrheit. Von einem Teutschen Bauers=Mann in Pennsylvanien. 8vo. 24 S.

Sets forth that the Lord who has protected us so long will also shield us hereafter without requiring our carnal arms. This pamphlet was gratuitously distributed.

[Hohburg, Christian.] Kurzer und erbaulicher Auszug oder: Denkwürdige Sprüche aus Christian Hohburgs Postilla Mystica über die Evangelium. 12mo. 311S.   G. S.

Christian Hohburg (1607 — 1675) came into serious conflicts with the church authorities on account of his mystic theology. He died as minister of a Mennonite congregation in Hamburg.

Kurze Beschreibung des Lebens und Todtes von Jacob Schmieblein aus Wollhausen im Luzerner Gebiet in der Schweiz, welcher im Jahr 1747 im Monath May die Woche vor Pfingsten in Luzern verbrannt worden. 16mo. 16 S.   H. S.

Eine Kurze Vermittelungs=Schrift, in sich haltende eine Ansprache an alle Menschen doch ins Besondere an die, die um Gott und göttlicher Dinge wegen mit Eiffer angezogen sind als mit Kriegs=Waffen für Göttliche Wahrheiten zu streiten. Gedruckt zu Germanton bey C. S. im Jahre, da die Gerichte Gottes augenscheinlich mit Macht anfangen, einzu= brechen. Zum Nutzen und Verbesserung des menschlichen Geschlechts. 16mo. 35 S.   H. S.

Jacob Lischys Reformirten Predigers zweyte Declaration seines Sinnes an seine Reformirte Religions=Genossen in Pennsylvanien. Auf Begeh= ren guter Freunde herausgegeben. 4to. 20 S.   H. S.

About Lischy see 1743.

Ein Mystischer das ist ein vor der alten Natur und Vernunfft und Eigenheit verborgener Seelen Spiegel, geschrieben aus Erkantnus und Erfahrung. 16mo. 62 S.   H. S.

Mystic and theosophic speculations in the vein of the Ephrata school.

Der Sigenische Catechismus oder ein Auszug aus dem Heidelberger Catechismus.

(Advertisement.)

Tersteegen, Geret. Warnungs=Schreiben wider die Leichtsinnigkeit. Aus dem Holländischen übersetzt. 12mo. 48 S.

Verschiedene Christliche Wahrheiten und Kurtze Betrachtung über das kürtzlich herausgegebene Büchlein, Genandt Lautere Wahrheit. Aufgesetzt zur Überlegung von einem Handwerksmann in Germanton. 8vo. 32 S.

Another thrust against "Plain Truth". This pamphlet, also, was given away.

Der Hoch=Deutsch Americanische Calender, Auf das Jahr . . 1749 u. f. w. 4to. 36 S.

The almanac for 1749 as well as later ones in the series of the Hist. Soc. are printed in red and black.

* Pensylvanische Berichte, Oder: Sammlung Wichtiger Nachrichten aus dem Natur= und Kirchen=Reich. H. S.

Ein Christ besuchet oft und gerne die Zions=Kinder nah und ferne. 8vo. 8 S.

(Hildeburn.)

Date and printer uncertain.

Philadelphia. Gotthard Armbrüster.

Böhm, J. Ph. Der Reformirten Kirchen in Pennsylvanien Kirchen=Ordnung, welche im Jahr 1725 von D. Joann Phillip Böhm, damahls von den versammelten Gliedern der Reformirten Kirchen einhellig erwählten Prediger aufgestellet, und vor der Menge der Glieder vorgelesen, welche alle Glieder vor nützlich und gut gehalten, und auch willig angenommen haben etc. Von Joann Phillip Böhm, Prediger zum Falckner=Schwamm und Whitpen. Philadelphia. Gedruckt bey Gotthard Armbriester, wohnhaft in der Arch=strasse. 8vo. Vorrede 8 S. Text 14 S. H. S.

(Hildeburn.)

Very rare. The very prolix title of the little book goes on to say that the Kirchen-Ordnung or liturgy being approved by the elders was submitted to the consideration of Walter DuBois and Henry Boel of New York and Vincent Antonides of Long Island, correspondents of the Classis at Amsterdam and on their recommendation sanctioned by the Classis. Being then adopted by the various Reformed congregations it worked well. The coetus of the Reformed churches in Pennsylvania, recognized by the synods of Holland, at the meeting on Sept. 28th 1748 ordered the liturgy to be printed.

Grammatica Anglicana concentrata, Oder Kurtzgefaßte Englische Grammatica, worinnen die zur Erlernung dieser Sprache hinlänglich nöthige Grundsätze auf eine sehr deutliche und leichte Art abgehandelt sind. 8vo. 118 S.

(Hildeburn.)

The English Grammar is followed on p. 97 by "A short Appendix of a German Grammar whereby an Englishman may easily obtain a knowledge of the German language."

Kurtze Verteidigung der Lautern Wahrheit gegen die sogenannte Unter= schiebliche Christliche Wahrheiten, welche der Buchdrucker C. S. in Germantown ohnlängst ausgestreuet. Vorgestellet in einem Brief von einem 3ten Handwerksmann in Philadelphia an seinen Freund im Lande geschrieben.

Wenn man des Narren Kopf im Mörser stieß wie Grütz.
So ließ sein Herz doch nicht von seiner Narren Mütz.
8to. 17 S.   H. S.

A Treatise showing the need we have to rely upon God as sole Protector of this Province. 8vo. 26pp.

(Hildeburn.)

Against Franklin's *Plain Truth.*

Verhandlungen des Coetus von Pensylvanien.

(Hildeburn.)

Neu=eingerichteter Americanischer Geschichts=Calender. Auf das Jahr 1749 u. s. w.

* Deutsche Wöchentliche Zeitung.

Not a single number of this paper has come to light and its title is not known. G. Armbruster advertised in the *Pennsylvania Gazette* of February 2, 1748 that he was publishing a German Newspaper once a fortnight. Christopher Saur remarks in his *Berichte* of May 16, that Armbruster's paper would, after May, 29. appear every week. He closes with the request, that dishonest subscribers who had never paid him would not play the same trick on Armbruster. It is not likely that the paper outlived its first year.

Philadelphia. Johann Böhm.

Hochreutiner, J. J.   Schwanen Gesang, Oder Letzte Arbeit des weiland Ehrwürdigen und Hochgelehrten Herrn Johann Jacob Hochreutiner, bestimmten Prediger der Reformirten Gemeinde zu Lancäster. . . Mit einer Zuschrifft versehen von Michael Slatter. 4to. 15 S.

Rev. J. J. Hochreutiner, sent to America by the Synod of Holland and preparing to accept a call to Lancaster, died in Philadelphia Oct. 14, 1748 by the accidental discharge of a gun.

It is very probable that Benjamin Franklin acquired in 1748 or early in 1749 the printing stock of Gotthard Armbrüster and continued with the aid of Johann Böhm the German book printing business in Arch Street. G. Armbrüster's name can not be authenticated on any prints after 1748, while the imprint of B. Franklin and J. Böhm is found on publications of 1749 and the two following years. From the *Hallische Nachrichten* (p. 384, new ed. p. 526) we learn that Franklin bought the outfit of a German printing establishment and with the help of a German foreman printed Luther's small catechism. The letter containing this information is dated April 11, 1749.

1749.

Germantown. Ch. Saur.

Kempis, Thomas A. Vier Bücher von der Nachfolger Christi.

H. S.

Thomas A. Kempis. The Christian Pattern, or the Imitation of Jesus Christ, being an Abridgement of the Works of Thomas A. Kempis. By a Female Hand. London Printed MDCC-XLIV. Germantown: Reprinted by Christophor Sowr. 12mo. 278 pp. G. S.— H. S.

Lischy, Jacob. V. D. M. Prediger der Reformirten Gemeinden über die Susquehanna in Pennsylvanien. Eine Warnende Wächter-Stimme an alle Gott und Jesum liebende Seelen. Hergenommen aus dem überaus wichtigen Evangelio von den Falschen Propheten. 8vo. 48 S.

H. S.

With severity and sarcasm Lischy inveighs against his former friends, the Moravians.

Treuherzige und Einfältige Anweisung, wie sich solche Gutwillige Seelen zu verhalten haben, welche theils von den groben Welt-Geistern und Lock-Vögeln zum Mitmachen, theils von denen Unlautern Seelen-Werbern und Neben-Buhlern unter guten Schein zu ihrer Nachfolge gereitzet, gelocket, angefochten und überlauffen werden. Dargelegt zur Prüfung, Verwahrung und Warnung von Einem durch Schaden gewitzigten Gemüth. 16mo. 40 S. H. S.

(Zubly, J. J.) Sie bekehren sich aber nicht recht. Eine Predigt.

Advertised in Saur's paper Sept. 1, 1749. About Rev. J. J. Zubly see the year 1746.

Der Hoch-Deutsch Americanische Calender, Auf das Jahr . . 1750 u. s. w. 4to. 36 S.

* Pensylvanische Berichte, Oder: Sammlung wichtiger Nachrichten aus dem Natur- und Kirchen-Reich. H. S.

In addition to the regular issue on the 16th of each month numbers were occasionally published on the 1st, but not numbered.

Philadelphia. Johann Böhm. (Franklin & Böhm?)

[Volck, Alexander.] Das Entdeckte Geheimnüß der Bosheit der Herrnhutischen Sekte, zu Errettung vieler unschuldigen Seelen, zur Warnung der mit Vorurtheilen eingenommenen Gutmeyner, und zur Offenbahrung der Verirrten und verwirrten Verführer vor dem Angesichte der ganzen Christenheit. Gesprächsweise dargelegt von Alethophilo und Timotheo Verino. Mit einer Zuschrift an seine Hoch=Ehrwürden, Hrn. Johann Philipp Fresenium, Predigern und Pastorn zu St. Catharinen in Frankfurt am Mayn.

This book, an unsparing denunciation of Count Zinzendorf and the Moravians, appeared originally in Frankfurt and Leipzig 1748. The reprint, of which only an imperfect copy has been available, was advertised in Saur's paper Dec. 1749.

Philadelphia. Franklin & Böhm.

Luther, M. Der Kleine Catechismus des sel. D. Martin Luther.

No copy of the book is known, but that it was printed by Franklin & Böhm in 1749 appears from *Hallische Nachrichten* p. 384 (New Edition p. 526).

Ein Jeder sein eigner Doctor, oder des armen Land Manns Artzt. In sich haltend: Wie sich jedermann durch schlechte und leichte Mittel von allen, oder doch von den meisten Krankheiten, die in diesem Climate gemein sind, curiren kan u. s. w. Zuerst in Englischer Sprache geschrieben und zum öfftern gedruckt, nun aber um seiner Vortrefflichkeit willen in das Teutsche übersetzt worden durch P. M. 16mo. 40 S.

G. S.

Neu=eingerichteter Americanischer Geschichts=Calender. Auf das Jahr 1750 u. s. w. Zum dritten mal ans Licht gegeben. 4to. 36 S.

H. S.

Printed in black and red. G. Armbrüsters printing establishment appears to have passed into the hands of Benjamin Franklin, who associated himself with Johann Böhm for the printing of German books.

* **Philadelphier Teutsche Fama.**

This paper is several times mentioned in Christopher Saur's *Berichte* of 1749 and 1750 in the course of a controversy. Saur speaks of Böhm's *Philadelphier Teutsche Fama* but it is probable that Franklin & Böhm's partnership covered also this paper.

1750.

Ephrata. Brüderschaft.

Liebreicher Zuruf der Väter, Freunden und Gönner in Europa gethan an die von Ihnen gesandte Hirten in Pensylvania an ihrem Lob= und Dank=Fest wegen deren glücklicher Ankunfft so jährlich fället auf den 15. Januarii. 4to. 28 S.

(Hildeburn.)

Has probably reference to the arrival of "awakened" recruits from Gimsheim in the Palatinate, in 1749. Among those that joined the Ephrata settlement at that time were Lohmann and Kimmel. See Chronicon Ephr. p. 186, Transl. p. 218—219.

Germantown. Christoph Saur.

Göttliche Liebes-Andacht mit einer Anweisung und Unterricht, wie man die Liebes-Andacht in der Stille und Ruhe des Gemüths üben soll vor GOTT. Samt einer Erklärung, worinnen die wahre und falsche Gemüths-Ruhe bestehe. 16mo. Vorrede 9 S. Text 53 S.

H. S.

Der Kleine Kempis, oder Kurtze Sprüche und Gebätlein. Aus denen meistens unbekannten Werklein des Thomas A. Kempis zusammengetragen zur Erbauung der Kleinen. Vierte Auflage. 16mo. 162 S.

Schule der Weisheit in Reimen oder Hochteutsches A. B. C. vor Schüler und Meister in Israel. 16mo. 144 S. H. S.

Der Hoch-Deutsch Americanische Calender. Auf das Jahr . . 1751 u. s. w. 4to. 36 S.

* Pensylvanische Berichte, Oder: Sammlung Wichtiger Nachrichten aus dem Natur- und Kirchen-Reich. (9½ x 7). H. S.

[*Fenelon.*] The Archbishop of Cambray's Dissertation on Pure Love. With an account of the Life and Writings of Madame Guion, the Lady for whose sake the Archbishop was banish'd from Court. . . . . . Together with an apologetic Preface. 8vo. xcvii & 120 pp. H. S.

Reprint of a London edition.

Philadelphia. Benjamin Franklin und Johann Böhm.

Neu-eingerichteter Americanischer Geschichts-Calender. Auf das Jahr 1751 u. s. w.

* Philadelphier Teutsche Fama.

See 1749.

1751.

Germantown. Christ. Saur. (Sauer.)

Ausbund, das ist: Etliche schöne Christliche Lieder, wie sie in dem Gefängnüß zu Bassau . . . gedichtet worden. 12mo. 812 S. G. S.

Appended are: Fünff schöne Geistliche Lieder. Gedruckt im Jahr 1752. 40 S. not found in the edition of 1742.

Eine Nützliche Anweisung Oder Beyhülfe vor die Teutschen um Englisch
zu lernen: Wie es vor Neu-Anfommende und andere im Land geboh=
rene Land= und Handwercks=Leute, welche der Englischen Sprache
erfahrne und geübte Schulmeister und Preceptores ermangelen,
vor das bequemste erachtet worden; mit ihrer gewöhnlichen Arbeit
und Werckzeug erläutert. Nebst einer Gramatic ver diejenigen, welche
in andern Sprachen und deren Fundamenten erfahren sind. 12mo.
287 S.   G. S.

Tersteegen, G.   Der Frommen Lotterie.

    Advertised in Saur's Paper.

Zublin, Johann Joachim.   Evangelisches Zeugnuß vom Elend
und Erlösung der Menschen, in zwey Predigten abgelegt. Von
Johann Joachim Zublin, Prediger bey einer englischen Gemeinde
ohnweit Carlesstade. 8vo. 32 S.   H. S:

    Carlesstade is probably a translation of Charlestown.

Der Hoch=Deutsch Americanische Calender, Auf das Jahr . . 1752
u. s. w.   4to. 36 S.

    This almanac contains the first instalment of the dialogues contiuued
from year to year between a new comer and an older inhabitant of Pennsylvania, on a variety of topics, such as religion, laws, customs, agriculture,
gardening, climate etc. In England and the provinces the Gregorian calender
was adapted in this year, hence it numbers only 355 days, eleven days being
skipped after the 2nd of September.

* Pensylvanische Berichte, Oder: Sammlung Wichtiger Nachrichten aus
dem Natur= und Kirchen=Reich.   H. S.

Philadelphia. Benjamin Franklin und Johann Böhm.

(Arndt.) Des Hocherleuchteten Theologi Herrn Johann Arndts wei=
land General=Superintendenten des Fürstenthums Lüneburgs u. s. w.
Sechs geistreiche Bücher vom Wahrem Christenthum. . . Neue Auf=
lage mit Kupfern, samt richtigen Anmerkungen, kräfftigen Gebetern
über alle Capitel und einem sechsfachen Register. 8vo. Vorrede
u. s. w. 32 S. Text 1356 S. 65 Kupfer.   H. S.

    This is the largest book printed in Philadelphia during the last century
The American preface is written by the Lutheran minister, Rev. J. A
Christoph Hartwig, the subscription list contains 512 names, among them
those of prominent Lutheran and Reformed clergymen, which goes to show
that the publication was countenanced by the churches. But the sects, also,
took very kindly to the writings of Arndt, who in Germany had been
arraigned for his leaning towards mysticism and other unorthodox isms.
The plates inserted in the American edition were imported.

Philadelphia. Benjamin Fräncklin.

Neu-eingerichteter Americanischer Geschichts-Calender. Auf das Jahr 1752 (Welches ein Schaltjahr von 355 Tagen ist.) u. s. w. 4to. 40 S.   G. S.

Johann Böhm died in July 1751 and thus B. Franklin, spelled "Fräncklin", became the sole representative of the firm. The printing office, as is stated on the title page of this almanac, was still in Arch street.

* Deutsche und Englische Zeitung.

Known only through the following advertisement in the *Pennsylvania Gazette* of Sept. 12th and later dates.

"At the German Printing Office in Arch Street is now printed every Fortnight a Dutch and English Gazette, containing the freshest Advices, foreign and domestick with other entertaining and useful Matter in both Languages, adapted to the Convenience of such as incline to learn either. Subscribers to pay five Shillings per Annum."

This was the first bilingual paper in America. The English text was very likely a reprint of that in Franklin's *Pennsylvania Gazette*. The statement in Thomas' *History of Printing* (2d edition vol. II. p. 144) followed by Hildeburn (*Issues of the Press in Pennsylvania*, vol. I, p. 265), to the effect that the paper was printed by G. Armbruster, cannot be verified. The German almanac for 1752, which must have been issued at this time, has Franklin's imprint and it is altogether improbable that two German printing establishments, both in Arch Street, existed then in Philadelphia.

1752.

Ephrata.

Beissel, C. Erster Theil der Theosophischen Lectionen, betreffende die Schulen des einsamen Lebens. 4to. Vorrede 2 S. Text 432 S.   G. S.

Turgid and confused utterances on ascetic, mystic and theosophic doctrines. The volume also contains *Theosophische Sprüche* and *Theosophische Gedichte*. No second part was published.

Germantown. Christ. Saur.

Evangelisches Zeugnuß von der falschen Fleisches-Religion in allen Seeten der Christenheit nach ihrem Ursprung, eigentlichem Wesen und dreifacher Stütze. 16mo. 16 S.   H. S.

(Geistreiche Lieder, welche sowohl bey dem öffentlichen Gottesdienste in denen Reformirten Kirchen der Hessisch-Hanauisch-Pfälzisch-Pensylvanischen und mehreren andern angräntzenden Landen, als auch zur Privat-Andacht und Erbauung nützlich können gebraucht werden. Nebst Joachim Neandri Bundes-Liedern mit beygefügten Morgen-Abend- und Communion-Gebätern, wie auch Catechismo und Symbolis. Nach dem neuesten Gesangbuch, welches gedruckt zu Marburg bey Joh. H. Stock, nun zum ersten mal gedruckt zu Germanton bey

Chriſtoph Saur. 12mo. Geſangbuch 562 S. u. Reg. Catechiſmus, Gebäter, Evangelien und Epiſteln, Zerſtörung Jeruſalems u. ſ. w. 123 S.   H. S.

First Reformed hymn-book printed in America.

Thomas von Jmbroich. Bekantnuß eines Chriſten. 20 S. Ein wahrhafftiger Bericht von den Brüdern im Schweitzerland 46 S. Fünf ſchöne Geiſtliche Lieder 40 S.

These are the contents of a supplement belonging to and bound with the "*Ausbund*", published 1751.

Der Kleine Catechiſmus des ſel. Dr. Martin Luthers. Nebſt den gewöhn= lichen Morgen= Tiſch= und Abend=Gebeten. . . Nebſt einem Anhang der ſieben Buß=Pſalmen, einem Geiſtlichen Liede und das Ein mal Eins. 16mo. 140 S.   G. S.

[Mühlenberg, H. M.] Unpartheyiſche Gedanken in Reimen bey Einweihung einer Evangeliſchen Kirche in Germanton. Mitgetheilt von einem Fremblinge unter Meſach, den 1. October 1752. Fol. 4 S.   H. S.

That H. M. Muhlenberg was the writer of this dedicatory poem appears from *Hallische Nachrichten*, N. Ed. p. 466—469 where the text is reprinted. The enlarged Lutheran church at Germantown was solemnly dedicated Oct. 1, 1752.

Steiner, J. Conrad. Ref. Pred. in Germantown. Wächter=Stimm aus dem verwüſteten Sion in Penſylvanien an deſſen Lehrer und Wächter, insbeſonder an das geſamte Volck insgemein. 4to. 16 S.

Rev. J. C. Steiner of Winterthür, came to Pennsylvania in 1749 and obtained the favor of a part of Schlatter's congregation, finally supplanting the latter as pastor of the Ref. congregation. The above "Watchman's call" is written in verse.

Der Hoch=Deutſch Americaniſche Calender, Auf das Jahr . . 1753 u. ſ. w. 4to. 40 S.

* Penſylvaniſche Berichte, Oder: Sammlung Wichtiger Nachrichten aus dem Natur= und Kirchen=Reich.   H. S.

Lancaſter. H. Müller & S. Holland.

Circular=Schreiben der Vereinigten Reformirten Prediger in Pennſylvanien an die daſige ſämmtliche Reformirten Gemeinen, darin ſie kürtzlich darlegen, wie der große Jehovah die von S. E. Mich. Slatter, V. D. M. an unſere Chriſtl. Kirchenväter übernommene Commiſſion zu ihrer Rettung und Hülfe in Gnaden geſegnet und wie ſolches von ſothanen Gemeinen ſolle gebührend erkant, mit Dankſagung ange=

nommen werben. Zu allgemeiner Nachricht herausgegeben von G. M. Weiß, J. P. Leydich, J. Lischy. 4to. 11 S.

Exceedingly rare. A copy is in the Reformed Library at the Hague.

The Rev. M. Schlatter, after five years' work in Pennsylvania, went, at the request of the Reformed synod, in 1751 to Europe for the purpose of presenting the cause of the destitute Reformed Churches in America and to solicit aid. He was successful to the amount of £12,000, mostly contributed in Holland.

* Die Lancasterische Zeitung: Oder: Ein Kurtzer Begriff der Hauptsächlichsten Ausländisch= und Einheimischen Neuigkeiten. Fol. 13 x 8½.

A bilingual paper, the first column in German, the second in English. At first it was issued by H. Müller and S. Holland at the New Printing Office in King's Street. The twelfth and following numbers were printed by S. Holland, at the Post Office in King's Street. It is possible, that the printer H. Müller is identical with Henrich Miller, who will be mentioned under the year 1760.

Philadelphia. Benjamin Franklin.

Neu=eingerichteter Americanischer Geschichts=Calender. Auf das Jahr 1753.

As the series of this almanac was continued, Franklin was presumably the publisher. Whether the paper, begun in 1751, was also continued, is not known.

1753.
Germantown. Chr. Saur.

Die Kleine geistliche Harfe.

Hymnbook for Mennonites.

Die Neue Acte enthaltend was ein jeder Beamter, als der Feldmesser, Sheriff, Coroner und die übrigen zu Lohn haben sollen.

Advertisement.

Neu= vermehrt= und vollständiges Gesang=Buch, worinnen sowohl die Psalmen Davids nach D. Ambrosii Lobwassers Uebersetzung hin und wieder verbessert als auch 700 auserlesener alter und neuer Geistreichen Lieder begriffen sind. Welche anjetzo sämtlich in denen Reformirten Kirchen der Hessisch=Hanauisch=Pfälzischen und vielen andern angrenzenden Landen zu singen gebräuchlich in nützliche Ordnung eingetheilt. Mit dem Heidelbergischen Catechismo und erbaulichen Gebätern versehen. 12mo. Psalmen 214 S. Lieder 562 S. u. Reg. Heidelberger Catechismus 2c. 123 S.   H. S.

The "Lieder" or hymns were printed 1752.

Der Hoch=Deutsch Americanische Calender, Auf das Jahr . . 1754 u. s. w. 4to. 40 S.   H. S.

* Penſylvaniſche Berichte, Oder: Sammlung wichtiger Nachrichten aus
dem Natur= und Kirchen=Reich. H. S.

The fatal Consequences of the unscriptural Doctrine of Predesti-
nation and Reprobation. With a caution against it. Written
in High Dutch by M. K. and translated by Desire. 16mo.
14 pp.

Grew, T. Mathematical Professor. The Description and Use of
the Globes, celestial and terrestrial. With a variety of
examples. 16mo. 60 pp. H. S.

Theophilus Grew was professor at the Academy,

Siegvolck, Paul. The Everlasting Gospel, commanded to be
preached by Jesus Christ, Judge of the Living and the Dead
unto all creatures. Mark XVI. 15, Concerning the eternal
redemption found out by Him. Written in German by Paul
Siegvolck and translated into English by John S. 16mo.
vii and 152 pp.

Pleads for the doctrine that all souls are finally saved. A reprint of the
German original was published by Ch. Sour in 1768.

Der letzte Wille des hochfürſtlichen Printzen Diederichs von Anhalt Deſſau.,
des alten Regierenden Fürſten von Deſſau und Preuſſiſchen General=
Feldmarſchall ſein Sohn, geſchrieben in Jahr 1753. Fol. 1 S.
H. S.

A poem on the vanity of earthly things. Publisher and year of publication not certain.

Lancaſter. S. Holland.

* Die Lancaſterſche Zeitung: Oder: Ein Kurzer Begriff der Hauptſächlichſten
Ausländiſch= und Einheimiſchen Neuigkeiten.

The last (31st) number of the paper, in the possession of the Historical
Society of Pennsylvania, is dated June 5, 1753.

Philadelphia. Anton Armbrüſter.

Benkendorf, Henricus. Seliger Marter Stand der erſten Chriſten
oder von den Zehen Haupt=Verfolgungen der erſten Chriſten Neues
Teſtaments u. ſ. w. 12mo. 326 S. G. S.

Habermann, Joh. Das groſſe Gebetbuch.

Advertisement in the Lancaſterſche Zeitung.

Joh. Habermann or Avenarius (1516—1590), Lutheran minister and
Prof. of theology at Jena and Wittenberg, wrote a Hebrew grammar and
other linguistic works; his prayer book, of which there was a large and a
small edition, attained great popularity, also in America.

Neu=eingerichteter Americanischer Geschichts=Calender — Auf das Jahr 1754 u. s. w. Zum Erstenmal ans Licht gegeben. Philadelphia. Gedruckt und zu finden bei Anton Armbrüster, wohnhaft in der Archstrasse.   G. S.

Anton Armbrüster, a brother of Gotthard A., now appears as the sole publisher of this almanac and calls the issue of this year the first. He gave the title page a new cut representing multitudinous objects of heaven and earth strangely jumbled together. It is not unlikely, however, that Benjamin Franklin was still the owner of the press and types in the Arch Street office, which A. Armbrüster used.

1754.

Ephrata. Brüderschaft.

[Beissel, C.] Paradisisches Wunder=Spiel, welches sich in diesen letzten Zeiten und Tagen in denen Abend=Ländischen Welt=Theilen als ein Vorspiel der neuen Welt hervorgethan. Bestehende in einer gantz neuen und ungemeinen Sing=Art auf Weise der Englischen und himmlischen Chören eingerichtet. Da dann das Lied Mosis und des Lamms, wie auch das hohe Lied Salomonis samt noch mehrern Zeugnüssen aus der Bibel und andern Heiligen in liebliche Melodyen gebracht. Wobey nicht weniger der Zuruf der Braut des Lamms, samt der Zubereitung auf den herrlichen Hochzeit=Tag trefflich praefigurirt wird. Alles nach Englischen Chören Gesangs=Weise mit viel Mühe und großem Fleiß ausgefertiget von einem Friedsamen, der sonst in dieser Welt weder Namen noch Titel suchet. Ephrata Sumptibus Societatis. 1754. Folio. 212 S. u. Reg.
                                                                                  S. W. P.—H. S.

Printed on writing paper. Most of the space is given to staff lines intended to be filled out by written notes. Provision is made for choruses of four voices, in some pieces for six and even seven voices. The text over' the staff consists partly of hymns, partly of adaptations from Solomon's Song and the Revelation of St. John. Altogether there are 49 pieces, 20 of which are also found among the hymns of the later Wunderspiel of 1766. The *"Friedsame"* on the title page is *Conrad Beissel* who was called in the cloister, *Vater Friedsam Gottrecht.*

Bunian, Johann. Eines Christen Reise nach der seeligen Ewigkeit. Zwei Theile. 12mo. 280 und 264 S.   H. S.

Freame, John. Scripture-Instruction; Digested into several sections by way of question and answer. With a preface relating to Education. 16mo. 162 pp.
                                                                                  Hildeburn.

Reprint of the Londen edition of 1713.

Germantown. (Germanton.) Chriſt. Saur.

Hildebrand, Johannes. Ein Geſpräch zwiſchen einem Jüngling und einem Alten von dem Nutzen der gottſeeligen Gemeinſchafften. 12mo. 24 S.

> About Hildebrand see 1742, 1743.

Der Wunderbare bußfertige Beichtvater und Seel=Sorger Herr M. Aaron, Prieſter der Großen Stadt Babel. Herausgegeben von C. A. einem Exulanten welcher um der Wahrheit willen vertrieben. 16mo. 36 S.

> Sale catalogue.

Der Hoch=Deutſch Americaniſche Calender. Auf das Jahr . . 1755 u. ſ. w. 4to. 48 S.

*Penſylvaniſche Berichte, Oder: Sammlung Wichtiger Nachrichten ꝛc. Fol. 1754.

> Though enlarged and now regularly issued twice a month the price of the paper was not raised.

Germantown. *Christoph Sower, Jr.*

Christian Education. Exemplified under the Character of Paternus instructing his only Son. 12mo. 7 pp.

The Pennsylvania Town and Countrymen's Almanac for 1755. 16mo.

> These English almanacs of small size appeared till 1760 and perhaps later.

Philadelphia. [A. Armbrüſter.]

Neu=eingerichter Americaniſcher Geſchichts=Calender. Auf das Jahr 1755. Zum zweyten mal ans Licht gegeben.

1755.

Ephrata. Brüderſchafft.

Nachhall zum Geſang der einſamen Turtel Taube. Enthaltend eine neue Sammlung Geiſtlicher Lieder. 8vo. 112 S.   H. S.

> The *Turteltaube* appeared 1747.

Germantown. (Germanton.) Chriſtoph Saur.

Ein Bettler und doch kein Bettler, Ein jeder ein König, wann er will. In Engliſcher ſprach gedruckt zu Philadelphia 1749. Und zur Erwägung und Nutzen der Deutſchen überſetzt. 16mo. 45 S.

> H. S.

J. Bunians Pilgrims= oder Christen Reise aus dieser Welt nach der Zukünfftigen. Der dritte Theil. 16mo. 144 S.   H. S.

Bunyan, J. Das angenehme Opfer oder die Vortrefflichkeit eines verbrochenen Herzens. 16mo. 151 S.

> Bound together with the preceding.

[Crisp, Stephen.] Eine Kurtze Beschreibung einer langen Reise aus Babylon nach Bethel. Zweyte Auflage. 16mo. 38 S.   G. S.

> First German edition appeared 1748.

[Kemper, Henry.] Treuhertzige Erinnerung und Warnung bestehend in vielen Klag=Reden vom Verfall des Christenthums im äußerlichen Gottesdienst. 16mo. 12 u. 78 S.   G. S.

Das Kinder=Büchlein in den Brüder=Gemeinen. 16mo. 16, 210 u. 62 S.

Das Neue Testament Unsers Herrn und Heylandes Jesu Christi. Ver=teutscht von D. Martin Luther. 12mo. 562 S.   H. S.

> Second edition, with a preface of Christopher Saur.

[Saur, Ch.] Eine zu dieser Zeit höchst nöthige Warnung und Erin=nerung an die freye Einwohner der Provintz Pensylvanien von Einem, dem die Wohlfahrt des Landes angelegen und darauf bedacht ist.   H. S.

> An appeal to the Germans to assert and guard their rights as freemen in the face of nativistic schemes.

[Skougal, H.] Das Leben Gottes in der Seele des Menschen. 16mo. 21 S.

Verschiedene alte und neuere Geschichten von Erscheinungen der Geister und etwas von dem Zustand der Seelen nach dem Tode. Nebst verschiedenen Gesichtern solcher die auch jetzo noch im Leben sind. Dritte und vermehrte Auflage. 12mo. 201 S.   G. S.

Der Hoch=Deutsch Americanische Calender, Auf das Jahr . . 1756 u. s. w. 4to. 48 S.   H. S.

* Pensylvanische Berichte, Oder: Sammlung Wichtiger Nachrichten aus dem Natur= und Kirchen=Reich. Fol. (13 x 8 i.)   H. S.

Philadelphia. Anton Armbrüster.

[Smith, W.] Eine Kurtze Nachricht von der Christlichen und Liebreichen
Anstalt, welche zum Besten und zur Unterweisung der Armen Teutschen
und ihrer Nachkommen in Pennsylvanien und anderen daran gräntzen=
den Englischen Provinzien in Nord=America errichtet worden ist.
Herausgegeben auf Befehl derer zur Ausführung dieser Sache
bestimmten Herrn General Trustees. 4to. 16 S.   H. S.

> This is a German translation of Wm. Smith's *Brief History of the Rise and
> Progress of the Charitable Scheme etc.* It was this scheme that found in
> Christopher Saur a vigorous adversary. He insisted that behind the cloak
> of charity political intentions were lurking. For interesting details see.
> Harbaugh's *Life of Michael Schlatter* and W. H. Smith's *Life and Correspond-
> ence of Rev. Wm. Smith*, vol. I, p. 52 — 79.

Philadelphia. Benj. Fränklin u. Anton Armbrüster.

Neu=eingerichteter Americanischer Geschichts=Calender.   Auf das Jahr
1756.   Zum Drittenmal ans Licht gegeben.

* Philadelphische Zeitung von allerhand Auswärtig= und einheimischen
merkwürdigen Sachen. Fol.

> At the bottom of the fourth page: Gedruckt und zu finden bey B. Fränklin
> General Postmeister und Anthon Armbrüster in der britten Strasse zwischen der
> Marck= und Erb=Strasse.

> This paper was one of the publications of the "Society for propagating
> Christian knowledge among the Germans in Pennsylvania", which was
> subsidized by wealthy Englishmen and managed in Pennsylvania by a Board
> of Trustees, consisting of James Hamilton, William Allen, Richard Peters,
> Benjamin Franklin, Conrad Weiser and Rev. Wm. Smith, D. D. The
> latter was the most active promoter of the enterprise. The same society
> established a number of German free schools in German settlements of
> Pennsylvania. An avowed purpose of the Society was to counteract the
> influence of Christopher Sower. In 1754 the Trustees resolved to set up a
> German press and to print a paper, almanacs and other popular publications,
> Benjamin Franklin's offer to sell them his German printing establishment
> for a sum 25 pounds under its ascertained value, was accepted.

> The editorship of the Philadelphische Zeitung was offered to Rev. H. M.
> Muhlenberg, who declined and proposed his colleague, the Rev. Johann
> Friederich Hundshub for the place. The latter accepted and edited the
> paper probably as long as it existed.

1756.

Ephrata. Brüderschafft.

Ein Angenehmer Geruch der Rosen und Lilien, die im Thal der Demuth
unter Dornen hervor gewachsen. Alles aus der brüderlichen Gesell=
schafft in Bethania. Im Jahr des Heils 1756.

Darauf ein zweiter Titel:

Ein Angenehmer Geruch der Rosen und der Lilien, die im Thal der
Demuth unter den Dornen hervor gewachsen. Alles aus der schwes=

terlichen Geſellſchafft in Saron.   Im Jahr des Heils 1756.   4to.
26 S. und Anhang von 28 S.   PHILA. LIBRARY.

    Saron was the convent of the Sisters.

Das Bruderlied oder ein Ausfluß Gottes und ſeiner Liebe aus der
Himmliſchen und Paradiſiſchen Gold=Ader oder Brunnen des Lebens
entſprungen.   Aus der Brüderlichen Geſellſchaft in Bethanien entſproſ=
ſen und herfürgebracht.   4to. 30 S.   H. S.

    Bethania was the convent of the brethren.   The *Bruderlied* is the joint
effort of a number of brethren, each contributing his say in the same metre
and general tenor.

Germantown.   (Germanton.)   Chriſt. Saur.

Chamberlain, Thomas.   Eine Erinnerung an die Engliſche
Nation, daß ein jeder die rechte Zeit wahrnehmen ſoll.   Geſchehen
von einem Prediger, welcher ſeine eigene Leichenpredigt gehalten.
Eine Warnung vom Himmel an alle boshafte Sünder auf Erden.
12mo. 14 S.   H. S.

    Translation from the English.

Dickinſon, Jonathan.   Die Göttliche Beſchützung iſt der Menſchen
gewiſſeſte Hülfe und Beſchirmung zu allen Zeiten auch in den gröſſeſten
Nöthen u. Gefahren.   Aus Erfahrung gelernet.   Bey einer merck=
würdigen Geſchichte, da verſchiedene Perſonen aus der groſſen Waſſers
Gefahr errettet worden, in dem ſie nicht nur Schiffbruch erlitten,
ſondern auch aus dem noch grauſameren Rachen der Canibalen oder
Menſchenfreſſern in Florida ſind befreyet worden.   12mo. 98 S.

                                             H. S.

    The incident here recounted happened in 1696.   The fourth English
edition of the book appeared in Philadelphia 1751.

Eine Erzehlung von den Trübſalen nnd der Wunderbahren Befreyung ſo
geſchehen an William Flemming und deſſen Weib Eliſabeth, welche
bey dem verwichenen Einfall der Indianer über die Einwohner im
groſſen Wald (Grät Grov) bey Cannagobſchick in Penſylvanien ſind
gefangen genommen worden.   12mo. 98 S.   G. S.

    Translated from an English original printed in Lancaster.

Jmrie, D.   Des Ehrwürdigen Lehrers David Jmries, Predigers in
St. Mungo in Schottland, Send=Schreiben an ſeinen Freund in
Edinburg, verkündigend die baldige Erfüllung der groſſen und ſchröck=
lichen und auch herrlichen Erfolgungen.   12mo. 26 S.   H. S.

    Translation from the English.

Der Hoch=Deutſch Americaniſche Calender.   Auf das Jahr . . 1757
u. ſ. w.   4to. 48 S.

*Penſylvaniſche Berichte, Ober: Sammluug wichtiger Nachrichten, aus
    dem Natur= und Kirchenreich.   H. S.

[*Fenelon.*] The uncertainty of a death-bed repentance. By the
    Bishop of Cambray. 12mo. 16 pp.   G. S.—H. S.

Zubly, J. J. The Real Christians Hope in Death or an account
    of the edifying Behaviour of several Persons of Piety in their
    last Moments. 12mo. ix and 187 pp.   G. S.

Germantown. *Christ. Sower, Jr.*

The Nature and Design of Christianity Extracted from a late
    author. 12mo. 16 pp.   G. S.—H. S.

A Pattern of Christian Education agreeable to the Precepts and
    Practice of our Blessed Lord and Saviour Jesus Christ.
    Extracted from a pious author. 12mo. 16 pp.
                                      G. S.—H. S.

We find that Christopher Sower, Jr., even before the death of his father,
which occurred in 1758, had charge of the printing and publishing business
of English issues.

Philadelphia. B. Fränklin u. A. Armbrüſter.

Acrelius, Iſrael. Der Todt als eine Seligkeit. Rede bei der am
    12. Februar 1756 geſchehenen Beerdigung Herrn Matthias Heinzel=
    manns, treu fleißig geweſenen Zweyten Evangeliſch Lutheriſchen
    Predigers in Philadelphia. Aus dem Engliſchen überſetzt von Joh.
    Fr. Handſchuh, Evang. Luth. Prediger, nebſt des Ueberſetzers kleiner
    Rede. 16mo. 31 S.

Rev. I. Acrelius was provost of the Lutheran churches on the Delaware.
Rev. Johann Dietrich Matthias Heintzelmann, assistant of Mr. Brunnholtz,
in the German Lutheran Church, Philadelphia, died February 9, 1756.

Hollatz, Dav. Die Gebahnte Pilgerſtraße nach dem Berg Zion und
    Himmliſchen Jeruſalem.
                                        Advertisement.

Kurtzer Begriff oder leichtes Mittel zu Gott zu beten oder mit Gott zu
    reden.
                                          Advertisement.

[Seougal, H.] Das Leben Gottes in der Seele des Menſchen oder die
    Natur und Vortrefflichkeit der Chriſtlichen Religion. Auf Veranſtal=
    tung der von einer löblichen Geſellſchaft in London ernenten General
    Truſtees aus dem engliſchen ins teutſche überſetzt, nebſt einer in ihrem
    Namen geſtellten Vorrede. 8vo. 21 u. 28 S.   G. S.—H. S.

The same book Christ. Saur had printed in the preceding year. The preface of the Franklin & Armbrüster edition was written and undersigned by the Rev. Wm. Smith or, as he is called here, "Willhelm Schmidt", the chairman of the Trustees of the Society for propagating Christian knowledge among the Germans of Pennsylvania.

Treuherßige Erinnerung unb Warnung. Klagreben vom Verfall bes Christenthums.

Neu=eingerichteter Americanischer Geschichts=Calender. Auf bas Jahr 1757.

*Philabelphische Zeitung von allerhanb Auswärtig= unb einheimischen merckwürbigen Sachen.

1757.

Germantown. Chr. Saur.

Der Inhalt von ben verschiebenen Conferentzen, welche einige Freunde in Philabelphia mit etlichen Inbianern gehalten, um eine Vorbereitung zum Frieben zu machen. . . Wie auch ber Inhalt ber Conferentzen mit ben Inbianern zu Eston in ben Monathen July unb November 1756. 4to. 55 S.

Hildeburn.

Der Inhalt von ben verschiebenen Conferentzen, welche mit ben Inbianern gehalten worben zu Eston in bem Monath July unb August 1757. 4to. 36 S. H. S.

Everard, John, D. D. Some Gospel Treasures, or the Holiest of all Unveiling; Discovering yet more the Riches of Grace and Glory to the Vessels of Mercy etc. In several Sermons, preached at Kensington and elsewhere. 2 vols. 4to. 268 and 280 pp. G. S.—H. S.

The Germantown reprint is finer than any of the original editions which appeared in London 1653, 1659 and 1679. Everard was a Puritan and a Mystic.

Der Hoch=Deutsch Americanische Calender. Auf bas Jahr . . 1758 u. f. w. 4to. 48 S.

* Pensylvanische Berichte, Ober: Sammlung Wichtiger Nachrichten aus bem Natur= unb Kirchenreich. H. S.

Philabelphia. B. Franklin unb A. Armbruster.

Regeln unb Articuls zu besserer Regierung unb Aufführung Jhro Majestät Garben zu Pferbe unb zu Fuße unb aller bero anberer Kriegsvölcker in Grossbritanien unb Irland Herrschaften jenseits bes Meeres unb in

ben auswärtigen Ländern. Vom 24 Mertz 1755 Auf Jhro Majestät
Befehl öffentlich herausgegeben und auf Veranstaltung der General
Trustees, so zur Aufrichtung englischer Schulen unter den Teutschen
in Pennsylvanien verordnet sind, zum Besten der unter Jhrer Majestät
regulären und Provinzialen Truppen in Nord Amerika stehenden
Teutschen aus dem Englischen ins Teutsche übersetzt. Philadelphia.
Gedruckt von B. Fränclin und A. Armbrüster iu Mertz 1757.
12mo. 46 S.

It seems strange that the trustees of the "Society for propagating Christian
Knowledge among the Germans in Pennsylvania" should use their trust
funds for printing Rules and Articles of War. But the Society, while
professedly charitable and religious, had also political aims, countenancing
the fighting Germans during the Indian War. The Royal American
regiment consisted mainly of Germans. The German *sects* sided with the
Quakers for peace.

Der Psalter Davids.

Advertised in the *Philadelphia Zeitung.*

Verordnungen des Coetus von Pennsylvanien.

Hildeburn from information of Rev. Mr. Dubbs. The same title occurs
in 1748.

Neu=eingerichteter Americanischer Geschichts=Calender. Auf das Jahr
1758. Zum fünften mal ans Licht gegeben.

* Philadelphische Zeitung von allerhand Auswärtig= und einheimischen
merkwürdigen Sachen.

This paper probably came to an end with the number issued Dec. 31,
1757, which contained the German translation of an article offensive to the
Quaker majority of the Assembly. It was written by Wm. Moore for the
Pennsylvania Gazette, which was not molested for its publication. Rev.
Wm. Smith, being chairman of the Trustees who published the German
paper, was held responsible for its contents and finally put into prison by
order of the Assembly, who had a spite against him. Anton Armbrüster
was also called to account, but only to extort from him the admission that
Smith had caused the insertion of the German translation of Moore's paper.

1758.

Germantown. (Germanton.) Christ. Saur.

Ein Spiegel der Eheleute. Nebst schönen Erinnerungen vor ledige Per=
sonen, welche willens sind, sich in den Stand der Ehe zu begeben . .
Vorgestellt in einem Gespräch zwischen einem Jüngling und Meister.
16mo. 32.   H. S.

Gellatly, A. Some Observations upon a late Piece entitled.
The Detection detected etc. 8vo. 204 pp.
                                          ・ Hildeburn.

Der Hoch=Deutsch Americanische Calender, Auf das Jahr . . 1759
u. s. w. 4to. 48 S. H. S.

* Pensylvanische Berichte, Oder: Sammlung Wichtiger Nachrichten aus
dem Natur und Kirchenreich. Fol. H. S.

> Christoph Saur, Sr., died Sept. 15, 1758 at the age of 64 years. His only
> son, also named Christoph, who till then had been in charge of the bindery,
> stepped into his place and conducted the business upon the same plan and
> with the same conscientious scrupulosity as his father.

Philadelphia. Anton Armbrüster.

Fränckel, D. H. Eine Danck=Predigt wegen des wichtigen und wunder=
vollen Siegs, welchen Se. Königl. Maj. in Preussen am 5ten
December 1757 über die der Anzahl nach ihm weit überlegene gesamte
Oesterreichische Armee in Schlesien preißwürdig erfochten. Gehalten
am Sabbath den 10ten desselben Monats von David Hirschel Fränckel,
Ober Rabbi. 8vo. 16 S.

Hildeburn.

Neu=eingerichteter Americanischer Geschichts=Calender. Auf das Jahr
1759. Zum sechsten mal ans Licht gegeben.

Philadelphia. ?

Des Kinder=Büchleins Tom. VII, d. i. Ein Versuch zu einem Losungs=
Büchel aus der Bibel. Aufs Jahr 1758. Barby Gedruckt im Jahr
1758. Zum andernmahl gedruckt zu Philadelphia 16mo. 121 S.

H. S.

Moravian.

1759.

Ephrata. *Typis Societatis.*

M. Tobias Wagners Abschieds=Rede an seine Lutherische Gemeinden in
Pennsylvanien, welche er zu unterschiedlichen Zeiten alle 14 Tage oder
4 Wochen bedienet, vornehmlich in 1. Richmond von 1743 bis 1759.
2. Ruscombaner von 1849 bis 1759. 3. Windsor von 1758 bis
1759. 4. Earltown von 1748 bis 1755. 5. Lancaster von 1751
bis 1753. 6. Bern von 1745 bis 1750. 7. Dulpehakin von 1743
bis 1746. 8. Allemängel von 1749 bis 1754. 9. Der Protestan.
Kirche von 1744 bis 1746. 10. Freunds Kirche von 1744 bis 1746.
11. North Kill von 1744 bis 1746. 12. Elsaß von 1748 bis 1752.
13. Reading, etliche mal angenommen, etliche mal abgedanckt. 8vo.
39 S. H. S.

> For a biographical notice of Tobias Wagner see Hallische Nachrichten
> New Ed. p. 433 — 438.

Germantown. (Germanton.) Chriſtoph Saur.

Habermann, J. und Caspar Naumann: Chriſtliche Morgen=
und Abend=Gebäter. Auf alle Tage in der Wochen. .Durch Joh.
Habermann. Samt andern ſchönen Gebätern, wie auch D. Naumanns
Kern aller Gebäter und ſchönen Morgen= nub Abend= und andern
Liedern. 24mo. 62 u. 55 S.

Vollſtändiges Marburger Geſang=Buch; Zur Uebung der Gottſeligkeit in
649 Chriſtlichen und Troſtreichen Pſalmen und Geſängen Hrn. D.
Martin Luthers und anderer Gottſeliger Lehrer. Ordentlich in XII.
Theile verfaſſet. Auch zur Beförderung des ſo Kirchen= als Privat=
Gottesdienſtes. Mit erbaulichen Morgen= Abend= Buß= Beicht und
Communion=Gebätlein vermehret. 16mo. 12, 527 u. 16 S.

H. S.

The first Lutheran hymnbook published in America.

Der Hoch=Deutſch Americaniſche Calender. Auf das Jahr . . 1760
u. ſ. w. 4to. 48 S. H. S.

* Penſylvaniſche Berichte, Oder: Sammlung Wichtiger Nachrichten aus
bem Natur und Kirchenreich.

[*Benezet Anthony.*] Observations on the Inslaving, importing
and purchasing of Negroes. With some advice thereon
extracted from the Yearly Meeting Epistle of London for the
present year. 8vo. 15 pp. G. S.

Bromley, Thomas. The way to the Sabbath of Rest or the Soul's
Progress in the Work of the New Birth. 8vo. viii, 60 pp.
G. S.
Reprint from a London Edition.

Bromley, Thomas. The Journeys of the Children of Israel, as
they are recorded and in their Names and Historical Passages
comprise the great and gradual Work of Regeneration. 8vo.
p. 61 — 187. G. S.
Bound with the preceding book and paging continued.

Bromley, Thomas. A Treatise of Extraordinary Dispensations
under the Jewish and Gospel Administrations. 8vo. p. 188
— 280. G. S.
Bound with the two preceding books and paging continued.

Hartley, Thomas. A Discourse on Mistakes concerning Religion, Enthusiasm, Experiences etc. G. S.

> Reprint from a London edition. Thomas Hartley, (1707—1784), Rector of the church at Winwick, Northamptonshire, was a friend of E. Swedenborg, some of whose books he translated into English.

𝔓𝔥𝔦𝔩𝔞𝔡𝔢𝔩𝔭𝔥𝔦𝔞. Teutſche Buchdruckerey.

(𝔐iller u. 𝔚eiß.)

Die Erzählungen von Maria le Roy und Barbara Leininger, welche viertehalb Jahr unter den Indianern gefangen geweſen und am 6ten May in dieſer Stadt glücklich angekommen. Aus ihrem eigenen Munde niedergeſchrieben und zum Druck befördert. 8vo. 14 S.

H. S.

> The narrative is entirely authentic and illustrates the perils and sufferings of white settlers during the Indian Wars.

> The connection of Anthony Armbrüster with Benjamin Franklin came to an end in 1759 and the German printing office passed into the hands of Peter Miller and Ludwig Weiss, conveyancers. Armbrüster continued in their employ as compositor.

> Peter Miller, born at Neu-Saarwerden, Rhenish Palatinate, was a scrivener, notary public and justice of the peace in Philadelphia. From 1764 till 1772, he was Vice-President and from 1787 — 1789 Attorney of the German Society. He died in 1794. Ludwig Weiss, his partner, was born in Berlin 1717 and educated in the Moravian Seminary at Lindheim. He studied law, emigrated in 1755 and settled in Philadelphia as conveyancer and lawyer. Weiss took a very active interest in public life. In 1764 he took the side of the proprietaries against B. Franklin, in 1776 he was a staunch supporter of the revolutionary party, in 1782 he bravely denounced the massacre of Indians at the Muskingam as a fiendish outrage. He was one of the founders of the German Society, its first attorney (1764 — 1777), vice-president in 1781 and president in 1782. His death occurred in 1796.

Neu-eingerichteter Americaniſcher Geſchichts- und Haus Calender. Auf das Jahr . . 1760. Zum ſiebentenmal ans Licht gegeben.

1760.

𝔊ermantown. Chriſtoph Saur.

Evangelien und Epiſteln auf alle Sonntage wie auch auf die hohen Feſte. . . Nebſt der Hiſtorie von der Zerſtörung der Stadt Jeruſalem, vermehret und verbeſſert. 16mo. 94 S. H. S.

Das Kleine Davidiſche Pſalterſpiel der Kinder- Zions. 12mo. 6, 547, 23 S. H. S.

> See remarks on the first edition of 1744.

[Mack, Alexander.] Eine Anmuthige Erinnerung zu einer Christlichen Betrachtung Von der Wunderbaren Allgegenwart des Allwissenden Gottes. 8vo. 7 S.

Hildeburn.

Date doubtful.

Der Psalter des Königs und Propheten Davids. Zweite Auflage.

See 1746.

Der Hoch=Deutsch Americanische Calender, Auf das Jahr . . 1761 u. s. w. 4to. 48 S.

G. S.—H. S.

*Pensylvanische Berichte, Oder: Sammlung Wichtiger Nachrichten aus dem Natur= und Kirchenreich. Fol.

[*Benezet, A.*] Observations on the Inslaving, importing and purchasing of Negroes etc. Second edition. 16mo. 16pp.

H. S.

See 1759.

Certain agreements and concessions made, concluded and agreed upon by and between the contributors to a Sum of Money for erecting and establishing a School House and School in Germantown. 4to. 8 pp.

Hildeburn.

These arrangements resulted in the establishment of the Germantown Academy, which was opened in September 1761. It embraced a German and an English department.

Dell, W. Christ's Spirit a Christian's Strength. . . . Two Sermons.

Dell, W. The Stumbling Stone, wherein the University is reproved. 12mo.

Dell was a Puritan clergyman in Cromwell's time, for a while chaplain in Lord Fairfax's army.

(*Fenelon.*) The Uncertainty of a Death Bed Repentance. 8vo. 16 pp.

Philadelphia. Henrich Miller.

Höchst merkwürdige Prophezeyung von wichtigen Kriegs= und Welthändeln: in welcher vornehmlich von dem glorwürdigen Könige von Preussen geweissagt wird. Aus einer uralten Lateinischen Handschrift, so in einem berühmten Europäischen Büchersaale verwahrt wird. Mit einem Versuch einer Erklärung. 4to. 8 S.

A most Remarkable Prophecy concerning Wars and Political
Events; especially the Glorious King of Prussia. Taken
from an ancient Latin Manuscript said to be deposited in the
Bodleyan Library. .With an attempt towards an Expla-
nation. 4to. 8 pp.

Hildeburn.

Henrich Miller born 1702 at Rhoden in the Principality of Waldeck,
was a professional printer almost from boyhood. He was a passionate
traveller, and in course of time worked as printer in Zurich, Leipzig, Altona,
London, Hamburg, Amsterdam, Rotterdam, Antwerp, Brussels, Paris,
Philadelphia, (in 1742), Marienburg where he established a business, again
in England, Scotland, Philadelphia (1751, employed by Benjamin Franklin).
Went back to Germany, set up in London a press of his own and in 1760
reached Philadelphia for the third time. He printed many German and
English books, retired from business in 1779 and died in Bethlehem, March
31, 1782. His religious convictions and sympathies were on the side of the
Moravians.

Philadelphia. *Peter Miller & Co.*

Catalogus Bibliothecae Loganianae : Being a choice Collection
of Books, as well in the Oriental, Greek and Latin, as in the
English, Italien, Spanish, French .and other Languages,
given by the late James Logan, Esq. etc. 8vo. 116 pp.

H. S.

Koffler, John Frederick. A Letter from a Tradesman in Lancaster
to the Merchants of the Cities of Philadelphia, New York
and Boston respecting the loan of Money to the Government.
16mo. 3, 14 pp.

Hildeburn.

A Collection of the Laws of the Province of Pennsylvania, now
in Force. Vol. II. Philadelphia, By Peter Miller & Company at the German Printing Office in Race street, 1760.
Fol. xii & 464 pp.   ·   H. S.

Philadelphia. Teutsche Buchdruckerey.

Neu=eingerichteter Americanischer Geschichts= und Haus=Calender. Auf
das Jahr 1761.

(Ephrata?)

König, Simon. (Eine Schrift über Ephrata.)
Die Chronik von Ephrata (p. 225) bemerkt: Er (Simon König) hat
von seiner Aufnahme eine eigene Schrift herausgegeben, darinnen er
die Gemeinschaft von Ephrata die vornehmste in der ganzen Welt
genennet.

Place and printer not known. Nor is the year quite certain.

1761.

Ephrata. Brüderschaft.

Abgeforderte Relation oder Erscheinung eines entleibten Geistes, dem Publico zur Nachricht getreulich aus dem Munde derer, die von Anfang bis ans Ende mit interessiret, aufgeschrieben. 12mo. 39 .S

H. S.

Spiritistic manifestations and visions are also told of in the *Chronicon Ephratense*.

Germantown. Christoph Saur.

Dilworth, W. H. Das Leben und heroische Thaten des Königs von Preußen, Friedrichs des III. von seiner Geburth an bis zum Ende des 1760sten Jahres u. s. w. Zuerst in Englischer Sprache herausgegeben durch W. H. Dilworth 1758 und nun ins Deutsche übersetzt und vermehrt. 12mo. 288 S.

Frederick the Great figures through the whole book as Frederick III. Only 165 pages contain the translation of Dilworth's book, the rest is a compilation from later accounts.

Die Naturalisations-Form derjenigen, welche ohne Eid mit dem Quäkeratteft naturalisirt werden.

Das Neue Testament Unsers Herrn und Heylandes Jesu Christi u. s. w. Dritte Auflage. 12mo. 562 S.

See year 1745.

Der Hoch-Deutsch Americanische Calender, Auf das Jahr . . 1762 u. s. w. 4to. 48 S. G. S. — H. S.

The "Kräuterbuch", or lessons in botany, was commenced in the almanac of this year and continued every year till 1778.

* Pensylvanische Berichte, Oder: Sammlung Wichtiger Nachrichten aus dem Natur- und Kirchenreich. Fol. H. S.

Philadelphia. Teutsche Buchdruckerey in der Räs-Strasse.

Neu-eingerichteter Americanischer Geschichts- und Haus-Calender auf . . 1762. Zum neuntenmal ans Licht gegeben. G. S.

Philadelphia. Henrich Miller.

Des Landmanns Advocat. Das ist: Kurtzer Auszug aus solchen Gesetzen von Pensylvania und England, welche daselbst in völliger Kraft, und einem freyen Einwohner auf dem Lande höchst nöthig und nützlich zu wissen sind. . . Zum besten der hiesigen Deutschen in ihre Muttersprache übersetzt. 8vo. viii u. 170 S. nebst Reg.   H. S.

Steiner, J. C. Schuldigstes Liebes= und Ehren=Denkmahl, Unserm weyland Allergnädigsten und Glorwürdigsten Könige von Großbritanien, Georg II, nach Seiner Majestät töblichem Hinschiede, so erfolgt den 25sten October 1760, aufgerichtet in der Hoch=deutschReformirten Gemeine zu Philadelphia . . in einer öffentlichen Trauerrede über die Worte Deut. 35, 5—8, von Johann Conrad Steiner, Reformirten Prediger zu Philadelphia, den 1. Februar 1761. 8vo. 31 S.   H. S.

Das Wunder ohne Maßen: Wie sich hat martern laßen der Schöpfer fürs Geschöpf. . . Die Leidens= und Todesgeschichte des Herrn der Herrlichkeit. 16mo. 16 S.   H. S.

Die wunderthätige Kraft der Kleider und Hohe Würde der Kleidermacher, nach Anleitung des Sprüchworts: Kleider machen Leute. 16mo. 16 S.   H. S.

Luther's Small Catechism, translated into English by Rev. C. M. Wrangel.

> See Hallische Nachrichten. Old Ed. p. 876. Charles Magnus von Wrangel, Provost of the Swedish churches on the Delaware, an intimate friend of Rev. H. M. Mühlenberg, came to Pennsylvania in 1759, returned to Sweden in 1768 and died in 1786.

The Miraculous Power of Clothes and Dignity of the Taylors. Being an Essay on the words: Clothes make Men. A Satire translated from the German.

Hildeburn.

Observations on the Conversion and Apostleship of St. Paul. By the Hon. George Lyttelton, Esq. London. Philadelphia Reprinted by Henry Miller in Second str. 8vo. 79 pp.

Hildeburn.

A short, easy and comprehensive Method of Prayer. Translated from the German. 12mo. 36 pp.

Hildeburn.

> Attributed by J. Watson to Johann Kelpius. See year 1763.

1762.

Ephrata. Brüderschaft.

Neu=vermehrtes Gesäng der einsamen Turtel=Taube. Zur gemeinsamen
Erbauung gesammlet und ans Licht gegeben. 12mo. Vorrede 3 S.
Text 329 S. Register 3 S.   S. W. P.

Of the 183 hymns, contained in this volume, 80 were written by C. Beissel,
the rest by other inmates of the cloister. Nearly all hymns were in 1766
reprinted in the Paradisische Wunderspiel. An exception was made with
those of Kroll, Landert, S. König and Maria Eicher.

M. Valentin Wudrians, seel., Creutz=Schule, in sich haltende: Eine
schöne Christliche Unterweisung von dem lieben Creutz. Vor alle
Creutz=Brüder und Schwestern . . zusammengetragen von einem
wohl geprüfften Creutz=Bruder und Nachfolger Jesu Christi. Ephrata
Drucks und Verlags der Brüderschafft. (Auf der letzten Seite:)
Impressum Ephratae in Comitatu Lancastriensi Typis Soci-
atatis per Godofredum Zeusingerum, Kistrino-Brussum anno
post partum virginis millesimo septingentesimo sexagesimo
secundo. 8vo. Vorrede 3 S. Text 465 S. Reg. 3 S.   G. S.

Valentin Wudrian (1584—1625) occupied the pulpit in Pomerania,
Mecklenburg, and Hamburg and was for some time Professor of Hebrew at
Greifswalde. The cast of his meditations is somewhat sombre but has
nothing in common with the mysticism of the Ephrata brethren. About
Godfrey Zeusinger of Küstrin nothing could be ascertained. In the very
next year (1763) a J. George Zeisiger turns up in Ephrata; should there
be any connection between the two?

Germantown. Christoph Saur.

Habermann, Johann, von Eger, weiland Prediger und Superin=
tendent in Zeitz. Kleines Christlich Gebätbuch.   G. S.

See 1753.

Neu=Eingerichtetes Gesang=Buch in sich haltend eine Sammlung (mehren=
theils alter) schöner lehrreicher und erbaulicher Lieder, welche von
langer Zeit her bei den Bekennern und Liebhabern der Glorien und
Wahrheit Jesu Christi biß anjetzo in Uibung gewesen. u. s. w. Auf
Kosten vereinigter Freunden. 12mo. 760 S.   G. S.—H. S.

Hymnbook of the Schwenkfelders.

Eine Nützliche Anweisung, Oder Beyhülffe vor die Teutschen um Englisch
zu lernen. 8vo. 4, 287, 4 S.   H. S.

A new edition of the book printed in 1751.

Der Psalter des Königs und Propheten Davids. 3te Ausgabe.

Vollständiges Marburger Gesang=Buch zur Uebung der Gottseligkeit, in
    649 Christlichen und Trostreichen Psalmen und Gesängen u. s. w.
    12mo. 527 S. u. Reg.

First edition appeared in 1759.

Der Hoch=Deutsch Americanische Calender, Auf das Jahr . . 1763.
    G. S.— H. S.

* Germantauner Zeitung, Oder: Sammlung Wahrscheinlicher Nachrichten
    aus dem Natur= und Kirchenreich, wie auch auf das allgemeine Beste
    angesehene nützliche Unterrichte und Anmerkungen.

Chr. Saur finding that his published news did not always prove true
inserted on the title before the word *News* "probable", so as to clear his
conscience. In the absence of any file or single copies of the paper during
the following years it is not known how long the modified title was retained.

Philadelphia. Anton Armbrüster.

Lampe, Dr. Friedrich Adolph. Erste Wahrheits=Milch für Säug=
    linge am Altar und Verstand. Oder kurzgefaßte Grund=Lehren des
    Reformirten Christenthums. 12mo. Vorrede 4 S. Text 40 S.
    Hildeburn.

Neu=eingerichteter Americanischer Geschichts= und Haus=Calender. Auf
    . das Jahr 1763.

Printed either by A. Armbrüster or by Armbrüster & Hasselbach.

* Philadelphische Fama.

The second *Fama* would, like the first of 1749 and 1750, have remained
unknown to us, were it not for a newspaper controversy. H. Miller in his
Staatsbote ruthlessly assailed A. Armbrüster and his *Fama* (pöbelhafter Narr,
Mischmasch zu schlecht für Wahnwitzige, hottentottisches Geschmier) "to
pay him back in his own coin."

Philadelphia. A. Armbrüster und N. Hasselbach.

Zwölff Sibyllen Weissagungen, Viel wunderbarer Zukunft von Anfang
    bis zum Ende der Welt besagend, Auch der Königin von Saba dem
    König Salamon gethane Prophezeyung Wie auch merklicher künftiger
    Dinge, von St. Brigitten, Cyrillo, Methodio, Joachimo, Bruder
    Reinhard, Johann Lichtenberger und Bruder Jacob aus Spanien
    beschrieben. Philadelphia. Gedruckt und zu haben bey A. Armbrüster
    und H. Hasselbach in Moravian Alley nächst der Bruder Kirche.

Philadelphia. Nicolaus Hasselbach.

Der Psalter des Königs und Propheten Davids, verteutschet von D. Martin
    Luther. Gedruckt und zu finden bey Nicolaus Hasselbach in der

Second Straffe zwischen Räß und Weinstraffe. 1762. 16mo. 239 S.

Little is known of N. Hasselbach. In Saur's paper (Aug. 1, 1755) he is mentioned as "paper maker in the late Mr. Koch's paper mill on the Wissahicken." In 1762 he turns up in Philadelphia as printer, in 1763 he removed his business to Chestnut Hill, opposite to the "Wirthshaus zum Schiff." Afterwards he went to Baltimore. In 1762 he was associated with Ant. Armbrüster, their office being in Moravian Alley (Bread st) next door to the Moravian church.

Philadelphia. H. Miller.

Geistlicher Irrgarten mit vier Gnadenbrunnen. Fol. 1 S.   H. S.

The typographical arrangement with its turns and geometrical intricacies forms the labyrinth, the text furnishes the spiritual lesson.

Der Heilige und Sichere Glaubensweg eines Evangelischen Christen. The Holy and Sure way of Faith of an Evangelical Christian. With 4 copper-plates.

(Advertisement.)

German and English printed in opposite columns.

Klagen eines Theils der Evangelisch-Lutherischen Gemeinglieder zu Philadelphia wider einige dermalige Aeltesten der Gemeine. Fol. 4 S.   G. S.

The complainants aver that the funds of the Church are used by the elders in an arbitrary and wasteful manner and propose an annual election of the elders by majority of votes as a remedy.

A. B. C. und Buchstabier Buch.

(Hildeburn.)

Der Neueste, Verbessert- und Zuverläßige Calender Auf das 1763ste Jahr Christi, Welches ein gemein Jahr von 365 Tagen ist. Darin enthalten die Wochen- Monaths- und Merkwürdige Tage; des Monden Auf- und Untergang; seine Zeichen, Grade und Viertel; die Aspecten der Planeten, samt der Witterung, des Siebengestirns Aufgang, Südplatz und Untergang; Auf- und Untergang der Sonnen, nebst der Fluth und dem hohen Wasser zu Philadelphia; Und andere gewöhnliche Calender-Arbeit. Wie auch Geschichten, Sittenlehren, lustige und angenehme Erzählungen u. s. w. Vornemlich auf den Pennsylvanischen Horizon berechnet; Jedoch in den angrenzenden Landschaften ohne merklichen Unterschied zu gebrauchen. Zum Erstenmal herausgegeben.   H. S.

*Der Wöchentliche Staatsbote, Mit den neuesten Fremden und Einheimisch- Politischen Nachrichten; Samt den von Zeit zu Zeit in der Kirche und Gelehrten Welt sich ereignenden Merkwürdigkeiten. (Fol. 13 x 8)   G. S.

First number published on 18. January. The printing office, at first on the S. E. corner of Second and Race Sts. was in December moved to a house in Second Street, between Race and Vine Streets, till then occupied by the printer Nicholas Hasselbach, who removed his business to Chestnut Hill, north of Germantown.

Philadelphia. Peter Miller u. Co.

Katechismus ober Kurzer Unterricht christlicher Lehre, wie berselbe in benen Reformirten Kirchen und Schulen der Churfürstlichen Pfalz, auch anderwärts getrieben wirb. Mit Zeugnissen ber heiligen Schrift erklärt und bestätigt. Nach vorhergegangener Collation mit allen Exemplarien gebruckt bei Peter Miller u. Comp. MDCCLXII.

The Charter and Acts of Assembly of the Province of Pennsylvania. 2 vols. Fol. First vol. 21, 4, 164 pp. Second vol. 3, 116, 13 and 32 pp.   H. S.

Edited by Lewis Weiss and Charles Brockden.
An edition in smaller size appeared in the same year.

1763.
Chestnut Hill. N. Hasselbach.

Der Ehrliche Kurzweilige Deutsche Americanische Geschäfts und Haus=Calender auf das Jahr 1764 u. s. w. Tschesnüt=Hüll. Gebruckt und zu haben bey N. Hasselbach, gegenüber bem Wirthhaus zum Schiff.

Whether Hasselbach's Almanac appeared in any other year is not known.

Ephrata. J. George Zeisiger.

The Christian's Duty, to render to Caesar the Things that are Caesar's, considered with regard to the payment of the present Tax of Sixty Thousand Pounds granted to the King's use. 16mo. 28 pp.

Hildeburn.

Reprint of a pamphlet, which was originally published in Philadelphia 1756. As place of printing the fictitious name Parthenopolis (i. e. Virgin City) is given, by which Ephrata is occasionally designated.

Barba, A. A. Gründlicher Unterricht von ben Metallen, barinnen beschrieben wird wie sie werben in ber Erben generirt und was man insgemein babey finbet. In zwei Büchern vormals im Spanischen beschrieben durch Albano Alonzo Barba, Pfarrherr zu St. Bernardi, Kirchspiel der Kaiserlichen Stabt Potosi im Königreich Peru. Hernach ins Englische übersetzt durch Edward, Graff von Sanperich. Zum erstenmal ins Hoch=beutsche übersetzt und zum Druck befördert von G. R., bieser Kunst Beflissenen. 12mo. 198 S. Mit einem Bilde.

The book may have been printed on the cloister press but is no cloister publication. Philadelphia German papers of a later date contain advertisements of George Zeisiger who kept a school in Quarry Street and was very likely identical with the J. George Zeisiger of Ephrata.

Ephrata. Brüderschafft.

(Benezet, A.) Eine kurtze vorstellung des theils von Africa, welches bewohnt wird von Negroes, darinnen beschrieben wird die fruchtbarkeit desselben Landes, die gutartigkeit dessen einwohner und wie man daselbst den sclavenhandel treibt. Zweymal in Engländischer sprache und nun zum drittenmal, und das der Hoch-teutschen Nation zur mitleidenblichen betrachtung des Zustandes ihrer armen mit-geschöpfen in ihrer Sprache heraus gegeben. Ephrata Drucks der Societät auf Kosten etlicher freunden. 8vo. 107 S.   G. S.

Germantown. Christoph Saur.

Biblia, Das ist: Die Heilige Schrift Altes und Neues Testaments, Nach der Teutschen Uebersetzung D. Martin Luthers. 4to. 992 u. 277 S.
                G. S.

In his preface Christ. Sower remarks: "So then the Holy Writ, called the Bible, appears on the American continent for the second time in the German language to the renown of the German nation, no other nation being able to claim that the Bible has been printed in their language in this division of the globe."

Der Kleine Darmstädtische Catechismus Herrn D. Martin Luthers nebst beygefügten Fragstücken für diejenige sonderlich, welche christlichem Gebrauch nach confirmiret werden und hernach zum ersten mal das heilige Abendmahl gebrauchen. 16mo.

Neu-vermehrt und vollständiges Gesang-Buch, u. s. w. Zweyte Auflage. 12mo. Psalmen 208 S. Geistreiche Lieder 536 S. Heidelberger Catechismus ꝛc. 24 S. Evangelien und Episteln 82 S.

The first edition appeared 1753.

Das Neue Testament Unsers Herrn und Heylandes Jesu Christi. Verteutscht von D. Martin Luther. Mit jedes Capitels kurtzen Summarien. Auch beygefügten vielen richtigen Parallelen. Vierte Auflage. 12mo. 4 u. 679 S.   G. S.

Otterbein, W. Die heilbringende Menschwerdung und der herrliche Sieg Jesu Christi über den Teufel und Tod. Vorgestellt in einer im J. 1760 in der Reformirten Kirche zu Germantown öffentlich gehaltenen erbaulichen Predigt. 8vo. 15 S.

About Wm. Otterbein (1726—1813), a distinguished minister of the Reformed Church see Rev. H. J. Dubbs in *Reformed Quarterly Review,* January 1884, and *Historical Manual of the Ref. Church,* p. 214 and 599.

Schabalie, J. P.   Die Wandlende Seel, das ist: Gespräch der Wandlenden Seelen mit Adam Noah und Simon Cleophas; verfasset die Geschichten von der Erschaffung der Welt an biß zu und nach der Zerstörung Jerusalems. . . Durch Johann Philipp Schabalie' in Niederländischer Sprach geschrieben; Anjetzo aber in die Hochdeutsche Sprach übersetzt von B. B. B.   12mo. 8, 463, 25 S.

Schabalie, a Mennonite minister of Alkmaer and Amsterdam published the Dutch original of the Wandering Soul in 1635. He makes the participants of great biblical events tell their own story in an entertaining and picturesque manner. Noah's story of his narrow escape, of his botanical and zoological storehouse and the good conduct of the imprisoned brutes is pleasant to read. The German translation attained in America great popularity, went through many editions and is yet in demand.

Zeugnis der Wahrheit, Oder: eines Christen Gedancken von der vergangenen und von der künfftigen Reformation. Erstlich in Franckfurt u. Leipzig 1760, nun aber zu Germantown gedruckt bey Chr. Saur. 8vo. 40 S.   G. S.

About the shortcoming of churches and doctrined theology in building up true Christianity.

Der Hoch=Deutsche Americanische Calender. Auf das Jahr . . 1764 u. s. w.   4to. 48 S.   G. S.— H. S.

* Germantauner Zeitung. Oder: Sammlung u. s. w.
    See 1762.

(*Defoe, D.*)   The Dreadful Visitation, in a short Account of the Progress and Effects of the Plague.   16mo. 16 pp.
                                                                      (Hildeburn.)

(*Kelpius, J.*)   A short easy and comprehensive method of prayer. Translated from the German by a lover of internal Devotion. Second edition.   12mo. 3 pp.   H. S.

Watson's manuscript Annals of Philadelphia contain the following remark: "I have seen a second edition of a small book on Prayer by Kelpius, which had been printed in Germantown in 1763 by C. Sower. It had been translated into English by Dr. C. Witt." Kelpius was the so called Hermit of the Wissahickon. He died in 1708.

Friedensthal bei Bethlehem. *Johann Brandmüller.*

Grube, Bernhard Adam.   Evangelien-Harmonie, in die Delaware Sprache übersetzt.

B. A. Grube, a Moravian Missionary (b. 1715, d. 1805) came to Pennsylvania 1746.

Johann Brandmüller, b. at Basle in 1704, learned the printer's trade of his uncle, joined the Moravians in 1739, made his first journey to Pennsylvania in 1741 and found a permanent home near Bethlehem in 1743. He died 1777. He set up a printing press, which was obtained from London, in 1761 at Friedensthal, Northampton County.—See John W. Jordan's Note in *Pennsylvania Magazine*, vol. VI, p. 250.

[*Grube, B. A.*] Dellawaerisches Gesang-Büchlein. 8vo.

Hildeburn.

A hymnbook in the language of the Delaware Indians.

Philadelphia. Anton Armbrüster.

, in Moravian Alley.

Funck, Henrich. Eine Restitution Oder eine Erklärung einiger Hauptpuncten des Gesetzes: Wie es durch Christum erfüllet ist u. s. w. 4to. 4 u. 308 S. G. S.

H. Funck was a prominent minister of the Mennonites. His book, printed after his death, treats of biblical archæology, chronology and interpretation.

Neu=eingerichteter Americanischer Geschichts= und Haus=Calender auf das Jahr 1764.

* Philadelphische Fama.

A. Armbrüster was again in monetary trouble. He writes to Benjamin Franklin, June 18, 1763: "I do assure you, the distress is very great and if you do not rescue me I shall be a great sufferer in my business, but I expect your generous disposition will prevent it." (Franklin's Correspondence, Philosophical Society of Penna.)

Tunes in Three Parts. For the several Metres of Dr. Watt's Version of the Psalms etc. 12mo. 43 pp. H. S.

A word in Season to all Protestants of all denominations throughout Great Britain, Ireland and America. 8vo. 7 pp.

Reprint of an anti-catbolic pamphlet, published in London.

Philadelphia. Henrich Miller.

Catechismus Oder Anfänglicher Unterricht Christlicher Glaubens=Lehre. 12mo. 4 u. 146 S. G. S.

A Schwenkfelder Catechism.

Die Lehr=Texte der Brüder Gemeine und insonderheit der Kinder. Aus den Briefen Pauli an die Gemeinen aus den Heiden. Zweyte Auflage. Zum Gebrauch des Jahres 1764. 8vo. 48 S. H. S.

Printed for the Moravians.

Die Täglichen Loosungen der Brüder=Gemeine für das Jahr 1764. 8vo. 46 S. u. Register. H. S.

Steiner, Johann Conrad. Die Herrliche Erscheinung des HERRN JESU zum Allgemeinen Welt=Gericht samt desselben Folgen für die Gerechten und Ungerechten auf die endlose Ewigkeit. In Achtzehn Predigten. Nebst der dem sel. Verfasser am 7. Julii des verflossenen Jahrs gehaltenen Leichen=Rede; und Kurtzer Nachrichten von dessen Lebens=Unständen. 8vo. vi. 478 S. G. S.

Der Neueste, Verbessert= und Zuverläßige Americanische Calender. Auf das 1764ste Jahr Christi, u. s. w. Zum Zweytenmal herausgegeben. H. S.

* Der Wöchentliche Philadelphische Staatsbote. Fol. H. S.
    See 1762.

[*Ritzema, J.*] Aan den Eeerwaarden Do Joannes Leydy, Predi-kant in N. Brunswyck. 8vo. 38 pp. H. S.

A Hymnbook for the Children belonging to the Brethren's Congregations. 12mo. xxx & 64 pp. H. S.
    Hildeburn.
    Moravian.

1764.

The year 1764 was one of great stir and strife and its literary record reflects the boisterous tide of events. The principal cause of contention was the unsettled Indian problem. Hostile Indians continued their outrages in the frontier districts and the Assembly was severely censured for its apathy. There was a small Indian settlement on the Conestoga, numbering about twenty heads, inclusive of women, children and old men. They are said to have been peaceful; but some young people of Paxton Township (Dauphin County) and Donegal Township (Lancaster County) thinking otherwise, deliberately killed six on the Conestoga, Dec. 14, 1763, and the rest who had meantime found shelter in the Lancaster Workhouse, in this place of refuge, not sparing women, children nor age. These were the "Paxton boys", so much written on in 1764. They were Irish Presbyterians, a fact brought out prominently in some of the pamphlets. Other Indians, christianized by the Moravians, were taken to Philadel-phia for better protection and lodged in the barracks. The Pax-ton Boys, mounted and armed, set out for Philadelphia and halted in Germantown, Feb. 5, 1764. The excitement in Phila-delphia was immense, even Quakers joined the militia called out

to resist the invaders. The difficulty was peaceably settled by a
conference of influential citizens of Philadelphia with the leaders
of the Paxton boys. The old quarrel between the Assembly and
the Proprietaries culminated in 1764 in a petition of the Assembly
to the King, requesting him to abolish the Proprietary system
and vest the appointment of Governors directly in the Crown.
A number of speeches and pamphlets on both sides of the question
were published. In the fall of the year Assembly men for Philadelphia City and County had to be elected and that was another
occasion for a flood of political pamphlets. Benjamin Franklin
who had been member of the Assembly for fourteen years was
defeated, strong appeals having been made to the Germans, not
to vote for him. His appointment as agent of the Assembly, to
plead before Parliament for the abolition of proprietary government led to the publication of protests and these were met with
repartees.—When Benjamin Franklin reached England quite
another unexpected issue loomed up, the *Stamp Act*, which
became the great sensation of 1765.

Ephrata. Brüderschaft.

Von der Historia des Apostolischen Kampffs, Zehen Bücher, wie sie der
Abdias anfänglich in Hebräischer Sprache beschrieben, Eutropius aber
ins Griechische und Julius Africanus ins Lateinische übersetzt haben,
u. s. w. Vormals -in Amsterdam, nun aber in Ephrata gedruckt
durch die Brüderschafft auf Kosten der Brüder in Canetgotschicken.
12mo. 388 S.   G. S.

The Conogocheague creek is a rivulet in Franklin County, Pa., in the
vicinity of which Dunkers had settled, part of whom favored the religious
notions and customs of the Ephrata brethren. Friendly relations between
the Franklin County or "Antietum" baptists and those of Ephrata were
established (see *Chronicon Ephratense*, p. 223, transl. 259) in 1762 and thus
it came to pass that the brethren on the Conogocheague had their printing
done by their Ephrata friends.

Des Jüngers Nicodemi Evangelium von unsers Meisters und Heylandes
Jesu Christi Leyden und Auferstehung. 12mo. 52 S.   G. s.

Forms an appendix to the preceding volume. The first American
edition of the apocryphal gospel of Nicodemus appeared in Ephrata 1748.

(Ephrata?)

Historische Nachricht von dem neulich in Lancaster County durch unbekante
Personen ausgeführten Blutbade über eine Anzahl Indianer, welche
Freunde dieser Provinz waren. Aus dem Englischen übersetzt. 8vo.
31 S.   H. S.

No place of publication given on the title.

A Letter from Batista Angeloni, who resided many years in London, to his Friend Manzoni, wherein the Quakers are politically and religiously considered. To which is added, The Cloven foot discovered. Ephrata. 8vo. 8 pp.

PHILA. LIBRARY.

Against the Quakers. As the names on the title page are fictitious, so also the imprint may be a mask. Another edition of the same book makes Carolina the place of publication.

Germantown. Chriſtoph Saur.

Die allmächtige Errettungs-Hand Gottes aus den wilden Meeres Wellen; Wunderbar erwiesen an einer Anno 1735 d. 10den October von Altona nach London ſchiffenden Frauens-Perſon. 16mo. 14 S.

H. S.

Chriſtliche Morgen und Abend Gebäter, Auf alle Tage in der Wochen durch D. Joh. Habermann. Samt andern ſchönen Gebätern. Wie auch D. Neumanns Kern aller Gebäter. 24mo. 62 u. 55 S.

Das Kleine Davidiſche Pſalterſpiel der Kinder Zions u. ſ. w. Zum britten mal ans Licht gegeben. 12mo. 6, 570, 24 u. 4 S.

H. S.

First edition 1744. The third of 1764 is enlarged.

Die Regeln der Teutſchen Geſellſchaft in Philadelphia. 8vo. 8 S.

. The German Society of Pennsylvania was founded December 26, 1764. The officers elected were: Heinrich Keppele, President; Peter Miller, Vice-President; Blasius Daniel Mackinet and Joh. Wm. Hoffmann, Secretaries; Jacob Winey, Treasurer; Ludwig Weiss, Attorney; David Schäfer, Christian Schneider, Jacob Bertsch, Phil. Ulrich, Jos. Kaufmann, Johann Odenheimer, Directors.

[Terſteegen, G.] Das Anhangen an Gott, ein Unterricht des Albertus Magnus, geweſenen Biſchoffs zu Regensburg. 16mo: 17 u 56 S.

H. S.

Der Hoch-Deutſch Americaniſche Calender. Auf das Jahr . . 1765 u. ſ. w.

H. S.—G. S.

* Germantauner Zeitung, Oder: Sammlung u. ſ. w.

* Ein Geiſtliches Magazien, Oder: Aus den Schätzen der Schrifftgelehrten zum Himmelreich gelehrt, bargereichtes Altes und Neues.

The numbers of this religious Magazine were not dated; they appeared between 1764 and 1770 and were given away, not sold. It is the first religious periodical printed in America. In one of the early numbers the publisher states, that the type used was made in Germantown.

Anmerkungen über Ein noch nie erhört und gesehen Wunder=Thier in Pennsylvanien, genannt Streit= und Strauß=Vogel. Herausgegeben von einer Teutschen Gesellschaft freyer Bürger und getreuer Unter= thaner Seiner Groß=Brittanischen Majestät. Gedruckt in diesem Jahr.

For the existing government and against B. Franklin.

Eine zu dieser Zeit Höchstnöthige Warnung an die freye Einwohner der Provinz Pennsylvanien von Einem, dem die Wohlfahrt des Landes angelegen und darauf bedacht ist. Fol. 2 S.   H. S.

Directed against a scheme to restrict the free suffrage of the Germans. The date of publication is not stated.

Protestation gegen die Bestellung Herrn Benjamin Franklins zu einem Agenten für diese Provinz.

Followed by

(Franklin, B.) Anmerkungen über eine neuliche Protestation gegen die Bestellung Hrn. Benjamin Franklins zu einem Agenten für diese Provinz. Folio. 4 S.

Philadelphia. Anton Armbrüster.

Eine Anrede an die Deutschen Freyhalter der Stadt und County Phila= delphia. 8vo. 8 S.   H. S.

In favor of abolishing the proprietary government. A. Armbrüster moved in 1764 from Moravian Alley (Bread st. between Second and Third st.) to Arch st.

Etliche merkwürdige Puncten betreffende die Verwechselung des Govern= ments, gerichtet an die deutschen Einwohner der Provinz Pennsyl= vanien.

Hildeburn.

Eine Historische Beschreibung von den letzhin geschehenen Unruhen zwischen den Hintern Einwohnern d. Provinz Pennsylvanien und denen zu Philadelphia. Aus dem Englischen ins Hochteutsche übersetzt. 8vo. 8 S.

Merkwürdige Nachricht von F. W. Autenrieths Ehrlichen Abkunft, gott= losen Leben und gerichtlichen Tode, als eines verlorenen und wieder= gefundenen Sohns.

Hildeburn.

Seiner Königlichen Erhabensten Majestät im Hohen Rath nahe sich diese demüthigste Vorstellung und Bitte von Seiner Majestät gehorsamst=

68

getreuen Unterthanen, ben freyen Einwohnern ber Provinz Pennsyl=
vanien. Fol. 2 S.

H. S.
Hildeburn.

A petition to have the proprietary government remain as it was.

Zwey wahrhafte neue Zeitungen von ganz besondere Himmelszeichen
u. s. w.   4to. 4 S.

H. S.

Gives an account of remarkable heavenly signs (coffin, fiery rods, sculls,
serpent and pyramid) witnessed near Riga and Elbing in May 1763.

An bie Freyhalter unb Einwohner ber Stabt unb County Philabelphia
beutscher Nation.   4to. 4 S.

Eine anbere Anrebe an bie beutschen Freyhalter ber Stabt unb County
Philabelphia von etlichen von ihren Lanbsleuten.   8vo. 8 S.

H. S.

In favor of abolishing the proprietary government.

Ein schön weltlich Lieb. Melobie: Ein Solbat bin ich eben unb steh vor
meinem Feinb.   4to. 10 S.

A burlesque on the Quakers taking up arms to protect the Indians in
Philadelphia. The first verse begins: Ihr Quäcker seyb gelaben, frisch auf
unb kommt heran, Zum Denckmahl eurer Thaten hengt ihr ben Degen an.

Neu=eingerichteter Americanischer Geschichts= unb Haus=Calenber.   Auf
bas Jahr 1765.

* Philabelphische Fama.

It is stated in Thomas' History of Printing, second edition, vol. 1, p. 248,
that Armbrüster again failed in 1764 and could not recover his standing as
master printer. There are, however, publications with his imprint till the
year 1767.

An Address to the Freeholders and Inhabitants of the Province
of Pennsylvania In answer to a paper called the Plain
Dealer.   8vo. 12 pp.

P. S.

Against the Proprietary government.

An Answer to the Pamphlet entitled The Conduct of the Paxton
Men impartially represented.   Wherein the generous Spirit
of the Author is manifested . . and the spotted garment
pluckt off.   8vo. 28 pp.

H. S.

The Paxton Men, who massacred the Conestoga Indians, among them
women and children, are denounced as murderers.

Kinnersley, E. A course of Experiments in that curious and entertaining Branch of Natural Philosophy, called Electricity; Accompanied with explanatory lectures, in which Electricity and Lightning will be proved to be the same thing. By Ebenezer Kinnersly, M. A. Prof. of English and Oratory in the College and Academy of Philadelphia. 8vo. 8 pp.

Hildeburn.

An Historical Account of the late Disturbance between the Inhabitants of the back settlements of Pennsylvania and the Philadelphians. 8vo. 8 pp. H. S.

An apology for the country mob that on the 8th of February approached Philadelphia, threatening the lives of Christianized Indians, whom the Moravians had for better safety taken to Philadelphia.

A letter from a Gentleman in Transylvania to his friend in America giving some account of the late disturbances that happened in that government.

Hildeburn.

The Maybe or some observations occasioned by reading a Speech delivered in the House of Assembly the 14th of May last. 8vo. 7 pp. H. S.

In favor of a change of government.

Observations on a late Epitaph in a letter from a Gentleman in the Country to his Friend in Philadelphia. 8 pp.

The Paxton Boys, a Farce, Translated from the Original French. By a Native of Donegal. 16mo. 16 pp.

PHILA. LIBRARY.

Two editions were published in the same year.

The Quakers Assisting to preserve the Lives of the Indians in the Barracks vindicated and proved to be consistent with Reason, agreeable to our Law etc. 16mo. 16 pp.

Defence of the stand taken by the Quakers in protecting the Indians from violence.

Remarks upon the delineated Presbyterian play'd Hob with; or Clothes for a stark Naked Author. 8vo. 8 pp. H. S.

Hildeburn.

Tunes in three parts, for the several metres in Dr. Watt's version of the Psalms. Second adition (sic!) 12mo. viii & 44 pp. H. S.

The Universal Peace-Maker or Modern Author's Instructor.   By
   Philanthropos.   8vo. 15 pp.

   Quite general reflections on the beauties of peace and Union.

A. Armbruster printed in 1764 from fifteen to twenty more
   pamphlets in English on which his name does not appear.

Philadelphia. Henrich Miller.

Dickinson, J.   Eine Rede gehalten im Hause der Assembly der Provinz
   Pennsylvanien am 24. May 1764 . . Bey Gelegenheit einer Bitt-
   schrift, die auf Befehl des Hauses aufgesetzt und damals in Ueberlegung
   genommen war, worin Seine Majestät um eine Veränderung des
   Gouvernements dieser Provinz ersucht wird. . . Aus dem Englischen
   übersetzt. 8vo. xvi und 35 S.

   In favor of the existing proprietary government.

Galloway.   Die Rede Herrn Joseph Galloways, eines der Mitglieder
   des Hauses für Philadelphia County, zur Beantwortung der Rede,
   welche Hr. John Dickinson gehalten im Hause der Assembly der Prov.
   Pennsylvanien, am 24. May 1764, u. s. w.   Audi et alteram
   partem. 8vo. 44, 4 u. 46 S.   H. S.

   In favor of abolishing the proprietary system of government.

Eine Neue Anrede an die Deutschen in Philadelphia.—„Salbe deine
   Augen mit Augensalbe". Gedruckt zur Zeit und in dem Jahr Da
   Einer wider'n Andern war. 4to. 4 S.   H. S.

Eine dem Hochedlen Herrn Gouvernör und der Landesversammlung der
   Provinz Pennsylvanien übergebene Erklärung und Vorstellung von
   den bedrängten und in Todesgefahr stehenden Einwohnern an den
   Grenzen dieser Provinz: Worin die Uhrsachen ihrer letztherigen Unzu-
   friedenheit und Kummers angezeigt werden: Samt den Beschwerungen
   die sie ausgestanden haben und um deren Abschaffung sie unterthänig
   bitten. Aus dem Englischen übersetzt. 8vo. 16 S.   H. S.

Des Ehrw. Hrn. Philip Widders, ehmaligen Chur-Pfälzischen Reformirten
   Kirchenraths und Pfarrherrn in Mannhein Sechs und zwanzig
   Passions-Predigten.

                                                      Hildeburn.

Gemein-Litaney der Vereinigten Brüder.   Zum Gebrauch der Pennsylvanischen Gemeinen. 8vo. 8 S.

   A Moravian litany. The year of its publication is not certain.

Der Lockvögel Warnungsgesang vor den Stoßvögeln: Oder Nöthige
Beantwortung der sogenannten Getreuen Warnung gegen die Lockvögel.
8vo. 8 S.

> In favor of the existing government; against B. Franklin's policy.

Eine Lustige Aria über die letztgeschehene Unruhen in Philadelphia. 4to.
1 Blatt.

Hildeburn.

> The printer's name is not mentioned.

Der Neueste, Verbessert= und Zuverläßige Americanische Calender Auf
das 1765ste Jahr Christi u. s. w. Zum Drittenmal herausgegeben.

H. S.

* Der Wöchentliche Philadelphische Staatsbote. Fol. H. S.

Getreue Warnung gegen die Lockvögel. Samt einer Antwort auf die
andere Anrede an die deutsche Freyhalter der Stadt und County von
Philadelphia. Durch Germanicus. „Behalte was du hast." 8vo.
15 S.

H. S.

> For the proprietaries and against the re-election of Franklin. The friends
> of the latter had tried to smooth down Franklin's offence against the Ger-
> mans in calling them *boors*, by suggesting that *boor* was the same as Bauer,
> i. e. peasant, but *Germanicus* (probably non de plume of L. Weiss) declares
> that the proper equivalent for *boor* is Bauerntölpel and strongly advises his
> German countrymen not to vote for Franklin. *H. Keppele*, one of the
> elders of Zions church was on the anti-Franklin Ticket, which the congre-
> gation voted for "unitis viribus". Franklin was defeated.

Protestation gegen die Bestellung Herrn Benjamin Franklins zu einem
Agenten für diese Provinz. Fol. 1 S. H. S.

> Among the signers of this protest is Henrich Keppele.

1765.

Ephrata.

Beissel, C. A Dissertation on Mans Fall. Translated from the
High-German Original. 8vo. 37 pp.

> The vignette on the title page represents an altar with a nest of unfledged
> swallows opening their bills for food which the older swallows are bringing.
> Inscription of the altar: *Non omnibus simal.* Circular legend around the
> picture: *Invenit Hirundo Nidum Jehovah Altaria tua. Deliciae Ephratenses.*
> This strange book rehearses in very uncouth language the theory of
> mystic writers concerning the fall of man. Originally the male and female
> essence were united in one individual (Adam), but through his fault the
> "divine Sophia", the womanly constituent of his being, became dissociated
> and fled. A fleshly companion, Eve, was created for him. Redemption is
> effected through Christ, the Virgin's son, with whose aid we can recover
> the lost female essence and lead a virgin life.

Germantown. Chrift. Saur.

Arnd, Johann. Des Gottseligen und Hocherleuchteten Lehrers, Hrn. Johann Arnds, Weiland General=Superintendentens des Fürstenthums Lüneburg, Paradieß=Gärtlein, Zur Uebung des wahren Christenthums durch Geistreiche Gebäter in die Seele zu pflanzen. u. s. w. 16mo. Vorrede 32 S. Text 531 S. u. Register.

G. S.

Die Erste Frucht der Teutschen Gesellschaft. Ein Lands=Gesetz, worin noch fernere Verordnungen hinzu gethan werden zu demjenigen Landes Gesetz, welches den Titel führet: „Ein Landes=Gesetz, worin verboten wird, daß von den Teutschen sowohl als andern Passagieren nicht zu viele mit einander in ein Schiff gepackt und hieher überge= bracht werden mögen" nebst einem Auszug aus demselben Landes= Gesetz. Auf Verordnung der Teutschen Gesellschafft aus dem Englischen übersetzt. 8vo. 15 S.

G. S.

A petition of the German Society to the Assembly for better protection of immigrants during their passage and after their arrival was laid before that body January 11, 1765. A bill based upon it was passed February 13, but failed to get the signature of Governor John Penn. A law not covering all points to which the German Society had called attention, but on the whole acceptable, was passed May 18, 1762 and was hailed as the "First Fruit of the German Society". For further details see *Seidensticker, Geschichte der Deutschen Gesellschaft.*, p. 46—49.

Saur, Christoph. Werthefte Landes=Leute, sonderlich in Philadel= phia, Bucks und Berck's County. Fol. 2 S.

An address of Christopher Sower's on the political questions of the day. He disapproves of a change of government and favors a convention to petition the King for the repeal of the Stamp Act.

Der Hoch=Deutsche Americanische Calender, Auf das Jahr . . 1766 u. s. w. 4to. 48 S.

G. S.—H. S.

* Germantauner Zeitung, Oder: Sammlung u. s. w.

Antwort auf Hrn. Fränklins Anmerckungen über ein ohnlängst herausge= kommenes Protestations=Schreiben. Uebersetzt aus dem Englischen. 12mo. 27 S.

G. S.

Severe Strictures on Benjamin Franklin. The publisher's name and place are not mentioned.

Philadelphia. Anton Armbrüster.

Evangelischer Unterricht, wie die Confirmation, d. i.: Die Tauf=Bunds Erneuerung . . anzustellen. Gedruckt in Stuttgart und Tübingen. In Philadelphia nachgedruckt von Anton Armbrüster in der Räs= Straffe.

H. S.

Neu=eingerichteter Americanischer Geschichts= und Haus=Calender. Auf
das Jahr 1766.

An Account of a surprizing Phenomenon, which appeared in the
City of Philadelphia and different places of Pennsylvania on
Saturday, the 2d of February 1775. 4to. 4 pp.

It was simply a meteor.

The Christian Letter to Presbyterian, Church and Quaker. 8vo.
12 pp. H. S.

Philadelphia. Henrich Miller.

An die Deutschen vornehmlich die zum Wählen berechtigten in Philadelphia,
Bucks und Bercks County. Fol. 2 S. H. S.

In defence of B. Franklin against the aspersions of Ch. Saur.

Etwas aus der Schatzlade des Alterthums. Das ist: Ein Christlicher
Gesang von dem Leben und Regierung Unseres Hochverdienten Herrn
Jesu Christi seith dessen Erscheinung im Fleisch bis auf unsere Zeiten.
8vo. 8 S. H. S.

Die Geheiligten Wissenschaften unter dem Kreutze. Ein Traum. 8vo.
8 S. H. S.

A reprint.

Der Neueste, Verbessert= und Zuverläßige Americanische Calender. Auf
das 1766ste Jahr Christi u. s. w. Zum Viertenmal herausgegeben.

Little vignettes with the constellation of the zodiac for every month and
rude figures representing seasonable occupations make their first appearance
in the almanac for 1766.

* Der Wöchentliche Philadelphische Staatsbote. Fol. H. S.

See 1762.

When the passage of the stamp act was announced Miller suspended the
publication of the Staatsbote "until it would appear, whether means can be
found to escape from the chains forged for the people and from unbearable
slavery." The suspension lasted only two weeks, from Oct. 28. to Nov. 18.

A Catalogue of Books belonging to the Union Library Company
of Philadelphia. 12mo. 40 pp. H. S.

Godfrey, J. Juvenile Poems on Various Subjects. With the
Prince of Parthia, a Tragedy. 4to. xxvi & 223 pp. H. S.

1766.

Ephrata. Typis et Consensu Societatis.

Parabiſiſches Wunder=Spiel, welches ſich in dieſen letzten Zeiten und
Tagen in denen Abenbländiſchen Welt=Theilen, als ein Vorſpiel der
neuen Welt hervorgethan: Beſtehend in einer neuen Sammlung
anbächtiger und zum Lob des groſen Gottes eingerichteter geiſtlicher
und ehebeſſen zum Theil publicirter Lieder. (Vignette wie in
Dissertation 1765.) 4to. Vorrede 7 S. Text 472 S. u. Reg.

G. S.—H. S.—S. W. P.

This is the last and most extensive collection of Ephrata hymns, numbering 725, of which not a few are of considerable length. Most of them had
been printed before in the Franklin hymnbooks (1730—1736) and in the
Turteltaube. The preface, probably written by Peter Miller, touches upon
the salient points of the Ephrata religion, the organization and peculiar
features of the community and the merits of Conrad Beissel. The *Wunderspiel* itself has four divisions, the first, Beissel's own, contains 441 hymns
all written by him, the 72 hymns of the second division were contributed
by the brethren, except a few taken from Fr. Rock's and G. Tersteegen's
writings; the third, which has the fragrant heading: *Ein angenehmer Geruch
der Lilien und Rosen,* is the poetical offering of 100 hymns by the sisters, and
the last, numbering 111 hymns, came from the wider circle of devotees who
were connected with the Ephrata establishment.

Altogether there were about thirty-five men and twenty-five women who
felt inspired by the sacred muse, a fact to which an edition of the *Turteltaube*
with names printed under the text gives the clue. For fine texture of
thought and neat versification brother Jaebez, (Peter Miller) surpasses all
others.

Friedensthal bei Bethlehem. *Johann Brandmüller.*

Zur Christ-Nacht. 8vo. 7 S. H. S.

Germantown. Chriſt. Saur.

Die Regeln der Teutſchen Geſellſchaft in Philadelphia. 12mo. 8 S.

P. S.

Since the issue of the first edition in 1764 some changes had been made
in the Rules.

Der Hoch=Deutſche Americaniſche Calender, Auf das Jahr . . 1767
u. ſ. w. 4to. 48 S. G. S.—H. S.

*Germantauner Zeitung, Ober: Sammlung u. ſ. w.

Philadelphia. Anton Armbrüſter.

Der Kleine Katechismus des ſel. D. Martin Luthers u. ſ. w. Sechſte und
vermehrte Auflage. Gedruckt und zu haben bey Anton Armbrüſter
in der Räßſtraſſe ohnweit dem Grünen Baum. H. S.

Philadelphia ben 19ten May 1766.　　　　　　　　　　　H. S.

　An account of the repeal of the Stamp Act is headed by an allegorical
cut and followed by twenty-six lines of verse disposed in two columns.

Neu=eingerichteter Americanischer Geschichts= und Haus=Calender.　Auf
das Jahr 1767.

Philadelphia.　Henrich Miller.

Mühlenberg, H. M.　Ein Zeugniß von der Güte und Ernst Gottes
gegen sein Bundesvolk in alten und neuen Zeiten und des Volkes
Undankbarkeit, gelegentlich des Dankfestes wegen Aufhebung der
Stempel=Acte, 1. August 1766.

Verbesserte A. B. C. oder Namenbücher nach der richtigen Buchstabier=Art.
　　　　　　　　　　　　　　　　　　　　　　　　　　(Hildeburn.)

Die Verhörung Doctor Benjamin Franklins vor der hohen Versammlung
des Hauses der Gemeinen von Groß=Brittanien, die Stämpel=Act ꝛc.
betreffend.　Aus dem Englischen übersetzt.　12mo. 43 S.　G. S.

Der Neueste, Verbessert= und Zuverläßige Americanische Calender.　Auf
das 1767ste Jahr Christi u. s. w.　Zum Fünftenmal herausgegeben.

*Der Wöchentliche Philadelphische Staatsbote.　Fol.　　　H. S.

　The repeal of the stamp act was heralded in an extra leaf, headed by the
verses:
　　　　　Den Herren lobt und benedeyt,
　　　　　Der von der Stämpel Act uns hat befreyt.

Benezet, A.　A Caution and Warning to Great Britain and her
　Colonies in a short Representation of the calamitous State of
　the enslaved Negroes in British Dominions.　8vo. 35 pp.
　　　　　　　　　　　　　　　　　　　　　　H. S.

Christian Piety, freed from the many Delusions of Modern
　Enthusiasts of all Denominations.　Daily Conversations
　with God exemplified in the Life of Armelle Nicolas.　12mo.
　22 pp.　　　　　　　　　　　　　　　　　H. S.

　Reprint from a London edition.

Evans, N.　The Love of the World incompatible with the Love
　of God.　A Discourse.　8vo. 22 pp.
　　　　　　　　　　　　　　　　Hildeburn.

Law, Wm.　An Extract from a Treatise by Wm. Law, M. A.
　called the Spirit of Prayer; or, the Soul rising out of Vanity
　of Time into the Riches of Eternity.　8vo. 48 pp.

Roberts, D. Some Memoirs of the Life of John Roberts. Written by his son Daniel Roberts. Fifth Edition. 8vo. 67 pp.

H. S.

Originally printed in London and Bristol.

Thoughts of the Nature of War and its repugnancy to the Christian Life. 8vo. 30 pp. ·H. S.

Zubly, J. J. Sermon on the Repeal of the Stamp Act.

Advertisement.

Publisher unknown.

* Wahre und wahrſcheinliche Begebenheiten auf ungeſtempfelten Papier weil kein geſtempfeltes zu haben iſt.

(Cassel.)

Number of a newspaper, dated March 5, 1766 without place of issue and printer's name, as the publication was an infringement on the stamp act.

1767.
Ephrata.

The Family Prayer Book. Containing Morning and Evening Prayers for Families and private Persons. Together with the Church-Catechism collected and published chiefly for the Use of Episcopal Congregations of Lancaster, Pequea and Caernarvon. Ephrata. Printed for William Barton. 12mo. 40 pp.

Followed by

Directions for a devout and decent Behaviour in the Public Worship of God. 27 pp.

The Church Catechism. 8 pp.

Friedensthal bei Bethlehem. *Johann Brandmüller.*

Die täglichen Loosungen der Brüder-Gemeinde für das Jahr 1767. Gedruckt bey Bethlehem in der Fork Dellawar. H. S.

Ein Psalm zum grossen Sabbath. Fol. 4 pp.

Germantown. Chriſtoph Saur.

Ausbundt, Das iſt: Etliche ſchöne Chriſtliche Lieder. Zum Drittenmal aufgelegt in Pennſylvanien u. ſ. w. 12mo. 10, 812, 6 u. 96 S.

See 1742.

Kurße Unterweiſung vor Kleine Kinder. 16mo. 48 S. G. S.

Der Hoch=Deutsche Americanische Calender. Auf das Jahr . . 1768
u. s. w. 4to. 48 S. ·

G. S.— H. S.

* Germantauner Zeitung, Oder: Sammlung u. s. w.

Philadelphia. Anton Armbrüster.

Der Gantze Psalter des Königs und Propheten Davids. Verdeutscht von
D. Martin Luther. 12mo. 350 S.

Neu=eingerichteter Americanischer. Stadt und Land Calender. Auf das
Jahr . . 1768. Zum funfzehendenmahl ans Licht gegeben. . .
Gedruckt und zu haben bey Anton Armbrüster in der Räß Strasse
ohnweit dem grünen Baum=Wirth.

Printed in black and red. It is questionable whether the series of these
almanacs extended beyond this year.

The Gospel explained according to the III. Chapter of St. John,
3d verse. Delivered in five propositions.

Hildeburn.

Philadelphia. Henrich Miller.
(Zweite Straße.)

Auszug aus einer Rede Thomas Hartleys, eines Lehrers der Englischen
Kirche, über die Mißbegriffe, die Religion betreffend. Aus dem
Englischen übersetzt. 8vo. 8 S.

Der Kleine Katechismus Lutheri mit der Ordnung des Heils und dem
Würtembergischen Kurzen Kinder=Examen u. s. w.

Die Täglichen Loosungen der Brüder=Gemeine für das Jahr 1768.
16mo. 42 S.

H. S.

Der Neueste, Verbessert= und Zuverläßige Americanische Calender. Auf
das 1768ste Jahr Christi u. s. w.

* Der Wöchentliche Philadelphische Staatsbote. Fol.

H. S.

The vignette at the top of the title was slightly changed on and after
February 25, the mounted post=boy, instead of carrying a scroll with the
inscription "Novae" blows a horn.

Daily Conversation with God, exemplified in the Holy Life of
Armelle Nicolas . . deceased in Bretaigne in the year 1671.
. 12mo. 16 pp.

De Foe, D. The dreadful Visitation: In a short account of the progress and effects of the plague·the last time it spread in the City of London. 16mo. 16 pp.

The Emptiness and Vanity of a Life spent in the pursuit of worldly profit, ease or pleasure, etc. 16mo. 16 pp. H. S.

Extract from an address in the Virginia Gazette March 19, 1767. 8vo. 4 pp.   H. S.
Hildeburn.

The Genuine Letter from the Baptist Association met in Philadelphia.
Hildeburn.

1768.

Ephrata. Brüderschafft.

Ein Lob-Lied dem in GOTT geehrten Vatter Friedsam zum Andencken abgesungen. Als die ehrwürdige Jungfrau und Schwester ATHA-NASIA seinen Hingang aus der Zeit mit einem Liebesmahl beehrte. Geschehen den 29ften August 1768.

Conrad Beissel, the head of the Ephrata convent, died, upward of 77 years old, on the 6th of July 1768. Sister Anastasia (Thome) one of the hymnwriters, was a Swiss woman, whose earthly love and pious resignation are the subject of a pleasing episode in the Ephrata chronicles.

Germantown. (Germanton.) Chr. Saur.

Schabalie, J. P. Die Wandlende Seel durch Johann Schabalie in Niederländischer Sprache beschrieben; anjetzo aber in die Hochteutsche Sprach übersetzt. 12mo. 463 S.

See 1763.

Der Psalter des Königs und Propheten Davids, verteutschet von D. Martin Luther. Fünfte Auflage. 24mo. 252 S.   G. S.

Siegvolck, Georg Paul. Das von Jesu Christo, dem Richter der Lebendigen und Todten, aller Creatur zu predigen befohlene Ewige Evangelium von der durch Ihn erfundenen Ewigen Erlösung, wodurch Alles, was da heisset Teufel, Sünde, Hölle und Tod endlich gantz und gar vernichtiget und also alle Geschöpfe, die von Gott sehr gut erschaffen worden, nach genügsam geoffenbahrter Göttlichen Straff-Gerechtigkeit, wiederum in ihre uranfängliche Reinigkeit und Seligkeit gebracht werden sollen. 12mo. 9 u. 175 S.

An English translation of this plea for universal salvation was published by Saur in 1753.

Der Hoch=Deutsche Americanische Calender. Auf das Jahr . . 1769
    u. s. w. 4to. 48 S.   G. S.—H. S.

* Germantauner Zeitung, Oder: Sammlung u. s. w.
    See 1762.

Philadelphia. H. Miller.

Der Heidelbergische Catechismus Samt der Haus=Tafel.

Die Lehr=Texte der Brüder=Gemeine und insonderheit der Kinder für das
    Jahr 1769. 8vo. 39 S.   H. S.

Die Täglichen Loosungen der Brüder=Gemeine für das Jahr 1768.
                                        H. S.

Der Psalter des Königs und Propheten Davids, verteutschet von D.
    Martin Luther. 16mo. 252 S.   G. S.

Ein schön Lied von dem Schweizerischen Erz=Freyheitsfohn Wilhelm
    Tellen, dem Urheber der löbl. Eydgenossenschaft. Samt einem
    andern Liede von dem Ursprung und Herkommen der Schweizer.
    12mo. 14 S. (nicht paginirt.)   H. S.

Der Neueste, Verbessert= und Zuverläßige Americanische Calender Auf
    das 1769ste Jahr.

* Der Wöchentliche Pennsylvanische Staatsbote. Fol.   H. S.
    For *Philadelphische* the designation *Pennsylvanische* was substituted this
    year.

The Baptist Association held in Philadelphia the 11. 12. & 13.
    day of October 1768 to the Churches thereunto belonging.
    Fol. 3 pp.
                                      Hildeburn.

1769.

Ephrata. Typis Societatis.

(Roosen, Gerhard.) Christliches Gemüths=Gespräch von dem Geist=
    lichen und seligmachenden Glauben und Erkäntnüß der Wahrheit so
    zu der Gottseligkeit führet etc. 8vo. 168 S.   G. S.
    Mennonite tract on Religion and religious institutions, arranged in the
    form of questions and answers.

Germantown. Chriſtoph Saur.

(Terſteegen.) Geiſtliches Blumen-Gärtlein Inniger Seelen, u. ſ. w.
Fünfte und vermehrte Edition. Nebſt der Frommen Lotterie. 16mo.
526 S. u, Reg.   G. S.

    First edition 1747.

Das Neue Teſtament Unſers Herrn und Heylands Jeſu Chriſti. Verteutſchet von D. Martin Luther. Sechſte Auflage. 12mo. 529 S.

Siegvolck, Georg Paul. Das von Jeſu Chriſto, dem Richter der
Lebendigen und Todten, aller Creatur zu predigen befohlene Ewige
Evangelium u. ſ. w. 12mo. 175 S.

    See 1768. The issue of 1769 was not designated as a second edition and
    appears to be identical with that of 1768.

Der Hoch-Deutſche Americaniſche Calender. Auf das Jahr . . 1770
u. ſ. w. 4to. 48 S.   G. S.—H. S.

*Germantauner Zeitung, Oder Sammlung u. ſ. w.

The Sentiments and Plans of the Warren Association.   4to. 4 pp.

Philadelphia. Henrich Miller.

Die Geſchichte der Tage des Menſchen-Sohnes von der Marter-Woche an
bis zu Seiner Himmelfahrt. . . Zu haben mit oder ohne Wilcocks
Honigtropfen. 16mo. 88 S.

Die Lehr-Texte der Brüder-Gemeine, und inſonderheit der Kinder, für das
Jahr 1770.

                                   (Hildeburn.)

Die Täglichen Looſungen der Brüder-Gemeine für das Jahr 1770.

Der Neueſte, Verbeſſert- und Zuverläßige Americaniſche Calender Auf
das 1770ſte Jahr, u. ſ. w.

* Der Wöchentliche Pennſylvaniſche Staatsbote. Fol.   H. S.

Anno Regni Georgii III. Regis Magnae Britaniae, Franciae et
Hiberniae Nono. At a General Assembly of the Province of
Pennsylvania, begun and holden at Philadelphia the four-
teenth day of October A. D. 1768 . . and from thence continued by Adjournment to the eighteenth day of February
1769. Fol. 101 pp. And from thence continued by Adjournments to the twenty-seventh day of May 1769. p. 105
—108.   H. S.

1770.

Ephrata, Brüderschaft.

(Roosen, Gerhard.) Christliches Gemüthsgespräch von dem Geistlichen und seligmachenden Glauben u. s. w. 12mo. 248 S.

Printed with the *Ernsthafte Christenpflicht*.

Die Ernsthafte Christenpflicht, darinen schöne Gebäter, darmit sich fromme
Christen-Hertzen zu allen Zeiten und in allen Nöthen trösten können.
12mo. 99 S.   G. S.—H. S.

First edition 1745.

Germantown. Chr. Saur.

Deigendesch, J. Nachrichters: Oder Nützliches und aufrichtiges Roß-
Artzney-Büchlein. . Auch wird gelehret einige Composita selbsten
zu machen, insonderheit das sympatetische Pulver und dessen Appli-
cirung wie auch der Freyschnitt mit dem Klettenstock.; Welchem
annoch beygefüget ein Anhang von Rind-Viehs Artzeneyen, u. s. w.
Von einem Scharffrichter Johannes Deigendesch. 24mo. 209 S.
u. Reg.

Dock, Christoph. Eine Einfältige und gründlich abgefaßte Schul-
Ordnung, darinnen deutlich vorgestelt wird, auf welche Weiße die
Kinder nicht nur in denen in Schulen gewöhnlichen Lehren bestens
angebracht, sondern auch in der Lehre der Gottseligkeit wohl
unterrichtet werden mögen. Aus Liebe zu dem menschlichen Geschlecht
aufgesetzt durch den wohlerfahrenen und lang geübten Schulmeister,
Christoph Dock. Und durch einige Freunde des gemeinen Bestens den
Druck übergeben. Die Zweyte Edition. 8vo. Saur's Vorrede
6 S. Text 34 S.   G. S.

Two editions of the book were published in 1770. For a full account of
Chr. Dock and his works see Pennypacker's *Historical and Biographical
Sketches*. While this early and interesting specimen of German-American
pedagogics was written by Schoolmaster Dock in the year 1750, it was not
published, as we learn from Ch. Saur's preface, till 1770, after the author
had passed away.

Frantzen, M. Einfältige Lehr-Betrachtungen und Kurtzgefaßtes Glau-
bens-Bekänntniß des gottseligen Lehrers Michael Frantzen, weyland
gewesenen Vorstehers der Täuffer-Gemeine in Canestogoe. 16mo.
47 S.   G. S.

Religious ordinances and moral precepts of the Dunkers, partly in
doggerel rhyme, partly in prose.

Lucius, Samuel. Die Parabisische Alve der Jungfräulichen Keusch=
heit, welche Gott giebet allen, die da sind aus dem Glauben an den
Herren Jesum: Wobey gelehret wird, wie dieses Himmlische Gewächs
mit Christi Dornen=Cron als einem Leb=Hag umzäunet werden müsse,
damit es nicht von der höchst=schädlichen gifftigen Fleisches=Lust
verderbet werde. Gesammlet und ausgepresset von Gratinao
Christophilo. 12mo. 304 S.   G. S.

> Rev. 'Samuel Lucius or Lutz of Berne (1674—1750) wrote a number of
> books in an affected flowery style.

Vollständiges Marburger Gesang=Buch u. s. w. 12mo. Anweisung 10 S.
Text 470 S. Register 13 S. Anhang 82 S.   H. S.

> See 1759 and 1762.

Der Hoch=Deutsche Americanische Calender, Auf das Jahr . . 1771
u. s. w. 4to. 48 S.   G. S.—H. S.

* Germantauner Zeitung, etc.

Philadelphia.   H. Miller.

Francke, A. H. Der heilige und sichere Glaubensweg eines Evangeli=
schen Christen.—The Holy and Sure way of Faith of an Evangelical Christian. Second Edition. 16mo. 16 pp.   H. S.

> German and English on alternate pages. Augustus Hermann Francke
> was the famous founder of the Halle orphanage.

Der Kleine Catechismus des sel. D. Martin Luthers. Nebst den gewöhnli=
chen Morgen= Tisch= und Abend=Gebethern u. s. w. Siebente
Auflage. 12mo. 4 u. 144 S.

Die Lehr=Texte der Brüder=Gemeine für das Jahr 1771. 8vo. 64 S.

Liturgische Gesänge der Brüder=Gemeinen, auf neue revidirt. 16mo.
48 S.

Secombe, J. Eine zu Halifax den 3ten July 1770 gehaltene Predigt
an die hoch=deutsch Reformirten Gemeine zu Lüneburg in Nova Scotia.
Aus dem Englischen übersetzt.

> Advertised in the Penns. Staatsbote.

Die Täglichen Loosungen der Brüder=Gemeine für das Jahr 1771.
8vo. 58 S.

Ziguerer, C. Prediger zu Grusch in Graubünden. Theologisches Bedenken zur Beantwortung der Frage: Woher das jetzige Verderben der Christenheit in Lehr und Leben komme? 8vo. 46 S.   H. S.

Der Neueste, Verbessert= und Zuverläßige Americanische Calender. Auf das 1771ste Jahr u. s. w.

* Der Wöchentliche Pennsylvanische Staatsbote. Fol.

David, E. Offers of Christ. No Gospel Preaching. To which is added a Word of advice to a young Gospel minister.
H. S.

Elmer, J. Dissertatio Medica Inauguralis de Sitis in Febribus causis et remediis. 23 pp.   P. S.

Votes and Proceedings of the House of Representatives of the Province of Pennsylvania, met at Philadelphia 14th of Oct. A. D. 1769 and continued by adjournments. Fol. p. 113—201.

The same p. 205—300.

Zubly, J. J. Funeral Sermon on the Death of George Whitefield.
Advertisement.

1771.
Ephrata. Albert Conrad Reben.
Der Americanische Calender auf das 1772ste Jahr Christi . . Ephrata mit Bewilligung der Brüderschaft gedruckt von Albert Conrad Reben. 4to. 40 S.

Whether this almanac appeared for other years is not known.

Germantown. Christ. Saur.

Deigenbesch, Johannes. Nachrichters: Oder Nützliches und auf= richtiges Roß=Artzney Büchlein. Von einem Scharfrichter Johannes Deigenbesch. Zweyter Druck. 16mo. 209 S. Register und An= hänge 19 S.   G. S.

Schabalie, Johann Philipp. Die Wandlende Seel, Das ist: Gespräch der Wandlenden Seelen mit Adam, Noah und Simon Cleophas u. s. w. Die Zweite Auflage. 12mo. Vorrede 4 S. Text 463 S. u. Register.   G. S.

Der Weg der Gottseligkeit oder Empfindungen und Erfahrungen im Christenthum auf dem Wege zum Himmel.

According to Mr. A. C. Cassel this essay appeared also in the first number of the Geistliche Magazien for 1772.

Der Hoch=Deutsche Americanische Calender. Auf das Jahr . . 1772 u. s. w. 4to. 48 S. G. S.—H. S.

* Die Germantowner Zeitung.

Philadelphia. Henrich Miller.

Die Lehr=Texte der Bruder=Gemeinde und insonderheit der Kinder für das Jahr 1772.

Hildeburn.

Wohl=eingerichtetes Vieh=Arzney=Buch, worin enthalten die Wartung und Pflege, sowohl als die Krankheiten und Heilungsmittel 1. Der Pferde, 2. Des Rindviehes, 3. Der Schafe, 4. Der Schweine, 5. Der Gänse und Hühner. 12mo. 10 u. 184 S. G. S.

Der Neueste, Verbessert= und Zuverläßige Americanische Calender. Auf das 1772ste Jahr Christi u. s. w. Zum Zehntenmal herausgegeben.

* Der Wöchentliche Pennsylvanische Staatsbote. Fol.

Name of place and printer not given.

Furman, Moore. An das Publicum. Fol. 4 S. H. S.

A vindication of the writer's character, that had been assailed by Isaac Wikoff.

1772.

Ephrata.

Der Christliche Calender.

Hildeburn.

Germantown. Christoph Saur.

Neu= vermehrt= und vollständiges Gesang=Buch, worinnen sowohl die Psalmen Davids, nach D. Ambrosii Lobwassers Uebersetzung, hin und wieder verbessert, als auch 730 auserlesener alter und neuer geistreichen Lieder begriffen sind, u. s. w. Dritte Auflage.

The first edition of this Reformed hymnbook appeared in 1753, the second in 1763.

Eine nützliche Anweisung oder Beyhülffe vor Deutsche um Englisch zu lernen. . . Nebst einer Grammatic vor diejenigen, welche in andern Sprachen und deren Fundamenten erfahren sind. Dritte Auflage. 12mo. Vorrede 2 S., Text 262 S., Appendix 4 S.   H. S.
>   See 1751 and 1762.

Der Hoch=Deutsch Americanische Calender, Auf das Jahr . . 1773 u. s. w.   4to. 48 S.   G. S.—H. S.

*Die Germantauner Zeitung.

Philadelphia. *William Mentz.*

Goldsmith, O. The Vicar of Wakefield. A Tale. Supposed to be written by himself. Philadelphia. Printed for William Mentz and sold by most of the Booksellers in America. 2 vols. 12mo. 180 pp.

> Wm. Mentz arrived in America 1754 and opened a bookstore in Philadelphia. His son and grandson were printers and publishers.

Philadelphia. Henrich Miller.

Die Artikel der Patriotischen Gesellschaft.   PHILA. LIBRARY.
> The year of publication is not certain.

Die Lehr=Texte der Brüder=Gemeine für das Jahr 1773. 8vo. 72 S.
>   H. S.

Die Loosungen der Brüder=Gemeine für das Jahr 1773. 8vo. 55 S.
>   H. S.

Tersteegen, G. Die Kraft der Liebe Christi. Angepriesen und angewiesen in einer Erweckungs=Rede über 2 Corinth. 5, 14. gehalten am 18. Oct. 1751 zu Mühlheim. 8vo. 64 S.

Der Neueste, Verbessert= und zuverläßige Americanische Calender. Auf das 1773ste Jahr Christi u. s. w.

* Der Wöchentliche Pennsylvanische Staatsbote. Fol.

Bachmair, *John James M. A.* A complete German Grammar in two Parts, the first, containing the *Theory* of the Language through all the parts of Speech, the second part is the *Practice* in as ample a manner as can be desired. 8vo. Preface 2 pp. Text 313 pp. and Index.   G. S.

> The first edition of Bachmair's Grammar appeared in London 1751, the third in 1771. Of the latter the American edition of 1772 is a reprint. It remained for a long time the standard German Grammar.

Votes and Proceedings of the House of Representatives of the Province of Pennsylvania. (From October 14, 1771 on.) Fol. p. 303—412. H. S.

Druďer unbekannt.

Otto, Johann Heinrich. Ein geiſtlich Lied auf Paul Springs Selbſtmord mit einer Piſtole, ſo ſich im Jahr 1772 im Monat September in Lancaſter County, Cocalico Township, zutrug. Fol. 1 S. H. S.

1773.

Ephrata. Brüderſchaft.

Deliciae Ephratenses. Pars I. Oder des ehrwürdigen Vatters, Friedſam Gottrecht, Weyland Stiffters und Führers des Chriſtlichen Ordens der Einſamen in Ephrata in Pennsylvania Geiſtliche Reden. 4to. 340 S. G. S.

A posthumous publication of Conrad Beissel's addresses on high grade mysticism. The writer fluctuates between paroxysms of mental agony and transports of ecstatic joy, attempts to peer into the mysteries of creation and human destiny and constructs a system of theosophy of "such stuff as dreams are made on." Biblical history, the phenomena of nature and sexual relations furnish him material for fanciful allegories.

A different book was the *Lectiones*, of which the *Chronicon Ephratense* remarks as follows: "At this time (about 1735) the *Lectiones* were first instituted in the Settlement; namely, the *Vorsteher* (Conrad Beissel) ordered that weekly, on the evening of the sixth day, every one should examine his heart before God, in his own cell, and then hand in to the *Vorsteher* a written statement of his spiritual condition, which he read at the meeting of the congregation on the following Sabbath. These confessional papers were called *Lectiones* and several hundred of them were afterwards published, in printed form" (Transl. of the *Chronicon* p. 81.)

It is not unlikely that the publication alluded to in this remark is the *Theosophishe Lectionen*, printed in 1752, in which case the contents of that book should not be credited, as has been done, to Conrad Beissel, but to his disciples.

Germantown. Chriſtoph Saur.

Der Kleine Kempis oder Kurze Sprüche und Gebätlein aus denen meiſtens unbekannten Werďlein des Thomas a Kempis zuſammen getragen zur Erbauung der Kleinen. Fünfte Auflage. 16mo. 10 u. 155 S.

First edition in 1750.

Terſteegen Geiſtliches Blumen=Gärtlein Inniger Seelen; Oder kurze Schluß=Reimen, Betrachtungen und Lieder. Sechſte Auflage. 24mo. 12 u. 547 S. H. S.

As far as we know only two editions were previously printed in America, viz. in 1747 and 1769.

Der Hoch=Deutsch Americanische Calender, Auf das Jahr . . 1774
u. s. w. 4to. 48 S. G. S.—H. S.

* Die Germantauner Zeitung.

Philadelphia. Henrich Miller.

Frühauf, Daniel. Beschreibung der bevorstehenden Partial Monds=
Finsterniß, so aus dem Meridian zu Philadelphia sichtbar seyn wird
den 7ten April im Jahr 1773. 8vo. 16 S. PHILA. LIBRARY.

Die Lehrtexte der Brüder=Gemeine für das Jahr 1774. H. S.

Die Täglichen Loosungen der Brüder=Gemeine für das Jahr 1774. 48 S.

Publicus. An die guten Einwohner in Pennsylvanien. Fol. 2 S.

Zum 29sten August 1773. 4to. 4 S.

> A memorial psalm.

Der Neueste, Verbessert= und Zuverläßige Americanische Calender. Auf
das 1774ste Jahr Christi u. s. w.

* Der Wöchentliche Pennsylvanische Staatsbote. Fol. H. S.

Votes and Proceedings of the House of Representatives. Met at
Philadelphia Oct. 14th 1772 and continued by adjournments.
Fol. p. 415—498.

1774.

Friederichs=Stadt. (Frederick, Md.) Matthias Bartgis.

Der Erfahrene Americanische Haus= und Stall=Arzt.

Germantown. Christoph Saur.

Fenning, Daniel. Der Geschwinde Rechner, Oder: Des Händlers
nützlicher Gehülfe; in Kauffung und Verkauffung allerley Sachen
sowohl im Grossen als Kleinen. 8vo. 280 S. H. S.

Gruber, Eberhard Ludwig. Grundforschende Fragen, welche denen
neuen Täufern im Wittgensteinischen, insonderheit zu beantworten
vorgelegt waren, sammt beygefügten kurzen und einfältigen Antworten
auf dieselben, vormals schriftlich heraus gegeben von einem Aufrichti=
gen Mitglied der Gemeine zu Wittgenstein. Zweyte Auflage.
16mo. 58 S. G. S.—H. S.

The, writer who called himself *Aufrichtiges Mitglied*, was *Alexander Mack, Sr.* and the New Baptists of Wittgenstein were the Dunkers who organized their Society in 1708 at Schwarzenau under Al. Mack's lead. E. L. Gruber, to whose questions Mack published this reply in 1713, was at the head of the "Inspired" at Marienborn and Schwarzenau. See M. Goebel's Articles on the "Inspired" in Niedner's Zeitschrift für historische Theologie 1854 — 1857.

Mack, Alexander. Kurtze und einfältige Vorstellung der äussern, aber doch heiligen Rechten und Ordnungen des Hauses Gottes, vorgestellt in einem Gespräch unter Vater und Sohn. Zweyte Auflage. 16mo. Vorbericht u. Vorrede 20 S., Text 134 S. G. S.

A concise statement of the faith, moral precepts and congregational rules of the Dunkers. The preface gives a history of their origin. The writer, Alexander Mack, Jr., born at Schwarzenau in 1712, immigrated in 1729 with the fraction of the Dunkers, who had found a refuge in Rüstringen, Ost Friesland. He became in Pennsylvania one of their ministers and influential leaders.

Nachdrückliche Buß=Stimme und Warnungs=Posaune vom Himmel an alle boßhaften Sünder auf Erden. Oder Thomas Chamberlains letzte Leichen=Rede. Aus dem Englischen. 16mo. 22 S.

Vollständiges Marburger Gesangbuch in 680 christlichen und trostreichen Psalmen und Gesängen. Vierte Auflage.

Der Hoch=Deutsch Americanische Calender. Auf das Jahr . . 1775 u. s. w. 4to. 48 S.

* Die Germantauner Zeitung.

Fenning, Daniel. The Ready Reckoner; or Trader's most useful Assistent, in buying and selling all sorts of commodities either wholesale or retail, etc. 8vo. 280 pp.

A reprint of the seventh London edition.

Lancaster. Frantz Bailey.

Erzehlung derer durch Samuel Brand verübten gantz unmenschlichen Thaten und seiner darauf erfolgten Hinrichtung. 8vo. 34 S.

Geschichte von der Pfaltz=Gräfin Genovefa.

Hildeburn.

According to Thomas' History of Printing (Second Ed. vol. I, p. 322) the widow of N. Hasselbach (the printer who, in 1763, moved his business from Chestnut Hill to Baltimore) sold the printing materials of her deceased husband to William Goddard in Baltimore, who again disposed of them to F. Bailey in Lancaster.

Philadelphia. Henrich Miller.

An die Einwohner der Stadt und County Philadelphia. 4to. 1 Blatt.
                                                        H. S.

> Appeal to the people of Philadelphia to suspend all business on the first
> of June to show sympathy with the people of Boston on account of the
> oppressive Port Bill.

An das Volck in Pennsylvanien. Erster Brief. Unterzeichnet: Ackermann.
Fol. 2 S.   H. S.

Auszüge aus den Stimmungen und Verhandlungen des Americanischen
   Congresses vom Vesten Lande, gehalten zu Philadelphia den 5ten
   September 1774. . . Herausgegeben auf Befehl des Congresses und
   aus dem Englischen übersetzt. 16mo. 96 S.   H. S.

Der Kleine Catechismus des sel. Dr. Martin Luthers. Achte Auflage.
   Mit einer neuen Tabelle vermehrt.

Die Lehr-Texte der Brüder-Gemeine für das Jahr 1775. 8vo. 60 S.
                                                        H. S.

Die Täglichen Loosungen der Brüder-Gemeine für das Jahr 1775.
   8vo. 55 S.   H. S.

Pomp, N. V. D. M. Kurzgefaßte Prüfungen der Lehre des Ewigen
   Evangeliums: Womit deutlich gezeiget wird, daß man die Wiederbringung aller Dinge in der Heiligen Schrift vergeblich suchet.
   12mo. Vorbericht 16 S., Text 200 S.   G. S.

> Written to refute P. Siegvolck's arguments for universal salvation (See
> 1753 and 1769). Nicholas Pomp was a minister of the Reformed church
> who came to America in 1765. He occupied the pulpit at Falckner Swamp,
> Baltimore, Indianfield etc. and died at Easton 1819.

Ein Schreiben an die Einwohner der Provinz Quebec. Auszug aus dem
   Protocoll des Congresses. 8vo. 14 S.

Thoma Wilcocks köstlicher Honig-Tropfen aus dem Felsen Christo u. s. w.
   In Englisch und deutscher Sprache gedruckt.
                                                        Hildeburn.

Der Neueste, Verbessert- und Zuverläßige Americanische Calender. Auf
   das 1775ste Jahr Christi u. s. w.

* Der Wöchentliche Pennsylvanische Staatsbote. Fol.   H. S.

Bachmair, J. J.   A Complete German Grammar.

Hildeburn.

See 1772.

Votes and Proceedings of·the House of Representatives of the Province of Pennsylvania. Beginning the 15th day of October 1744. Vol. IV. Fol. 856 pp.

1775.

Parthenopolis. (Ephrata).

Inwendige Glaubens= und Liebes=Uebung einer Seelen gegen Gott und deſſen Gegenwart. Kurtz und einfältig entworfen und angewieſen. Parthenopolis. Gedruckt Anno 1775 vor Jacob Kimmel. **H. S.**

Jacob Kimmel, one of the leaders of the "Gimsheim awakening" joined the Ephrata settlement in 1751 and died there at a great age in 1784.

Germantown. Chriſtoph Saur.

Hoch=Deutſches Lutheriſches A. B. C. und Namen=Büchlein. Für Kinder welche anfangen zu lernen.

Das Neue Teſtament unſers Herrn und Heylandes Jeſu Chriſti.   Siebente Auflage. 12mo. 529 S. u. Reg.   **G. S.**

Der Hoch=Deutſch= Americaniſche Calender, Auf das Jahr . . 1776 u. ſ. w.   4to. 48 S.

* Die Germantauner Zeitung.

Lancaſter. Frantz Bailey.

Der Gantz Neue. Verbeſſerte Nord=Americaniſche Calender.   Anf das 1776ſte Jahr Chriſti u. ſ. w.   Zum Erſtenmal herausgegeben und verfertigt von Anthony Sharp. 4to. 36 S.   **G. S.**

The plate of the title page is the same that had done service for Armbruster's and Franklin's German almanacs. The cone of light proceeding from the angel's trumpet has in different years different inscriptions.

Philadelphia. Henrich Miller.

An die Einwohner in Jrland von den Abgeordneten der Vereinigten Colonien im General=Congreß zu Philadelphia d. 16. May 1775. 12mo. 16 S.   **H. S.**

Feſt=Pſalm zum 29. Auguſt 1775. 8vo. 4 S. H. S.

Die Lehr=Texte der Brüder Gemeine für das Jahr 1776. 8vo. 68 S.

Die Täglichen Looſungen der Brüder=Gemeine für das Jahr 1776. 8vo. 60 S. H. S.

Eine kurtzgefaßte Hiſtoriſche Nachricht von den Kämpfen der Schweitzer für die Freyheit. 8vo. 16 S.

A timely publication evidently prompted by the political aspects of the period.

Pitt. Des Hoch=Edlen Grafen von Chatam Rede, gehalten im Hauſe der Lords den 20ſten Januar 1775. Bey Gelegenheit eines Vor= ſchlags zu einer Abdreſſe an Seine Mäjeſtät, den König, daß derſelbe unvorzüglich Befehle ertheilen möge, ſeine Truppen von Boſton ſogleich wegzuziehen, um die Gemüther ſeiner guten Unterthanen zu beruhigen.

Schreiben des Evangeliſch=Lutheriſchen und Reformirten Kirchen=Rathes wie auch der Beamten der Teutſchen Geſellſchaft in der Stadt Philadelphia an die Teutſchen Einwohner der Provinzen Neu=York und Nord=Carolina. 8vo. 40 S. H. S.

The publication of this pamphlet, authorized by the official boards of the German Churches and the German Society in Philadelphia, committed those bodies to the measures of Congress and the cause of the American Revolution.

The avowed object of the publication was to furnish the Germans in the Provinces of New York and North Carolina with information on the important issues of the day and to induce them to support Congress. As to the Germans in Pennsylvania they are represented as doing everything to sustain the measures of Congress, in organizing militia companies and corps of Yeagers, ready to march wherever and whenever summoned. The chairman of the committee which issued the pamphlet was Ludwig Weiss, Solicitor of the German Society.

Eine kurze und aufrichtige Erklärung an unſere wohlmeinende Aſſembly und alle andere hohe und niedrige in der Regierung und alle andere Freunde und Einwohner dieſes Landes, denen dies zu Geſicht kommen mag, ſowohl Engliſche als Deutſche. Den 7. November 1775. H. S.

The printer's name is not stated; it was probably H. Miller.

Der Neueſte, Verbeſſert= und Zuverläßige Americaniſche Calender auf das 1776ſte Jahr Chriſti. G. S.

* Der Wöchentliche Pennſylvaniſche Staatsbote.   H. S.

In March the title was changed into: Henrich Millers Pennſylvaniſcher Staatsbote. From this time till July 26, 1776 the paper appeared twice a week (Tuesday and Friday) on half a sheet, to satisfy the eagerness for news. It was then the only bi-weekly in Philadelphia.

Carmichael, Rev. John. A Self-defensive War lawful, proved in a sermon preached at Lancaster in the Presbyterian Church on Sabbath Morning June 4, 1775. 8vo. 34 pp.

Jones, David. Defensive war in a just Cause sinless. A Sermon preached on the day of the Continental Fast at Tredyffryn in Chester County. Published by request. 8vo. 27 pp.
                                                                            H. S.

Minutes of the Philadelphia Association. 8vo. 11 pp.
                                                                   Hildeburn.

Votes and Proceedings of the House of Representatives of the Province of Pennsylvania. Beginning 14th of October 1758. Vol. V. Fol. 560 pp.   H. S.

Zubly, J. J. The Law of Liberty. A Sermon on American Affairs preached at the opening of the Provincial Congress of Georgia.—With an Appendix giving a concise account of the struggles of Switzerland to recover Liberty. 8vo. 21 pp.

In spite of this blast for liberty, the Rev. J. J. Zubly sided afterwards with the Loyalists.   .

(*Zubly, J. J.*) Great Britain's Right to tax her Colonies.

Zubly, J. J. Pious Advice. Sermon on the Faith.
                                                              Advertisement.

Zubly, J. J. Letter to Mr. Frinck. Thoughts on the Day of Judgment.   •   ˙
                                                              Advertisement.

1776.
Ephrata.

Schneeberger, A. Das Raben-Geſchrey. Durch Br. Andreas auf Antitum. (Ein Lied von 10 Strophen.)

Schneeberger, B. Die Stimme der Turteltaube, durch Schw. Barbara Schneeberger. (Ein Lied von 8 Strophen.)

Andrew Schneeberger was the founder of the Snowhill Monastic Society, near Antietam in Franklin Co. Pa. It closely resembled the Ephrata community in its religious tenets, mode of worship, customs and ascetic seclusion.

Germantown. Chrift. Saur.

Biblia, Das ift: Die ganze Göttliche Heilige Schrift Alten und Neuen
Teftaments nach der Deutfchen Ueberfetzung D. Martin Luthers.
Dritte Auflage. 4to. 992 u. 227 S. u. Regifter. G. S.

> The first edition appeared 1743, the second 1763. In the preface to the
> third edition Ch. Saur could still say, that the German was the only
> European language in which, so far, the Bible had been printed in America.

Habermann, J. Chriftliche Morgen= und Abend=Gebäter u. f. w.
wie auch D. Neumanns Kern aller Gebäter. 24mo. 62 u. 55 S.
H. S.

Die Kinder Bibel. 24mo. 24 u. 463 S. H. S.

Der Hoch=Deutfch=Americanifche Calender. Auf das Jahr . . 1777
u. f. w. 4to. 48 S.

* Die Germantowner Zeitung. Herausgegeben von Chriftoph Saur und
Sohn.

> The number published July 3rd, property of Mr. A. H. Cassel, contains
> the following announcement, relating to the adoption by Congress, on July
> 2nd, of the resolution, which led two days after to the Declaration of Inde-
> pendence. „Geftern hat der Veftländifche Congreß die Vereinigten Colonien Freye
> Unabhängliche Staaten zu feyn erklärt."

Germantown. Chriftoph Saur, der Jüngere.

Das Alte Zeugniß und die Grund=Sätze des Volkes fo man Quäfer nennet,
erneuert in Anfehung des Königs und der Regierung und wegen den
nunmehr herrfchenden Unruhen in biefem und andern Theilen von
America. An das Volk überhaupt gerichtet. Germantown gedruckt
bey Chriftoph Saur, dem Jüngern, auf Koften der Verfaffer. 8vo.
8 S. H. S.

> Translation of a paper, issued by the Quakers "The Ancient Testimony"
> etc., setting forth the grounds of their loyalty to the King.
> Christoph Saur, Jr. (the third) whose name appears on the imprint of
> this and the following Germantown publications, was born June 27, 1754
> and died July 3, 1799. It is very likely, that his father wearied by the
> troublous times withdrew in 1776 from active business, leaving its manage-
> ment to younger hands. While he, in obedience to his religious principles,
> was an unflinching non-resistant, his sons, Christopher and Peter, became,
> as we shall see, identified with the Loyalists.

Barclay, Robert. Apologie Oder Vertheidigungs=Schrift der wahren
Chriftlichen Gottesgelahrtheit, wie folche unter dem Volk, fo man
aus Spott Quäfer, das ift, Zitterer nennet, vorgetragen und gelehret
wird. . . Nach der zweyten lateinifchen und neunten Englifchen
Herausgebung ganz von neuen ins Deutfche überfetzt. 12mo.
797 S. u. Regifter. G. S.

First German translation of Barclay's famous book in defence of the
Quakers. The first Latin edition appeared 1676, the first English in 1678.

Geßner, Salomon. Der Tod Abels. In fünf Gesängen. 12mo.
157 S. G. S.

Lancaster. Frantz Bailey.

Der Ganz Neue Verbesserte Nord=Americanische Calender. Auf das
1777ste Jahr. Zum Zweytenmal herausgegeben und verfertiget von
Gottlieb Himmelsbewunderer. 4to. 36 S. G. S.

Lancaster. Matthias Bartgis.

Der Allerneueste Nord=Americanische Calender auf das Jahr 1777. Zum
erstenmal herausgegeben.

The completeness of the title is doubtful. See Bartgis Almanac for
the next year.

Philadelphia. Henrich Miller.

Freylinghausen, J. A. Ordnung des Heyls, nebst einem Ver=
zeichniß der wichtigsten Kern=Sprüche der Heil. Schrift u. s. w.
Hildeburn.

John Anastasius Freylinghausen (1670—1739) was a renowned theologian
and hymnwriter of the pietistic school.

Kurze Angaben von dem Verfahren der Convention des Staats von
Pennsylvanien, gehalten zu Philadelphia d. 15. July 1776. Fol.
17 S. H. S.

Die Repräsentanten der Vereinigten Staaten von America im Congreß
versammlet. An das Volk überhaupt und an die Einwohner
Pennsylvaniens und der angrenzenden Staaten insbesondere. Fol.
1 Blatt. H. S.

This proclamation, dated 10th of December 1776, was issued in English
and German, when the approach of the English army by way of New
Jersey, threatened Philadelphia.

Zum 24sten Juni 1776. 4 S. (Herrnhutischer Fest=Psalm.)

Der Neueste, Verbessert= und Zuverläßige Americanische Calender. Auf
das 1777ste Jahr Christi, u. s. w.

* Henrich Millers Pennſylvaniſcher Staatsbote. Fol.

. Miller's *Staatsbote* was the only Philadelphia paper which appeared on
Friday and as the fourth of July 1776 fell on a Thursday, the *Staatsbote* was
the first paper, that gave publicity to the fact, that Independence had been
declared. In the next issue on the following Tuesday an extra leaf brought
the full text of the Declaration of Independence in German, printed in
large conspicuous type.

After the 30th of July the *Staatsbote* was published only once a week, at
first on a full sheet, but after December 19th on a half sheet, an indication
of the bad times then setting in.

Minutes of the Baptist Association, held at the Scots Plains, N. J.
October 15th and 16th 1776. 8vo. 7 pp.

Hildeburn.

Minutes of the Proceedings of the Convention of the State of
Pennsylvania, held at Philadelphia, the 15th day of July
1776. Fol. 67 pp.

Resolutions directing the Mode of levying Taxes on Non-Asso-
ciators.

Hildeburn.

Rules and Articles for the Government of the Pennsylvania
Forces.

Hildeburn.

Also printed in German.

View of the Title to Indiana, a Tract of Country on the River
Ohio, etc. 8vo. 46 pp.   PHILA. LIBRARY.

Votes and Proceedings of the House of Representatives of the
Province of Pennsylvania. Beginning Oct. 14th 1767.
Vol. VI. Fol. 766 pp.   H. S.

Zeisberger, David. Essay of a Delaware-Indian and English
Spelling-Book for the use of the Schools of the Christian
Indians on Muskingum River. 8vo. 2 & 113 pp.   H. S.

The following issues which appeared without the printer's name,
were presumably printed by H. Miller, both in German and
English.

Der Alarm: Oder Eine Erweckungs-Zuſchrift an das Volk von Penn=
ſylvanien, über den neuerlichen Schluß des Congreſſes, um alle von
der Krone Großbrittanien hergeleitete Macht und Gewalt abzuſchaffen.
4to. 4 S.   H. S.

An die Unter=Officiers und Gemeinen der verschiedenen Companien Associators, die zur Stadt und zu den Freyheiten von Philadelphia gehören. Fol. 2 S.   H. S.

> A section of the Associators, i. e. citizen soldiers before and during the revolution, consisted of Germans. In 1776 Michael Schubert was the presiding officer und Heinrich Kämmerer the Secretary of the German Associators.

Regiments=Verfassung von Pennsylvanien. 8vo. 16 S.   H. S.

Philadelphia. Melchior Steiner & Carl Cist.

(Paine, Thomas.) Gesunde Vernunft an die Einwohner von Amerika über folgende wichtige Gegenstände: 1. Von dem Ursprung und der Absicht der Regierung überhaupt mit kurzen Anmerkungen über die Englische Landesverfassung. 2. Von Monarchie und Erb= folge. 3. Gedanken über den gegenwärtigen Zustand Americanischer Angelegenheiten. 4. Von der jetzigen Stärke von America. Aus dem Englischen übersetzt. 8vo. viii u. 70 S.   H. S.

> Melchior Steiner, the son of the Ref. Minister Conrad Steiner in Philadelphia, learned the printer's trade in Henry Miller's establishment. Carl Cist, a native of St. Petersburg, had been occupied in the office of the *Staatsbote* as editor. Their partnership formed in 1776 was dissolved in 1781. They took as printers and publishers the place vacated by Henry Miller. Steiner withdrew from the printing business in 1794 and died at Washington in 1807. Charles Cist died in 1805.

In der Assembly, ben 12ten December 1776.

> Call for volunteers and offer of bounties.

Extracts from the Proceedings of the Provincial Conference of Committees for the Province of Pennsylvania, held at Carpenter's Hall, Philadelphia June 18, 1776. 4to. 6 pp.   H. S.

The Fall of British Tyranny: or, American Liberty triumphant. 8vo. viii & 66 pp.   H. S.

Four letters on interesting subjects. 8vo. 2 & 24 pp. H. S.

[*Paine, Thomas.*] The American Crisis. Number I. By the author of Common Sense. 8vo. 8 pp.

> The first number of "The American Crisis" opening with the famous words "These are times that try men's souls" was published Dec. 19, 1776. Three others appeared in 1777.

Printer unknown.

A German broadside dated Bucks County 14. Dec. 1776, denouncing the British and Hessian troups for outrages committed during their march through Jersey.

1777.

Albany (?)

Proclamation. Sintemal der König von Grossbrittanien hat Mittel gefunden etc.

This proclamation, dated White Plains, Nov. 16, 1777 and signed: Israel Putnam, appeals to Hessian and other mercenaries of the English Government to abandon the British cause and lead a peaceable, useful life among the freemen of America. Printed in Max Eelking's *Deutsche Hülfstruppen,* vol. I, p. 232 and Ratterman's *Deutsch-Amerikanisches Magazin,* vol. I, p. 401.

Germantown. Chriſtoph Saur.

Das Kleine Davidiſche Pſalterſpiel der Kinder Zions u. ſ. w. Zum Vierten mal ans Licht gegeben. 12mo. 572 S. u. Reg.   G. S.

See 1744.

Vollſtändiges Marburger Geſangbuch, zur Uebung der Gottſeligkeit, in 680 chriſtlichen und troſtreichen Pſalmen und Geſängen, u. ſ. w. Fünfte und vermehrte Auflage. 12mo. 522 S., Reg. u. 78 S.

G. S.

The first American edition appeared 1759.

Germantown. (Chriſtoph Saur u. Peter Saur.)

Emmerich, A. An die Deutſchen in Amerika.

A passionately worded appeal to the Germans in America to stand by England. In another paper, given to the public, the writer as violently answers Gen. Putnam's proclamation. Emmerich, a Hessian by birth, was a zealous loyalist. At the outbreak of hostilities he returned to Germany and enlisted an independent corps (Freicorps) of sharpshooters (Jägers) in aid of the English cause. Only little is known of his military record. After the war he returned to Hessia; loyal to his hereditary sovereign he entered 1809 into a plot against King Jerome, failed and was shot near Cassel. See Max Eelking's *Deutsche Hülfstruppen,* vol. I, p. 232 and Rattermann's *Deutsch-Amerikanisches Magazin,* vol. I, p. 399.

Der Kleine Catechiſmus des ſel. Dr. Martin Luthers, nebſt den gewöhn= lichen Morgen= Tiſch= und Abend=Gebätern u. ſ. w. 24mo. 4 u. 140 S.   H. S.

Der Hoch=Deutsch=Americanische Calender, Auf das Jahr . . 1778.
Zum Vierzigstenmal herausgegeben. 4to. 48 S.

> This almanac contains a poem dwelling upon the misfortunes of the
> country, which are attributed to the folly and sins of the people.

* Die Germantowner Zeitung. Diese Zeitung wird alle Wochen heraus=
gegeben von Christoph Saur, jun. und Peter Saur.

> Number 689, dated March 19, 1777, is in possession of the Hist. Soc. of
> Penna. Christ. Saur, Jr., states in it that he has removed to a house
> adjoining the Quaker Meeting House and will there continue his business.

Lancaster. Frantz Bailey.

Bekanntmachung. Bey seiner Excellenz, G. Waschington, Esq., General
und oberster Befehlshaber über die Völker der Vereinigten Staaten.

> Translation of Washington's proclamation from Valley Forge (Dec. 20,
> 1777) enjoining the threshing of grains at specified times.

Der Gantz Neue Verbesserte Nord=Americanische Calender. Auf das
1778ste Jahr u. s. w.

> The inscription of the angel's trumpet blast is "Trübsal". (calamity.)

An die Hochgeehrten Glieder der Assembly, des Pennsylvanischen Staats.
1 Blatt.

Hildeburn.

Lancaster. Matthias Bartgis.

Der Allerneuste Americanische Calender. Auf das Jahr . . 1778.

> On the fifth page follows the second title:

Der Hinckend= und Stolpernd= doch eilfertig= fliegend= und laufende
Americanische Reichs= Bott, das ist der Allerneuste Verbesserte und
Zuverläßigste Americanische Reichs= Staats= Kriegs= Siegs= und
Geschichts=Calender, Auf das Jahr nach der Gnadenreichen Geburt
unsers Herrn und Heylandes Jesu Christi 1778 u. s. w. Zum
Zweytenmal herausgegeben.

> Title from a copy in possession of Mr. H. Heilman in Lebanon.
> The funny exuberance of the title is probably meant as a burlesque on
> other almanacs.

Philadelphia. Henrich Miller.

Der Neueste, Verbessert= und Zuverläßige Americanische Calender. Auf
das 1778ste Jahr Christi u. s. w. Zum Sechszehntenmal heraus=
gegeben.

* Henrich Müllers Pennsylvanischer Staatsbote. Fol.

> After the battle on the Brandywine, when the English army approached Philadelphia, Henry Miller, like other revolutionary printers, took flight, leaving his printing office in charge of his housekeeper. In June 1778, a short time before the evacuation of Philadelphia, his press and types were seized and taken to New York.

Philadelphia. Christ. Saur, jr. u. Peter Saur.

Proclamation. Eine durch Seine Excellenz, Sir William Howe, Ritter vom Bad, General und Oberbefehlshaber u. s. w. herausgegebene Proclamation. 'PHILA. LIBRARY.

> Dated 8th October 1777 offering a land bounty to recruits for the Provincial corps then raising. Hildeburn.

> This proclamation may have been the first presswork which Christ. Saur, Jr. and Peter Saur did in Philadelphia after the city had fallen into the hands of Howe's army.

* Der Pennsylvanische Staats Courier, oder einlaufende Wöchentliche Nachrichten. Diese Zeitung wird alle Wochen herausgegeben von Christoph Saur, Jr. und Peter Saur in der Zweyten Straße.

> The *Pennsylvanische Staats Courier*, which supported the English side, appeared only during the time of the occupation of Philadelphia by the English and had for its patrons probably the Hessians, who formed a considerable part of the invading army. Our knowledge of this paper is derived from a partial reprint of the number dated May 6, 1778, in Prof. Schlözer's *Briefwechsel*, (vol. 3, p. 260—267), a monthly, published in Göttingen, Germany. An extract, full of wild effusions against the "rebels", is also found in the *Pennsylvanische Zeitungsblat* of Feb. 18, 1778 printed at Lancaster.

Place and Printer unknown.

Braun. Ein Lied welches auf die Bestürmung und Einnahme des Forths Mont-Gomery, den 6ten Octobris Anno 1777 von einem Anspacher Grenadier Namens Braun poesirt wurde.

> Title in Döhla's Tagebuch and kindly communicated by Mr. H. A. Rattermann, Cincinnati. Döhla gives the text and leaves us to infer that the song was printed.

Philadelphia. Steiner & Cist.

Eine Acte zur Anordnung der Miliz der Republik Pennsylvanien. Aus dem Englischen übersetzt. 8vo. 28 S.

Catechismus, Oder: Kurzer Unterricht Christlicher Lehre, wie derselbe in denen Reformirten Kirchen und Schulen der Chur=Fürstlichen Pfalz, auch anderwärts getrieben wird. Mit Zeugnissen der heiligen Schrifft erklärt und bestätigt. 8vo. 286 S.

Zuſchrift aus der Verſammlung der Repräſentanten des Staates von Newyork an die, welche ſie dazu beſtellt haben. Aus dem Engliſchen überſetzt. 8vo. 21 S.

Pamphlet in favor of Independence. It was printed in Philadelphia, because there was no German printing office in the State of New York.

An Address to General St. Clair's Brigade at Ticonderoga.

Hildeburn.

(*Paine, T.*) The American Crisis. Number II. By the author of Common Sense. 8vo. p. 9 to 24. Number III. 8vo. p. 27 to 56. Number IV. (published pratis). 8vo. p. 57 to 60.
H. S.

The second number was issued January 13th, the third April 19th, the fourth, after the battle on the Brandywine September 12, 1777.

In Council. Philadelphia, April 9, 1777. To the People of Pennsylvania. Folio. 1 leaf.

"An address on a rumored movement 'of the Royal troops towards Philadelphia."

Several other resolutions of the Council were printed by Styner & Cist.

Observations on the Slaves and Indented Servants inlisted in the Army and in the Navy of the United States. Fol. 2 pp.
H. S.

(*Rush, Benj.*) Observations upon the present Government of Pennsylvania. In four letters to the People of Pennsylvania. 8vo. 24 pp.
PHILA. LIBRARY.

(Drucker nicht angegeben.)

An das Publicum. Im Sicherheits-Rath. Philadelphia den Erſten Januar 1777. Fol. 1 S. Unterzeichnet Thomas Wharton, Jr.
H. S.

Upon the arrival of about a thousand Hessians taken prisoners at Trenton, this proclamation was issued in English and German, warning the people not to show any resentment against the irresponsible tools of tyranny and greed.

1778.

Lancaſter. Franz. Bailey.

Artikel des Bundes und der immerwährenden Eintracht zwiſchen den Staaten von Neu-Hampſchire, Maſſachuſſets-Bay, Rhode-Eyland und Provindence Plantagen, Connecticut, Neu-York, Neu-Jerſey,

Pennſylvanien, Delaware, Maryland, Virginien, Nord=Carolina, Süd = Carolina und Georgien. Aus dem Engliſchen überſetzt. 16mo. 16 S.

Hildeburn.

Der Ganz Neue Verbeſſerte Nord=Americaniſche Calender. Auf das 1779ſte Jahr u. ſ. w. Verfertigt von David Rittenhaus. H. S.

> The winged angel on the allegorical cut of the title page holds in one hand a medallion portrait of Washington, in the other a tuba, from which a blast proceeds with the reading: *Des Landes Vater*. No earlier instance of the designation of Washington as the Father of his Country is known.

* Das Pennſylvaniſche Zeitungsblat. Oder: Sammlung Sowohl Aus= wärtig als Einheimiſcher Neuigkeiten. H. S,

> The first number appeared Wednesday, February 4th, the last, June 24th 1778. The time of publication, therefore, falls within the period of the English occupation of Philadelphia. Upon the petition of prominent German citizens the Supreme Executive Council of Pennsylvania paid for 500 copies.

Lancaſter. Matthias Bartgis.

Der Allerneueſte Nord=Americaniſche Calender. . . Auf das Jahr 1779 u. ſ. w.

> The fourth issue of Bartgis almanac (for 1780) appeared in Frederick City, Md. and it is possible that also the almanac for 1779, of which no copy is at hand, was published there.

Lancaſter. Theophilus Coſſart.

Geſpräch zwiſchen Doctor Beale und dem Jehemmo.

Hildeburn.

Der Republikaniſche Calender auf das 1779ſte Jahr Chriſti. Zum Erſtenmal herausgegeben. Gedruckt und zu finden bey Theophilus Coſſart und Compagnie in Lancaſter nahe bey der Priſon und gerade gegenüber den brey grünen Bäumen. G. S.

Philadelphia. Johann Dunlap

in der Markt=Straſſe.

Der Hoch=Deutſch Americaniſche Calender, Auf das Jahr . . 1779 u. ſ. w. Zum ein und vierzigſten mal herausgegeben.

> John Dunlap, a Philadelphia printer, bought part of the confiscated effects of Christopher Saur's establishment and continued the publication of the almanac in the old style and with the old title for several years.

Philadelphia. Henrich Miller.

Henrichs Millers des Buchdruckers in Philadelphia nöthige Vorstellung an die Deutschen in Pennsylvanien. H. S.

Avis au Public.— To the public. Oeffentliche Bekanntmachung. Fol. 1 S.

> A French officer, Col. De la Balme, offers employment to the destitute in workshops twenty-eight miles from Philadelphia. The bill of fare for their breakfast, dinner and supper is quite liberal, wages are not mentioned.

Der Neugestellte, Verbessert= und Zuverläßige Americanische Staats= Calender. Auf das 1779ste Jahr Christi u. s. w.

* Henrich Millers Pennsylvanischer Staatsbote.

> After the English had left Philadelphia, Miller returned and having found help resumed on the 5th of August the publication of the *Staatsbote*, at first on a half sheet, but after a couple of weeks in full size.

Philadelphia. Christoph und Peter Saur.

Kunze, Johann Christoph, Ev. Luth. Pred. zu Philadelphia. Einige Gedichte und Lieder. 12mo. 42 u. 132 S. G. S.

> This volume of poetry is dedicated to the Swedish Society, *Pro Fide et Christianismo*, of which Rev. J. C. Kunze had been elected a member. The book was printed during the English occupation of Philadelphia, but the poems were written long before and, therefore, contain no allusion to the events of the times. Johann Christian Kunze, born 1744, died 1807, Pastor of Zion's Church in Philadelphia 1770—1784, Trustee and Professor at the University of Pennsylvania 1780—1784, Pastor of Lutheran Christ Church in New York 1784—1807, Prof. of Oriental Languages in Columbia College 1784.

* Der Pennsylvanische Staats = Courier oder einlaufende Wöchentliche Nachrichten.

> See 1777.

Philadelphia (?)

Thormann. Ein Lied welches in unsern Winter=Quartier zu Phila= belphia auf die Rebellen gemacht worden ist. Von einem Anspacher Mousquetier Namens Thormann.

> Title from *Döhla's Tagebuch*, kindly communicated by Mr. H. A. Ratter- mann, Cincinnati, The poem, which consists of four stanzas, each of eight lines, appears to have been printed, but no clue is given as to time and place. Its spirit is sufficiently indicated by the first four lines:
>
> „Hat sich das Prahlen schon verlohren
> Euch Herren vom Congreß gesagt,
> Ist euch das Maul schon zugefroren,
> Da ihr kaum einen Schritt gewagt!"

Druckort unbekannt.

Apel. Ein Lied, welches auf die Ein- und Ausfahrt der französischen Flotte zu New-Port und des Attacks mit den Rebellen auf der Insul Rhode-Island, den 29ften August im Jahr 1778 vorgefallen ist, von dem Mousquetier Apel von Capitain Eyles Compagnie angefertigt.

Title from *Döhla's Tagebuch*, like the preceding, furnished by Mr. H. A. Rattermann.

Friedrich und Sichart. Ein Lied über die herzoglich Braunschweig. Truppen nach America in engl. Sold gehend, vom Jahr 1776 bis 1777, nehmlich zwey Feldzüge so sie gethan und endlich sich am 17. October 1777 bey Soratoga in Albanien unter Commando der Generale Bourgayne und Riedesel an den Rebellen-General Gates zu Kriegsgefangenen ergeben mußten.

Begins: Braunschweig ist ein schöner Ort. Title from *Döhla's Tagebuch*. See above.

Philadelphia. Steiner & Cist.

In der General Assembly von Pennsylvania. Samstags den 28ten November 1778. Fol. 1 Blatt.

Hildeburn.

In der General Assembly von Pennsylvanien. Fol. 1 S.

Public information on the call of a constitutional convention to meet at Lancaster in June 1779.

(*Brown, Wm.*) Pharmacopoeia Simpliciorum et Efficaciorum in usum Nosocomii militaris ad exercitum Foederatarum Americae Civitatum pertinentis.

A copy is in the library of the Surgeon General's office. The little book, the first Pharmacopœia of the United States, contains hundred prescriptions, made use of in the military hospital at Litiz.

York. *Henrich Miller.*

"Henry Miller translated into German the Address of Congress to the States of America in order that it might be read to various congregations, as ordered by Congress." Pennsylvania Magazine. Vol. 16, p. 436.

This occurred when during the occupation of Philadelphia by the enemy Congress held its session in York.

1779.

Friederich=Stadt, Md. Matthias Bartgis.

Der Allerneuste, Verbesserte= und Zuverläßige Americanische Reichs=
Staats= Kriegs= Siegs= und Geschichts=Calender, Auf das Jahr
. . 1780 u. f. w. Vornehmlich nach dem Märylandischen Horizont
berechnet. Zum Vierten mal herausgegeben. G. S.

> On the outside page there is a very rough cut, representing the "limping
> messenger" before a comfortable looking couple. Over him floats a ring
> with the inscription: Der hinkende Bot and on the top of the page there is
> another title: Märylandischer Kalender auf das Jahr 1780.

Lancaster. Francis Bailey.

Der Ganz Neue Verbesserte Nord=Americanische Calender. Auf das
1780ste Jahr Christi u. f. w.

Lancaster. Theophilus Coffart.

Der Republikanische Calender auf das 1780ste Jahr Christi.

Philadelphia. Johann Dunlap.

Der Hoch=Deutsch= Americanische Calender, Auf das Jahr u. f. w.
1780. 4to. 32 S. G. S.—H. S.

* Deutsche Zeitung.

> Title not known. A defective number of the paper, in possession of
> the Hist. Soc. of Penna., has at the close of the last page these lines:
> Philadelphia: Gedruckt und zu haben von Johann Dunlap in der Englischen
> und Deutschen Buchdruckerey. The Text shows that the number was published
> in February 1779.

Philadelphia. *William Mentz.*

Memorable Accidents and unheard of Transactions containing an
account of several strange Events etc.

> Translated from the French.

A Narrative of Colonel Etau Allen's Captivity etc. 8vo. 64 pp.

Hildeburn.

Philadelphia. Henrich Miller.

An das Volk in Pennsylvanien. Erster Brief. Fol. 2 S.

Der Neugestellete und Verbesserte Americanische Staats=Calender. Auf das 1780ste Jahr Christi. Zum Zwanzigstenmal herausgegeben.

G. S.

The number of the series is two years ahead. The Description of Philadelphia, usually contained in Miller's almanac, is this year followed by bitter complaints about the havoc which the British had wrought during the occupation of the city.

* Henrich Millers Pennsylvanischer Staatsbote.

The *Staatsbote*, commenced in 1762, went out of existence in 1779. In the number of April 21. Miller intimates that the time for withdrawing from business is near at hand and on the 26th of May he takes a formal and affectionate leave from his readers and friends, feelingly alluding to his advanced age of 80 years and the many troubles that he had in the latter years gone through.

Philadelphia. Steiner & Cist.

Die Täglichen Loosungen der Brübergemeine für das Jahr 1780. 8vo. 58 S.

H. S.

Americanischer Haus= und Wirthschafts=Calender auf das 1780ste Jahr Christi.

* Philadelphisches Staatsregister, enthaltend die neuesten Nachrichten von den merkwürdigsten In= und Ausländischen Kriegs= und Friedens= Begebenheiten; nebst verschiedenen andern gemeinnützigen Anzeigen Fol. 16½ x 10¼.

Steiner and Cist's printing office was in Second Street above Race. The first number of this paper was issued July 21, 1779.

Already in 1776 Steiner and Cist, then located in the house, formerly occupied by Ludwig Sprögel in Second Street above Arch, proposed to publish a German paper if 500 subscribers could be obtained in advance. There is no indication that they printed a paper at that time, Henry Miller's *Staatsbote* closed its career May 26th, and Dunlap's German paper must have expired soon after, for we are advised in the "Address to the German Public", printed in the first number of the *Staatsregister*, that at that time not a single German paper existed in Philadelphia.

There are a few numbers of the *Staatsregister* in the library of the Philosophical Society. It did not live long and was followed in 1781 by Steiner and Cist's *Philadelphische Correspondenz*.

(*Morris, Gouverneur.*) Observations on the American Revolution. 8vo. 122 pp.

Miller, J. A Treatise of Artillery. To which is prefixed an Introduction with a Theory of Powder applied to Fire-Arms. 32 plates. 8vo. Introduction 40 pp., text 215 pp.

PHILA. LIBRARY.

1780.

Lancaſter. Francis Bailey.

Der Gantz Neue Verbeſſerte Nord=Americaniſche Calender. Auf das 1781ſte Jahr Chriſti.

Ein ſchön Geiſtlich Lied. 4to. 1 S.
> The year is uncertain.

Koppelberger, Johannes. Ein neues Lied. Fol. 1 S.
> An acrostic on the name of Leonard Detweiler. Year and place uncertain.

Lancaſter. Theophilus Coſſart & Comp.

Der Republikaniſche Calender auf das 1781ſte Jahr Chriſti.

Philadelphia. Johann Dunlap.

Der Hoch= Deutſch=Americaniſche Calender. Auf das Jahr 1781. 4to. 32 S.

Philadelphia. Steiner & Ciſt.

Die Täglichen Looſungen der Brüdergemeine für das Jahr 1781. H. S.

Americaniſcher Haus= und Wirthſchafts=Calender auf das 1781ſte Jahr Chriſti. Zum Zweytenmal herausgegeben. 4to. 40 S.

* Philadelphiſches Staatsregiſter.

Buchanan, James. A Regular English Syntax. 8vo. xxiii & 165 pp. H. S.
> Reprint from a London Edition.

Matlack, T. An Oration delivered March 16, 1780 before . . the American Philosophical Society at Philadelphia. 4to. 27 pp. H. S.

Perrin, John. The Practice of the French Pronunciation alphabetically exhibited. 8vo. iv & 108 pp. · H. S.

1781.

Lancaſter. Francis Bailey.

Der Ganz Neue Verbeſſerte Nord-Americaniſche Calender. Auf das 1782ſte Jahr Chriſti.

Lancaſter. Theophilus Coſſart & Comp.

Der Republikaniſche Calender, auf das 1782 Jahr Chriſti. 4to. 32 S.

H. S.

Philadelphia. Johann Dunlap.

Der Hoch- Deutſch- Americaniſche Calender, Auf das Jahr 1782. 4to. 32 S.

H. S.

Philadelphia. Steiner und Ciſt.

Das Kleine Davidiſche Pſalterſpiel der Kinder Zions u. ſ. w. 12mo. 6 S., 575 S. u. Regiſter.

G. S.

See 1744.

Cullen, W. First lines of the Practice of Physic. 8vo. Pref. etc. xv., text 388 pp.

The firm Steiner & Cist was dissolved in 1781, each partner continuing his business on his own account, Steiner in Race Street between Second and Third Streets, Cist in Market Street between Fourth and Fifth Streets.

Philadelphia. Carl Ciſt.

Americaniſcher Haus- und Wirthſchafts-Calender auf das 1782ſte Jahr Chriſti.

After dissolving partnership Cist and Steiner published almanacs, each in his own name, which at first had the same title and very nearly the same contents.

Brown, W. Pharmacopoeia Simpliciorum et Efficaciorum in usum Nosocomii Militaris ad exercitum Foederatarum Americae civitatum pertinentis. Autore Gulielino Brown M. D. Editio altera.

See 1778. A copy of this second edition, in possession of the late Chas. A. Heinitsch in Lancaster, was used by Prof. J. M. Maisch for a reprint, which originally appeared in the American Journal of Pharmacy in 1884.

A Short Introduction to Latin Grammar, for the use of the University and Academy of Pennsylvania.

A German Advertisement of the book is found in the *Philadelphische Correspondenz* of September 19, 1781.

Philadelphia. Melchior Steiner.

Helmuth, Justus Heinrich Christian. Empfindungen des Herzens in einigen Liedern. 12mo. Vorrede 8 S., Text 81 S.

G. S.

> The Rev. J. H. C. Helmuth was born 1745, arrived from Halle with Rev. John Fred. Schmidt 1769, accepted a call to the Lutheran church in Lancaster, and in 1779 to that in Philadelphia. After holding this office for forty years he resigned it in 1820 and died 1825. His religious poetry is of the sentimental and tearful kind.

Kunze, Johann Christophi. Etwas vom rechten Lebenswege. 8vo. Widmung u. Vorbericht 10 S.—243 S. G. S.

> Some copies of the same book have the title: Ein Wort·für den Verstand und das Herz vom rechten und gebanten Lebenswege. It is dedicated to Peter, Freiherrn von Hohenthal, Oberconsistorialrath und Domänenpräsidenten in Sachsen.

Die Täglichen Loosungen der Brübergemeine für das Jahr 1782. 8vo. 62 u. 69 S. u. Reg. H. S.

Americanischer Haus= und Wirthschafts=Calender auf das 1782ste Jahr Christi. Zum Drittenmal herausgegeben. Rees=straffe zwischen der Zweyten= und Drittenstraffe.

> Identical with Cist's.

* Gemeinnützige Philadelphische Correspondenz. Diese Zeitung wird alle Mittwochen herausgegeben von Melchior Steiner, Buchdrucker in der Rees=straffe, zwischen der Zweyten und Dritten Straffe zu Philadelphia; für zwey harte Thaler des Jahres, wovon die Hälfte beim Einschreiben bezahlt wird. H. S.

> The first number was issued May 21, 1781. The paper was edited for some time by the Lutheran ministers Rev. J. C. Kunze und Rev. J. H. C. Helmuth.

Wesley, J. Hymns and Spiritual Songs, intended for the use of Real Christians of all denominations. 12mo. 136 pp.

Wesley, John & Charles. Collection of Psalms and Hymns. 12mo. 144 pp.

Druckort unbekannt.

Saur, Christoph. Ein Einfältiges Reim=Gedicht, welches Christoph Saur gemacht hat auf seinen Namen und Geburts=Tag, als er sechzig Jahr alt war den 26sten September 1781. 8vo. 4 S.

Hildeburn.

> An acrostic on Ch. Saur's name.

1782.

Lancaſter. Francis Bailey.

Der Gantz Neue Verbeſſerte Nord=Americaniſche Calender. Auf das 1783ſte Jahr Chriſti. 4to. 36 S.   G. S.

Philadelphia. Carl Ciſt.

Americaniſcher Haus= und Wirthſchafts=Calender auf das 1783ſte Jahr Chriſti.

Mackenzie, H. Julia de Roubigne. A Sentimental Novel. In a Series of Letters. 16mo. 2 vols.

Hildeburn.

Philadelphia. Theophilus Coſſart.

Der Republikaniſche Calender auf das 1783ſte Jahr Chriſti. Zum Fünftenmal herausgegeben.

Hildeburn.

Formerly printed in Lancaster.

Philadelphia. Joseph Crukſhank.

Der Neue, Verbeſſert= und Zuverläſſige Calender. Auf das 1783ſte Jahr Chriſti. Zum Erſtenmal herausgegeben.

Judging by the title and the woodcut, representing the city of Philadelphia, Joseph Crukshank's almanac was intended to take the place of Henry Miller's.

Philadelphia. Johann Dunlap.

Der Hoch=Deutſch=Americaniſche Calender auf das Jahr . . 1783.

Philadelphia. Melchior Steiner.

Eine Acte zur Incorporirung der zur Unterſtützung nothleidender Deutſchen beyſteuernden Deutſchen Geſellſchaft. 8vo. 30 S.   G. S.

The German Society, founded December 26, 1764 was incorporated September 20, 1781.

Kunze, J. C. Lobet den Herren, der zu Zion wohnet! Bey dem erſtmaligen Wiederbeſuche der durch den Feind inwendig verwüſtet geweſenen, aber durch den Segen Gottes wieder völlig hergeſtellten Evangeliſch=Lutheriſchen Zions=Kirche, zu Philadelphia, den 22ſten September 1782. 8vo. 4 S.

Zions Church was used by the English during the occupation (1777—1778) for hospital purposes and the interior had been entirely ruined. On the resumption of divine service the worshipers had to provide for their seats as well as they could by bringing chairs; the congregation was too poor to undertake repairs on the scale required. When at length, in 1782, the church had been renovated, the joyous event was celebrated by thanksgiving services.

Kunze, J. C. Eine Rede von den Abſichten und dem bisherigen Fortgange der privilegirten Deutſchen Geſellſchaft.

A copy of the original has not turned up. A reprint is found in *Schöpff's Reise durch die Vereinigten Staaten,* vol. I, p. 613.sqq. The speaker gives a retrospect of the doings of the German Society and dwells upon its enlarged sphere of action, the recently granted charter empowering it to apply a part of its income to educational objects. Kunze himself had been instrumental in securing this change.

Die Täglichen Looſungen und Lehrterte der Brüdergemeine für das Jahr 1783. 8vo. 51 u. 63 S.

Hildeburn.

Americaniſcher Haus- und Wirthſchafts-Calender auf das 1783ſte Jahr Chriſti. Zum Viertenmal heraus gegeben. 4to. 40 S.　G. S.

* Gemeinnützige Philadelphiſche Correſponden;. (16 x 10).　H. S.

Published every Wednesday, till July, then every Tuesday.

Paine, Thomas. Letter addressed to the Abbe Raynal on the Affairs of North-America, in which the Mistakes in the Abbe's Account of the Revolution of America are corrected and cleared up. 8vo. 77 pp.

Hildeburn.

1783.

Lancaſter. (*Printer not mentioned.*)

Der Difinitive Friedens-Tractat zwiſchen Großbrittanien und den Vereinigten Staaten von America; unterſchrieben zu Paris den 3ten September 1783. Fol.

Hildeburn.

Lancaſter. Francis Bailey.

Der Ganz Neue Verbeſſerte Nord Americaniſche Calender auf das 1784ſte Jahr Chriſti.　G. S.

Philadelphia. Carl Ciſt.

Der Pſalter des Königs und Propheten Davids, verteutſchet von D. Martin Luther. 24mo. 252 S.　H. S.

Wahrheit und Guter Rath an die Einwohner Deutschlands, besonders in
Hessen. 12mo. 35 S.   P. S.

> An appeal to the Hessians and other Germans in the service of England,
> not to return under the despotic sway of their respective sovereigns, who
> had basely sold them, but to become American citizens and settle in South
> Carolina where land is offered them on easy terms. The book closes with
> a spirited German poem of an American Grenadier addressed to Hessians
> and others in 1777.

Webb, E. Einige Glaubens-Bekenntnisse und göttliche Erfahrungs-
Proben in einem Send-Schreiben von Elisabetha Webb an Anton
Wilhelm Böhm, Capellan zum Prinzen Georg von Dänemark. Aus
der Englische Sprache übersetzt von J. M. Jorck. 12mo. 55 S.
(Im Anschluß daran) Branntwein und Verderben. 12mo. 22 S.
                                                            G. S.

> A. W. Böhm was the first Lutheran court chaplain to the royal house-
> hold in London. He died 1722 and was succeeded by Dr. Ziegenhagen.

Americanischer Stadt und Land Calender auf das 1784ste Jahr Christi.
4to. 40 S.   G. S.

Buchanan, J. A Regular English Syntax. Wherein is exhibited
the Whole Variety of English Construction, etc. 12mo.
xxxi & 197 pp.
                                                       Hildeburn.

Cullen, W. First Lines of the Practice of Medicine. Part II.
Containing Nervous Diseases.
                                                       Hildeburn.

[*Rush, Benjamin.*] Observations upon the present Government
of Pennsylvania. First printed in 1777.
                                                       Hildeburn.

Rush, Dr. Benjamin. A Syllabus of a Course of Lectures on
Chemistry, for the use of the Students of Medicine in the
College of Philadelphia. 12mo. 39 pp.
                                                       Hildeburn.

Philadelphia. Johann Dunlap.
Der Hoch-Deutsch Americanische Calender auf das Jahr . . 1784 u. f. w.

Philadelphia. Melchior Steiner.
Benezet, Anton. Kurzer Bericht von den Leuten, die man Quäker
nennet, ihrem Ursprung, ihren Religionsgründen, und von ihrer
Niederlassung in America. Aus dem Englischen übersetzt. 12mo.
45 S.   H. S.

Das Neue Testament unsers Herrn und Heylandes Jesu Christi, nach der Deutschen Uebersetzung D. Martin Luthers. 12mo. 533 S. u. Register.

H. S.

Die Täglichen Loosungen und Lehrtexte der Brüdergemeine für das Jahr 1784. 8vo. 128 S.

H. S.

Americanischer Haus= und Wirthschafts=Calender auf das 1784ste Jahr Christi. Zum Fünftenmal herausgegeben.. 4to. 40 S.

G. S.

* Gemeinnützige Philadelphische Corresponbenz. Fol. (16 x 10).

H. S.

[*Fletcher, John.*] An Appeal to Matter of Fact and Common Sense. Or a Rational Demonstration of Man's corrupt and lost Estate. 12mo. 271 pp.

G. S.

A reprint.

Philadelphia.

Beschreybung von den 13 Vereinigten Provinzen, welche nunmehr einen freyen Staat oder eine Republik ausmachen.

Mentioned as a Philadelphia print in *Döhla's Tagebuch*, p. 442—450 of the original manuscript. The publication of the *Tagebuch* in Rattermann's *Deutsch-Americanisches Magazin*, Cincinnati 1887, was not brought to a close, the passage in which Döhla dilates on the contents of this German *Description of the 13 provinces now constituting a Republic*, was kindly furnished by Mr. Rattermann.

Printer not known ; time uncertain.

Ein Neu Trauer=Lied. Wie man vernommen von einem Menschen der vom Tod ist wiederkommen. Die Melodie thut so anfangen: Ihr Sünder kommt gegangen. 1 Blatt. Fol.

Hildeburn.

1784.

Ephrata.

Ein Denckmahl aufgerichtet zum heiligen Andencken der H. Jungfrau und Schwester Melania in Saron, als sie den 11ten September 1784 ein erbauliches Liebesmahl vor die Gemeinschaft gehalten. 1 Blatt. 4to.

A hymn sung in honor of sister Melania, an inmate of the Ephrata cloister. She died at the age of 87 years September 19th 1813.

Friedrich=Stadt, Md. Matthias Bärtgis.

Der Verbesserte Hoch=Deutsche Americanische Land und Staats Calender.
Auf das Jahr . . 1785. Zum erstenmal herausgegeben.

Germantown. Leibert und Billmeyer.

Bläser, P. Ein Brief, Weiland von Peter Bläser an seinen Freund
Michael Billmeyer, Buchdrucker in Germantown, worin er ihm einen
Bericht ertheilt, wie es ihm in seiner Gegend ergangen ist, daß man
ihm wie auch andern, seines tugendsamen Betragens halber den
Unnamen Strabler beygelegt habe u. s. w.

> The year of this publication is not certain. Mr. I. D. Rupp, marked on
> his copy: "Written about the year 1780 — 1784."

> Peter Bläser came to America before 1780. He was school teacher in
> Oley, Berks County from 1784—1790, in Manheim, Lancaster County, from
> 1790—1807, and in a school attached to the Friedenskirche in Cumberland
> County from 1807—1809. In the latter year he moved to York County
> near East Berlin, where he died 1813 at the age of 78 years. A German
> poem in doggerel verse, entitled: „Ein Trauergedicht über den Schaden
> Josephs" forms a part of the pamphlet.

Der Kleine Catechismus des sel. Dr. Martin Luther.

Das Lutherische und Reformirte A. B. C. und Namenbüchlein.

Der Psalter des Königs und Propheten Davids, verdeutschet von Dr.
Martin Luther. Erste Auflage. 16mo. 252 S.   H. S.

Der Hoch=Deutsche Americanische Calender. Auf das Jahr 1785. Zum
Erstenmal herausgegeben. 4to. 40 S.   G. S.

> Peter Leibert, a Dunker, and his son-in-law Michael Billmeyer, a Luth-
> eran, established 1784 in Germantown a printing house which may be con-
> sidered as a renewal of the Saur concern, which had come to an end in 1778.
> The almanacs resemble in every respect those printed by Saur, but are
> numbered as a new series. Much of the confiscated stock of Christopher
> Saur was acquired by the new firm.

Lancaster. Jacob Bailey.

Evangelium Nicodemi, Oder: Historischer Bericht von dem Leben Jesu
Christi, welches Nicodemus, ein Rabbi und Oberster der Jüden
beschrieben . . Viel schöne Stücke und Geschichte dabey zu finden,
welche die Evangelisten nicht beschrieben haben. 8vo. 247 S.

G. S.

Der Gantz Neue Verbesserte Nord=Americanische Calender. Auf das
1785ste Jahr Christi. 4to. 36 S.

Philadelphia. Francis Bailey.

Die Regierungsverfassung der Republik Pennsylvanien, wie solche von der zu dem Zweck erwählten und vom 15. Juli bis zum 28. September von Tag zu Tag in Philadelphia gehaltenen Convention bestgesetzt worden. Aus dem Englischen übersetzt. 8vo. 47 S.　　G. S.

Philadelphia. Carl Cist.

Kurze Fragen Ueber die Christliche Glaubens-Lehre. Nach Heil. Schrift-Zeugniß beantwortet und bewähret. Den Christlichen Glaubens-Schülern zu einem anfänglichen Unterricht nützlich zu gebrauchen. 8vo. 10 u. 140 S.　　H. C.

> The book presents the Schwenkfelder view of Christian doctrines and precepts.

Die Wunderbare Geschichte von Ambrose Gwinnet. Aus dem Englischen.

Americanischer Stadt und Land Calender auf das 1785ste Jahr Christi. 4to. 40 S.

[*Bordley, J. B.*] A Summary View of the Courses of Crops, in the Husbandry of England and Maryland with a comparison of their products etc. Sq. 8vo. 22 pp.　　G. S.

Chambaud, L. Fables Choisies. A l'usage des Enfants. 12mo. Preface. 93 & 66 pp.　　G. S.

Philadelphia. Klein und Reynolds.
(Carter's Alley.)

Der Kleine Catechismus des sel. Dr. Martin Luthers. 24mo. 139 S.
　　G. S.

Fortitude or the Power of Love.
　　Hildeburn.

Philadelphia. Melchior Steiner.

Freimüthige Gedanken über die sogenannte „Anrede von der Minorität im Rath der Censoren" denen freyen und unabhängigen deutschen Bürgern des Staats von Pensylvanien übergeben von Einem freyen deutschen Bürger des Staats. Folio. 2 S.　　H. S.

Kunze, J. C. Eine Aufforderung an das Volk Gottes in Amerika zum frohen Jauchzen und Danken. An dem von einem Erlauchten Congreß wegen erhaltenen Friedens und erlangter Unabhängigkeit auf ben 11ten December 1783 ausgeschriebenen Dankfeste in der Zionskirche zu Philadelphia vorgestellt und auf Verlangen verschiedener Zuhörer dem Druck übergeben; nebst dem Anhange einer andern Predigt ähnlichen Inhalts und an dem Dank= und Bettage des Jahres 1779 gehalten von Johann Christoph Kunze, der heil. Schrift Doctor, Professor der orient. und der deutschen Sprache auf der Univers. zu Philadelphia und Ev. Luther. Pred. daselbst. 8vo. 101 S.

G. S.

Rev. J. C. Kunze accepted in 1784 a call to Christ Church in New York. No further German publications from his pen are known to exist.

Die Regierungsverfassung der Republik Pennsylvanien, wie solche von der General Convention, die zu dem Zweck erwählet und vom 15ten Juli, 1776, bis zum 28sten September, 1776, in Philadelphia gehalten wird, vestgesetzt worden. Aus dem Englischen übersetzt. 8vo. 49 S.

Tagebuch des Raths der Censoren, versammlet zu Philadelphia, am Montage, den Zehnten November 1783. Aus dem Englischen übersetzt. Fol. 147 S.

Americanischer Haus= und Wirthschafts=Calender auf das 1785ste Jahr Christi. 4to. 40 S.

* Gemeinnützige Philadelphische Correspondenz.

H. S.

The History of the Old and New Testament, interspersed with Moral and Instructive Reflections chiefly taken from the Holy Fathers. By J. Reeve. 8vo. vi & 436 pp.

Hildeburn.

1785.

Ephrata. ——

Die Ernsthafte Christenpflicht. Darinnen Schöne Geistreiche Gebäter, damit sich Fromme Christen=Herzen zu allen Zeiten und in allen Nöthen trösten können. 12mo. 199 S.

First edition in 1745.

Friedrichs=Stadt, Md. Matthias Bartgis.

Der Verbesserte Hoch=Deutsche Americanische Land und Staats Calender. Auf das Jahr . . 1786.

Germantown. Leibert & Billmeyer.

Ausbund, das ist: Etliche schöne Christliche Lieder, wie sie in dem Gefäng=
nüß zu Passau u. s. w. hin und her gedichtet worden. Zum vierten
mal aufgelegt in Pennsylvanien. 12mo. 812 S., Register und
Anhang 103 S.   G. S.

> First edition in 1742.

Funk, Ch. Ein Aufsatz oder Vertheidigung von Christian Funk gegen
seine Mitbiener der Mennoniften Gemeinschaft. 16 S.   H. S.

> Christian Funk, a Mennonite, son of Henry Funk (see 1763), held that
> it was not contrary to the peace principles professed by Mennonites, to pay
> the taxes imposed by government for defraying war expenses. For this he
> incurred *Vermeidung* (ex-communication) and a split of the Mennonites
> was the consequence.

Der Hoch=Deutsch Americanische Calender. Auf das Jahr 1786. 4to.
40 S.

* Die Germantauner Zeitung. Diese Zeitung wird alle 14 Tage, Dienstag
Nachmittags herausgegeben. Fünf Schilling des Jahres. Fol.
16 x 9½.   H. S.

> The first number of the resuscitated *Germantauner Zeitung* appeared on
> the 8th of February 1785. It came out every fortnight till July 20th 1790,
> when it became a weekly. The Assembly selected it for publishing its
> proceedings, a favor, which Melchior Steiner, the publisher of the *Gemein-
> nützige Philadelphische Correspondenz*, complained of, on the ground that
> Leibert and Billmeyer had not supported the cause of the republic during
> the revolution. How long it existed has not been ascertained. It had a
> wide circulation, being sold by agents in Philadelphia, Lancaster, Middle-
> town, York, Hanover, Lebanon, Lititz, Reading, Kutztown, Emaus, Allen-
> town, Easton, New Germantown, (N. J.), Albany and New York. In the
> latter city it had 160 subscribers.

Lancaster. Jacob Bailey.

Der Gantz Neue Verbefferte Nord=Americanische Calender. Auf das
1786ste Jahr Christi.

Philadelphia. Carl Cift.

Americanischer Stadt und Land Calender auf das 1786ste Jahr Christi.
4to. 40 S.

Philadelphia. Melchior Steiner.

Americanischer Haus= und Wirthschafts=Calender auf das 1786ste Jahr
Christi. Zum Siebenten mal herausgegeben. 4to. 40 S.

* Gemeinnützige Philadelphische Correspondenz.

Printer not known.

Kunze, J. C. Rudiments of the Shorter Catechism of Luther, chiefly for the use of Lutheran congregations in America, to which is annexed an Abridgement of the Principles of the Evangelical Religion.

Title from W. J. Mann: Life and Times of Muhlenberg, p. 445.

1786.

Ephrata. (Klosterpreſſe.)

Chronicon Ephratense. Enthaltend den Lebens=Lauf des ehrwürdigen Vaters in Chriſto, Friedſam Gottrecht, Wehland Stifters und Vor= ſtehers des geiſtlichen Ordens der Einſamen in Ephrata in der Graffſchafft Lancaster in Pennsylvania. Zuſammen getragen von Br. Lamech und Agrippa. Ephrata. Gedruckt Anno MDCC-LXXXVI. 4to. 250 S.   H. S.

This biography of Conrad Beissel, the founder of the Ephrata cloister, is the principal source for the history of that remarkable and unique institution. Brother Lamech's secular name was Jacob Gass. Who brother Agrippa was, can not be stated.

An English translation of the *Chronicon* by Rev. Max Hark was published in Lancaster 1890.

Etliche Anmerkungen über den Zuſtand und Gemüths=Beſchaffenheit Der Indianiſchen Einwohner dieſes Welttheils. Aus dem Engliſchen überſetzt. 8vo. 44 S.

Followed by:

Die merkwürdige Indianer=Predigt oder Verantwortung auf eine Predigt, von einem Schwediſchen Missionario gehalten worden an der Conestoga im Jahre 1710. Ephrata 1786.

Kurz gefaßtes Nützliches Schul=Büchlein, die Kinder zu unterrichten im Buchſtabiren, Leſen und auswendig lernen, u. ſ. w. Zwehte Auflage. Ephrata. Gedruckt und zu haben bei dem Schulmeiſter, Drucker und Buchbinder. 48 S.

Friedrich=Stadt, Md. Matthias Bärtgis.

Der Verbeſſerte Hoch Deutſche Americaniſche Land und Staats Calender. Auf das Jahr . . 1787.

* Deutſche Zeitung.

Name not known. That Matthias Bartgis published a German paper in "Friederich Stadt" at this time, appears from a notice found in his "Maryland Chronicle and Universal Advertiser" of January 18, 1786,

quoted in Scharff's History of Western Maryland, vol. 1, p. 528, as follows:
"I purpose, should sufficient encouragement offer, to establish a Post from
this place to Winchester, to carry *my English and German News Papers* to
Funk's Town, Hager's Town, Sharpsburg, Shephard's Town, Martinsburg
and Winchester."

There are no data to show how long Bärtgis' paper was published.

Germantown. Leibert und Billmeyer.

Catechismus oder Kurzer Unterricht Christlicher Lehre. 24mo. 118 S.
German Reformed.

Der Kleine Catechismus des sel. Dr. M. Luther. Zweyte Auflage.

Erbauliche Lieder=Sammlung. Zum Gottesdienstlichen Gebrauch in den
Vereinigten Evangelisch=Lutherischen Gemeinen in Nord=America;
Gesamlet, eingerichtet und zum Druck befördert durch die gesamten
Glieder des hiesigen Vereinigten Evangelisch=Lutherischen Ministe=
riums. Erste Auflage. 12mo. 592 S. u. Reg.   G. S.

> This hymnbook published by authority of the Lutheran Synod, was
> compiled mainly by the aged Henry Melchior Muhlenberg, who closed his
> earthly career in 1788. It superseded the *Marburger Gesangbuch*, reprints
> of which had till then been used in the Lutheran congregations of North
> America. Muhlenberg wrote the preface in which he alludes to the forty-
> four years of his "toilsome pilgrimage" in the western continent and
> states the principles that guided him in the selection of hymns. The
> preface is signed by 25 members of the Lutheran Ministerium, headed by
> H. M. Muhlenberg, its Senior.

Kurze Andachten einer Gottsuchenden Seele auf alle Tage der Woche und
andere Umstände eingerichtet. Erste Auflage. 12mo. 128 S.
                                                  G. S.
> Bound together with the *Erbauliche Liedersammlung.*

Tagebuch der General Assembly der Republic Pennsylvanien (1786 —
1787).

Der Hoch Deutsche Americanische Calender. Auf das Jahr 1787. 4to.
40 S.

* Die Germantauner Zeitung. Fol. 16 x 9½.   H. S.

Lancaster. Jacob Bailey.

Der Ganz Neue Verbesserte Nord=Americanische Calender. Auf das
1787ste Jahr Christi.

Philadelphia. Carl Cist.

Broot, Mary. Gründe für die Nothwendigkeit eines stillen Harrens beym öffentlichen Gottesdienst. 8vo. 38 S. G. S.

Translation of a Quaker tract, printed in London and reprinted in Philadelphia.

Phipps, Joseph. Abhandlungen über die Natur und Wirkung der Christlichen Taufe, Communion u. s. w. 8vo. 63 S. G. S.

Translation from the English. Joseph Phipps, an English Quaker was the author of several works on religious subjects.

Americanischer Stadt und Land Calender auf das 1787ste Jahr Christi. 4to. 40 S. G. S.

The Art of Speaking.

Title from an advertisement in Cist's Almanac.

Philadelphia. Melchior Steiner.

Die ersten Früchte der Singeschule der Evangel. Lutherischen Gemeine in Philadelphia. 16mo. 28 S. H. S.

Kirchen-Agende der Evangelisch-Lutherischen Vereinigten Gemeinen in Nord-Amerika. 8vo. 58 S.

The late Rev. W. J. Mann in his Life and Times of Henry Melchior Muhlenberg remarks: "The Liturgy published also in 1786 by synod, essentially harmonizes with the hymn-book of that year. It even more purely expresses the creed of genuine Lutheranism."

The object of both publications was to strengthen the bond of union of the German Lutheran congregation in N. A.

Americanischer Haus- und Wirthschafts-Calender auf das 1787ste Jahr Christi.

* Gemeinnützige Philadelphische Correspondenz. H. S.

1787.

Ephrata. (Klosterpresse.)

Das Ganz Neue Testament Unseres Herrn Jesu Christi. Recht gründlich verdeutschet. Anhang: Vier schöne Geistliche Lieder. 12mo. 192 S. G. S.

This is not Luther's translation, but one originally made in Switzerland.

Friedrich-Stadt, Md. Matthias Bärtgis.

Der Verbesserte Hoch Deutsche Americanische Land und Staats Calender auf d. Jahr 1788.

Germantown. (Germantaun.) Michael Billmeyer.

Das Neue Testament unsers Herrn und Heylandes Jesu Christi nach der Deutschen Uebersetzung D. Martin Luthers: Erste Auflage. 12mo. 537 S. u. Register. G. S.

The partnership of Leibert & Billmeyer was dissolved in August 1787; the latter continued the business as it had existed; Leibert opened a new printing office and began in the following year to publish on his own account.

Tagebuch der General Assembly der Republik Pennsylvanien. 1787 —1788. (Officielle Deutsche Uebersetzung.)

Der Hoch=Deutsche Americanische Calender auf das Jahr 1788. 4to. 40 S.

*Die Germantauner Zeitung.

Halifax, N. S. Anthon Henrich.

Der Neu=Schottländische Calender. Auf das Jahr Christi 1788. Zum Erstenmal herausgegeben.

The first German settlement in Nova Scotia dates back to 1749; it consisted mainly of soldiers, whose term of service had expired. A few years later (about 1752) the efforts of the Royal Commissioners to attract German settlers by offer of land grants and other advantages, stimulated German emigration to Novia Scotia to such a degree, that the promises had to be revoked. In 1761 a German Lutheran church was built in Halifax, of which Rev. B. M. Hausiehl became pastor in 1783. A copy of the Neu=Schottländische Calender for 1791 is in the collection of the German Society; we have no information, how long it was continued and what German books, if any, were printed at Halifax.

Lancaster. Albrecht und Lahn.

Der Neue Gemeinnützige Landwirthsschaft Calender. Auf das Jahr nach der heilbringenden Geburt unseres Herrn Jesu Christi 1788. Zum erstenmal herausgegeben. Lancäster. Gedruckt und zu haben bey Albrecht und Lahn in der neuen Buchdruckerey in der Queenstrasse.

Lancaster. Stiemer, Albrecht und Lahn.

* Neue, Unpartheyische Lancäster Zeitung und Anzeigs=Nachrichten. Fol. 16 x 10.

The *Neue, Unpartheyische Lancaster Zeitung* was the first paper in Lancaster, that lived beyond the experimental stage. It was the third German newspaper then published in Pennsylvania. Its first number appeared August 7, 1787. Mr. Anton Stiemer died April 18, 1788, after which time the paper was published by Albrecht and Lahn till 1790, when the firm changed to Albrecht & Comp. Jacob Lahn, a man of considerable literary equipment, was born in Frankfurt on the Main and had been a teacher of "languages and sciences" in Philadelphia before he went to Lancaster. He kept a bookstore; on his shelves he had, according to advertisement, about 800 volumes of the "newest and best German works" imported by him. John Albrecht was born at Bethlehem, Pa. in 1745, learned of Chr. Saur the art of printing and came to Lancaster in 1787. When he died in 1805 his business was continued by his sons.

Philadelphia. Carl Cist.

Americanischer Stadt und Land Calender auf das 1788ste Jahr Christi.

H. S.

Philadelphia. Melchior Steiner.

Etwas für Kleine und Grosse Deutsche Kinder.

Freiheitsbrief der Deutschen Hohen Schule (College) der Stadt Lancaster in dem Staate Pennsylvanien, nebst einer Anrede an die Deutschen dieses Staats von den Trusties der besagten Hohen Schule. 8vo. 16 S.

> The charter of Franklin College in Lancaster was granted by the General Assembly of Pennsylvania on the 16th of March 1787, at the earnest solicitation of the Rev. Drs. Helmuth, Weiberg, Hendel and H. E. Muhlenberg, the former two of Philadelphia, the latter of Lancaster. Franklin College was established with a view of giving to German speaking youths the advantages of higher education. The German department of the University of Pennsylvania, opened in 1780 through the efforts of Rev. J. C. Kunze, had the same object. As it was given up in 1786 or soon after, it looks as if Franklin college was called into life to assume the task abandoned by the University. Dr. Helmuth, of Zions church, was a leading man in both projects. For further information see Dr. J. H. Dubbs: *The Founding of Franklin College.* Philadelphia 1887.

Ordnung welche in Absicht der Procession und öffentlichen Gottesdienstes bey der Einweihung der Franklinischen Deutschen Hohen Schule in der Stadt und Grafschaft Lancaster zu beobachten.

Americanischer Haus= und Wirthschaft=Calender auf das 1788ste Jahr Christi.

* Gemeinnützige Philadelphische Correspondenz. H. S.

Druckort unbekannt.

An die Einwohner der County Northampton. Q. F. 1 S. H. S.

> A statement with figures to show frauds in the County Treasurer's office.

1788.

Ephrata.

Anhang zum Widerlegten Wiedertäufer.

Das Vergnügte Leben eines Einsamen, Namens Jörgel.
Glückselig ist der Mann
Der so wie Jörgel leben kan!

H. S.

(Mack, Alexander, Jr.) Apologia, Oder schrifftmäßige Verant=
wortung Etlicher Wahrheiten, herausgefordert durch eine neulich
aufgesetzte Schrifft unter dem Namen Der Wiederlegte Wiedertäufer.
Geschrieben für den Gemeinen Mann durch Theophilum. 8vo.
72 S.   H. S.

> Defence of Dunker doctrines and rites as scriptural. The book was
> printed at the expense of the "Brethren", i. e. Dunkers.

Friedrichs=Stadt, Md. Matthias Bärtgis.

Der Verbesserte Hoch Deutsche Americanische Land und Staats Calender
auf d. Jahr 1789.

Germantown. Michael Billmeyer.

Das Neue Testament.

Tagebuch der General Assembly der Republik Pennsylvanien. 1788
—1789. (Officielle Deutsche Uebersetzung).

Der Hoch=Deutsche Americanische Calender, Auf das Jahr 1789 u. s. w.

* Die Germantauner Zeitung. Fol. 16 x 9½.   H. S.

> Published once a fortnight.

Germantown. Peter Leibert.

Habermann, Joh. Geistliche Morgen= und Abendgebäter.

Der Kleine Kempis oder kurze Sprüche und Gebätlein u. s. w. des
Thomae a Kempis. Sechste Auflage. 16mo. 154 u. 12 S.

Liebliche und erbauliche Lieder von der Herrlichkeit und Ehre Christi.
12mo. 16 S.

> Contains among other specimens of religious poetry some poems of
> Johannes Kelpius, the Hermit on the Wissahickon, and of Christopher
> Saur.

Halifax, N. S. Anthon Henrich.

Der Neu=Schottländische Calender. Auf das Jahr Christi 1789. 4to.
40 S.

Lancaster. Stiemer, Albrecht & Lahn.

Reitz, J. H. Das Fürbilde der Heilsamen Worten vom Glauben und
Liebe, so in Christo Jesu ist. Zusammen gestellt von Johann H.
Reitzen. 16mo. 167 S.   H. S.

> J. F. Reitz, one of the Wittgenstein Separatists, is the author of the
> *Historie der Wiedergebornen.* 1717.

Lancaster. Albrecht und Lahn.

(Lavater.) Nachdenken über mich selbst. 12mo. 43 S.

Der Neue Gemeinnützige Landwirthschafts Calender auf . . 1789.

* Neue, Unpartheyische Lancäster Zeitung und Anzeigs=Nachrichten. Fol.
16 x 10.

Philadelphia. Carl Cist.

Robinson Crusoe. 16mo. 154 S.

> Appeared in English at the same time.

Americanischer Stadt und Land Calender auf das 1789ste Jahr Christi.

Philadelphia. Melchior Steiner.

Denkmal der Liebe und Achtung, welches Seiner Hochwürden dem Herrn
D. Heinrich Melchior Muhlenberg, verdienstvollesten Senior des Ev.
Luth. Ministeriums in Nord America und treu eifrigsten ersten
Lehrer an der St. Michaelis= und Zions=Gemeinde in Philadelphia
ist gesetzet worden. Samt desselben Lebenslaufe. 8vo. 60 S.

G. S.

> Rev. Henry Melchior Muhlenberg, the patriarch of the Lutheran church
> in America, died at Trappe October 7, 1787. The *Denkmal* contains a
> memorial sermon, preached by Dr. J. H. C. Helmuth in Philadelphia
> Oct. 21, 1787, and a notice of the principal events of Muhlenberg's life.

Kunze, J. Ch. Elisas betränter Nachruf bei der Hinwegnahme seines
Gottesmanns Elias. Gedächtnißpredigt auf Dr. H. M. Mühlenberg
gehalten in New=York von J. Ch. Kunze.

Tagebuch der Convention der Republik Pennsylvanien. 8vo. 30 S.

PHILOS. S.

> This was the convention that ratified the Federal Constitution.

Americanischer Haus= und Wirthschafts=Calender auf das 1789ste Jahr.

* Gemeinnützige Philadelphische Correspondenz. H. S.

> In the number of December 2, 1788, the publication of a *Universal History*
> in German is announced, contingent on a sufficient number of subscribers.

1789.

Ephrata.

Göttliche Wunderschrift, darinnen entdecket wird, wie aus dem ewigen
Guten hat können ein Böses urständen. 12mo. 31 S.

> According to statement of the preface, the book, which is profoundly
> mystical, was written 1760, when Conrad Beissel was still living. Was it
> written by him?

Friedrich Stadt. Matthias Bärtgis.

Der Verbesserte Hoch Deutsche Americanische Land und Staats Calender. Auf das Jahr 1790.

Germantown. M. Billmeyer.

Tagebuch der General Assembly der Republik Pennsylvanien. 1889 —1790. (Officielle Deutsche Uebersetzung).

Der Hoch=Deutsche Americanische Calender. Auf das Jahr 1790 u. f. w.

* Die Germantauner Zeitung. H. S.

Halifax, N. S. Anthon Henrich.

Der Neu=Schottländische Calender. Auf das Jahr Christi 1790. 4to. 40 S.

Lancaster. Albrecht und Lahn.

Der Neue Gemeinnützige Landwirthschafts Calender auf . . 1790.
* Neue, Unpartheyische Lancäster Zeitung und Anzeigs=Nachrichten.

Philadelphia. Carl Cist.

Neu=eingerichtetes Schul=Büchlein, darin die Jugend zu Erlernung der Buchstaben, des Buchstabirens und Lesens auf eine leichte, deutliche und gründliche Art angeleitet wird. Nach der Ebersdorfischen Ausgabe von 1784. 12mo. 92 S. G. S.

Americanischer Stadt und Land Calender auf das 1790ste Jahr Christi.

Philadelphia. Melchior Steiner.

Americanischer Haus= und Wirthschafts=Calender auf das 1790ste Jahr.

* Gemeinnützige Philadelphische Correspondenz.

Reading. Johnson, Barton und Jungmann.

* Neue Unpartheyische Readinger Zeitung und Anzeigs=Nachrichten. Fol. 17 x 11.

The first number appeared Wednesday, February 18th. The publishers express the hope, that their enterprise will be a success, considering that Reading is a flourishing town in one of the most populous counties of the State, which through the industry of the Germans has become "a garden of God". Children in the German schools now will study their lessons more eagerly, so that hereafter they may be able to read the German paper. Agents for receiving subscriptions were appointed in Reading, Kutztown, Maxitany, Kärgerstown, Bethlehem, Womelsdorf, Tulpehocken, Meyerstown, Lebanon, Lancaster and Germantown. This was the first newspaper printed in Reading.

The Ready Reckoner or the Trader's sure guide.   12mo. 195 pp.

P.

Printed in German and English.

1790.

Chestnut Hill. Samuel Saur.

Der Neue Hoch Deutsche Americanische Calender auf das Jahr Christi
1791. Zum Erstenmal heraus gegeben.   G. S.

Samuel Saur, the youngest of Christopher Saur's ten children, was born
March 30th 1767 in Germantown and died Oct. 12th 1820 in Baltimore.
He made his debut as a printer in Chestnut Hill, north of Germantown,
moved 1794 to Philadelphia and 1795 to Baltimore. Here he became
prominent as printer, publisher and type founder.

* Die Chesnuthiller Wochenschrift.   Diese Zeitung wird wöchentlich,
nemlich Mittwochs, herausgegeben von Samuel Saur, Buchdrucker
auf Chesnuthill, nahe bey dem 10ten Meilstein allwo die Readinger
und Nordwelscher Straffe zusammenkommen. 4to. 10 x 8.

The first number appeared on the 8th of October.

Ephrata.

Kurtzgefaßtes Arzney=Büchlein für Menschen und Vieh, darinnen CXXX
auserlesene Recepten.   H. S.

Schröder, Johann Georg. Merkwürdige Geschichte von einem
Menschen, der mit dem Teufel in einen Bund getreten auf 18 Jahr
und wieder durch Christum erlöset worden ist. Von Johann Georg
Schröder, D. D., evangel. Prediger in Maryland. 12mo. 48 S.

Friedrich Stadt, Md. Matthias Bärtgis.

Der Verbesserte Hoch Deutsche Americanische Land und Staats Calender.
Auf das Jahr . . 1791.

Germantown. Michael Billmeyer.

Anhang zu dem Gesangbuch der Vereinigten Evangelisch=Lutherischen
Gemeinen in Nord=Amerika. Enthaltend den Kleinen Katechismus
Lutheri, Evangelien und Episteln u. s. w. mit Kirchengebeten.
12mo. 80 S.   G. S.

Etliche Christliche Gebäte. 16mo. 163 S.

Lob und Anbetung des Gottmenschen am Tage der Einweihung einer neuen Orgel am 10. October 1790.

> Zions Church in Philadelphia received in 1790 a new organ, then the largest in America, built by D. Tanneberg in Litiz. The dedication sermon was preached by the pastor, Rev. J. H. C. Helmuth.

(Roosen, Gerhard.) Christliches Gemüths-Gespräch von dem geistlichen und seligmachenden Glauben. 16mo. 241 S.   G. s.

> Presents the Mennonite view of Christian doctrine and life, and contains some edifying songs (Erbauliche Lieder) of Christoph Dock, the schoolmaster. The same book was printed in Ephrata 1769 and 1770.

Tagebuch der General Assembly der Republik Pennsylvanien. 1790 —1791.

Der Hoch-Deutsche Americanische Calender, Auf das Jahr 1791 u. s. w.

* Die Germantauner Zeitung. 4to. 10 x 8.   H. S.

> The folio size of the paper was reduced to quarto and instead of appearing twice a month it became a weekly.

Germantown. Peter Leibert.

Hoch-Deutsches Lutherisches A. B. C. und Namenbüchlein.

Habermann, Johann. Christliche Morgen- und Abendgebeter. 16mo. 216 S.

Halifax, N. S. Anton Henrich.

Der Neu-Schottländische Calender auf das Jahr . . 1791. Zum Viertenmal herausgegeben.   G. S.

> It is not known how much longer this almanac was published.

Lancaster. Johann Albrecht & Comp.

Jesus und die Kraft seines Bluts ganz besonders verherrlicht an Johann Jost Weygand, einem armen Sünder, der einen Mord begangen u. s. w. 12mo. 232 S.   H. S.

Der Neue Gemeinnützige Landwirthschaft Calender auf . . 1791.

* Neue, Unpartheyische Lancäster Zeitung und Anzeigs Nachrichten.

> The change of the name of the publishing firm from Albrecht & Lahn to Albrecht & Comp. was made in March.

Lancaster. J. Bailey.

Historie von der unschuldigen heiligen Genoveva.

Philadelphia. Carl Cist.

Catechismus ober kurzer Unterricht ber chriftlichen Lehre für bie angehenbe
Jugend in ber Churfürftlichen Pfalz unb anbern reformirten Orten
zu gebrauchen. 16mo. 124 S.

Dell, W. Prüfung ber Geifter fowohl in ben Lehrern als in ben
Zuhörern, u. f. w. 12mo. 80 S. G. S.

> Wm. Dell (d. 1664) was a non-conformist preacher and chaplain in the
> army of Lord Fairfax. While not a Quaker, his works became popular.
> among them. Carl Cist, a Moravian, published several Quaker tracts
> in German.

Americanifcher Stabt unb Lanb Calenber auf bas 1791fte Jahr Chrifti.

Ausbrücke ber Wehmuth über ben Tob Dr. C. D. Weybergs.

> Rev. Casper Dietrich Weyberg, born in Switzerland, came to America
> about 1762 und accepted a call to the pastorate of the Reformed church in
> Philadelphia in Nov. 1763. During the revolution he took a decided stand
> for independence. He died August 21, 1790 and was buried in Franklin
> Square.

Philadelphia. M. Steiner.

* Gemeinnützige Philabelphifche Correfponbenz.

> In October 1790 the name of the paper was changed into: Neue Philabel-
> phifche Correfponbenz, and its issue was doubled to twice a week. At the
> same time a new editor took charge of it and a general improvement was
> promised.

* Der General=Poftbothe an bie Deutfche Nation. 4to.

> A specimen number of the *Postbothe* in 8vo. size appeared Nov. 27, 1789.
> During the first six months of 1790 it came out twice a week and was then
> discontinued. Its long and rather heavy articles on historical subjects were
> ill suited for a newspaper. The editor was Magister Friedrich C. Reiche,
> who is mentioned in Von Bülow's book *Der Freistaat von Nord-America*
> (1797) as an instance of shipwrecked talent. He wrote, also, *Fifteen
> discourses on the marvellous works of Nature*, published 1792.

Reading. Bartan unb Jungmann.

* Neue Unparthepifche Reabinger Zeitung unb Anzeigs=Nachrichten. Fol.
17 x 11.

> See 1789.

1791.

Cheftnut Hill. Samuel Saur.

Ein ganz neu eingerichtetes Lutherifches A. B. C. Buchftabier= unb
Namenbuch zum nützlichen Gebrauch beutfcher Schulen. H. S.

> The same book appeared in Philadelphia with the imprint: David Saur
> and Wm. Jones, Buchbinder unb Buchhändler, 73 Race Street.

(Crisp, Stephen.) Eine Kurze Beschreibung einer Langen Reise aus Babylon nach Bethel. Dritte Auflage. 12mo. 24 S.   G. S.

Das Kleine Davidische Psalterspiel der Kinder Zions. Zum sechstenmal ans Licht gegeben. 12mo. 572 S. u. Register.

Angebunden:

Die Kleine Harfe. Zum erstenmal ans Licht gegeben. 12mo. 56 S.
    G. S.
    See 1744.

Der Neue Hoch Deutsche Americanische Calender. Auf b. J. 1792.

* Die Chesnuthiller Wochenschrift. 4to. (10 x 8).

Ephrata.

Kurzgefaßtes Arzney-Büchlein für Menschen und Vieh. Darinnen 128 auserlesene Recepte nebst einer prognostischen Tafel. In Wien gedruckt. In Ephrata nachgedruckt. 16mo. 24 S.

Der bußfertige Beicht-Vater und Seel-Sorger, Aaron, Priester in der grosen Stadt Babel, Wie er zur Erkenntniß seiner Sünde kommen und dieselbe bereuet u. s. w. Von C. A. Ein um die Wahrheit willen Vertriebener. Ephrata. Gedruckt auf Kosten der Liebhaber. 16mo. vi u. 47 S.   H. S.

Friedrich Stadt, Md. Matthias Bärtgis.

Der Verbesserte Hoch Deutsche Americanische Land und Staats Calender. Auf das Jahr 1792.

Germantown. Michael Billmeyer.

Die Spuren der Güte Gottes in der deutschen evangelischen lutherischen Gemeinde in Philadelphia. 12mo. 36 S.   G. S.

Tagebuch der Ersten Sitzung des Zweyten Hauses der Representanten der Republik Pennsylvanien, welche in Philadelphia, am Dienstag, den sechsten Tag Decembers im J. 1790 ihren Anfang nahm. Aus dem Engl. übersetzt. Fol. 327 S. u. Anhang (gedruckt 1792) 33 S.
    G. S.

Tagebuch des Senats der Republik Pennsylvanien. 1790—1791.

Weichenhan, Erasmus. Chriſtliche Betrachtungen über die Evange=
liſchen Texte, ſo man pfleget zu leſen an denen Sontagen und hohen
feſten. 4to. Vorrede 6 S., Text 785 S.   G. S.

> The work reflects the religious views of the Schwenkfelders. The writer
> who was minister at Langen-Bielau in Silesia, where he died 1594, left it
> in manuscript and it was not printed till 1672 in Sulzbach. The German-
> town reprint "at the expense of united friends" is a very creditable piece
> of bookmaking as to typography, paper and binding. The preface is dated
> Montgomery County Feb. 12, 1791.

Der Hoch=Deutſche Americaniſche Calender, Auf das Jahr 1792 u. ſ. w.

* Die Germantauner Zeitung. 4to. 10 x 8.   H. S.

Germantown. Peter Leibert und Sohn.

Terſteegen, G. Geiſtiges Blumengärtlein inniger Seelen. Siebente
Auflage. 12mo. 534 S. u. Regiſter.

> See 1747.

The Christians Duty, exhibited in a Series of Hymns collected
from various Authors. Designed for the worship of God and
for the edification of Christians. Recommended to the
Serious of all Denominations by the Baptists of Germantown.
12mo. 320 pp.   H. S.

> A Dunker hymnbook.

Lancaſter. Albrecht & Comp.

Döring, Friedrich Chriſtlieb. Daß das Evangelium von Jeſu
Chriſto, nach Römer 1.16 noch immer eine Kraft Gottes ſey,
erläutert durch das Beyſpiel ſeines eigenen Bruders Auguſt Salomon
Dörings. Zweyte Auflage. 12mo. 65 S.   G. S.

> The original of this reprint appeared in Germany. The writer was a
> minister, whose brother had killed a boy and was executed for his crime.
> An English translation was published by C. Cist in 1792.

Der Neue Gemeinnützige Landwirthſchafts Calender auf das Jahr .
1792.

* Neue, Unpartheyiſche Lancäſter Zeitung und Anzeigs=Nachrichten.

Lancaſter. Jacob Bailey.

Evangelium Nicodemi, oder Hiſtoriſcher Bericht von dem Leben Jeſu Chriſti
welches Nicodemus, ein Rabbi u. ſ. w. beſchrieben. 12mo. 95 S.

Angebunden:

Teſtament und Abſchrift der Zwölf Patriarchen, der Söhnen Jacobs
u. ſ. w. 12mo. 113 S.

Philadelphia. Carl Cist.

Benezet, Anton. Kurzer Bericht von den Leuten, die man Quäker nennet, ihrem Ursprung, ihren Religionsgründen, und von ihrer Niederlassung in America. Aus dem Englischen übersetzt. 12mo. 36 S.   G. S.

Der Kleine Catechismus des sel. D. Martin Luther u. s. w. 16mo. 128 S.

Das Neue Testament.

Der Psalter des Königs und Propheten Davids u. s. w. 16mo. 251 S.   G. S.

Penn, Wilhelm. Forderung der Christenheit vors Gericht. Eine Freundliche Heimsuchung in der Liebe Gottes 2c. Sendbrief an alle diejenigen, die unter der Christlichen Confession und von den äusser=lichen Secten und Gemeinen oder Kirchen abgesondert sind. Send=brief an alle diejenigen, die von dem Tage ihrer Heimsuchung empfindlich seyn geworden. In die Hochdeutsche Sprache treulich transferiret. 12mo. Vorrede 9 S., Text 119 S.   G. S.

Mason, Benjamin. Ein Licht das aus der Dunkelheit leuchtet. Antwort auf Franz Herr's Schrift. 12mo. 53 S.   H. S.

Americanischer Stadt und Land Calender auf das 1792ste Jahr.

Philadelphia. Melchior Steiner.

Kunze, D. Johann Christoph. Der 119. Psalm, genau nach der Grundsprache übersetzt.

* Neue Philadelphische Correspondenz.   H. S.
     Appeared every Tuesday and Friday.

Philadelphia. Joh. Zeller, 89 Race St.

Beschreibung einer ungeheuren großen Schlange, Anaconda genannt.
       Advertisement.

Reading. Barton und Jungmann.

Die Gesichte des Isaac Cheilds welches er gesehen hat, betreffend das Land seiner Geburt. 12mo.

* Neue Unpartheyische Readinger Zeitung und Anzeigs=Nachrichten. Fol. 17 x 11.

1792.

Chesnuthill. Samuel Saur.

Brobbeck, Christian. Geistiges Wetter=Glöcklein, Oder Christliche Donner= und Wetter=Gebäter auf allerley Fäll, andächtigen Herzens mit Fleiß zusammengetragen von Christian Brobbeck.　　H. S.

Hirte, Tobias. Ein Neues, auserlesenes gemeinnütziges Hand= Büchlein. 12mo. 96 S.　　H. S.

Die Kleine Harfe, gestimmt von unterschieblichen Liedern und Lobgesängen, welche gehöret werden von den Enden der Erden zu Ehren der Gerechten.　　G. S.

[Mack, Val.] Ein Gespräch zwischen einem Pilger und Bürger auf ihrer Reise nach und in der Ewigkeit. 12mo. 72 S.

Verschiedene alte und neuere Geschichten von Erscheinungen der Geister u. s. w. Vierte Auflage. 12mo. 168 S.　　G. S.

　　First edition 1744.

Eine kurze Beschreibung einer langen Reise von Babylon nach Bethel. 12mo. 24 S.　　G. S.

Die Wege und Werke Gottes in der Seele. 12mo. 59 S.　　H. S.

Der Neue Hoch Deutsche Americanische Calender. Auf das Jahr 1793.

* Die Chesnuthiller Wochenschrift.

Ephrata.

(Martin, G. A.) Christliche Bibliothek, enthält dasjenige was allen Pilgern auf der Reise nach der verlorenen Herrlichkeit zu wissen nöthig ist. Herausgegeben durch deinen Getreuen Aufrichtigen Mitbruder. 8vo. 148 S.

　　The initials of the last three words are those of the author's name, Georg Adam Martin. An autobiographical account of his conversion, spiritual life and connection with the Ephrata convent is found in the thirty-first chapter of the *Chronicon Ephratense.*

Römeling's (C. A.), gewesenen Predigers zu Haarburg, Nachricht Seiner von GOTT geschehenen völligen Herausführung aus Babel. Wie auch Treuherzige Erweckungs=Stimme zum Ausgang aus Babel, Deme angehängt ein Theosophischer Entwurf von denen zwey Er=

Kețern, Vernunft und Eigenliebe, und G. Arnold's Heilſame Wahrnehmung jețiger Zeiten, wie auch ein Stüď aus G. T. Steegens von der Myſtiť und ein Tractat vom innern Leben und der reinen Liebe GOTTES. Ephrata, gedruďt im Jahr 1792. 8vo. 466 u. 96 S.

Christian Anton Römeling, Lutheran minister at Harburg, from 1701 — 1710, was, on account of his leaning to pietistic and mystical religion, excommunicated and banished. In Holland, where he found a refuge, he joined the Mennonites. His book was originally printed in Frankfurt and Leipzig 1710. The appended tracts of *Arnold* and *Tersteegen* have a mystical drift quite in accord with the religious temper of Ephrata. They were also separately printed there.

(Tersteegen, G.) Vom Chriſtlichen Gebrauch der Lieder und des Singens. 12mo. 56 S. G. S.

Merkwürdige Prophezehung eines Einſiedlers, welcher 15 Jahre allein in der Wüſten gewohnet. Entdeďt von Dr. Peter Schneider. Gedruďt für den Verfaſſer.

Place of issue not stated, but probably Ephrata.

Friedrich Stadt, Md. Matthias Bärtgis.

Der Verbeſſerte Hoch=Deutſche Americaniſche Land und Staats Calender. Auf d. Jahr 1793.

Germantown. M. Billmeyer.

Ein wohl eingerichtetes A. B. C. Buchſtabir= und Leſebuch zum Gebrauch deutſcher Schulen.

Tagebuch des Dritten Hauſes der Repräſentanten der Republiť Pennſyl= vanien. 1791 — 1792.

Tagebuch des Senats der Republiť Pennſylvanien. 1791 — 1792.

Der Hoch=Deutſche Americaniſche Calender. Auf das Jahr 1793 u. ſ. w.

* Die Germantowner Zeitung. H. S.

Germantown. Peter Leibert.

Eine nüßliche Anweiſung oder Beyhülfe vor die Teutſchen um Engliſch zu lernen. Vierte Auflage. 12mo. 282 S. u. Regiſter. H. S.

Züblin, J. J. Evangeliſches Zeugniß vom Elend und Erlöſung der Menſchen, in zwey Predigten abgelegt. Vierte Auflage.
See 1751.

Lancaſter. Johann Albrecht und Comp.

Der Neue Gemeinützige Landwirthſchafts Calender auf das Jahr . . 1793.

* Neue, Unpartheyiſche Lancaſter Zeitung und Anzeigs=Nachrichten.

Philadelphia. Carl Ciſt.

Dell, W. Lehre von der Taufe, die von ihren alten und neueren Ver=
fälſchungen befreyet und nach iher urſprünglichen Reinigkeit und
Wahrheit wieder hergeſtellt wird. Aus dem Engliſchen überſetzt.
12mo. 63 S. G. S.

    With an appendix:

(Sewell, W.) Zwei Sendſchreiben aus Sewells Geſchichte der
Quäker. 32 S.

Dell, Wilhelm. Prüfung der Geiſter ſowohl in den Lehrern als in
den Zuhörern, u. ſ. w. 12mo. 80 S. G. S.

    See 1790.

Americaniſcher Stadt und Land Calender auf das 1793ſte Jahr Chriſti.

Philadelphia. Steiner & Kämmerer.

Americaniſcher Haus und Wirthſchafts=Calender auf das 1793ſte Jahr
Chriſti. Zum Zwölftenmal herausgegeben. G. S.

    No almanacs of this series were published for 1791 and 1792. On Novem-
ber 6, 1792 Steiner entered into partnership with H. Kämmerer, a paper
dealer and prominent officer of the German Society.

* Neue Philadelphiſche Correſpondenz. H. S.

    Since October 1790 this paper had appeared twice a week, on Tuesdays
and Fridays. After May 15, 1792, the Friday issue was discontinued. On
November 6th the name of the firm was changed to *Steiner* and *Kämmerer*
and from November 27th the word *Neue* was ommitted in the name of the
paper.

Philadelphia. Wm. Woodhouſe.

McPherſon's Vorleſungen über philoſophiſche Sittenlehre. Ueberſetzt
von G. F. Götz.

    G. F. Götz was a contributor to the Philadelphische Correspondenz.

Reading. Barton und Jungmann.

* Neue Unpartheyiſche Readinger Zeitung und Anzeigs=Nachrichten.

1793.

Chesnut Hill. Samuel Saur.

Gabriel, P. Kurzer Bericht von der Pest, dessen Uhrsprung, Zeichen und Eigenschaft; wie auch einige Hausmittel, Recepte, Rauchwerke und politische Verordnungen bey ansteckenden Krankheiten. 12mo. 56 u. 10 S.. G. S.

> The reprint of this book written about 1640 by Peter Gabriel, Inspector of the Court Gardens in Stuttgart, was prompted by the yellow fever epidemic in Philadelphia, which is noticed in an appendix.

Geschwinder Rechner oder des Händlers nützlicher Gehülfe.

Der Neue Hoch deutsche Americanische Calender. Auf b. J. 1794.

* Die Chesnuthiller Wochenschrift..

Federal or New Reckoner.

Easton. Jacob Weygandt.

* Neuer Unpartheyischer Eastoner Bothe und Northampton Kundschafter.

> Mr. Ethan A. Weaver, Philadelphia, has a photographic copy of No. 270, published November 13, 1798. The first number consequently must have appeared five years and ten weeks before that date. The paper had four pages of three columns each.

Ephrata.

Der Psalter des Königs und Propheten Davids, verteutscht von D. Martin Luther. 12mo. 252 S. H. S.

Wurde abgesungen den 31sten August 1793 bey B. A. S. auf dem jährlichen Fest an der Antitum. Fol. 1 S.

> This heading is followed by a song of fifteen stanzas. The letters B. A. S. stand for Brother Andrew Schneeberger, who was the founder of the Snowhill Monastic Institute in Franklin County.

Anonymus's Travels from Europe to America and some Visions of Many Heavenly Mansions in the house of God. H. S.

Bolton, James. Treatise on Universal Restoration. H. S.

Friedrich Stadt, Md. Matthias Bärtgis.

Der Verbesserte Hoch Deutsche Americanische Land und Staats Calender. Auf b. J. . . 1794.

* Der General Staatsbote.

It is possible that the paper which M. Bartgis is said to have published at Frederick in 1786, was continued and called *Der General Staatsbote*, a name attributed to a German paper published at Frederick in 1793 every other week. How long it appeared cannot be stated, the history of German printing in Maryland remaining yet in the dark.

Germantown. Peter Leibert.

Gerhard Tersteegens Lebensbeschreibung. 12mo. 87 S.   G. S.

Des seligen Gerhard Tersteegens hinterlaßene Erklärung seines Sinns seinem Testamente beygelegt. 12mo. 8 S.   G. S.
Bound with the foregoing book.

Hirte, Tobias. Der Freund in der Noth, Oder Zweyter Theil des Neuen Auserlesenen Gemeinnützigen Hand=Büchleins Für die Deut=schen in America. 16mo. 94 S.   G. S.

Germantown. Michael Billmeyer.

Helmuth, J. H. Christian. Betrachtung der Evangelischen Lehre von der Heiligen Schrift und Taufe; samt einigen Gedanken von den gegenwärtigen Zeiten. 12mo. Vorrede 6 S. 336 S.   G. S.

Tagebuch des Vierten Hauses der Repräsentanten der Republik Pennsyl=vanien. 1792—1793. Amtliche Deutsche Uebersetzung.

Tagebuch des Senats der Republik Pennsylvanien. 1792—1793.

Der Hoch=Deutsche Americanische Calender. Auf das Jahr 1794 u. s. w.

* Die Germantauner Zeitung.   H. S.

Hanover, (M'Alisters Stadt.) York County. H. Willcocks.

Eine Controversia oder Disputations=Schreiben, welches in Hanover Stadt, York County, geführet worden im Jahr 1793 zwischen einem Lutherischen Prediger und etliche Handwerksleute, welche die Lehre der Wiederbringung aller Dinge glauben.   H. S.

Lancaster. Albrecht & Comp.

Gespräch im Reich der Todten über die Begnadigten auf Erden und über die Seligen im Himmel, zwischen zwey Hocherleuchteten seligen Männern Gottes, nämlich Gerhard und Jacob aus dem Bergischen. 12mo. 226 S.   G. S.

Der Neue Gemeinnützige Landwirthschafts Calender auf das Jahr 1794.

* Neue, Unpartheyische Lancäster Zeitung und Anzeigs=Nachrichten.

Philadelphia. Carl Cist.

Americanischer Stadt und Land Calender auf das 1794ste J. Christi.

Philadelphia. Steiner und Kämmerer.

Eine Acte zur Incorpirung der deutschen Gesellschaft in Pennsylvanien. 8vo. 21 S.   G. S.

Helmuth, J. Ch. H. Kurze Nachricht von dem sogenannten Gelben Fieber in Philadelphia. 12mo. 104 S.   G. S.

> The German population of Philadelphia suffered terribly from the ravages of the yellow fever. By statistics given in the appendix it appears that the Lutheran congregation lost in August, September and October 625 members, children included.

Zimmermann, J. Georg. Von der Einsamkeit.

Americanischer Haus= und Wirthschafts=Calender auf das 1794ste Jahr Christi.

* Philadelphische Correspondenz.   H. S.

> On May 7th the bi-weekly issue of the paper on Tuesdays and Fridays was resumed.

Reading. Jungmann und Gruber.

Beyspiele Märkwürdiger Bekehrungen, in der Geschichte des Barons von Dyherrn und der Johanna Cisch. 12mo. 28 u. 23 S.   H. S.

> Translated from the English.

* Neue Unpartheyische Readinger Zeitung und Anzeigs=Nachrichten.

1794.

Chesnuthill. Samuel Saur.

Carey, M. Eine kurze Nachricht von dem bösartigen Fieber, welches kürzlich in Philadelphia grassirt, samt Nachricht von der Pest in London und Marseille. Uebersetzt von Carl Erdmann. 8vo. 105 S.   G. S.

> Contains a list of names of those who died in Philadelphia of yellow fever in August, September and October 1793.

* Die Chesnuthiller Wochenschrift.

> The number dated April 24th was printed in Philadelphia 71 Race ("Rees") st., foreshadowing the publication of the paper in Philadelphia.

Easton. Jacob Weygand.

* Neuer Unpartheyischer Eastoner Bothe und Northampton Kundschafter.

Ephrata. Salomon Mayer.

Frage. Die Salbung. 16mo. 12 S.

Merkwürdige Prophezeyung eines Einsiedlers, welcher 15 Jahre allein in der Wüsten gewohnet. Entdeckt von Dr. Peter Schneider. Zum brittenmal gedruckt. 12mo. 22 S.

> Probably printed in Ephrata. See 1792.

Friederich Stadt, Md. Matthias Bärtgis.

Der Verbesserte Hoch Deutsche Americanische Land und Staats Calender. Auf das Jahr . . 1795.

Germantown. Peter Leibert.

Dr. Joh. Habermanns von Eger Christlich Gebät=Buch. 12mo. 284 S. u. Reg.

Schabalie, Philipp. Die Wandlende Seel. Dritte Auflage. 12mo. 463 S. u. Register.

Germantown. M. Billmeyer.

Tagebuch des Fünften Hauses der Repräsentanten der Republik Pennsylvanien 1793—1794.

Tagebuch des Staats der Republik Pennsylvanien. 1793—1794.

Der Hoch=Deutsche Americanische Calender. Auf das Jahr 1795 u. s. w.

* Die Germantauner Zeitung.

Harrisburg. Benjamin Mayer und Conrad Fahnestock.

* Die Unpartheyische Harrisburgh Zeitung.

> According to Dr. Wm. H. Egle's History of Dauphin and Lebanon Counties the first number of this paper was published March 1, 1794. In politics it was democratic.

Lancäster. Johann Albrecht & Comp.

Fliegender Brief evangelischer Worte an die Jugend von der Glückseligkeit
solcher Kinder und jungen Leute, die sich frühzeitig bekehren. 12mo.
Vorrede 16 S., Text 218 S.   G. S.

 A reprint.

Der Neue Gemeinnützige Landwirthschafts Calender auf das Jahr . .
1795.

* Neue, Unpartheyische Lancäster Zeitung und Anzeigs=Nachrichten.

[Menno Simon.] Ein Fundament und Klare Anweisung von der
seligmachenden Lehre unseres Herrn Jesu Christi u. s. w. durch M.
S. Gedruckt in Europa 1575. Pennsylvanien, gedruckt im Jahre
Christi 1794. 12mo. 675 S. u. Reg.   G. S.

 This important work of Menno Simon has been repeatedly reprinted in
Pennsylvania. J. Bär of Lancaster published an edition in 1835.

Philadelphia. Carl Cist.

Americanischer Stadt und Land Calender auf das 1795ste J. Ch.

Philadelphia. Samuel Saur.

Prophetische Muthmaßungen über die französische Revolution.—Erzählun=
gen von Joseph II., Kaiser von Deutschland. 12mo. 88 S.
                H. S.

 Samuel Saur removed in this year from Chestnut Hill to 71 (O. N.)
Race Street, Philadelphia.

Von dem Durchschauen und Beharren in das vollkommene Gesetz der
Freyheit. Predigt zum Besten der in der türkischen Sclaverey
seyenden Americaner.

 Advertised in S. Saur's Philadelphia Weekly. The fact that charity was
invoked in various ways for Americans held in captivity by the Turks
reminds of remarkable changes in the conditions of America and Turkey.

Der Neue Hoch Deutsche Americanische Calender auf das Jahr 1795.
Zum fünftenmal herausgegeben.

* Das Philadelphier Wochenblat. Diese Zeitung wird wöchentlich, nem=
lich Dienstags herausgegeben von Samuel Saur, Buchdrucker Num.
71 in der Reesstrasse, zwischen der Zweyten und Drittenstrasse, zu
Philadelphia, für Drey Schilling und Neun Pens des Jahres. 4to.
10 x 8.

 In the beginning of the year the paper appeared as the *Chesnuthiller
Wochenschrift.*

Philadelphia. Gedruckt für David Saur.

Ein ganz neu eingerichtetes A. B. C. Buchstabir= und Namenbuch. 12mo.
94 S.   G. S.

The memorial verses with little wood cuts for each letter of the alphabet
were translated from the *New England Primer* and while intended to
be edifying could in our time but raise a smile; e. g. Auf Gottes Stimme
hören Wallfische in den Meeren.—Uriahs schönes Eheweib War des Davids
Zeitvertreib. The latter lines read in the New England Primer: Uria's
beauteous wife made David seek his life.

Philadelphia. Steiner & Kämmerer.

Regeln der incorporirten Deutschen Gesellschaft.   G. S.

Americanischer Haus= und Wirthschafts Calender auf das 1795ste. Jahr
Christi.

Helmuth, J. H. C. Die Bruderliebe in Philadelphia gegen die
Armen Brüder. Rede gehalten am 3. Februar 1794 als am Gedächt=
nißtage der Gesellschaft zur Unterstützung Hülfsbedürftiger Haus=
armen. 8vo. 16 S.   G. S.

* Philadelphische Correspondenz.

Published twice a week.

Philadelphia.

Mühlenberg, F. A. Rede bei der Feier des 20sten Septembers.

The charter of the German Society received the signature of the Speaker
of the Assembly, Frederick A. Muhlenberg, on the 20th of September 1781.
Hence this day was for some time annually celebrated, an address being
delivered on the occassion. In 1794 F. A. Muhlenberg was President of
the German Society, and of his address, as we know by the minutes, 300
copies were printed, none of which, however, has come to light.

Reading. Jungmann & Gruber.

* Neue Unpartheyische Readinger Zeitung und Anzeigs=Nachrichten.

1795.

Baltimore. Samuel Saur.

A. B. C. Buchstabir und Namenbuch zum nützlichen Gebrauch deutscher
Schulen.

Bunian, Joh. Der heilige Krieg, Wie derselbe geführet wird von
Christo wider den Teuffel. 12mo. 304 S.

Eine neue Charte und sinnliche Abbildung von der engen Pforte und dem schmalen Wege der zum ewigen Leben führet und von der weiten Pforte und dem breiten Wege der zum Verderben führet. Fol. 2 S.

Curiously arranged text interspersed with allegorical pictures. The second closely printed page contains the Key.

Des Johann Lassenius Politische Geheimniß Vieler hin und wieder heutigen Tages einreißenden unartigen Atheisten, in einigen Gesprächen entdeckt und entworfen. 16mo. 195 S.   H. S.—G. S.

A satirical exhibit of selfish and unscrupulous maxims.

Der Neue Hoch=Deutsche Americanische Calender auf das Jahr Christi 1796.

* Deutsche Zeitung.

The name of Saur's paper, published in Baltimore, has not been ascertained, nor is the year of its first appearance certain. In the almanac for the year 1800 Samuel Saur referring to his paper says, that he has been publishing it for considerable time (geraume Zeit) and that it is issued three times a week on a half sheet.

Easton. Jacob Weygandt.

* Neuer Unpartheyischer Eastoner Bothe und Northampton Kundschafter.

Ephrata. Salomon Mäyer.
(Neue Buchdruckerey.)

Das Kleine Davidische Psalterspiel der Kinder Zion's. 12mo. 575 S. u. Register.

Angebunden:

Das allerneuste Harfenspiel u. s. w. von P. Ely, C. Grosch u. s. w. 12mo. 45 S.

Das Neue Testament. Erste Auflage. 12mo. 528 S.

The cheap and famous Farrier.   H. S.

Pennsylvanischer Calender. Auf das 1796ste Jahr Christi. 4to. 40 S.
      G. S.

First issue.

Friederich Stadt, Md. Matthias Bärtgis.

Der Verbesserte Hoch Deutsche Americanische Land und Staats Calender. Auf das Jahr . . 1796.

Germantown. Michael Billmeyer.

Erbauliche Lieder=Sammlung zum gottesdienstlichen Gebrauch der vereinigten ev. luth. Gemeinden. Zweyte Auflage. 12mo. 602 S. G. S.

First edition in 1786.

Kurze Andachten einer gottsuchenden Seele. Zweyte Auflage. 12mo. 28 S.

Das Neue Testament. Zweite Auflage. 12mo. 537 S.

Tagebuch des Senats der Republik Pennsylvanien. 1794—1795.

Der Hoch=Deutsche Americanische Calender. Auf das Jahr 1796 u. s. w.

* Die Germantauner Zeitung.

Germantown. Peter Leibert.

Habermann, Dr. J. Christliche Morgen= und Abend=Gebeter auf alle Tage in der Woche, wie auch Magister Neumanns Kern aller Gebeter und Geistlicher Stundenwecker.   H. S.

Der Kleine Kempis oder kurze Sprüche und Gebätlein. Siebente Auflage. 16mo. 180 S.   H. S.

Hagerstown, Md. Johann Gruber.

* Der Deutsche Waschington Correspondent.

John Gruber who had been engaged in the printing business in Philadelphia went in 1795, at the solicitation of Gen. Ringold, to Hagerstown and started there a German paper called the *German Washington Correspondent*. It was continued a number of years but was not a permanent success. See Scharff, *History of Western Maryland*, vol. 2, p. 1141. J. Gruber (1768—1857) was the son of Johann Adam Gruber who has been noticed on page 13.

Harrisburg. Benj. Meyer u. Conrad Fahnestock.

* Die Unpartheyische Harrisburg Zeitung.

Lancaster. Johann Albrecht & Comp.

Der Neue Gemeinnützige Landwirthschafts Calender auf das Jahr . . 1796. Zum Neuntenmal herausgegeben.

* Neue, Unpartheyische Lancäster Zeitung und Anzeigs=Nachrichten.

Philadelphia. Carl Cist.

Otterbein, Georg Gottfried. Lesebuch für Deutsche Schulkinder. Mit Veränderungen und Zusätzen zum Gebrauch Nord=Americanischer Schulen. Herausgegeben von Carl Gotthold Reichel in Nazareth. 12mo. 220 S.   G. S.

Americanischer Stadt und Land Calender auf das 1796ste Jahr Christi.

Philadelphia. Steiner u. Kämmerer.

Auserlesene Fabeln des Aesop. Nach der englischen Ausgabe des Herrn R. Dodsley übersetzt von Gustav F. Goetz, drei Theile mit mehr als 150 wohlgerathenen schönen Kupferstichen geziert.

Catechismus, Oder: Kurzer Unterricht christlicher Lehre wie derselbe in denen Reformirten Kirchen und Schulen Deutschlands wie auch in America getrieben wird. 286 S.   H. S.

Endreß, Christian. Einige vermischte Gedanken über Regierungs= form in Beziehung aufs Christenthum. Eine Rede gehalten vor der Gesellschaft zur Unterstützung hülfsbedürftiger Hausarmen der lutherischen Gemeinde. 8vo. 12 S.   G. S.

Die Grundregeln der Gesellschaft zur Beyhülfe und Unterstützung der armen alten und kranken Glieder der Deutschen Evangelisch=Lutheri= schen Gemeine in Philadelphia. 8vo. 12 S.   G. S.

Tagebuch des Sechsten Hauses der Repräsentanten der Republik Penn= sylvanien: 1794 — 1795.

Americanischer Haus= und Wirthschafts=Calender auf das 1796ste Jahr Christi.   H. S.

* Philadelphische Correspondenz.
    Published twice a week.

Reading. Jungmann und Gruber.
* Neue unpartheyische Readinger Zeitung und Anzeigs=Nachrichten.

1796.

Baltimore. *G. Keating*.

Dem Andenken Deutscher Dichter und Philosopher gewidmet, von Deutschen in Amerika. Erster Band. 8vo. 324 S.
     G. S.

The preface, dated Philadelphia and Baltimore, announces a series of volumes, comprising the works of famous German writers. But only one volume appeared. It is dedicated to Washington and contains Gessner's *Tod Abels*, *Dophnis* and *Die Nacht*. G. Keating was probably the publisher only, while the very neatly executed print (in Roman type) was the work of Samuel Saur.

Baltimore. Samuel Saur.

Der Psalter des Königs und Propheten Davids.

Der Neue Hoch=Deutsche Americanische Calender auf das Jahr 1797.

* Deutsche Zeitung.
    See 1795.

Easton. Jacob Weygandt.

* Neuer Unpartheyischer Eastoner Bothe und Northampton Kundschafter.

Ephrata. Benjamin Mäyer.

William Beables Lebensbeschreibung nebst Ermordung seiner Familie und sich selbst. 16 S.

Das Fromme Mägdelein oder Elternsegen.

Gemeinnützige Sammlung zum Gebrauch der Deutschen in Amerika, Vornehmlich der Landleute in Pennsylvanien. 8vo. 136 S.

H. S.

A German letter writer and form book.

Merkwürdige Prophezeyung eines Einsiedlers u. s. w. Vierte Auflage. See 1792.

Der Weg zum Glück, Oder: Das Leben von Dr. Benjamin Franklin beschrieben von ihm selbst. 16mo. 135 S.

G. S.

Pennsylvanischer Calender. Auf das 1797ste Jahr Christi.

Friedrich Stadt, Md. Matthias Bärtgis.

Der Verbesserte Hoch Deutsche Americanische Land und Staats Calender. Auf das Jahr. . 1797.

Germantown. Michael Billmeyer.

Ein wohl eingerichtetes A. B. C.- Buchstabir= und Lesebuch zum Gebrauch deutscher Schulen. 12mo. 120 S.

Der Hoch=Deutsche Americanische Calender, Auf das Jahr 1797 u. s. w.

* Die Germantauner Zeitung.

Germantown. Peter Leibert.

Bunian, Joh. Eines Christen Reise nach der Seligen Ewigkeit. Zwey Theile. 12mo. 240 u. 225 S.

H. S.

Kurze Beschreibung von den Leben und Sterben von Joh. Bunyan. 26 S.

H. S.

Gedanken über die Rechtmäßigkeit der Kriege. Aus dem Englischen übersetzt. 31 S.

H. S.—G. S.

Denounces war, commands everlasting peace. The original appeared the same year in London and was reprinted in Philadelphia.

Germantown.

The New-England Primer, much improved, Containing a Variety of easy lessons. 24mo.

The German translation of the memorial verses was noticed under the year 1794. The first are the well known: "In Adam's fall we sinned all."

Hagerstown. Johann Gruber.

* Der Deutsche Washington Correspondent.
See 1795.

Harrisburg. B. Meyer u. C. Fahnestock.

* Die Unpartheyische Harrisburg Zeitung.

Lancaster. Joh. Albrecht & Comp.

Die Christliche Haushaltung. Uebersetzt aus dem Griechischen Original. 12mo. 48 S.   H. S.

Becker, Christian Ludwig. Die Religion Jesu, eine sanfte Religion, vorgestellt in der Einweihungsrede der Deutsch-reformirten Kirche in Lancaster von Dr. C. L. Becker.

> C. L. Becker, D. D., was born 1756, came to America 1793, was pastor in Easton 1794—1795, in Lancaster 1795—1806, in Baltimore 1806—1818, in which year he died.

Der Neue Gemeinnützige Landwirthschafts Calender auf das Jahr . . 1797.

* Neue, Unpartheyische Lancäster Zeitung und Anzeigs-Nachrichten.

Lancaster. William und Robert Dickson.

Allein, Joseph. Grundlegung zum Thätigen Christenthum. Aus dem Englischen übersetzt. 12mo. 332 S.   G. S.

> Allein, an English clergyman, lived 1633—1668.

Philadelphia. Carl Cist.

Ein herzlicher Gruß in evangelischer Liebe. 12mo. 24 S.

> A Quaker tract.

Americanischer Stadt u. Land Calender auf das 1797ste Jahr Cristi.

Philadelphia. Henrich Schweitzer.

Goetz, Johann Nepomuck. Predigt von der Heiligkeit Christlicher Tempel, am jährlichen Gedächtnißtage der feierlichen Eröffnung der allerseligsten Dreyfaltigkeitskirche der Teutschen christ-katholischen Gemeine. Gehalten am 20. November 1796 von Johann Nepomuk Goetz, Weltpriester und vormaliger Professor und Prediger an der Kais. Königlichen Akademie zu Wienerisch Neustadt.

> Trinity Church, 6th and Spruce Street, Philadelphia, opened for service on the 22d of November 1789.

Philadelphia. Steiner. u. Kämmerer.

Eine kurze Betrachtung über die Feier des Tages des Herren. 12mo. 16 S.   H. S.

Das gute Kind vor und nach der Schule. 16mo. 24 S.   H. S.

Tagebuch des Siebenten Hauses der Repräsentanten der Republik Penn=
sylvanien.

Americanischer Haus= und Wirthschafts=Calender auf das 1797ste Jahr
Christi.

* Philadelphische Correspondenz.

> Published twice a week.

Philadelphia.   Neal u. Kämmerer.

Noth und Hülfsbüchlein für Bauersleute.

Philadelphia.

Eine ganz neue und sehr merkwürdige Reisebeschreibung oder zuver=
lässige und glaubwürdige Nachrichten von den westlichen bis jetzt noch
unbekannten Theilen von America. Von Don Antonio Decalves.
Gedruckt und zu haben bey den Herren Buchhändlern. 12mo.
82 S.   G. S.

> A fancy drawn account of the unexplored West.

Reading.   Jungmann u. Gruber.

* Neue Unpartheyische Readinger Zeitung und Anzeigs=Nachrichten.   Fol.
17 x 11.

Reading.   Jacob Schneider u. Georg Gerrish.

* Der Unpartheyische Reading Adler. „Wir suchen kein lob aus den
grundsätzen einiger Parthey, hoffen es aber durch unser anliegen
für das gemeine beste, zu verdienen." Herausgegeben von Jacob
Schneider und Georg Gerrish in der Deutsch= und Englischen Buch=
druckerey in Reading in der Pennstraße. Fol.   11 x 17.

> The first number of the *Adler*, now the oldest German paper in America,
> appeared November 29, 1796. The name of George Gerrish, one of the
> original publishers, was dropped after the issue of the second number and
> the publishing firm was till June 27. 1802, Schneider and Comp. Then it
> changed to Schneider & Ritter and in 1804 to Ritter and Comp. The
> partner was Charles A. Kessler, who died 1823. Ritter died in 1851. A
> son of Kessler, who had inherited his mother's share, bought in 1857 also
> the Ritter interest in the business and became sole proprietor. He
> conducted the business till 1864, when he transferred it to William S. Ritter,
> (a nephew of the former proprietor John Ritter) and Jesse H. Hawley.
> The paper was now again published under the old firm name, Ritter &
> Comp. Since the dissolution of the partnership in 1874, Mr. William S.
> Ritter (b. 1828) has the sole charge of the *Adler* concern. The name of
> the paper underwent some modifications, until it was called *Der Readinger
> Adler;* also the motto and the eagle clutching a scroll, were changed, but
> the loyalty of the *Reading Adler* to the democratic party has during a
> century remained immutable.

York, Pa. Solomon Mayer.

* Die York Gazette.

See Carter and Glossbrenner's History of York County, p. 96.

1797.

Baltimore. Samuel Saur.

Das Kleine Davidische Psalterspiel der Kinder Zions u. s. w. 12mo.
572 S. u. Reg. Zweyte Verbesserte Auflage. G. s.

Samuel Saur's first edition appeared 1791. By other publishers the
same book had been printed in 1744, 1760, 1764, 1777, 1781 and 1795.

Die Kleine Harfe, gestimmet von unterschieblichen lieblichen Liedern oder
Lob=Gesängen, welche gehöret werden von den Enden der Erden zu
Ehren der Gerechten. Zweyte Auflage. 12mo. 55 S. u. Reg.
G. s.

Appendix to the Kleine Davidische Psalterspiel.

Der Neue Hoch=Deutsche Americanische Calender auf das Jahr Christi
1798.

* Deutsche Zeitung.

See 1795.

Easton. Jacob Weygandt.

* Neuer Unpartheyischer Eastoner Bothe und Northampton Kundschafter.

Ephrata. Benjamin Meyer.

Kurzgefaßtes Arzney=Buch . . für Menschen und Vieh. 12mo. 23 S.

Die Kinder im Walde. 16mo. 15 S.

Der Psalter des Königs und Propheten Davids.

Ephrata. Salomon Mäyer.

Merkwürdige Prophezeyung eines Einsiedlers. Fünfte Auflage.

See 1792.

Pennsylvanischer Calender. Auf das 1798ste Jahr Christi. G. s.

Friedrich=Stadt, Md. Matthias Bärtgis.

Der Verbesserte Hoch Deutsche Americanische Land und Staats Calender.
Auf b. J. 1798.

Germantown. Michael Billmeyer.

Das Kleine Davidische Psalterspiel u. s. w. 572 S. u. Reg., Anhang
20 S.

Tagebuch des Senats der Republik Pennsylvanien. 1796—1797

Der Hoch-Deutsche Americanische Calender. Auf das Jahr 1798 u. s. w.

* Die Germantauner Zeitung.

Hägerstown, Md. Johann Gruber.

Der neue Nord-Americanische Stadt und Land Calender. Auf das Jahr unseres Heylandes Jesu Christi 1798. Zum Erstenmal heraus=
gegeben.

> On the cover leaf there is an emblematical design and over it another title, viz.: Der Volksfreund und Hägerstauner Calender auf 1798. The engraver's name on the copperplate print is: J. F. Reiche, Philadelphia.

* Der Deutsche Washington Correspondent.

> See 1795.

Hanover, York Co. Stellingius u. Lepper.

* Die Pennsylvanische Wochenschrift.

> Established in April 1797, discontinued in 1805.

Harrisburg. B. Meyer u. C. Fahnestock.

* Die Unpartheyische Harrisburg Zeitung.

Lancaster. Albrecht und Lahn.

Tagebuch des achten Hauses der Repräsentanten der Republik Pennsyl=
vanien.

Lancaster. Johann Albrecht u. Comp.

Der Gemeinnützige Landwirthschafts Calender auf das Jahr . . 1798.

Tagebuch des Achten Hauses der Repräsentanten der Republik Pennsyl=
vanien.

* Neue, Unpartheyische Lancaster Zeitung und Anzeigs=Nachrichten.

Philadelphia. Carl Cist.

Heins, H. A. Von den wohlthätigen Absichten der deutschen Gesell=
schaft von Pennsylvanien. Rede gehalten d. 20. September 1796.

G. S.

Americanischer Stadt und Land Calender auf das 1798ste Jahr Christi.

Philadelphia. H. Kämmerer, jun. u. Comp.

Der Vereinigten Staaten Calender auf das Jahr Jesu Christi 1798.

G. S.

> This almanac took the place of M. Steiner's Haus und Wirthschafts Calender. As will be seen the publishing firm changed repeatedly in the following years.

Philadelphia. Steiner u. Kämmerer.

Das neue und verbefferte Gefang=Buch, worinnen die Pfalmen Davids famt einer Sammlung alter und neuer Geiftreicher Lieder . . enthalten find. Nebft einem Anhang des Heydelbergifchen Catechis= mus, wie auch erbaulicher Gebäter. Nach einem Synodal Schluß zufammengetragen und eingerichtet vor die Evangelifch=Reformirten Gemeinen in den Vereinigten Staaten von America. 12mo. 148 u. 585 S. u. Reg., Catechismus 33 S. G. S.

> Heretofore the Reformed Churches of America had been contented with reprints of foreign hymn-books (See 1752, 1753, 1763, 1772). A Synod having been constituted independent of that of Holland in 1793, one of the first steps taken was a resolution to have a new hymn-book compiled, adapted to the needs of American Reformed congregations. The committee appointed to carry this resolution into effect performed their task in a conservative spirit and the collection printed in 1797 was the result. See Rev. J. H. Dubbs' *Historical Manual of the Ref. Church in the U. S.*, p. 256— 258.

* Philadelphifche Correfponden.

Reading. Jungmann u. Comp.

Die Blut=Fahne ausgeftedt zur Warnung politifcher Wegweifer in America. Von Peter Porcupine. 8vo. 198 S. G. S.

> A translation of Wm. Cobbett's (Peter Porcupine) *The bloody Buoy thrown out as a warning to the political pilots of America*. The book dwells upon the horrors of the French revolution and was written to array the Democratic party for its sympathies with French notions of liberty.

Reading. Jungmann u. Gruber.

* Neue Unparthehifche Reabinger Zeitung und Anzeigs=Nachrichten.

Reading. Jacob Schneider u. Comp.

Stilling, H. Die Gefchichte Florentins von Fahlenborn. 3 Theile. 12mo. 128, 97, 105 S.

* Der Unparthehifche Reabinger Abler.

> The change of Reabing into Reabinger was made January 17th.

York, Pa. Salomon Maher.

* Die York Gazette.

1798.

Baltimore. Samuel Saur.

Winchefter, E. Der merkwürdige Lebenslauf, die Sonderbare Be= kehrung und Entzüdungen des ohnlängft bey Germantown in Penn= fylvanien wohnenden und unlängft verftorbenen Dr. Benneville.

> Dr. George De Benneville, b. 1703 in London had an eventful life in France, studied medicine in Germany, arrived 1741 in America and prac- ticed medicine in Berks County. He died 1793.

Der Neue Hoch=Deutsche Americanische Calender auf das Jahr Christi
1799. G. S.

* Deutsche Zeitung.
See 1795.

Easton. Jacob Weygandt u. Sohn.

* Neuer Unpartheyischer Eastoner Bothe und Northampton Kundschafter.

Friedrich=Stadt, Md. Matthias Bärtgis.

Der Verbesserte Hoch Deutsche Americanische Land und Staats Calender
auf das Jahr 1799.

Germantown. Michael Billmeyer.

Tagebuch des Senats der Republik Pennsylvanien. 1797—1798.

Tagebuch des neunten Hauses der Repräsentanten der Republik Pennsylvanien.

Der Hoch=Deutsche Americanische Calender. Auf das Jahr 1799 u. f. w.

* Die Germantauner Zeitung.

Hägerstown, Md. Johann Gruber.

Der neue Nord=Americanische Stadt und Land Calender. Auf das Jahr
1799.

* Der Deutsche Waschington Correspondent. (?)

Hanover, York Co. Stellingius u. Lepper.

* Die Pennsylvanische Wochenschrift.

Harrisburg. B. Meyer u. C. Fahnestock.

* Die Unpartheyische Härrisburg Zeitung.

Lancaster. Johann Albrecht u. Comp.

Das merkwürdige Leben, Krankheit, Tod und Begräbniß der französischen
Freyheit und Gleichheit samt der letzten Rede beym Begräbniß
derselben etc. herausgegeben von einem ehrlichen Deutschen.

Der Neue Gemeinnützige Landwirthschafts Calender auf das Jahr
1799.

* Der Deutsche Porcupein und Pennsylvanische Anzeigsnachrichten.
This new and very odd name, which Albrecht gave to his paper till then
called *Unpartheyische Lancaster Zeitung*, unmistakably indicated its affiliation
with the Federal party. It was borrowed from the *Peter Porcupine's Gazette*
which Wm. Cobbett had started in Philadelphia in 1797 in support of
extreme Federal principles and in opposition to the French notions of

liberty, which the Republican or Democratic party was believed to favor. The *Reading Adler*, then, as ever since, a pillar of democracy, did not miss the opportunity of poking fun in a most provoking way at the "Deutsche Stachelschwein" published in Lancaster.

Philadelphia. Carl Cift.

Webb, C. Einige Glaubens = Bekenntniffe und göttliche Erfahrungs= Proben u. f. w. Zweyte Ausgabe. 12mo. iv, 48 S. G. s.
> See 1783.

Americanifcher Stadt und Land Calender auf das 1799fte Jahr Chrifti.

Philadelphia. J. R. Kämmerer u. Comp.

Der Vereinigten Staaten Calender auf das Jahr Jefu Chrifti 1799. H. S.

Philadelphia. H. u. J. R. Kämmerer.

* Philadelphifches Magazin oder Unterhaltender Gefellfchafter für die Deutfchen in Amerika. 4to. 48 S.
> A belletristic German Monthly, probably the first published in America.

Philadelphia. H. Schweitzer.

Bericht des Präfidenten der Ver. Staaten an die beiden Häufer des Congreffes am 3. April 1798.

(Cobbet, W.) Der Fortgang der Menfchenfreffer oder die Greuel eines franzöfifchen Einfalls. Von Peter Porcupine. 8vo. 44 S. H. S.

Götz, J. Moralphilofophifche Rede über Aufrechterhaltung des Staates, von Johann Götz, vormaligem Profeffor und Prediger an der Kaiferl. Königl. Academie zu Wienerifch Neuftadt. 8vo. 22 S. H. S.

Der Kleine Catechismus des fel. D. Martin Luther. 12mo. 144 S. H. S.

Verhaltungsbefehle an Charles Cotesworth Pincney, John Marfchall und Elbridge Gerry, Außerordentliche Abgefandte und bevollmächtigte Minifter an die franzöfifche Republik. Aus dem Englifchen überfetzt. 8vo. 54 S. PHILOS. S.

Neuer Hauswirthfchafts Calender. Auf das Jahr 1799. Zum erftenmal herausgegeben.

* Die Pennfylvanifche Correfpondenz.
> This paper succeeded Steiner's *Philadelphifche Correspondenz*. It was a bi-weekly, appearing Tuesday and Friday evening, and was printed at the S. W. corner of 4th and Race Sts. H. Schweitzer, was in 1800 Secretary of the German Society. He died 1810.

Philadelphia.

Erdmann, C. Das Gelbe Fieber in Philadelphia im Jahre 1798.

Reading. Gottlob Jungmann u. Comp.

Neuer Haußwirthschafts Calender, Auf das gnadenreiche Jahr u. s. w.
   1799. 4to. 48 S.   G. S.
     First issue of this almanac.

* Neue Unpartheyische Readinger Zeitung und Anzeigs=Nachrichten.

Reading. Schneider u. Comp.

* Der Unpartheyische Readinger Adler.

York, York Co. Salomon Mäyer.

Pennsylvanischer Calender.   G. S.

* Die York Gazette.

1799.

Baltimore. Samuel Saur.

Felbinger, Jeremias. Christliches Handbüchlein. Dritte Auflage.
   12mo. 129 S.   G. S.

Mack, A. Rechte und Ordnungen des Hauses Gottes. Dritte Auflage.

(Mack, A.) E. L. Grubers Grunforschende Fragen u. s. w. nebst
   Antworten. Dritte Auflage. 12mo. 40 S.   G. S.
     The foregoing three Dunker tracts are combined in one volume. The
     last two were noticed under the year 1774.

Der Neue Hoch=Deutsche Americanische Calender auf das Jahr Christi
   1800.   G. S.
     Reference is made in this almanac to the German newspaper which
     S. Saur published in Baltimore.

* Deutsche Zeitung.
     See 1795.

Easton. Jacob Weygandt u. Sohn.

* Neuer Unpartheyischer Eastoner Bothe und Northampton Kundschafter.

Friedrichs=Stadt, Md. Matthias Bartgis.

Der Verbesserte Hoch=Deutsche Americanische Land und Staats Calender.
   Auf das Jahr . . 1800.

Germantown. (Germantoun.) Michael Billmeyer.

Das neue und verbesserte Gesangbuch, worrinnen die Psalmen Davids
   samt einer Sammlung alter und neuer Geistreicher Lieder enthalten
   sind, nebst einem Anhang des Heidelberger Catechismus wie auch
   erbaulicher Gebäter. Nach einem Synodal Schluß zusammengetragen

und eingerichtet für die Evangelisch-Reformirten Gemeinen der Ver.
Staaten in America. Zweyte Auflage. 12mo. 148 u. 585 S. u.
Reg., Catechismus 26 S.   G. S.
> See 1797.

Tagebuch des Senats der Republik Pennsylvanien. 1798—1799.

Der Hoch-Deutsche Americanische Calender, Auf das Jahr 1800 u. s. w.
4to. 32 S.

* Die Germantauner Zeitung.

Hägerstaun, Md. Johann Gruber.

Sasse, Bernhard Heinrich. Geistliche Lieder. 12mo. 42 S.
> Originally published in Minden 1786.

Der neue Nord-Americanische Stadt und Land Calender, Auf das Jahr
. . 1800.

Hanover, York Co. Stellingius u. Lepper.

* Die Pennsylvanische Wochenschrift.

Harrisburg. B. Meyer u. C. Fahnestock.

* Die Unpartheyische Härrisburg Zeitung.
> Between the words *Härrisburg* and *Zeitung* there is a cut representing the
> rising sun with the word **Morgenröthe** across the rays.

Lancaster. Johann Albrecht u. Comp.

Ernstlicher Ruf an die Deutschen in Pennsylvanien.
> A political pamphlet in favor of the Federal party.

Tagebuch des zehnten Hauses der Repräsentanten der Republik Pennsylvanien.

Der Neue Gemeinnützige Landwirthschafts Calender auf das Jahr . .
1800.

* Der Deutsche Porcupein und Pennsylvanische Anzeigsnachrichten.
> See 1798.

Lancaster. Christian Jacob Hütter.

* Der Lancaster Correspondent. Fol. (14 x 10.) Motto: Frey, standhaft und gemäßigt.
> This paper supported the Democratic party. Its first number appeared
> May 25, 1799, the last, September 3, 1803. A complete file is in the
> Mechanics Library in Lancaster, partial files in the office of the *Reading
> Adler* and the library of the Hist. Society of Penna.

Libanon. Jacob Schnee.

Der wohlerfahrene Baum-Gärtner oder gründliche Anweisung zur Behandlung der Obstbäume.

Philadelphia. Carl Cist.

Vollständiges Marburger Gesangbuch in 615 christlichen und trostreichen Gesängen zur Uebung der Gottseligkeit u. s. w. Neue und' von Druckfehlern sorgfältig gereinigte Ausgabe. 12mo. 262 S. G. S.

An edition in small type of the Lutheran *Marburger Gesangbuch*, of which the first American edition appeared in 1759.

Americanischer Stadt und Land Calender auf das 1800ste Jahr Christi.

Philadelphia.

Joseph R. Kämmerer u. G. Helmboldt, jun.

Der Vereinigten Staaten Calender auf das Jahr Jesu Christi 1800.

Philadelphia. Henrich Schweitzer.

Spiegel für alle Menschen oder Nutzanwendungen über das Evangelium St. Matthäi. 8vo. 70 S. H. S.

Neuer Hauswirthschafts Calender. Auf das Jahr 1800.

* Die Pennsylvanische Correspondenz.

Reading. Gottlob Jungmann u. Comp.

Neuer Haußwirthschafts Calender. Auf das gnadenreiche Jahr u. s. w. 1800.

* Neue Unpartheyische Readinger Zeitung und Anzeigs=Nachrichten.

Reading. Schneider u. Comp.

* Der Unpartheyische Readinger Adler.

York. Andreas Billmeyer.

* Der Volksberichter.

According to Carter and Glossbrenner's History of York County the first number appeared July 25, 1799. Andrew Billmeyer was the brother of Michael B., the printer in Germantown, who also hailed from York County.

York. Salomon Mayer.

Myseras, Lambrecht. Empfindungen und Erfahrungen der From= men auf dem Wege nach dem Himmel. Aus dem Holländischen übersetzt. 12mo. 395 S. H. S.

* Die York Gazette.

1800.

Baltimore. Samuel Saur.

Der Neue Hoch=Deutsche Americanische Calender auf das Jahr Christi 1801. 4to. 40 S.

* Deutsche Zeitung.

See 1795. It is very likely that S. Saur continued to publish his paper during the following years, though nothing is known of it.

Eaſton. Jacob Weygandt u. Sohn.

* Neuer Unpartheyiſcher Eaſtoner Bothe u. ſ. w.

Ephrata. J. Baumann.

Ein Geſpräch betreffend des Sabbaths, zwiſchen einen Täufer, Rogeraner, Römiſchem Katholik und Kirchenmann. 16mo. 32 S.

> The Rogerenes were seventh day Baptists of a certain type, founded by John Rogers of Connecticut.

Friedrich Stadt, Md. Matthias Bärtgis.

Der Verbeſſerte Hoch Deutſche Americaniſche Land und Staats Calender. Auf b. J. 1801.

Germantown. Michael Billmeyer.

Geiſtiges Blumen-Gärtlein inniger Seelen. Achte und vermehrte Auflage. 564 S. u. Regiſter.

Der Hoch-Deutſche Americaniſche Calender. Auf das Jahr 1801.

* Die Germantauner Zeitung.

Hägerstaun, Md. Johann Gruber.

Der neue Nord-Americaniſche Stadt und Land Calender, Auf das Jahr 1801.

Hanover, York Co. Stellingius u. Lepper.

* Die Pennſylvaniſche Wochenſchrift.

Harrisburg. Benjamin Meyer.

* Die Harrisburger Morgenröthe.

> Under this new name the *Unpartheyische Harrisburg Zeitung* appeared since August 18th.

Lancaſter. Albrecht und Comp.

Tagebuch des Senats der Republik Pennſylvanien.

Der Neue, Gemeinnützige Landwirthſchafts Calender. Auf das Jahr . . 1801.

Der Americaniſche Staatsbothe und Lancäſter Anzeigs-Nachrichten.

> Appeared every Wednesday. It was published as a continuation and with the running number of the *Deutsche Porcupein.*

Lancaſter. Chriſtian Jacob Hütter.

Waſhingtons Ankunft im Elyſium. Eine dialogiſirte Skizze nebſt Gedichten. Von einem bewunderer des erblaßten Helden.

Der neue allgemein nützliche Volks-Calender auf das Jahr Chriſti 1801. Zum erſtenmal herausgegeben. 4to. 40 S.

> Jacob Hütter, whose printing office was at the corner of King and Market sts., advertises in this almanac that he has in his store 8000 volumes of the latest and best German authors for sale.

* Der Lancaster Correspondent.

    See 1799.

Philadelphia. *Charles Cist.*

Ogden, *John.* An excursion into Bethlehem and Nazareth.

Americanischer Stadt= und Land=Calender auf das 1801ste Jahr Christi.

Philadelphia. Helmbold u. Geyer.

Des Aristocraten Catechismus. Ein wunderschönes Büchlein, erbaulich zu lesen für Junge und Alte.

    Advertised in the *Lancaster Correspondent.*

Der Vereinigten Staaten Calender auf das Jahr Jesu Christi 1801.

    John Geyer, (1778—1835) was a man of prominence in Philadelphia, 1809 Associate Judge, 1811 Alderman, 1813 Mayor, 1825 Register of Wills. The German Society elected him treasurer 1807—1810. He retired to private life in 1830.

Philadelphia. Heinrich Schweizer.

Der Kleine Reformirte Katechismus. 16mo. 144 S.

Neuer Hauswirthschafts Calender. Auf das Jahr 1801.

* Die Philadelphische Correspondenz.

Reading. Gottlob Jungmann u. Comp.

Neuer Haußwirthschafts Calender. Auf das gnadenreiche Jahr 2c. 1801. Zum brittenmal herausgegeben.

* Neue Unpartheyische Readinger Zeitung und Anzeigs=Nachrichten.

    No. 571 mentioned in the *Readinger Adler* January 28th.

Reading. Jacob Schneider u. Comp.

Der gemeinützige Americanische Calender auf das Jahr 1801. Zum erstenmal herausgegeben.

* Der unpartheyische Readinger Adler.

York. Andreas Billmeyer.

* Der Volksberichter.

York. Salomon Mayer.

Tagebuch der Ersten Sitzung des Elften Hauses der Repräsentanten. Folio.

* York Gazette.

1801.
Baltimore. Samuel Saur.

Der Geschwinde Rechner.

The Ready Reckoner.

Der Neue Hoch=Deutsche Americanische Calender auf das Jahr Christi
1802. 4to. 40 S.

Easton. Jacob Weygandt u. Sohn.

*Neuer Unpartheyischer Eastoner Bote u. s. w.

Ephrata. J. Baumann.

Das geistliche Vogel=Gesang von allerley Vögelen, was dieselben vor
Natur und Wesen an sich haben. 12mo. 13 S.

Friedrich Stadt, Md. Matthias Bärtgis.

Der Verbesserte Hoch=Deutsche Americanische Land und Staats Calender.
Auf das Jahr . . 1802.

Germantown. Michael Billmeyer.

Der Hoch=Deutsche Americanische Calender auf das Jahr 1802.

* Die Germantauner Zeitung.

Hägerstaun, Md. Johann Gruber.

Der neue Nord=Americanische Stadt und Land Calender, Auf das Jahr
. . 1802.

Hanover, York Co. Stellingius u. Lepper.

* Die Pennsylvanische Wochenschrift.

Harrisburg. Benjamin Meyer.

* Die Harrisburger Morgenröthe.

Der Americanische Calender auf 1802.

Lancaster. Johann Albrecht.

Tersteegen, G. Weg der Wahrheit, die da ist nach der Gottseligkeit;
bestehend aus zwölf bey verschiedenen Gelegenheiten aufgesetzten
Stücken und Tractätlein, nebst einer Zugabe. Sechste (und die erste)
Amerikanische Auflage. 12mo. 500 S.
  The year of publication is not certain.

Tagebuch des zwölften Hauses der Repräsentanten der Republik Pennsyl=
vanien.

Tagebuch des Senats der Republik Pennsylvanien. 1800—1801.

Der Neue, Gemeinnützige Landwirthschafts Calender auf das Jahr 1802.

* Der Americanische Staatsbothe und Lancäster Anzeigs=Nachrichten.

Lancaster. Christian Jacob Hütter.

Der Neue allgemein nützliche Volks=Calender auf das J. Christi 1802.

* Der Lancaster Correspondent.

Philadelphia. Carl Cist.

Americanischer Stadt und Land Calender auf das Jahr 1802.

Philadelphia. Helmbold u. Geyer.

Der Vereinigten Staaten Calender auf das Jahr Jesu Christi 1802.

Philadelphia. Henrich Schweitzer.

Der Psalter des Königs und Propheten Davids. Verteutschet von Dr. M. Luther. 16mo. 252 S.

Neuer Hauswirthschafts Calender, Auf das Jahr 1802.

* Die Philadelphische Correspondenz.

Reading. Jungmann u. Brückman.

Neuer Haußwirthschafts Calender auf das gnadenreiche Jahr u. s. w. 1802.

* Neue Unpartheyische Readinger Zeitung und Anzeigs-Nachrichten.

Reading. Jacob Schneider u. Comp.

Der gemeinützige Americanische Calender auf das Jahr Christi 1802. Zum zweytenmal herausgegeben. 4to. 40 S.

Outside title: Neuer Readinger Calender aufs Jahr 1802.

* Der Readinger Adler.

The qualification „Unpartheyische" was dropped in this year.

York. Andreas Billmeyer.

Gespräche zwischen einen Lehrer und Zuhörer über unsere jetzigen Zeiten und über das Wort der Weissagung davon. Von H. P. A. 12mo. 155 S.

* Der Volksberichter.

York. Solomon Mayer.

* Die York Gazette.

1802.

Baltimore. Samuel Saur.

Der Neue Hoch Deutsche Americanische Calender auf das Jahr Christi 1803.

Easton. Christian J. Hütter.

Tagebuch des Senats der Republik Pennsylvanien. 1801—1802.

Easton. Jacob Weygandt u. Sohn.

* Neuer Unpartheyischer Eastoner Bothe u. s. w.

Friedrich Stadt, Md. Matthias Bärtgis.

Der Verbesserte Hoch=Deutsche Americanische Land und Staats Calender.
Auf das J. 1803.

Germantown. Michael Billmeyer.

Der Hoch=Deutsche Americanische Calender auf das Jahr 1803.

* Die Germantauner Zeitung.

Hägerstaun, Md. Johann Gruber.

Der neue Nord=Americanische Stadt und Land Calender, Auf das Jahr
. . 1803.

Hanover, York Co. Stellingius u. Lepper.

* Die Pennsylvanische Wochenschrift.

Harrisburg, Pa. Benjamin Meyer.

Das Neue Testament.

* Die Harrisburger Morgenröthe.

Lancaster. Johann Albrecht.

Das eifrige Christenthum oder Thomas Watsons kräftige Ermahnung.
16mo. 269 S.   H. S.

Der Neue, Gemeinnützige Landwirthschafts Calender auf das Jahr 1803.
4to. 40 S.

Die täglichen Loosungen und Lehrtexte der Brüdergemeine für 1803.

* Der Amerikanische Staatsbothe und Lancäster Anzeigs=Nachrichten.

Lancaster. Christian J. Hütter.

* Der Lancaster Correspondent.

Norristown. David Sower.

* Der Norristowner Bote.
        Existed less than a year. (Hist. of Montgomery County).

Philadelphia. Carl Cist.

Americanischer Stadt= und Land=Calender auf das Jahr 1803.

Philadelphia. G. Helmbold & J. Geyer.

Der Vereinigten Staaten Calender. Auf das Jahr Jesu Christi 1803.

Philadelphia. Heinrich Schweitzer.

Hochdeutsches Lutherisches A. B. C und Namen=Büchlein.

Neuer Hauswirthschafts Calender. Auf das Jahr 1803.

* Die Philadelphische Correspondenz.

Reading. G. Jungmann & Comp.

Neuer Haußwirthschafts=Calender. Auf das gnadenreiche Jahr u. f. w. · 1803.

* Neue Unpartheyische Readinger Zeitung und Anzeigs=Nachrichten.

Reading. Jacob Schneider & Comp.

Einige kurzweilige Historien.

Die Höhle des Todes, eine Erzählung aus dem Englischen.

Die Lust=Rose, bestehend aus einer Sammlung der schönsten Arien und Lieder.

Reading. Schneider & Ritter.

Der Gemeinüzige Americanische Calender auf das Jahr 1803. Zum Drittenmal herausgegeben.

> The change in the name of the firm was made June 27th.

* Der Readinger Adler.

York. Andreas Billmeyer.

* Der Volksberichter.

York. C. Mäyer.

* Die York Gazette.

[Pennsylvania.] Snowden & McCorkle.

Tagebuch des dreizehnten Hauses der Repräsentanten der Republik Pennsylvanien.

1803.

Baltimore. Samuel Saur.

Der Neue Hoch=Deutsche Americanische Calender auf 1804.

Der hundertjährige Calender von 1799 bis 1899. 16mo. 80 S.

Easton. Jacob Weygandt & Sohn.

* Neuer Unpartheyischer Eastoner Bothe u. f. w.

Friedrichs=Stadt, Md. Matthias Bärtgis.

Der Verbesserte Hoch Deutsche Americanische Land und Staats Calender auf d. J. . . 1804.

* Die Hornisse.

> J. Thomas Sharff, *History of Western Maryland*, I, p. 528 says:
>
> He (M. Bartges) also printed and published from 1803 to 1813 a paper called *The Hornet* in English and German with the Motto:
> > To the Republicans I will sing
> > But Aristocrats shall feel my sting.

Germantown. Michael Billmeyer.

. Erbauliche Liedersammlung zum gottesdienstlichen Gebrauche. Dritte
Auflage. 12mo. 602 S. u. Register.

Kurze Andachten einer gottsuchenden Seele. 12mo. 80 S.

Die kleine geistliche Harfe der Kinder Zions u. s. w. Erste Auflage.
Auf Verordnung der Mennonisten Gemeinden. 12mo. 412 S.
u. Register.

Das Neue Testament. Dritte Auflage. 12mo. 537 S.

Der Hoch-Deutsche Americanische Calender auf 1804.

* Die Germantauner Zeitung. (?)

Hägerstaun, Md. Johann Gruber.

Der neue Nord-Americanische Stadt und Land Calender, Auf das Jahr
1804.

Hanover, York Co. Stellingius & Lepper.

* Die Pennsylvanische Wochenschrift.

Harrisburg, Pa. Benjamin Meyer.

* Die Harrisburger Morgenröthe.

Lancaster. Johann Albrecht.

Der Neue, Gemeinnützige Landwirthschafts Calender auf das Jahr 1804.
4to. 40 S.

* Der Americanische Staatsbothe und Lancäster Anzeigs-Nachrichten.

Lancaster. Christian Hütter.

* Der Lancaster Correspondent.

    This paper reached its end with the number issued on Sept. 3, 1803,
in which the publisher feelingly remarks, that he had lost by the venture
about five thousand dollars. Undaunted he went to Easton where he
succeeded better.

Philadelphia. Carl Cist.

Americanischer Stadt- und Land-Calender auf das Jahr 1804.

Philadelphia. G. Helmbold & J. Geyer.

Der Vereinigten Staaten Calender auf das Jahr Jesu Christi 1804.

Philadelphia. Henry Schweitzer.

A collection of Hymns for the use of the Christian Indians of
the Mission of the United States Brethern of N. America,
translated by David Zeisberger.

Neuer Hauswirthschafts Calender. Auf das Jahr 1804.

* Die Philadelphische Correspondenz.

Reading. Jungmann u. Comp.

Neuer Hauswirthschafts Calender auf 1804.

Reading. Jungmann u. Brückmann.

* Neue Unpartheyische Readinger Zeitung und Anzeigs=Nachrichten.

Reading. Schneider und Ritter.

Tagebuch des Senats der Republik Pennsylvanien. 1802—1803.

Tagebuch des vierzehnten Hauses der Repräsentanten der Republik Pennsylvanien.

* Der Readinger Adler.

York. Christian Schlichting.

* Die York Gazette.

> The time when the York Gazette passed into the hands of C. Schlichting is not certain.

York. S. Mäyer.

Büchlein des Hans Frummann, welcher von Himmel und Hölle zeuget und die Gotteslästerer vor der heißen Hölle treulich warnet. 12mo. 54 S.

H. S.

> Bartholomaeus Ringwaldt, the famous hymnwriter (1530—1600), published in 1582 "*Neue Zeittung, so Hans Fromman mit sich aus der Hellen und dem Himmel bracht hat*". Ringwaldt's book being not at hand, it cannot be stated, how closely it was followed in the York publication, which is written in verse, as probably the original was. A new edition of the same book was printed in 1815.

1804.

Baltimore. Samuel Saur.

Der Neue Hoch Deutsche Americanische Calender auf . . 1805.

Easton. Jacob Weygandt & Sohn.

* Neuer Unpartheyischer Eastoner Bothe u. s. w.

Ephrata. Baumann und Cleim.

[Bergholder]. Nützliche und erbauliche Anrede an die Jugend von der wahren Buße. Zum zweytenmal herausgegeben. 12mo. 92 S.

Das durch viele Curen bestätigte und sicher befundene Pferdearzneibüchlein.

Friedrich Stadt, Md. Matthias Bärtgis.

Der Verbesserte Hoch Deutsche Americanische Land und Staats Calender. Auf . . 1805.

Germantown. Michael Billmeyer.

Catechismus Oder Kurzer Unterricht Christlicher Lehre. 16mo. 116 S.

Der Hoch-Deutsche Americanische Calender auf das Jahr 1805.

* Die Germantauner Zeitung. (?)

Hägerstaun, Md. Johann Gruber.

Der neue Nord-Americanische Stadt und Land Calender. Auf das Jahr
. . 1805.

Hanover, York Co. Stellingius & Lepper.

* Die Pennsylvanische Wochenschrift.

Harrisburg. Benjamin Meyer.

Seelen-Medicin oder Vier geistreiche Tractätchen zum Unterricht Heilsbe-
gieriger Seelen.

* Die Harrisburger Morgenröthe.

Lancaster. Johann Albrecht.

Ein Unpartheyisches Gesangbuch. Auf Begehrung der Mennonisten gedruckt.
8vo. 415 S. u. 17 S. Register.

Tersteegen, Gerhard. Weg der Wahrheit, die da ist nach der
Gottseligkeit. 16mo. 500 S.

Date uncertain.

Kurzer Inbegriff der Christlichen Lehre. Nebst einer Kurzgefaßten Kirchen-
geschichte. 16mo. 58 S. H. S.

Der Neue, Gemeinnützige Landwirthschafts Calender auf das Jahr 1805.

* Der Americanische Staatsbothe und Lancäster Anzeigs-Nachrichten.

Lancaster. Henrich u. Benjamin Grimler.

* Der Wahre Amerikaner. Eine Zeitung für den Bauer und Stadtmann.
Gedruckt alle Samstag. (10½ x 8½).

A democratic paper.

Philadelphia. Carl Cist.

Americanischer Stadt- und Land-Calender auf 1805.

Philadelphia. Johann Geyer.

Der Vereinigten Staaten Calender auf das Jahr 1805.

Philadelphia. Henrich Schweitzer.

Der Kleine Katechismus des sel. Dr. Martin Luther. 16mo. 141 S.

Wackerhagen, August. Kurzer Inbegriff der Christlichen Glaubens-
und Sittenlehre. 8vo. 288 S.

A list of subscribers is appended.

Neuer Hauswirthſchafts Calender. Auf das Jahr 1805.
>Contains a map and description of Louisiana.

* Die Philadelphiſche Correſponbenz.

Bachmair, John James M. A. A complete German Grammar.
3d American Edition. 8vo. 108 pp.

Reading. Jungmann und Brückman.
Neuer Hauswirthſchafts Calender auf das Jahr 1805. Zum erſtenmal
herausgegeben.

* Neue Unparteyiſche Readinger Zeitung und Anzeigs=Nachrichten.
>It is likely that this paper continued to appear till 1808, when *Der
Standhafte Patriot* took its place.

Reading. Schneider & Ritter.
Nach dem 25. März Johann Ritter & Comp.
* Der Readinger Abler.
>Johann Ritter's partner was Carl A. Kessler.

Reading. Johann Ritter & Comp.
Der gemeinüzige Americaniſche Calender. Auf das Jahr Chriſti 1805.
Zum Viertenmal herausgegeben.

York. Christian Schlichting.
* Die York Gazette.

Druckort unbekannt.
Nützliche und Erbauliche Anrede an die Jugend. 4to. 39 S.

C. Cline.
Tagebuch des Senats der Republik Pennſylvanien. 1803 — 1804.

Moyer & Atkinson.
Tagebuch des fünfzehnten Hauſes der Repräſentanten der Republik Penn=
ſylvanien.

1805.

Baltimore. Samuel Saur.
Der Neue Hoch Deutſche Americaniſche Calender auf das Jahr Chriſti 1806.

Easton. Christian Jacob Hütter.
* Der Northampton Correſpondent.
>C. J. Hütter, who in Sept. 1803 gave up the *Lancaster Correspondent* as a
>financial failure started in 1805 the *Northampton Correspondent*, which
>survives to the present day.

Easton. Jacob Weygand.

* Der Eastoner Deutsche Patriot und Landmanns Wochenblatt.
    „Wo Freyheit wohnt da ist mein Vaterland."— Franklin.
Diese Zeitung wird Mittwoch herausgegeben von Jacob Weygand in der Neuen Buchdruckerey zu Easton.

Easton. Samuel Longcope.

Tagebuch des Senats der Republik Pennsylvanien. 1804—1805.

> Samuel Longcope, the editor of an English paper in Easton, advertised in 1799 for proposals to print a German Weekly, in 4to. 8 pages, to be issued as soon as 300 subscribers were secured. The name of the paper was to be: *Der Tyrannenfeind.* It probably never appeared.

Tagebuch des sechzehnten Hauses der Repräsentanten der Republik Pennsylvanien.

Ephrata.

Nützliches und bewährt befundenes Roßarzeney Büchlein. 16mo.

Simson gegen die Philister oder die Reformation der Gerichtshändel.

Ephrata.

Gedruckt für J. u. R. Johnson, Philadelphia.

Der Kleine Catechismus des sel. D. Martin Luthers. 16mo. 138 S.

Friedrich Stadt, Md. Matthias Bärtgis.

Der Verbesserte Hoch Deutsche Americanische Land und Staats Calender. Auf d. J. . . . 1806.

Germantown. Michael Billmeyer.

Erbauliche Liedersammlung u. s. w. Vierte Auflage.
> Lutheran hymn-book. See 1786.

Kurze Andachten einer gottsucherden Seele. Vierte Auflage. 12mo. 23 S.

Plan einer Anstalt zur Erziehung der jungen Prediger in den Evangelischen Deutschen Lutherischen Gemeinden in Pennsylvanien und den benachbarten Staaten.

S ch a b a l i e. Die Wandlende Seel. Vierte Auflage.
> See 1763.

Der Hoch=Deutsche Americanische Calender. Auf das Jahr Christi 1806.

* Die Germantauner Zeitung. (?)

Hägerstaun. Johann Gruber.

(Gedruckt für Jacob D. Dietrich's Bücher Stohr.)

Der neue Nord=Americanische Stadt und Land Calender auf das Jahr . . 1806. Zum zehntenmal herausgegeben. 4to. 42 S.

Hanover. (York Co.) P. Lange & J. P. Stark.

* Die Hanover Gazette.

> Printed with the types and on the press of the suspended *York Gazette* till 1810, when Lange alone continued it. (*Gibson Hist. of York Co. 378*).

Hanover, York Co. Stellingius & Lepper.

Die Pennsylvanische Wochenschrift.

> Last number published in February.

Harrisburg. Benjamin Meyer.

* Die Harrisburger Morgenröthe.

Lancaster. Johann Albrecht.

Der Neue Gemeinnützige Landwirthschafts Calender auf 1806.

* Der Americanische Staatsbothe und Lancäster Anzeigs-Nachrichten.

Lancaster. Henrich und Benjamin Grimler.

* Der Wahre Amerikaner.

Philadelphia. Carl Cist's Wittwe.

Der Americanische Stadt und Land Calender auf 1806.

Philadelphia. Josef Forster.

* Der Pelican. Gedruckt und herausgegeben von Josef Forster, Cherry Alley zwischen der 5. u. 6. Straße.

> A paper more designed for useful information than news. See 1806.

Philadelphia. J. Geyer.

Abdresse der Committee, bestimmt von einer großen Anzahl Glieder der deutschen Lutherischen Gemeine in Philadelphia an die Corporation derselben nebst ihrer Antwort. 12mo. 27 S.   G. S.

> (German and English.)
>
> The question was whether alternate preaching in German and English should be introduced, or the Congregation be divided, St. Michael's Church being given up for English service. The committee favors the latter alternative.

Der Vereinigten Staaten Calender auf das Jahr 1806.

Philadelphia. H. Schweitzer.

Die Philadelphische Corresponbenz.

Reading.

Grundregeln der Reading Deutschen Lesegesellschaft.

> The Readinger *Deutsche Lesegesellschaft* (German Reading Club) existed till 1828 or longer.

Reading. Gottlob Jungmann.

Biblia, Das ist: Die ganze Göttliche Heilige Schrift Alten und Neuen
Testaments, nach der deutschen Uebersetzung D. Martin Luthers.
Erste Auflage. 4to. 1008 u. 227 S. G. S.

> The publisher calls attention in the preface to the fact that since 1776,
> when the third edition of Saur's Bible appeared, no German translation of
> the Scripture ,had been printed in America and ventures to predict, that
> this edition will he the last. He says: Ob aber eine Bibel in der nehmlichen
> Sprache in diesen Vereinigten Staaten ein andermal seine Erscheinung machen
> wird, ist vielem und großem Zweifel unterworfen, zumal die deutsche Sprache
> in demselben so außerordentlich schnell abnimmt. A noteworthy remark which,
> to judge by its style, might appear true enough.

Neuer Hauswirthschafts=Calender. Auf das Jahr 1806.

* Die Unpartheyische Readinger Zeitung und Anzeigs=Nachrichten.

Reading. Johann Ritter & Comp.

Der gemeinnützige Americanische Calender, Auf das Jahr 1806. Zum
fünftenmal herausgegeben.

Der neue Americanische Landwirthschafts Calender auf das Jahr Christi
1806. Zum erstenmal herausgegeben.

> The outside title is: Der Neue Readinger Calender.

* Der Readinger Adler.

Winchester, Va. Jacob D. Dietrichs.

Der Neue Americanische Stadt und Land Calender u. s. w. für 1806.
Zum viertenmal herausgegeben. Gedruckt für Jacob D. Dietrichs.

> Outside title: Washington Calender für das Jahr 1806. This almanac
> resembles in every particular that of Hagerstown.

York. Schlichting und Billmeyer.

* Der Wahre Republikaner.

> According to Gibson, History of York County, the first number appeared
> February 20, 1805. The paper was at first published by Schlichting &
> Billmeyer, later by Daniel Billmeyer alone till 1828.

1806.

Baltimore. Samuel Saur.

Der Neue Hoch Deutsche Americanische Calender auf 1807.

Easton. Christian Jacob Hütter.

Becker, Christian. Ein jeder Deutscher sein eigener englischer
Sprachmeister, oder der Deutschen bester Gesellschafter. Von Christian
Becker, deutscher Lehrer. 8vo. 80 S.

* Der Northampton Correspondent.

Easton. Jacob Weygand.

* Der Eastoner Deutsche Patriot und Landmanns Wochenblatt.

Ephrata. Johannes Baumann.

Stoll, Jacob. Geistliches Gewürz-Gärtlein heilsuchender Seelen oder kurz gefaßte Betrachtungen über einige auserlesene Sprüche der Heiligen Schrift in gebundenen Schlußreimen und Geistlichen Brosamen. 16mo. 190 S. u. Register.

A Dunker publication.

Ephrata. (?)

Langennecker, Christian. Eine Vertheidigung der Wahrheit u. s. w. Wie die rechte Taufe von Christus an seine Jünger und Nachfolger befohlen wurde. 12mo. 79 S. H. S.

Takes the side of the Dunkers against Bergholder. See 1804.

Friederich Stadt, Md. Matthias Bärtgis.

Der Verbesserte Hoch Deutsche Americanische Land und Staats Calender. Auf das Jahr 1807.

How much longer this almanac appeared is not known.

Germantown. Michael Billmeyer.

Eine Herzliche Anrede des Lehrers an seine Zuhörer in der deutschen Evang.-Lutherischen Gemeine in Germantaun.

Gebet-Büchlein, gestellet von einer Christum und sein Wort liebhabenden Seelen. 12mo. 271 S. u. Register.

A Schwenkfelder publication.

Der Hoch-Deutsche Americanische Calender auf 1807.

* Die Germantauner Zeitung. (?)

Hagerstown, Md. Jacob D. Dietrich.

Der neue Nord-Americanische Stadt und Land Calender Auf das Jahr . . 1807. Zum fünftenmal herausgegeben. .

The cut on the cover represents a mansoleum with the inscription *Washington*, a temple and a variety of allegorical designs. At the foot of the page there is another title: Der Washingtoner und Hagerstauner Calender. Dietrich's Winchester almanac, of which a copy for the year 1807 is at hand, differs only in title from that of Hagerstown. The almanac was advertised in a Cincinnati paper (Liberty Hall) as being in great demand in the States of Virginia, Maryland, Pennsylvania and Ohio.

Hanover, York Co. Stark u. Lange.

* Die Hanover Gazette.

Harrisburg. Benjamin Mayer.

* Die Harrisburger Morgenröthe.

Lancaſter. Johann Albrecht.

Tagebuch des ſiebzehnten Hauſes der Repräſentanten der Republik Penn=
ſylvanien.

Der Neue Gemeinnützige Landwirthſchafts Calender. Auf das Jahr
. . 1807.

Der Americaniſche Staatsbothe und Lancäſter Anzeigs=Nachrichten.

Johann Albrecht died August 15, 1806. He was born in Northampton
County in 1745, learned printing in Christopher Saur's office and settled
1787 in Lancaster. He left nine children of whom George and Peter continued their father's business for several years.

Lancaſter. Georg und Peter Albrecht.

D. Beckers Abſchiedrede gehalten in der Reformirten Kirche.

Der Himmliſche Wandersmann. Das Leben und Tod ſammt der letzten
Predigt von Johann Bunyan.

Lancaſter. Heinrich u. Benjamin Grimler.

Tagebuch des Senats der Republik Pennſylvanien. 1805—1806.

* Der Wahre Amerikaner. Eine Zeitung für den Bauer und Stadtmann.

Philadelphia. Carl Ciſt's Wittwe.

Americaniſcher Stadt und Land Calender auf das 1807ſte Jahr.

Philadelphia. H. Schweitzer.

* Die Philadelphiſche Correſpondenz.

Philadelphia. Joſef Forſter.

* Der Pelican.

Beginning with June 17th it appeared three times a week with the title:
Der Pelican. Eine Zeitung in deutſcher, engliſcher und franzöſiſcher Sprache
unter Leitung einſichtsvoller Kunſtfreunde. Advertised in the *Reading Adler*.

Philadelphia. Johann Geyer.

Der Vereinigten Staaten Calender auf das Jahr 1807. H. S.

Reading. Gottlob Jungmann.

Neuer Hauswirthſchafts Calender. Auf das Jahr . . 1807.

* Die Unpartheyiſche Readinger Zeitung.

Reading. Johann Ritter & Co.

Der Neue Americaniſche Landwirthſchafts=Calender. Auf das Jahr . .
1807.

* Der Readinger Adler.

Somerset. Friedrich Goeb. (?)

* Somerseter Zeitung.

"As early as 1806 a German newspaper known as the *Somerset Gazette* was published in Somerset, but by whom and how long we have not been able to learn", (History of Somerset County). This is verified by the *Readinger Adler* of December 2, 1806, where the *Somerseter Zeitung* is quoted. It is not unlikely that F. Goeb published this paper till at least 1830. See 1817 and 1829.

York. Schlichting u. Billmeyer.

* Der Wahre Republikaner.

1807.

Baltimore.

Der Neue Hoch Deutsche Americanische Calender auf 1808.

Cincinnati. Office of Liberty Hall.

Teutscher Calender.

Mr. H. A. Rattermann of Cincinnati found and furnished the following advertisement in the *Liberty Hall* of October 6th: "Just printed and for sale at the office of *Liberty Hall*, price 12½ cents, Teutscher Calender. Dutch Almanacs for the year 1808, from calculations for the Ohio valley and the West, by Robert Stubbs, Philomathes, rendered into the German by Edward H. Stall." This is as far as we know, the first German print of Cincinnati. No data are at hand to show how long the Cincinnati almanac was continued.

Easton. Christian Jacob Hütter.

* Der Northampton Correspondent.

Easton. Jacob Weygandt.

* Der Eastoner Deutsche Patriot und Landmanns Wochenblatt.

Germantown. Michael Billmeyer.

Das neue und verbesserte Gesangbuch, worinnen die Psalmen Davids samt einer Sammlung alter und neuer Geistreicher Lieder . . enthalten sind. Nebst einem Anhang des Heidelbergischen Catechismus u. f. w. Dritte Auflage. 52mo. 585 S. Reg. 26 S.

Das Neue Testament. Vierte Auflage. 12mo. 537 S. u. Reg.

Der Hoch-Deutsche Americanische Calender auf das Jahr 1808.

* Die Germantauner Zeitung. (?)

Hägerstown. Johann Gruber.

Jung, Dr. Johann Heinrich. Der Christliche Menschenfreund in Erzählungen für Bürger und Bauern. 12mo. 102 u. 94 S.

Schmucker, J. G. Die vornehmste Weissagungen der Heiligen Schrift und ihre Erfüllung. Durch J. Georg Schmucker, Ev. Lutherischen Prediger in Hägerstaun. 12mo. 80 S.

Der neue Nord-Americanische Stadt und Land Calender auf 1808. Zum zwölftenmal herausgegeben. 4to. 40 S.

* Hagerstauner Wochenschrift.

> We know by the *Reading Adler* of January 27, 1807 that Gruber was then publishing a German paper, but its name is not given. Perhaps it was still Der Deutsche Washington Correspondent, which has been noticed under the year 1795.

Hanover, York Co. Stark & Lange.

* Die Hanover Gazette.

Harrisburg. Benjamin Mayer.

* Die Harrisburg Morgenröthe.

Lancaster. Georg und Peter Albrecht.

Der Neue Gemeinnützige Landwirthschafts Calender auf das Jahr 1808.

* Der Americanische Staatsbothe und Lancäster Anzeigs-Nachrichten.

Lancaster. Heinrich u. Benjamin Grimler.

Tagebuch des Senats der Republik Pennsylvanien 1806—1807.

Tagebuch des achtzehnten Hauses der Repräsentanten der Republik Pennsylvanien.

* Der Wahre Amerikaner. Eine Zeitung für den Bauer und Stadtmann.

Lancaster, Ohio. Carpenter & Green.

* Der Westliche Adler von Lancäster. 8 x 11.

> First German paper published in Ohio. At the beginning it probably appeared every other week. The name was afterwards changed to Der Ohio Adler. Its news was taken, to a great extent, from German papers printed in Pennsylvania. Joseph Carpenter, one of the proprietors, belonged to the Zimmermann family of Lancaster, Pa. See Rattermann in *Der Deutsche Pionier*, vol. 16, p. 218.

Libanon. Jacob Schnee.

Neuer Hauswirthschafts-Calender. Auf das Jahr . . 1808. Siebenmal herausgegeben von Heinrich Schweitzer in Philadelphia und jetzt zum erstenmal, von J. Schnee in Libanon.

* Der Freie Lebanoner.

> "*Frei Lebanoner* was established by Jacob Schnee, January 1, 1807 and continued till 1809, when Jacob Stoever purchased it and changed its title to *Libanon Morgenstern*." Dr. Egle's Hist. of Dauphin and Lebanon Counties.

Norristown. David Sower.

Etliche neue geistliche Lieder. 12mo. 4 S.

Philadelphia.

Catechismus oder Kurtzer Unterricht Christlicher Lehre.

Die Grundregeln der Gesellschaft zur Beförderung der deutschen evangelisch=
lutherischen Gemeine in und bey Philadelphia.

Mentioned in Fürstenwörther's *Der Deutsche in Amerika.* 1818.

Hoch=Deutsches Lutherisches A. B. C. Büchlein.

Philadelphia. Johann Geyer.

Der Vereinigten Staaten Calender auf 1808.

* Die Philadelphische Correspondenz.

Philadelphia. Conrad Zentler.

Americanischer Stadt und Land Calender auf das 1808te Jahr Christi.

Conrad Zentler succeeded C. Cist in business and location, Second St.
below Race St.

Reading. Gottlob Jungmann.

Neuer Hauswirthschafts Calender. Auf das Jahr . . 1808. Zum
Elftenmal herausgegeben.

* Die Unpartheyische Readinger Zeitung und Anzeigs=Nachrichten. (?)

Reading. Johann Ritter & Carl Keßler.

Geseze der Republik Pennsylvanien in übersetzten Auszügen. Enthaltend
die brauchbaren öffentlichen Geseze bis zu dem Jahr 1805 einschließlich.
8vo. Vorrede u. s. w. 49 S., Text 766 S., Inhaltsverzeichniß
12 S. H. S.

Grundregeln der Readinger Deutschen Lesegesellschaft, gegründet im May
1804. Nebst dem Catalogus der Bücher, so der Gesellschaft eigen.
12mo. 43 S. G. S.

(Keßler, Carl.) Anfangsgründe der Rechenkunst. Zum Gebrauch
der deutschen Schulen in den Ver. Staaten und besonders in
Pennsylvanien. Von C. K.

Tersteegen, G. Geistliche Brosamen von des Herrn Tisch. Erste
americanische Auflage. 2 Bde. 295 u. 332 S.

The appendix contains a list of subscribers.

Der Neue Americanische Landwirthschafts Calender. Auf das Jahr 1808.

* Der Readinger Adler.

York. Andreas Billmeyer.

* Der Wahre Republikaner.

1808.

Baltimore. Christian Cleim.

Der Neue Hoch Deutsche Americanische Calender auf 1809.

Carlisle. F. Sanno.

Der Kleine Catechismus des sel. D. M. Luthers.   16mo. 134 S.

Neuer Hauswirthschafts=Calender auf . . 1809.   Zum erstenmal heraus=
gegeben.

Easton. Christian Jacob Hütter.

Becker, Christian.   Der allgegenwärtige deutsche Sprachlehrer des
Wortes Gottes, u. s. w.   8vo. 192 S.

* Der Northampton Correspondent.

Easton. Jacob Weygandt.

* Der Eastoner Deutsche Patriot und Landmanns Wochenblatt.

Ephrata. Johannes Baumann.

Die Ernsthafte Christenpflicht.   Darin Schöne Geistreiche Gebäter. 16mo.
204 S.
Printed for Amish congregations.

Germantown. Michael Billmeyer.

Das Neue Testament.   Fünfte Auflage.   12mo. 537 S.

Der Hoch=Deutsche Americanische Calender.   Auf 1809.

* Die Germantauner Zeitung.   (?)

Hägerstown. Johann Gruber.

Lobgesänge zu Ehren dem Heiligen und Gerechten in Israel.   24mo.
212 S.

Stilling, J.   Siegesgeschichte der Christlichen Religion.

Stilling, J.   Theobald oder die Schwärmer.

Der neue Nord=Americanische Stadt und Land Calender, Auf das Jahr
. . 1809.

* Hägerstauner Wochenschrift.   (?)

Hanover, York Co. Stark & Lange.

* Die Hanover Gazette.

Harrisburg. Benjamin Mayer.

Tagebuch des neunzehnten Hauses der Repräsentanten der Republik Penn=
sylvanien.

* Die Harrisburger Morgenröthe.

Lancaster. Georg und Peter Albrecht.

Auslegung der Wahren Taufe Jesu Christi.   12mo. 50 S.

Das letzte Bekenntniß von William Robinson.

Ein Unparthehisches Gesang=Buch, enthaltend geistreiche Lieder und Psalmen. Zweyte Auflage. 8vo. 448 S. u. 18 S. Register.

Der Neue Gemeinnützige Landwirthschafts=Calender. Auf das Jahr 1809.

* Der Americanische Staatsbothe und Lancäster Anzeigs=Nachrichten.

Lancaster. H. & B. Grimler.
Tagebuch des Senats der Republik Pennsylvanien. 1807—1808.

* Der Wahre Amerikaner. Eine Zeitung für den Bauer und Stadtmann.

Lancaster. Hamilton und Ehrenfried.
* Der Volksfreund. (Motto): Leset und denkt für euch selbst.

> The first number of the *Volksfreund* was issued August 9, 1808. After various changes in the publishing firm it was acquired in 1817 by Johann Bär, who consolidated it 1838 with the *Beobachter* and whose sons publish it to the present day. When it was established, it took strong grounds in favor of the Federal party.

Lancaster, Ohio. Carpenter & Green.
* Der Ohio Adler.

Libanon. Jacob Schnee.
Zeugniß eines Kindes von der Richtigkeit der Wege des Geistes, vorgestellt in einer mystischen und buchstäblichen Erklärung der Offenbahrung Jesu Christi, dem heiligen Johanni geschehen. 12mo. 635 u. 37 S.

Moller, Martin. Anweisung zum Christlichen Leben und seligen Sterben. Neue verbesserte Auflage. 12mo. 150 S.

> First published in 1593.

Neuer Hauswirthschafts=Calender. Auf das Jahr 1809.

* Der Freie Lebanoner.

Neumarket, Shenandoah Co., Virg. Ambrosius Henkel.
* Der Virginische Volksberichter und Neumarket Wochenschrift.

> First German paper published in Virginia. A scroll in the hand of a postboy who blows a horn has the inscription: Ich bring was Neu's, so gut ichs weiß.—How long the paper existed is not known.

Philadelphia. J. Adams für Jacob Johnson.
Der Psalter des Königs und Propheten Davids. 16mo. 252 S.

Philadelphia. Johann Geyer.
Der Vereinigten Staaten Calender auf 1809.

* Die Philadelphische Correspondenz.

Philadelphia. Conrad Zentler.
Kurzer Bericht von den Anstalten in den deutsch Evangelisch=Lutherischen Gemeinden in Pennsylvanien und einigen benachbarten Staaten, die Reise=Prediger; Erziehung junger Lehrer und Fürsorge für arme Prediger Wittwen betreffend. 12mo. 24 S.

Americanische Stadt und Land Calender auf das 1809te Jahr Christi.

* Der Amerikanische Beobachter, dem Handel und Landbau gewidmet. Motto: Die Wahrheit ist unsere Richtschnur und das Wohl des Vaterlandes unser Ziel.

> The first number appeared in September 1808.

Reading. Gottlob & J. E. Jungmann.

* Der Standhafte Patriot.

> According to Montgomery's Hist. of Berks County this paper was published till 1816.

Reading. Johann Ritter & Comp.

Der Neue Americanische Landwirthschafts-Calender. Auf 1809.

* Der Readinger Adler.

Staunton, Va. Eagle Office.

* Teutscher Virginischer Adler.

> No copy of this paper has been discovered, its existence is surmised from an advertisement in the Cincinnati *Liberty Hall*, March 26, 1808, kindly copied and furnished by Mr. H. A. Rattermann. The first number of the paper was to appear in January, 1808. The advertisement calls for subscribers and makes the publication of the *Adler* contingent on sufficient encouragement.

York. Andreas Billmeyer.

* Der Wahre Republikaner.

1809.

Baltimore. Christian Cleim.

Der Neue Hoch Deutsche Americanische Calender auf 1810.

* Der Baltimore Correspondent.

> The Reading Adler of Feb. 21. prints a German Yankee "Dudel" credited to the Baltimore Correspondent.

Carlisle. F. Sanno.

Stilling, H. Der Christliche Menschenfreund, in Erzählungen für Bürger und Bauern. 12mo. 109 S.

Neuer Hauswirthschafts-Calender auf das Jahr . . 1810.

Chambersburg. Joh. Herschberger. (?)

Der Neue Chambersburger Stadt und Land Calender für 1810.

Easton. Christian Jacob Hütter.

Becker, Christian. Der Deutschen allgegenwärtiger Englischer Sprachlehrer des Wortes Gottes für Lehrer und Schüler. Zweyter verbesserter und vermehrter Druck. 8vo. 107 S.

Unterricht für amerikanische Bauern, Weinberge anzulegen und zu unter=
halten.

* Der Northampton Correspondent.

Eaſton.   Jacob Weygandt.

* Der Eaſtoner Deutſche Patriot und Landmanns Wochenblatt.

It is not known how much longer this paper was published.

Friedrichſtadt.   M. Bärtgis.

Die Lebensbeſchreibung und merkwürdigen Handlungen von Georg Waſh=
ington.   Aus dem Engliſchen.   Mit Portrait.   12mo. 176 S.

Germantown.   Michael Billmeyer.

Der Hoch=Deutſche Americaniſche Calender.   Auf 1810.

* Die Germantauner Zeitung.   (?)

Hägerſtaun.   Johann Gruber.

Der neue Nord=Americaniſche Stadt und Land Calender.   Auf . . 1810.

* Hägerſtauner Wochenſchrift.

Hanover, York Co.   Stark & Lange.

* Die Hanover Gazette.

Harrisburg.   Benjamin Mayer.

Tagebuch des zwanzigſten Hauſes der Repräſentanten der Republik Penn=
ſylvanien.

* Die Harrisburger Morgenröthe.

Lancaſter.   Anton Albrecht.

Der Gemeinnützige Landwirthſchafts=Calender auf 1810.

* Der Americaniſche Staatsbothe und Lancäſter Anzeigs=Nachrichten.

Lancaſter.   Henrich und Benjamin Grimler.

[Romer, Ignaz.]   Das Geheimniß der Bosheit bis auf den Grund
aufgedeckt; nebſt Anzeige der Rettungsmittel der Kirche.   In einer
Erklärung der Offenbarung Jeſu Chriſti an Johannes.   8vo. 239 S.

* Der Wahre Americaner.   Eine Zeitung für den Bauer und Stadtmann.

Lancaſter.   Hamilton, Albrecht und Ehrenfried.

* Der Volksfreund.

Peter Albrecht entered the firm on the 17th of January and continued in
it one year.

Lancaſter, Ohio.   Carpenter & Green.

* Der Ohio Adler.

Libanon.   Heinrich B. Sage.

Kramb, Chriſtian.   Auf Erfahrung gegründete Vorſchriften um
Wolle, Leinen und Baumwolle zu färben.   16mo. 52 S.

Libanon. Jacob Schnee.

Winchester, E. Merkwürdiger Lebenslauf und Die Sonderbare Bekehrung und Entzückungen des ohnlängst bey Germantaun wohnenden
und verstorbenen Dr. George de Benneville. 16mo. 45 S.

First edition in Baltimore 1795.

Weems, M. L. Leben General Washingtons.

Neuer Hauswirthschafts-Calender. Auf das Jahr 1810.

Libanon. Jacob Stoever.

*Libanoner Morgenstern. Ein republikanisches Wochenblatt. Motto:
Die freye Mittheilung der Gedanken und Meinungen ist eins der
schätzbarsten Rechte der Menschheit.

Neu-Market, Virg. A. Henkel.

Das Virginische Kinderbuch.

Title from A. L. Gräbner's *Geschichte der Lutherischen Kirche in Amerika.*
Vol. 1, p. 611.

Philadelphia. Johann Geyer.

Der Vereinigten Staaten Calender auf 1810.

* Die Philadelphische Correspondenz.

Philadelphia. Johnson und Warner.

Kleine Erzählungen über ein Buch mit Kupfern oder leichte Geschichte für
Kinder. 24mo. 42 S.

Oeconomy oder Haushaltung des menschlichen Leibes. Illustrirt. Neue
Auflage. 12mo. 77 S.

Philadelphia. Conrad Zentler.

Helmuth, J. H. Ch. Etliche Kirchenlieder.

Die wunderbare Lebensbeschreibung und erstaunlichen Begebenheiten des
berühmten Helden Robinson Crusoe. Mit Holzschnitt. 16mo.
141 S.

Americanischer Stadt und Land Calender auf das 1810te Jahr Christi.

* Der Amerikanische Beobachter.

The first number appeared towards the close of 1809.

Reading.

Die letzten Worte und das Sterbebekenntniß der Susanne Cox welche am
10. Juni 1809 hingerichtet worden auf denen Commons der Stadt
Reading. 8 S.

Reading. Gottlob & J. E. Jungmann.

* Der Standhafte Patriot.

Reading. Johann Ritter & Comp.

Der Neue Americanische Landwirthschafts=Calender. Auf 1810.

Tagebuch des Senats der Republik Pennsylvanien. 1808—1810.

* Der Reabinger Abler.

York. Andreas Billmeyer.

* Der Wahre Republikaner.

Pennsylvania.

Leichenrede des Herrn Christoph Emanuel Schultze, Predigers in Tulpe=
haccon. Von George Lochmann A. M.

Title from a catalogue, where the place of publication and the publisher
are not mentioned.

1810.

Betrug der Methodisten.

Title from a catalogue which does not state the place of publication.

Hohmann, Georg. Ein schön geistig Lied von dem Nichtsseyn des
menschlichen Lebens. Neu verfasset und gedruckt für Georg Hohmann,
welcher seine Dienste anbietet, um Sprüche, Gebeter und Lieder auf=
zusetzen und um geneigte Kundschaft bittet. Fol. 1 S.

Place of publication unknown, year uncertain.

Das Leben und die Thaten des berühmten Till Eulenspiegel. Gedruckt
für den Spaß liebenden Käufer.

(Allentown). Stadt Northampton. Christian Jacob Hütter.

* Der Unabhängige Republikaner und Lecha Caunty Freiheits Freund.
Frey, standhaft und gemäßigt.

The first number of this paper which supported the democratic party was
issued July 17, 1810.

Baltimore. Magill u. Cleim.

Becker, Dr. Christian Ludwig. Prediger der Hochdeutsch Reformir=
ten Gemeine zu Baltimore. Sammlung Neuer Geistreicher Predigten
über verschiedene Texte aus der Heiligen Schrift. 12mo. 264 S.

Der Neue Hoch=Deutsche Americanische Calender auf . . 1811.

Carlisle. F. Sanno.

Helffenstein, J. C. Albertus. Eine Sammlung auserlesener
Predigten. 12mo. 434 S. u. Reg.

Neuer Hauswirthschafts=Calender auf . . 1811.

F. Sanno & A. Loudon proposed in 1810 to print a complete German-
English and English-German Grammar.

Chambersburg. Johann Herschberger.

Leben des Ehrw. J. Wesley.

Tagebuch des einundzwanzigsten Hauses der Repräsentanten der Republik Pennsylvanien.

Thomä Wilcocks Honigtropfen aus dem Felsen Christo. Erste Auflage. 12mo. 30 S.

Der Neue Chambersburger Stadt und Land Calender für das Jahr 1811.

Easton. Christian J. Hütter.

Becker, Christian. Der Deutschen Kinder Englisch= und Deutsches A. B. C.= Buchstabir= Lese= und Sprechbüchlein.

Rauch, Christian H. Des deutschen Bauers und Landmanns Rechenbuch und des Schullehrers Gehülfe. 16mo. 261 S.

* Der Northampton Correspondent.

Germantown. Michael Billmeyer.

Das Neue Testament. Sechste Auflage. 12mo. 537 S.

Der Psalter. Achte Auflage.

Ein wohl eingerichtetes deutsches A. B. C.= Buchstabir= und Lesebuch, zum Gebrauch deutscher Schulen. Vierte Auflage. 12mo. 120 S.
Illustrated by woodcuts and recommended by the ministers of the Lutheran and Reformed churches in Philadelphia.

Der Hoch=Deutsche Americanische Calender. Auf das Jahr Christi 1811.

Hägerstaun. Johann Gruber.

Der neue Nord=Americanische Stadt und Land Calender, Auf das Jahr . . 1811.

* Hägerstauner Wochenschrift. .

Hanover, York Co., Pa. Starck & Lange.

(Reich, Joh. Chr. Fr.) Beschäftigungen des Herzens mitt Gott, nebst einer Anweisung zur Uebung des Gebets. 8vo. 220 S.

* Die Hanover Gazette.

Harrisburg. Benjamin Meyer.

* Die Harrisburger Morgenröthe.

Lancaster. Anton Albrecht.

Der Gemeinnützige Landwirthschafts=Calender. Auf das Jahr 1811.

* Der Americanische Staatsbothe und Lancäster Anzeigs=Nachrichten.

Lancaster. Hamilton & Ehrenfried.

Becker, Christian Ludwig. Kurtzer Entwurf der christlichen Lehre. 12mo. 16 S.

* Der Volksfreund.

In April a hot quarrel ended the partnership of Hamilton and Ehrenfried; the firm became Hamilton & Comp. and Ehrenfried established a business of his own.

Lancaster. Hamilton & Comp.

Rebb, Georg, in Friedrichsburg. Eine Neue Entdeckung äußerst wichtig für Pflanzer und Landbauer. 8vo. 16 S.

Thomas von Kempen. Vier Bücher von der Nachfolgung Christi. (Anhang): Lebensbeschreibung Thomä von Kempen. 12mo. 295 u. 18 S.

Lancaster. Johann Ehrenfried.

Die Zerstörung Jerusalems. Uebersetzt aus dem Englischen von Wilhelm Reichenbach. 12mo. 132 S.

Thomas von Kempen. Vier Bücher von der Nachfolgung Christi. Mit Erlaubniß der Obern. 12mo. 417 S. u. 13 S. Register.

Melsheimer, C. T. Wahrheit der Christlichen Religion für Unstudirte.

Title from an advertisement announcing the book.

Lancaster. Henrich u. Benjamin Grimler.

Sasse, Bernh. Heinrich. Geistliche Lieder. 12mo. 122 S.

* Der Wahre Amerikaner. Eine Zeitung für den Bauer und Stadtmann.

Lancaster, Ohio. Carpenter & Green.

* Der Ohio Adler.

Libanon. Heinrich Sage.

Die Americanische Goldgrube, das ist: die Kunst des Lanndmanns seine zeitlichen Güter fünfzig bis hundertfältig zu vermehren. Lehrreiches Lese= und Rechenbuch. 8vo. 192 S.

Libanon. Jacob Schnee.

Seiler, D. Georg Friedrich. Biblische Religion und Glückseligkeitslehre. Erste Americanische Auflage. 12mo. viii u. 325 S.

Tagebuch des Senats der Republik Pennsylvanien. 1809—1810.

Weems, M. L. Das Leben des Georg Waschington mit Sonderbaren Anecdoten sowohl ehrenvoll für ihn selbst als auch nachahmungswürdig für seine junge Landsleute. Aus dem Englischen übersetzt. 12mo. 240 S.

Zusammenhang der Christlichen Lehre, nach Anleitung des Heidelbergischen Catechismi. 12mo. 42 S.

Neuer Hauswirthschafts Calender. Auf das Jahr 1811.

Libanon. Jacob Stoever.

* Libanoner Morgenstern.

Neu Market, Birg. Henkel.

Das Neu eingerichtete Gesang=Buch, bestehend aus einer Sammlung der besten Lieder zum Gebrauch des öffentlichen deutschen Gottesdienstes und anderer Uebungen der Gottseligkeit in den Ver. St. von Nord= America. 372 S.

Title from Gräbner's *Geschichte der Lutherischen Kirche in Amerika.*

Philadelphia.

Die Incorporations=Acte nebst den Nebenregeln der Mosheimischen Gesell= schaft von Philadelphia.

Title from Fürstenwärther's *Der Deutsche in America* 1818.

Philadelphia. Johann Geyer.

Der Vereinigten Staaten Calender auf das Jahr 1811.

Philadelphia. Jacob Meyer für Johnson & Warner.

Catechismus für die Jugend in Reformirten Schulen. 12mo. 108 S.

Philadelphia. Heinrich Schweitzer.

* Die Philadelphische Correspondenz.

H. Schweitzer died in 1810.

Philadelphia. Conrad Zentler.

Die gebahnte Pilgerstraße nach dem Berge Zion.

Helffenstein, Samuel. Kurze Unterweisung in der christlichen Religion nach dem Heidelbergischen Catechismus. 12mo. 60 S.

Helffenstein, Samuel. Lieder zur Erbauung. 12mo. 39 S.

Hollazens Evangelische Gedanken=Ordnung. Erste americanische Auflage. 12mo. 52 u. 220 S.

Americanischer Stadt und Land Calender auf das 1811te Jahr Christi.

* Der Amerikanische Beobachter.

Reading. Gottlob & J. E. Jungmann.

* Der Standhafte Patriot.

Reading. Johann Ritter & Comp.

Der Neue Americanische Landwirthschafts=Calender. Auf das Jahr 1811. 4to. 40 S.

* Der Readinger Adler.

Reading. H. B. Sage.

* Der Weltbote.

York. Andreas Billmeyer.

* Der Wahre Republikaner.

1811.

Allentown Stadt, Northampton. Carl L. Hütter.
* Der Unabhängige Republikaner und Lecha County Freyheits=Freund.

Baltimore. Christian Cleim.
Der Neue Hoch Deutsche Americanische Calender auf das J. 1812. (?)

Carlisle. Friedrich Sanno.
Neuer Hauswirthschafts=Calender. Auf das Jahr . . 1812. Zum
    Viertenmal herausgegeben. 4to. 40 S.

Chambersburg, Pa. Johann Herschberger.
Der Neue Chambersburger Stadt und Land Calender für das Jahr 1812.

Easton. Christian Jacob Hütter.
* Der Northampton Correspondent.

Ephrata. Jacob Ruth.
(Boehm.) Christosophia oder der Weg zu Christo 2c. Gestellet aus
    Göttlichem Erkenntniß durch Jacob Böhmen. Die erste Americanische
    Auflage. 1811 u. 1812. (Mit allegorischen Bildern). 12mo.
    395 S.

Friedrichstadt. C. T. Melsheimer.
Melsheimer, F. W. Wahrheit der Christlichen Religion für Un=
    studirte. 12mo. x, 327 S.

Germantown. Michael Billmeyer.
Erbauliche Lieder=Sammlung u. s. w. Vierte Auflage. 12mo. 607 S.
    u. Reg.
        See 1786.

Die Kleine Geistliche Harfe der Kinder Zions u. s. w. 12mo. 39 S.
    u. Reg. Zugabe einiger auserlesener Lieder. 20 S.

Sammlung alter und neuer geistreicher Gesänge. Zweyte Auflage.
    12mo. 412 S. u. Zugabe von 20 S.

Der Hoch=Deutsche Americanische Calender. Auf das Jahr Christi 1812.

Hägerstaun. Johann Gruber.
Der neue Nord=Americanische Stadt und Land Calender, Auf das Jahr
    . . 1812.

Hägerstaun. Gruber u. May.
* Hägerstauner Wochenschrift.
    Mentioned in the *Lancaster Volksfreund*, Dec. 31, 1811.

Hanover, York Co. Stark u. Lange.
* Die Hanover Gazette.

Harrisburg. Gleim & Wiestling.

Becker, Dr. Christian Ludwig. Kurzer Entwurf der Christlichen Lehre. Dritte verbesserte Auflage. 16mo. 21 S.

Der Hundertjährige Calender auf das Jahrhundert nach Christi Geburt 1799—1899.

* Die Harrisburger Morgenröthe.

 In 1811 John S. Wiestling, son of Dr. Samuel C. Wiestling, a native of Oschatz in Saxony who immigrated 1793, bought the printing establishment of Benjamin Mayer and soon after associated himself with Christian Gleim of "Lebanontown". Dr. Egle, *History of Dauphin and Lebanon Counties.*

Lancaster. Anton Albrecht.

Der Gemeinnützige Landwirthschafts-Calender. Auf das Jahr 1812.

* Der Amerikanische Staatsbothe und Lancaster Anzeigs-Nachrichten.

Lancaster. Joseph Ehrenfried.

Habermanns Christliches Gebätbuch. 16mo. 158 S.

Eine auserlesene Sammlung Geistlicher Lieder. Queerfolio. Mit Notenlinien.

Philip, Dietrich. Enchiridion, oder Handbüchlein in der Christlichen Lehre und Religion, zuvor gedruckt in Haarlem (Holland), jetzt aber auf das treueste übersetzt in die Hochdeutsche Sprache. 8vo. 568 S.

Lancaster. Wilhelm Hamilton u. Comp.

* Der Volksfreund.

Lancaster. Henrich u. Benjamin Grimler.

Christliches Gemüthsgespräch von dem geistlichen und seligmachenden Glauben. 12mo. 241 S.

* Der Wahre Amerikaner. Eine Zeitung für den Bauer und Stadtmann.

Lancaster, Ohio. Carpenter u. Green.

* Der Ohio Adler.

Libanon. Jacob Schnee.

Tagebuch des Senats der Republik Pennsylvanien. 1810—1811.

Tagebuch des zwei und zwanzigsten Hauses der Repräsentanten der Republik Pennsylvanien.

Neuer Hauswirthschafts Calender. Auf das Jahr 1812.

Libanon. Jacob Stöver.

Ein Lied eines Lehrers. 12mo. 408 S.

Die Reisen der Capitaine Lewis und Clarke unternommen auf Befehl der Regierung der Ver St. in den Jahre 1804, 1805 u. 1806. 12mo. 60 S.

Stilling, Heinrich. Theobald oder die Schwärmer. 2 Bde in 1. 12mo. 272 u. 192 S.

* Libanoner Morgenstern.

Neu-Market, Shenandoah Co., Virg. Ambrosius Henkel.
Der Christliche Catechismus. 16mo. 120 S.

Philadelphia. Johann Geyer.
Der Vereinigten Staaten Calender auf das Jahr 1812.

Philadelphia. *Johnson & Warner, Kimber & Conrad etc.* *Printed by Jacob Meyer.*

Bachmair, John James. A Complete German Grammar in two parts. Third Edition. 12mo. 138 pp.
> The old preface written by Henry Miller in 1772 is retained in this reprint.

Philadelphia. Jacob Meyer.
Regeln und Artikel der deutschen Amerikanischen Unterstützungs-Brüder-schaft.

Rules and Articles of the German American Mutual Assistance Society. Incorporated June 3, 1801. 12mo. 18 & 13 pp.

Philadelphia. Conrad Zentler.
Hollazin, David. Die Lehrart des heiligen Apostels Pauli in seinem Briefe an die Römer. 12mo. 30 S.

Bogatzky, C. H. von. Güldenes Schatzkästlein der Kinder Gottes. 12mo. vi, 365 S. Mit Anhang u. Reg.

Ansprache an die gesammten Glieder der deutsch-evangel. Lutherischen Gemeinen in Pennsylvanien und den benachbarten Staaten. 20 S.
> Contains a report of Rev. J. P. Hinkel about his missionary tour through Virginia and North Carolina.

Americanischer Stadt und Land Calender auf das 1811te Jahr Christi.

* Der Amerikanische Beobachter.

Reading. Gottlob Jungmann & Comp.
* Der Standhafte Patriot.

Reading. Joh. Ritter u. Comp.
Catechismus oder kurzer Unterricht christlicher Lehre, für die angehende Jugend in der Churfürstlichen Pfalz und andere Reformirten Orten zu gebrauchen. 16mo. 104 S.

Geistlicher Irrgarten. 1 Blatt, 12 x 13.

Leben, Thaten und Meinungen Dr. Martin Luthers. Erste Americanische von der dritten verbesserten Leipziger Auflage. 12mo. 162 S.

Der Neue, Americanische Landwirthschafts=Calender. Auf das Jahr . . 1812.

* Der Reabinger Adler.

Reading. Heinrich B. Sage.

Lebensbeschreibung von Heinrich Stilling, sonst Heinrich Jung genannt. 12mo. 408 S.

Merkwürdige Lebensbeschreibung des seeligen Gerhard Tersteegen. 12mo. 94 S.

* Der Weltbote.

York. Andreas Billmeyer.

* Der Wahre Republikaner.

1812.

Allentown, Pa. Joseph Ehrenfried & Heinrich Ebner.

* Der Friedensbothe und Lecha County Anzeiger.—Friede, holdes Kind des Himmels mit dem freundlichen Gesicht, Schwebe sanft vom Himmel nieder; weil' o weile länger nicht.

The first number appeared September 28, 1812. The *Friedensbote* opposed the war against England, hence its name.

Allentown. Carl L. Hütter.

* Der Unabhängige Republikaner und Lecha County Freyheits=Freund.

Chambersburg, Pa. Johann Herschberger.

Der Neue Chambersburger Stadt und Land Calender für das Jahr 1813.

Easton. Chr. Jac. Hütter.

Catechismus, oder: Kurzer Unterricht Christlicher Lehre, wie derselbe in benen Reformirten Kirchen und Schulen der Chur=Fürstlichen Pfalz und anderwärts getrieben wird. 12mo. 288 S.

* Der Northampton Correspondent.

Ephrata. Jacob Ruth.

Das heutige Signal; Oder: Posaunen=Schall! dem Freyen Abend=Lande zur Warnung und zum Trost!! zum Feyerabend sich vorzubereiten, wie solches im Rath der Wächter beschlossen und worauf mit Fleiß zu merken ist!! Gedruckt für den Autor, bey Jacob Ruth.

Germantown. Michael Billmeyer.

Catechismus, Oder: Kurzer Unterricht Christlicher Lehre. (Reformirt). 24mo. 118 S.

Habermanns Christliche Morgen= und Abend=Gebäter; Kaspar Neumanns Kern aller Gebäter. Dritte Auflage. 16mo. 54 u. 50 S.

Erbauliche Liedersammlung u. s. w.   Fünfte Auflage.   12mo. 327 S.
>The Lutheran hymnbook in small print.

Der Hoch=Deutsche Americanische Calender.   Auf das Jahr Christi 1813.
>This almanac brings the first instalment of a reprint of the sensational novel *Rinaldo Rinaldini*, the robber chief. For a number of years it constituted the principal reading matter of the almanac. What a fall from the stern ideals of Christoph Saur, the founder of the almanac!

Hägerstaun.   Johann Gruber & May.

Der neue Nord=Americanische Stadt und Land Calender, Auf das Jahr 1813.

* Hägerstauner Wochenschrift.

Hanover, York Co.   Stark & Lange.

* Die Hanover Gazette.

Harrisburg.   Gleim u. Wiestling.

* Harrisburger Morgenröthe.

Lancaster.   Anton Albrecht.

Der Gemeinnützige Landwirthschafts Calender.   Auf das Jahr 1813.

* Der Americanische Staatsbote und Lancaster Anzeigs=Nachrichten.

Lancaster.   Joseph Ehrenfried.

Taylor, Jer.   Die Lebensgeschichte unsers Herrn und Heylands Jesu Christi, wie auch Leben, Thaten und Tod der Heiligen Evangelisten und Apostel. 8vo. 209 S.

Lancaster.   Wilhelm Hamilton.

Mühlenberg und Schipper.   Deutsch=Englisches und Englisch= Deutsches Wörterbuch, Nebst einer deutschen Sprachlehre und den Grundregeln für Aussprache beider Sprachen. Gedruckt unter der unmittelbaren Aufsicht des Ehrwürdigen Doctor Heinrich Mühlenberg, Pfarrer der deutschen luth. Kirche zu Lancaster und Herrn Benedict J. Schipper, Sprachlehrer in der Franklin Academie. In zwei Bänden. 8vo.   G. S.

>For the first German Dictionary published in America this extensive work is a very creditable performance. Its pages are not numbered, they count up in the two volumes to more than 1500. The second appendix contains a list of words used by the Germans in Pennsylvania, partly adapted from the English, e. g. Fens, Flaur, partly through contact with the English, charged with a meaning not proper to them, e. g. gleichen to like, ausfallen to quarrel.

Rudiments of the German Language, with an appendix containing the pronunciation of the English letters, by B. J. Schipper, professor of languages in Franklin Academy, Lancaster. 44 pp.

Das Neue Testament.   Erste Auflage.   12mo. 572 S.

Zuschrift von Mitgliedern des Hauses der Repräsentanten im Congreß. 12mo. 48 S.

* Der Volksfreund.

Lancaster. Henrich u. Benjamin Grimler.

* Der Wahre Amerikaner. Eine Zeitung für den Bauer und Stadtmann.

Lancaster, Ohio.

* Der Ohio Adler.

Libanon. Jacob Schnee.

Tagebuch des drei und zwanzigsten Hauses der Repräsentanten der Republik Pennsylvanien.

Neuer Hauswirthschafts Calender. Auf das Jahr 1813.

Libanon. Jacob Stoeber.

* Libanoner Morgenstern.

Norristown. David Sower.

Nimrod, Hughes. Feierliche Warnung für alle Erdenbewohner. 8vo. 23 S.

The writer prophesies that one third of the human race will perish on June 4, 1812.

Philadelphia. Jacob Mayer.

Der kleine Catechismus des sel. Dr. M. Luthers. 16mo. 188 S.

Der Psalter u. s. w. 16mo. 216 S.

Philadelphia. Conrad Zentler.

Helffenstein, Ehrw. S. Bußprebigt über Jeremias 6. 8. Am 30. Juli 1812.

[Lieder.] Auf den Tod ihres unvergeßlichen theuren Lehrers Johann Friedrich Schmidt, abgesungen in der Zionskirche am 31. May 1812.

Rev. J. Fr. Schmidt was minister of St. Michael's and Zion's Church in Philadelphia from 1786—1812.

[Lieder.] Bey der Antrittsprebigt des Wohlehrwürdigen Friedrich D. Schäfer, abgesungen . . am 30. August 1812.

Rev. F. D. Schäfer was minister of the same churches from 1812—1834.

Die Grundregeln der Gesellschaft zur Beyhülfe und Unterstützung der armen alten und kranken Glieder der deutschen evangelisch-lutherischen Gemeinde in Philadelphia.

Americanischer Stadt und Land Calender auf das 1813te Jahr Christi.

* Der Americanische Beobachter.

* Evangelisches Magazin, unter der Aufsicht der deutschen Lutherischen Synode. Erster Band. 8vo. 248 S.

Reading. Gottlob Jungmann u. Comp.

* Der Standhafte Patriot.

Reading. Johann Ritter & Co.

Calvins Leben, Meinungen und Thaten. (Nachdruck.) 12mo. 164 S.

Mühlenberg, Ehrw. H. A. Bußtags=Predigt am 20. August 1812. 12mo. 22 S.

Tagebuch des Senats der Republik Pennsylvanien. 1811—1812.

Der neue, Americanische Landwirthschafts=Calender. Auf das Jahr . . 1813.

* Der Readinger Adler.

Reading. H. B. Sage.

* Der Weltbote.

York. Andreas Billmeyer.

* Der Wahre Republikaner.

1813.

Allentown. J. Ehrenfried u. Comp.

The Economy of Human Life, oder Haushaltungskunst des menschlichen Lebens. Erste Americanische Ausgabe Englisch und Deutsch. 12mo. 515 S.

* Der Friedensbothe und Lecha County Anzeiger.

Allentown. Carl L. Hütter.

* Der Unabhängige Republikaner und Lecha County Freyheits=Freund.

Carlisle. F. Sanno.

Tagebuch des vier und zwanzigsten Hauses der Repräsentanten der Republik Pennsylvanien.

Bachmair, J. J. A German Grammar, to which are also annexed Instructions for Germans to acquire a Knowledge of the English Language. 12mo. 324 & 133 pp.

Chambersburg, Pa. Johann Herschberger.

Der Neue Chambersburger Stadt und Land Calender für das Jahr 1814. Zum Fünftenmal herausgegeben.

Chambersburg. Friedrich W. Schöpflein.

* Der Redliche Registrator.

Easton. Christian Jacob Hütter.

Becker, Christian, Lehrer in Pennsylvanien. Deutsches Buchstabir= Lese= une Schreibebuch oder Deutsche Sprachlehre, enthaltend Buch=

ſtabir= Leſe= und Schreibelectionen.   Wie auch die Pennſylvaniſche
Methode u. ſ. w.   8vo.

A list of Subscribers.

*Der Northampton Correſpondent.

Germantown.   Michael Billmeyer.

Das Kleine Davidiſche Pſalterſpiel der Kinder Zions, u. ſ. w.   Dritte
verbeſſerte Auflage.   12mo. 572 S. u. Reg.

Angebunden :

Die Kleine Harfe.   12mo. 55 S.

Das neue und verbeſſerte Geſangbuch u. ſ. w.   Vierte Auflage.   12mo.
71 S. u. 300 S. u. Reg.

Reformed Hymnbook.   Edition in small type.

The Christian's Duty, in a Series of Hymns collected from various
authors.   Third Edition.

A Dunker hymnbook.

Der Hoch=Deutſche Americaniſche Calender.   Auf das Jahr Chriſti 1814.

Hägerstaun, Md.   Johann Gruber.

Der neue Nord=Americaniſche Stadt und Land Calender, Auf das Jahr
. . 1814.   4to. 42 S.

* Hägerstauner Wochenſchrift.

Hanover, York Co.   Stark u. Lange.

* Die Hanover Gazette.

Harrisburg.   Johann S. Wieſtling.

Textor, Fridrich Ludwig.   Vermächtniß an Theone, in moraliſchen
Bruchſtücken über wichtige Gegenſtände unſerer Ruhe.   Erſte Ameri=
caniſche Auflage.   12mo. 142 S.   G. S.

Harrisburg.   Gleim u. Wieſtling.

* Härrisburger Morgenröthe.

Lancaſter.   Anton Albrecht.

Der Gemeinnützige Landwirthſchafts=Calender.   Auf das Jahr 1814.

* Der Americaniſche Staatsbote.

Lancaſter.   Joſeph Ehrenfried.

(Reichenbach, W.)   Agathon.   Ueber Wahren Gottesdienſt.   Ein
Handbuch für nachdenkende Menſchenfreunde.

Reichenbach was a follower and expounder of Swedenborg.—In this year
Ehrenfried proposed to print a German literary Monthly.

Lancaſter.   B. Grimler.

Tagebuch des Senats der Republik Pennſylvanien.   1812—1813.

* Der Wahre Amerikaner.   Eine Zeitung für den Bauer und Stadtmann.

Lancaſter. Wm. Hamilton & Comp.

* Der Volksfreund.

Plitt, Johann. Abſchiedsprebigt gehalten am Sonntag, Oculi, b,
21. März 1813 in ber lutheriſchen Gemeinde zu Neu=Holland.

> Johann Plitt was minister of the Lutheran congregation in New Holland,
> Lancaster Co., from 1790 to 1813.

Melsheimer, F. V. Wahrheit ber Chriſtlichen Religion für Unſtubirte.
Aus verſchiedenen lehrreichen Schriften zuſammengetragen.

> Friedrich Valentin Melsheimer was from 1790 to the time of his death,
> 1814, minister of the Lutheran congregation at Hanover, York Co. In 1787
> and the following years he was one of the teachers at Franklin College in
> Lancaster.

Muhlenberg, H. E. Catalogus Plantarum Americae Septentrionalis. 8vo. 112 pp.

Lancaſter, Ohio.

* Der Ohio Abler.

Libanon. Jacob Stöver.

* Libanoner Morgenſtern.

Philabelphia. Conrab Zentler.

Das Gute Kind vor, in unb nach ber Schule. 24mo. 24 S.

Regeln ber zur Unterſtützung Nothleibenber Deutſchen im Staat Pennſyl=
vanien beyſteurenben beutſchen Geſellſchaft. 8vo. 13 S. G. s.

> German and English.

Neueingerichtetes Geſang=Buch enthaltenb eine Sammlung (mehrentheils
alter) erbaulicher Lieber. 12mo. 588 S. u. Reg.

> Schwenkfelder hymnbook.

Americaniſcher Stabt unb Lanb Calenber auf bas 1814te Jahr Chriſti.

* Der Americaniſche Beobachter. (?)

Evangeliſches Magazin. Unter ber Aufſicht ber Evangeliſch=Lutheriſchen
Synobe. Zweiter Banb. 8vo. 240 S.

Philabelphia. Conrab Zentler u. G. W. Menz.

Otterbein, Georg Gottfrieb. Leſebuch für beutſche Schulkinber.
2 Aufl. 12mo. 216 S.

Stark, Joh. F. Tägliches Hanbbuch in guten unb böſen Tagen.
Zweite Verbeſſerte Auflage. 12mo. 566 S.

Stark, Joh. F. Tägliches Gebetbüchlein für Schwangere, Gebärenbe
unb Sechswöchnerinnen u. ſ. w. 12mo. 132 S. (Mit bem vorigen
zuſammengebunben).

Verfaſſung unb Nebengeſetze ber Waſhington Wohlthätigkeits=Geſellſchaft.

Philadelphia. Conrad Zentler u. George Blake.

Choral-Buch für die Erbauliche Lieder-Sammlung der deutschen Evangelisch-
Lutherischen Gemeinen in Nord-Amerika. Auf Ansuchen des deutschen
Ev.-Luth. Ministeriums herausgegeben von der Corporation der St.
Michaelis- und Zions-Gemeine. Querfolio. 160 S.

Reading. Gottlob u. J. E. Jungmann.

* Der Standhafte Patriot.

Reading. Johann Ritter & Comp.

Spiegel für alle Menschen oder Nutzanwendungen aus dem Leben und
Wandel Christel Funks eines in seinem Leben treu gewesenen Menonisten
Predigers. 12mo. 54 S.

> A translation was published 1814 by J. Winnard in Norristown under the
> title: A mirror of all mankind or instructive examples from the life and
> conduct of Christian Funk, a faithful minister among the Menonists

Das Leben, die Mordthat, Verhör, Hinrichtung von Johann Schild.
Gedruckt für die Käufer. 16 S.

Der Neue, Americanische Landwirthschafts-Calender. Auf das Jahr . .
1814.

* Der Readinger Adler.

Reading. Heinrich B. Sage.

Vollständiges Gebet-Buch auf alle Zeiten in allen Ständen u. s. w.
12mo. 520 S.

* Der Weltbote.

Somerset, Somerset Co., Pa. Fr. Goeb.

Biblia, das ist: Die ganze Göttliche Heilige Schrift, Alten und Neuen
Testaments, nach der deutschen Uebersetzung Dr. Martin Luthers.
Nebst schicklichen Nutzanwendungen zu den fünf Büchern Mosis, dem
Hohelied Salomonis und der Offenbarung Johannis. Die Erste
Auflage. Fol. 527, 66, 169 S.   G. S.

> The first edition of the Bible printed west of the Alleghany mountains.

York. Andreas Billmeyer.

* Der Wahre Republikaner.

1814.

Allentown, Pa. Joseph Ehrenfried.

Der Friedensbothe und Lecha County Anzeiger.

Allentown. Carl L. Hütter.

* Der Unabhängige Republikaner und Lecha County Freiheits-Freund.

Baltimore, Md. William Warner.

Der Neue Baltimore Stadt und Land Calender. Auf das Jahr . . 1815. Zum erstenmal herausgegeben.

Chambersburg. Friedrich W. Schöpflin.

* Der Redliche Registrator.

Easton. Christian Jacob Hütter.

* Der Northampton Correspondent.

Hägerstown, Md. Gruber u. May.

Der Volksfreund und Hägerstauner Calender auf b. J. . . 1816. Zum neunzehntenmal herausgegeben.

> This is the same almanac that has been noticed in former years as: Der neue Nord=Americanische Stadt und Land Calender. The title as above given was printed on the cover page.

* Hägerstauner Wochenschrift.

Hanover, York Co. Stark & Lange.

* Die Hanover Gazette.

Harrisburg. Johann S. Wiestling.

Myseras, Lambrecht, in Middleburg, Empfindungen und Erfahrungen der Frommen auf dem Wege nach den Himmel. Aus dem Holländi= schen. Zweyte Americanische Auflage. 12mo. 408 S.

> See 1799.

* Die Harrisburger Morgenröthe.

Lancaster. Anton Albrecht.

Der Gemeinnützige Landwirthschafts=Calender. Auf das Jahr 1815.

* Der Amerikanische Staatsbote.

Lancaster. Wm. Hamilton u. Comp.

* Der Volksfreund.

Lancaster. Joseph Ehrenfried.

Der Blutige Schau=Platz oder Märtyrer=Spiegel der Tauffs=Gesinnten oder Wehrlosen Christen u. s. w., in Holländischer Sprache heraus= gegeben von T. J. V. Braght, nun aber sorgfältigst ins Hochdeutsche übersetzt und zum Zweytenmal ans Licht gebracht. Zweyte America= nische Auflage. Folio. 948 S. u. Register.

> The first edition appeared in Ephrata 1748.

Lancaster. Henrich u. Benjamin Grimler.

* Der Wahre Amerikaner. Eine Zeitung für den Bauer und Stadtmann.

> Henry Grimler died in 1814.

Lancaster, Ohio.

* Der Ohio Adler.

Libanon. Jacob Schnee.

Doctor Johann Habermanns Chriſtliches Gebetbüchlein. 16mo. 151 S.

Tagebuch des fünf und zwanzigſten Hauſes der Repräſentanten der Republik Pennſylvanien.

* Der Libanoner Morgenſtern.

Philadelphia. G. u. D. Billmeyer.

Erbauliche Lieder=Sammlung zum Gottesdienſtlichen Gebrauch in den Evangel.=Lutheriſchen Gemeinen in Pennſylvanien und den benach= barten Staaten u. ſ. w. Die Sechſte vermehrte mit einem Melodien Regiſter verſehene Auflage. 12mo. 626 S. u. Regiſter.

As an appendix follows:

Kurze Andachten einer gottſuchenden Seele. 26 S.

> Michael Billmeyer's two sons, George and Daniel, kept a bookstore in Philadelphia from 1814—1820 and during this time the Billmeyer publi- cations have a Philadelphia imprint, though actually printed in Germantown at the old place, now No. 5347 Germantown Avenue, which is still in good condition and the residence of George Billimeyer's daughter. Michael Billmeyer died 1836.

Das neue und verbeſſerte Geſangbuch, worinnen die Pſalmen Davids, ſamt einer Sammlung alter und neuer Geiſtreicher Lieder . enthalten ſind. Nach einem Synodal=Schluß zuſammen getragen und einge= richtet vor die Evangeliſch=Reformirten Gemeinen in den V. St. von America. Fünfte Auflage. 118 S., 585 S., Regiſter, und Catechis= mus 26 S.

> See 1797.

Der Hoch=Deutſche Americaniſche Calender. Auf das Jahr Chriſti 1815.

Philadelphia. James Stackhouse.

Catechismus oder kurzer Unterricht chriſtlicher Lehre. 12mo. 108 S.

> Reformed.

Neuer Hauswirthſchafts Calender auf das Jahr 1815.

Philadelphia. Conrad Zentler.

Richtiger Weg zum ewigen Leben. Erſte amerikaniſche Auflage. 16mo. 144 S.

Jubel der Deutſchen, Holländer und Schweitzer bey dem Feſt= und Gaſtmahl 24. Febr. 1814 nach der Leipziger Schlacht und den weiteren Fort= ſchritten der Alliirten.

> Mentioned in M. v. Fürstenwärther's book *Der Deutsche in Nord Amerika*. Stuttgart und Tübingen 1818.

Americaniſcher Stadt und Land Calender auf das 1815te Jahr Chriſti.

* Der Americaniſche Beobachter. (?)

Evangeliſches Magazin. Dritter Band. 8vo. 248 S.

Reading. J. G. Jungmann.

Des Evangelischen Predigers G. Millers kurze und deutliche Lehren. 12mo. 225 S.

* Der Standhafte Patriot.

Reading. Johann Ritter & Comp.

Tagebuch des Senats der Republik Pennsylvanien. 1813—1814.

Der Neue, Americanische Landwirthschafts-Calender. Auf das Jahr 1815.

* Der Readinger Adler.

Reading. Henrich B. Sage.

Jung, Dr. Johann Heinrich. (Stilling). Die Siegesgeschichte der christlichen Religion. Mit Nachträgen. 12mo. 522 u. 202 S.

* Der Weltbote.

Somerset, Somerset Co. Friedrich Goeb.

Das Neue Testament. Die erste Auflage. 12mo. 537 S. u. Reg.

Shellsburg, Bedford Co. Friedrich Goeb.

Somerseter Calender auf das Jahr 1815.

York. Andreas Billmeyer.

* Der Wahre Republikaner.

Druckort unbekannt.

Doll, Jos. Leichter Unterricht in der Vocal-Musik, auf drei Stimmen gesetzt, enthaltend die vornehmsten Kirchen-Melodien. Angezeigt im Reading Adler 31. Jan. 1815.

Hahn, Michael. Ein Sendschreiben. 12mo. 41 S.

1815.

Allentown, Pa. Joseph Ehrenfried.

* Der Friedensbothe und Lecha County Anzeiger.

Allentown. Carl L. Hütter.

* Der Unabhängige Republikaner und Lecha County Freyheits-Freund.

Baltimore. William Warner.

Der Neue Baltimore Stadt und Land Calender. Auf das Jahr 1816.

Chambersburg. F. W. Schöpflin.

* Der Redliche Registrator.

Eaſton. Chriſtian Jacob Hütter.

Tagebuch des ſechs und zwanzigſten Hauſes der Repräſentanten der Republik
Pennſylvanien

* Der Northampton Correſpondent.

Hägerstaun. Gruber u. May.

Jung, Dr. Heinrich, (Stilling). Nachtrag zur Siegesgeſchichte der
chriſtlichen Religion und einer gemeinnützigen Erklärung der Offen=
barung Johannis.

Der Volksfreund und Hägerstauner Calender, Auf das Jahr . . 1816.
Zum zwanzigſtenmal herausgegeben.

* Hägerstauner Wochenſchrift.

Hanover, York Co. Stark & Lange.

* Die Hanover Gazette.

Harrisburg. J. S. Wieſtling.

Geiſtlicher Luſtgarten frommer Seelen. Erſte Americaniſche Ausgabe.
. 12mo.. 215 S.

Harrisburg. Gleim u. Wieſtling.

* Die Harrisburger Morgenröthe.

Lancaſter. Anton Albrecht.

Der Gemeinnützige Landwirthſchafts=Calender auf das Jahr 1816.

* Der Americaniſche Staatsbote.

Lancaſter. Joſ. Ehrenfried.

Ausbund, das iſt: Etliche ſchöne Chriſtliche Lieder, wie ſie in dem Gefängniß
zu Baſſau in dem Schloß von den Schweizer=Brüdern u. ſ. w. ge=
dichtet worden. 12mo. 812 S. nebſt Anhängen.
    See 1742.

Herr, Joh. Der wahre und ſelige Weg oder gründliche Lehre aus
Gottes Wort. 16mo. 333 S.
    Rev. John Herr caused a split among the Mennonites.

* Der Volksfreund.

Lancaſter. Benjamin Grimler.

* Der Wahre Amerikaner. Eine Zeitung für den Bauer und Stadtmann.

Lancaſter. W. Hamilton.

Die Aufgehende Lilie, ein theoſophiſcher Discurs. Die Erſte Auflage.
12mo. 204 S.

Lancaſter, Ohio.

* Der Ohio Adler.

Libanon.

Lochmann, Georg. Abschiedsrede an die Glieder der evangelisch=
lutherische Gemeinde.

Rev. G. Lochmann accepted in 1815 a call to Harrisburg.

Libanon. Jacob Stöver.

Tagebuch des Senats der Republik Pennsylvanien. 1814—1815.

* Der Libanoner Morgenstern.

Philadelphia. G. u. D. Billmeyer.

Der Kleine Catechismus. 10te Auflage. 16mo. 128 S.

Der Psalter. Zehnte Auflage. 16mo. 251 S.

Der Hoch=Deutsche Americanische Calender. Auf das Jahr Christi 1816.

Philadelphia. Conrad Zentler.

Bemerkungen an die Mitglieder der Deutsch=Lutherischen Gemeine in und
um Philadelphia, darüber daß nur deutsch gepredigt wird, und beshalb
ihre Gemeine in Verfall geräth. (German and English). 12mo.
31 S.

Ansprache der incorporirten Mosheimischen Gesellschaft an alle Glieder der
deutschen evang.=lutherischen Gemeinden in und bey Philadelphia.

Title from Fürstenwärther's Der Deutsche in Nord=Amerika. The address
opposed the introduction of English preaching in the German Lutheran
churches.

Americanischer Stadt und Land Calender auf das 1816te Jahr Christi.

* Der Americanische Beobachter. (?)

* Evangelisches Magazin, unter der Aufsicht der Deutschen Evangelisch=
Lutherischen Synode. 8vo. 96 S.

Reading. Gottlob & J. E. Jungmann.

* Der Standhafte Patriot.

Reading. Johann Ritter & Comp.

Der Neue, Americanische Landwirthschafts=Calender. Auf das Jahr . .
1816.

* Der Readinger Adler.

On February 22, an extra was issued containing the proclamation of
peace.

Reading. H. B. Sage.

* Der Weltbote.

Schellsburg, Bedford Co. Friederich Goeb.

Somerseter Calender auf das Jahr 1816.

York. Andreas Billmeyer.

* Der Wahre Republikaner.

York. Carl T. Melsheimer & James Lewis.

* Der Unions Freund.

First number published January 19.

Druckort unbekannt.

Merkwürdige Nachricht von der Wunderbaren Entzückung des Hans Frummans, Gedruckt für Liebhaber. 16mo. 23 S.

A shorter version of the story in rhymes which S. Mayer in York published 1803. See p. 161.

1816.

Allentown. Carl L. Hütter.

* Der Unabhängige Republikaner und Lecha County Freyheits=Freund.

Allentown, Pa. Joseph Ehrenfried.

* Der Friedensbothe und Lecha County Anzeiger.

Baltimore. Schäffer u. Maund.

Das kleine Davidische Psalterspiel u. s. w. Erste verbesserte Auflage. 12mo. 600 S.

See 1744.

Die Kleine Harfe u. s. w. Erste Auflage. 12mo. 55 S.

Der Volksfreund und Baltimorer Calender, Auf das Jahr . . 1817. Zum erstenmal herausgegeben.

Baltimore. William Warner.

Der Neue Baltimore Stadt und Land Calender. Auf das Jahr 1817.

Carlisle. *Peterson.*

The *Volksfreund* in Lancaster mentions in 1816 Mr. Peterson of Carlisle among the publishers of German papers.

Chambersburg. F. W. Schöpflin.

Schreiack, Johann. Auszug aus Gen. Washington's Circular= Schreiben. Die Constitution der Vereinigten Staaten und die Constitution von Pennsylvanien. 12mo. 92 S.

* Der Redliche Registrator.

Easton. Christian J. Hütter und
Allentaun. Carl L. Hütter.

Das unentbehrliche Buch für die Deutschen Bürger in Nord=Amerika. Enthaltend eine gründliche Anweisung zur Erlernung der Englischen Sprache; Vorschriften zum Gebrauch von Geschäftsleuten aller Art, Quittungen, Notar, Obligationen, Vollmachten, Agriements, Tes= tamente u. s. w. Alles in Deutscher und Englischer Sprache. 8vo. 391 S.

Easton. Christian Jacob Hütter.

* Der Northampton Correspondent.

Hägerstaun. Gruber u. May.

Der Volksfreund und Hägerstauner Calender, Auf das Jahr . . 1817.

* Hägerstauner Wochenschrift.

How much longer Gruber & May published a German paper has not been ascertained.

Hanover, York Co. Daniel P. Lange.

* Die Hanover Gazette.

Harrisburg. Gleim & Wiestling.

* Die Harrisburger Morgenröthe.

Harrisonburg, Va. Laurenz R. Wartmann, Rockingham Co.

Burkholter, Peter. Eine Verhandlung von der äusserlichen Wasser=Taufe, und Erklärung einiger Irrthümer, wie auch von der Feuer=Taufe und wie in Christo das gesetzliche Osterlamm aufgehöret und das Abendmahl eingesetzt u. s. w. 16mo. 59 S.

Lancaster. Anton Albrecht.

Der Gemeinnützige Landwirthschafts=Calender. Auf das Jahr 1817.

* Der Amerikanische Staatsbote.

Lancaster. Joseph Ehrenfried.

Das Kleine Je länger je lieber. Ist ein kurzer Anhang zur Aufgehenden Lilie. 12mo. 16 S.

Lancaster. B. Grimler.

Tagebuch des sieben und zwanzigsten Hauses der Repräsentanten der Republik Pennsylvanien.

* Der Wahre Amerikaner. Eine Zeitung für den Bauer- und Stadtmann.

Lancaster. Wilhelm Hamilton u. Comp.

* Der Volksfreund.

Lancaster, Ohio. Eduard Schäffer.

Herzens Opfer, eine Sammlung Geistreicher Lieder. Herausgegeben von der Conferenz der Vereinigten Brüder in Christo. 16mo. 352 S. u. Register.

The United brethren in Christ, a sect split off the Reformed Church and in their usages approximating the Methodists, owe their origin (1805) to Rev. Wm. Otterbein and Rev. J. A. Gueting.

* Der Ohio Adler.

Libanon. Joseph Hartman.

* Der Unpartheyische Berichter. „Wir sind alle Republicaner, Wir sind alle Federalisten".

Libanon. Jacob Schnee.

Tagebuch des Senats der Republik Pennsylvanien. 1815—1816.

Neu=Market, Virg. A. Henkel.

Der christliche Catechismus, verfaßt zum Unterricht der Jugend in der
Erkenntniß der Christlichen Religion, samt Morgen= und Abend=
Gebäte u. s. w. Von Paul Henkel, Evangelischer Lehrer.

Title from Grübner's Geschichte der Lutherischen Kirche.

Henkel, Ambrosius. Das große A. B. C=Buch, enthaltend: das
A. B. C, Wurzelwörter mit ihren angehängten Ableitungssylben.
Nebst vielen Buchstabir= und Leseübungen, u. s. w.

Philadelphia. G. u. D. Billmeyer.

Catechismus oder kurzer Unterricht der christlichen Lehre. 16mo. 118 S.

Der Hoch=Deutsche Americanische Calender. Auf das Jahr Christi 1817.

Philadelphia. Kimber u. Sharpleß.

Kersey, Jessy. Eine kurze Darstellung, oder gründliche Lehre der
christlichen Religion. 12mo. 110 S.

A Quaker tract.

Philadelphia. Georg W. Mentz.
(Gedruckt bey Conrad Zentler.)

Der Psalter des Königs und Propheten Davids. Besonders für Schulen
eingerichtet. 12mo. 252 S.

Philadelphia. Conrad Zentler.

Evangelischer Brief an die Jugend. Von einem jungen Prediger. 12mo.
336 S.

Habermann, Dr. G. Christliches Gebet=Büchlein. 16mo.

Dr. Martin Luthers Catechismus, erklärt und mit den vornehmsten Beweis=
sprüchen der H. Schrift versehen, nebst einem Anhang für die Evangel.
Lutherischen Christen in dem englischen Nord=Amerika. Von Conrad
F. Temme, Prof. und Pastor zu Lüneburg in Nova Scotia und
wirkl. Mitglied der Societät in England.

A Lutheran Congregation in Lunenberg, Nova Scotia, existed already 1754.

Die täglichen Loosungen und Lehrterte der Brüdergemeine für das Jahr
1817.

Americanischer Stadt und Land Calender auf das 1817te Jahr Christi.

* Americanischer Beobachter. (?)

Evangelisches Magazin, unter der Aufsicht der Deutschen Evangelisch=
Lutherischen Synode. 8vo. 96 S.

Original Church Resolutions of the German Lutheran Congregation.

Counter Resolutions 1765. Translated and published in 1816.

The following two pamphlets are mentioned by Fürstenwärther: Der Deutsche in Nord-Amerika, p. 95 and were probably printed by C. Zentler.

Constitution der Gesellschaft zur Ausbreitung nützlicher und erbaulicher Aufsätze.

Grundregeln der jugendlichen Frauenzimmer-Gesellschaft der deutschen evang. lutherischen St. Michaelis und Zions-Gemeine in Philadelphia.

Reading. Carl A. Bruckman.

* Der Readinger Postbothe und Berks, Schuylkill und Libanon Counties Advertiser.

The paper was advertised already in 1815. Charles A. Bruckman was the son of the former publisher of the same name.

Reading. Gottlob & J. E. Jungmann.

* Der Standhafte Patriot.

G. Jungmann failed in this year, as appears from an advertisement in the *Adler*.

Reading. Joh. Ritter & Co.

Caesar, Simon. Der geschwinde Interessen Rechner. 12mo. 42 S.
The same in English.

Handbuch für Deutsche; Enthaltend Formen zu Handschriften u. s. w. 112 S.

Der Neue, Americanische Landwirthschafts-Calender. Auf das Jahr . . 1817. 4to. 36 S.

* Der Readinger Adler.

Reading. Heinrich B. Sage.

Hauptinhalt der Christlichen Lehre. Vierte Auflage. 12mo. 45 S.

Jung, H. Stilling. Theorie der Geister Kunde. Nachtrag: Apologie der Theorie der Geisterkunde. 8vo. 384 u. 72 S.

Der Vollständige Pferdearzt.

* Der Weltbote. (?)

Schellsburg, Bedford Co. Friedrich Goeb.
Der Somerseter Calender auf das Jahr 1817.

Somerset. Friedrich Goeb.

The publication of a German paper by F. Goeb in 1816 is attested by a remark in the *Lancaster Volksfreund*.

York, (York Co.) Carl A. Melsheimer u. James Lewis.
*Der Unions Freund.

Last number issued in October 1816.

York. Andreas Billmeyer.
*Der Wahre Republikaner.

1817.

Allentown. Carl L. Hütter.

Tagebuch des acht und zwanzigsten Hauses der Repräsentanten der Republik
Pennsylvanien.

*Der Unabhängige Republikaner und Lecha County Freyheits=Freund.

Allentown, Pa. Joseph Ehrenfried.
*Der Friedensbothe und Lecha County Anzeiger.

Baltimore. Schäffer u. Maund.

Das Gemeinschaftliche Gesangbuch zum gottesdienstlichen Gebrauch der
Lutherischen und Reformirten Gemeinden in Nord=America. Zweyte
Auflage. 12mo. 370 S.

Verfassung der Deutschen Gesellschaft von Maryland. Deutsch und
Englisch. 16mo. 21 S.

The German Society of Maryland was organized February 18, 1817.

Weems, M. L. Das Leben des George Waschington mit Sonderbaren
Anekdoten u. s. w. 12mo. 210 S., mit 8 Kupferstichen. H. S.

Americanischer Stadt= und Land=Calender. Auf das Jahr . , 1818.
Zum zweytenmal herausgegeben.

Baltimore. William Warner.

Der Neue Baltimore Stadt und Land Calender. Auf das Jahr 1818.

Chambersburg. F. W. Schöpflin.
* Der Redliche Registrator.

Easton. Christian J. Hütter.
*Der Northampton Correspondent.

Ephrata. (Jacob Pfautz.)

Ein schön Lied. 12mo. 15 S.

Hägerstaun. J. Gruber u. D. May.

Der Volksfreund und Hägerstauner Calender. Auf das Jahr . . 1818.

Hanover, York Co. D. P. Lange.
*Die Hanover Gazette.

Harrisburg. Gleim u. Wiestling.

* Die Harrisburg Morgenröthe.

Harrisburg? Charles Greer.

Tagebuch des Senats der Republik Pennsylvanien. 1816—1817.

Harrisonburg, Va. Laurentz Wartmann.

Bowman, Peter. Ein Zeugniß von der Taufe.

    A Dunker publication.

Lancaster. Anton Albrecht.

Der Gemeinnützige Landwirthschafts Calender auf das Jahr 1818.

* Der Americanische Staatsbote.

Lancaster. Jos. Ehrenfried.

An die Gott suchende und Jesu liebende Seelen. 8vo. 42 S.

Lancaster. Benjamin Grimler.

* Der Wahre Amerikaner. Eine Zeitung für den Bauer und Stadtmann.

Lancaster. Wm. Hamilton u. Comp.
Samuel Kling.

* Der Volksfreund.

    Col. Wm. Hamilton failed and the paper was sold by the Sheriff. In the number of September 10th Samuel Kling is named as publisher, from November 25, 1817, till March 31, 1818, the firm was S. Kling & Johann Bär. Hamilton died April 10, 1820.

Lancaster, Ohio.

* Der Ohio Adler.

Libanon. Joseph Hartmann.

* Der Unparthepische Berichter.

Neuberlin. Salomon Miller u. Heinrich Niebel.

Glaubenslehre und Kirchen=Zucht=Ordnung der Evangelischen Gemeinschaft, Nebst dem Zweck ihrer Vereinigung mit Gott und unter einander. Zwepte und verbesserte Auflage. 16mo. 144 S.

Philadelphia. G. u. D. Billmeyer.

Das kleine Davidische Psalterspiel der Kinder Zions. 4te Auflage. 12mo. 56 S.

Der Hoch=Deutsche Americanische Calender. Auf das Jahr Christi 1818.

Philadelphia. Benj. u. Thomas Kite.

Ernste Uebersicht der Gewohnheit des Krieges. 8vo. 46 S.

Philadelphia. Conrad Zentler.

Einfältige Unterhaltungen mit Gott. 12mo. 180 S.

Ein Exempel= und Liederbüchlein für betende Kinder. 16mo. 144 S.

Der 31ſte October 1817, zum feyerlichen Andenken an den 31ſten October 1517 mit Rührung begangen von der St. Michaelis und Zions Gemeinde in Philadelphia.   12mo. 80 S.

The Tercentennial of the Reformation was celebrated on October 31, the day when in 1517 Luther fastened his 95 theses on the portals of the Schlosskirche in Wittenberg.

Die täglichen Looſungen und Lehrterte der Brüdergemeine für das Jahr 1818.

Trial of Frederick Eberle and others at a Nisi Prins Court held at Philadelphia, July 1816, before the Hon. Jasper Yeates, Justice, for illegally conspiring together by all means lawful and unlawful "with their bodies and lives" to prevent the introduction of the English Language into the service of *St. Michael's* and *Zion's Churches*.   8vo. 240 pp.   G. S.

The defendants were found guilty.

Americaniſcher Stadt und Land Calender auf das 1818te Jahr Chriſti.

* Der Amerikaniſche Beobachter.   (?)

Evangeliſches Magazin, unter der Aufſicht der deutſchen Evangeliſch=Lutheriſchen Synode.   8vo. 88 S.

Reading.   Carl A. Bruckman.

* Der Readinger Poſtbothe.

Reading.   Johann Ritter & Comp.

Geſchichte des Americaniſchen Krieges von 1812.   Illuſtrirt.   Aus dem Engliſchen überſetzt.   8vo. 273 S.

Der Neue Americaniſche Landwirthſchafts=Calender.   Auf das Jahr . . 1818.

* Der Readinger Adler.

Reading.   H. B. Sage.

Engel, J. F.   Abſchiedspredigt, gehalten im October 1816 in den Gemeinen in und um Blumsberg, Columbia County.

Der vollſtändige Pferde=Arzt.   Herausgegeben von Sage und Rietze.   12mo. 108 S.

* Der Weltbote.

Schellsburg, Bedford Co.   Friedrich Goeb.

Der Somerſeter Calender auf das Jahr 1818.

Somerſet.   Friederich Goeb.

*Goeb's Zeitung in Somerset County is referred to in the *Reading Adler* of January 21.

York.   Andreas Billmeyer.

* Der Wahre Republikaner.

1818.

Allentown. Heinrich Ebner.

Economy of human life. Haushaltungskunst des menschlichen Lebens.

Merkwürdige Kriminal Geschichten. Mit mehreren Abbildungen geziert. 12mo. 176 S.

Allentown. Carl L. Hütter.

* Der Unabhängige Republikaner und Lecha County Freyheits=Freund.

Allentown, Pa. Joseph Ehrenfried.

* Der Friedensbothe und Lecha County Anzeiger.

Baltimore. Schäffer u. Maund.

Liturgie oder Kirchen=Agende der Ev. Lutherischen Gemeinen in Pennsyl= vanien und den benachbarten Staaten. 12mo. 103 S.

Spiegel des Trunkenbolds.

Der Volksfreund und Baltimorer Calender, Auf das Jahr . . 1819. Zum drittenmal herausgegeben.

Der Westliche Calender. Für die Westlichen Staaten neugerichtet. Auf das Jahr . . 1819. Zum erstenmal herausgegeben.

Baltimore. William Warner.

Der Neue Baltimore Stadt und Land Calender. Auf das Jahr 1819.

Chambersburg. F. Wilhelm Schöpflin.

(Bowman, Peter.) Ein Zeugniß von der Taufe. 16mo. 72 S.
A Dunker tract.

* Der Redliche Registrator.

Easton. C. J. Hütter u. Sohn.

Tagebuch des neun und zwanzigsten Hauses der Repräsentanten der Republik Pennsylvanien.

Tagebuch des Senats der Republik Pennsylvanien. 1817—1818.

* Der Northampton Correspondent.

Easton. Heinrich u. Wilhelm Hütter.

Der Northampton Bauern Calender auf das Jahr 1819. (Erstes Jahr.)

Hägerstaun. J. Gruber und D. May.

Der Volksfreund und Hägerstauner Calender, Auf das Jahr . . 1819.

Hamburg, Berks Co., Pa.

Unsers Herrn Jesu Christi Kinder=Buch oder Merkwürdige historische Beschreibung von Joachim und Anna, deren Geschlecht aus welchem sie geboren; item von ihrer Tochter der Jungfrau Maria. 16mo. 47 S.

Hanover, York Co. D. P. Lange.

* Die Hanover Gazette.

Harrisburg. Gleim u. Wiestling.

* Die Harrisburger Morgenröthe.

Harrisonburg, Virg. Laurenz Wartmann.

Braun, Joh. Circularschreiben an die deutschen Einwohner von Rockingham und Augusta und den benachbarten Counties. 12mo. x, 409 S.

> Historical and statistical information on bible societies and the service they do.

Lancaster. Anton Albrecht.

Der Gemeinnützige Landwirthschafts Calender. Auf das Jahr 1819.

* Der Americanische Staatsbote.

Lancaster. Johann Bär.

Jacoby, Daniel. Americanischer Rechnungs-Schlüssel oder Anfangs-Gründe der Rechenkunst. 12mo. 120 S.

* Der Volksfreund.

> Up to March 31, the publishers were Kling & Bär. With the number issued April 7th, J. Bär entered upon sole proprietorship. At the same time the printing office was moved to other quarters in North Queen St.

Lancaster. Joseph Ehrenfried.

Reichenbach, W. Agathon, Ueber Wahren Gottesdienst nach dessen allgemeinsten Grundwesen betrachtet. Ein Handbuch für nachdenkende Menschenfreunde. 12mo. 204 S.

Lancaster, Ohio.

* Der Ohio Adler.

Libanon. Joseph Hartmann.

* Der Unpartheyische Berichter.

Neu-Berlin, Pa. Salomon Miller u. Henrich Niebel
(für die Evangelische Gemeinschaft.)

Francke, A. H. Ein Tractat von der Menschenfurcht, dem Lehrstande gewidmet. 16mo. 144 S.

Die Geistliche Viole, oder eine kleine Sammlung alter und neuer Geistreicher Lieder, zum Gebrauch und Erbauung der Evangelischen Gemeinschaft. Erste Auflage. 16mo. 186 S.

> The Evangelical Association, founded by Jacob Albrecht about 1800, adopted certain features of the Methodist Church.

Neu Market, Shenandoah Co. Solomon Henkel.

Henkel, Ambrosius. Das kleine A. B. C. Buch, oder erste Anfangs-Büchlein mit schönen Bildern und deren Namen, nach dem A. B. C., um den Kindern das Buchstabiren leichter zu machen. (Vignette: Ein Mädchen und ein Knabe auf dem Wege zur Schule.)

Title furnished by Mr. H. A. Rattermann.

Kurzer Auszug von den Verrichtungen der Synode des Lutherischen Ministeriums, gehalten im Staat Nord Carolina, im J. 1817. 12mo. 14 S.

Philadelphia.

Muhlenberg, H. E. Catalogus plantarum Americae Septentrionalis. Editio secunda. 12mo. 122 pp.

Philadelphia. G. u. D. Billmeyer.

Der Hoch=Deutsche Americanische Calender. Auf das Jahr Christi 1819.

Philadelphia. Philipp Gagel.

Walz, C. L. Die Elemente der deutschen Sprache. 8vo. 64 S.

Walz was a Lutheran minister and Principal of the Francke Academy in Philadelphia.

Philadelphia. Conrad Zentler.

Brook, Mary. Gründe für die Nothwendigkeit eines stillen Harrens beym öffentlichen Gottesdienst.

Deutsches und Englisches A. B. C. und Buchstabir=Büchlein für Anfänger. 16mo. 32 S.

Hoch=Deutsches Lutherisches A. B. C. und Namen=Büchlein.

Americanischer Stadt und Land Calender auf das 1819te Jahr Christi.

An Act for Regulating the Importation of German and other Passengers. 12mo. 22 pp.

During the preceding years there had been shocking abuses in the passenger traffic to which the German Society called the attention of the Legislature. In consequence, a protective law was enacted. See *Seidensticker's History of the German Society*, p. 107—118.

Reading. Carl A. Bruckman.

Homan, Johann George. Die Land= und Haus=Apotheke, enthaltend die allerbesten Mittel sowohl für die Menschen als für das Vieh. Nebst einem großen Anhang von der Aechten Färberey. Erste americanische Auflage. 12mo. 169 S.

Contains a list of subscribers.

Testament und Abschrift der zwölf Patriarchen.

* Der Reabinger Postbothe.

Reading. Johann Ritter u. Comp.

Der Neue, Americanische Landwirthschafts Calender. Auf das Jahr . . 1819.

* Der Reabinger Adler.

Reading. Heinrich B. Sage.

Vollständiges Gebät=Buch auf alle Zeiten, in allen Ständen und bey allen Angelegenheiten nützlich zu gebrauchen. . . Aus den bekannten Gebät= Büchern der Herren Starke, Zollikofer und Schmolken zusammen gezogen. 12mo. 512 S.

* Der Weltbote.

Shellsburg, Bedford Co. Friedrich Goeb.

Der Somerseter Calender auf das Jahr 1819.

York. Andreas Billmeyer.

* Der Wahre Republikaner.

Druckort unbekannt.

Leben und Thaten des berüchtigten Räubers Johannes Bückler, genannt Schinderhannes. 16mo. 140 S.

Das Sterbe=Bekenntniß von Joseph Hare, einer der Posträuber die am 10. letzten September zu Baltimore hingerichtet wurden.

Der vollständige Bienen=Wärter oder nützliche Anweisung zur Bienen=Zucht.

1819.

Allentown. Henrich Ebner.

Krauß, Johann. Oeconomisches Haus= und Kunstbuch. Zusammen= getragen aus den besten englischen und deutschen Schriften. 12mo. 452 S.

Schwenkfeld. Einige christliche und lehrreiche Sendbriefe durch Caspar Schwenkfeld von Ossing. 8vo. 100 S.

Allentown. Carl Ludwig Hütter.

Verhandlungen der Deutsch=Evangelisch=Lutherischen Synode von Penn= sylvanien und dem benachbarten Staaten; gehalten zu Baltimore den 6. Juni 1819. 12mo. 18 S.

Der neue Allentauner Calender. Auf das Jahr . . 1820.

* Der Unabhängige Republikaner und Lecha County Freyheits=Freund.

Allentown, Pa. Joseph Ehrenfried.

* Der Friedensbothe und Lecha County Anzeiger.

Baltimore. Schäffer u. Maund.

Der Volksfreund und Baltimore Calender, Auf das Jahr 1820.

Amerikanischer Stadt= und Land=Calender. Auf das Jahr 1820. Zum 4ten mal herausgegeben.

Der Westliche Calender. Für die Westlichen Staaten neugerichtet. Auf das Jahr . . 1820. Zum Zweytenmal herausgegeben.

Chambersburg. F. W. Schöpflin.

* Der Redliche Registrator.

Easton. Christian J. Hütter u. Sohn.

Kurzer Begriff der Biblischen Geschichte. Ein Schulbuch für die Americanische Jugend und zum Gebrauch für Jedermann. 12mo. 116 S.

* Der Northampton Correspondent.

Easton. H. u. W. Hütter.

Der Northampton Bauern Calender auf das Jahr 1820.

Ephrata. Joseph Bauman.

Clavis universalis oder Schlüssel der Geheimnisse zur Offenbarung des
alten und neuen Bundes. 1818 u. 1819. 16mo. 224 S.

Copia eines Briefs; Wahre Erklärung von dem Beyfalls= oder Historischen
Glauben und dem Wahren und Seligmachenden Glauben. 12mo.
35 S.

Sangmeister, E. Mystische Theologie. Zweyter Theil.

Germantown. M. Billmeyer.

Hochdeutsches Lutherisches A. B. C. und Namen=Büchlein für Kinder,
welche anfangen zu lernen.

Catechismus oder Kurzer Unterricht Christlicher Lehre. 24mo. 118 S.

Das Neue Testament. Achte Auflage. 12mo. 537 S.

Der Hoch=Deutsche Americanische Calender. Auf das Jahr Christi 1820.

Hägerstaun. J. Gruber & D. May.

Der Volksfreund und Hägerstauner Calender auf das Jahr . . 1820.
Zum drey und zwanzigstenmal herausgegeben. 4to. 30 S.

Hanover, York Co. D. P. Lange.

* Die Hanover Gazette.

Harrisburg. Gleim u. Wiestling.

* Härrisburger Morgenröthe.

Harrisburg.

Address an die Einwohner von Dauphin County. 16mo. 11 S.
A political campaign address.

Lancaster. Anton Albrecht.

Der Gemeinnützige Landwirthschafts=Calender. Auf das Jahr 1820.

* Der Americanische Staatsbote.

Lancaster. Johann Bär.

Biblia, das ist: Die ganze Heilige Schrift Alten und Neuen Testaments.
Nach der deutschen Uebersetzung von Doctor Martin Luther. Nebst

dem dritten Buch der Maccabäer und Zugabe des dritten und vierten
Buchs Esra. Imgleichen: Eine kurz gefaßte Biblische Geschichte und
Lebensbeschreibung Doctor Martin Luthers. Fol. Bibl. Gesch. 100
S., Lebensb. M. Luthers 12 S., Altes Test. 638 S., Anhang 26 S.,
Neues Test. 227 S., Namen= und Zeitregister 92 S.

* Der Volksfreund.

Reinke, Abraham. Einige Worte oder Wohlgemeinter Rath an
Johannes Herr. Zweite Auflage.

Lancaster, Ohio.
* Der Ohio Adler.

Libanon. Joseph Hartman.
Tersteegen, Gerhard. Geistliche und erbauliche Briefe über das
inwendige Leben und wahre Wesen des Christenthums. Erste
Americanische Auflage. 2 Theile. 12mo. Vorbericht, I, 458 S.
II, 427 S.

* Der Unpartheyische Berichter.

Libanon. Jacob Stoever.
Tagebuch des Senats der Republik Pennsylvanien. 1818—1819.

Tagebuch des dreißigsten Hauses der Repräsentanten der Republik Penn=
sylvanien.

Neu=Market, Va. Salmon Henkel.
Henkel, Ambrosius. Das kleine A. B. C. Buch u. s. w. Zweite
Auflage.

New=York. Eduard Schäffer.
* Der Deutsche Freund.

This was the first attempt to establish a German paper in New York. It
proved no success. The following information is kindly furnished by Mr.
Rattermann, Cincinnati. Edward Schäffer, a nephew of the Rev. F. D.
Schäffer in Philadelphia, was born in Frankfurt on the Main, where he
became a printer. In 1817 or 1818 he emigrated to America with a complete
outfit for his business and after a short stay in Philadelphia went to New
York. Of the *Deutsche Freund* only a few numbers appeared. Schäffer then
proceeded to Western Pennsylvania and soon to Ohio. In 1821 he founded
in Canton *Der Westliche Beobachter*; in 1826 he removed to Germantown, Ohio,
where he continued his paper for a short time and then returned to Pennsylvania. See also *Der Deutsche Pionier*, vol. 16, p. 218.

There appears to be some error in the dates, as already in 1816 there
appeared in Canton, Ohio, a book with E. Schäffer's imprint.

Philadelphia. Philipp Gagel.
Walz, E. L. Die Elemente der Deutschen Sprache, von E. L. Walz,
Evangel. Luth. Prediger und Oberlehrer an der Fränkischen Academie
in Philadelphia, enthaltend ein neues A. B. C. Buch in Deutscher
und Englischer Sprache. 8vo. 64 S.

Philadelphia. Conrad Zentler.
Etwas für Alle und vornehmlich für unsere Jugend.

Die täglichen Loosungen und Lehrtexte der Brüdergemeine für das Jahr 1820.

Americanischer Stadt und Land Calender auf das 1820te Jahr Christi.

Reading. C. A. Bruckman.
1. Das Evangelium Nicodemus. 2. Eine schöne, anmuthige und lesenswürdige Begebenheit von der unschuldig bedrängten heiligen Pfalzgräfin Genovefa. 3. Geschichte von der Geduldigen Helena Tochter des Kaisers Antonius. Herausgegeben von Johann George Homan im Rosenthal nahe bey Reading. 12mo. 302 S.

* Der Readinger Postbothe.

Reading. Johann Ritter & Co.
Fränklins Werke, Leben und Meynungen von Dr. Benjamin Fränklin. Mehrentheils von ihm selbst geschrieben.

Handbuch für Deutsche, enthaltend Formen zu Handschriften u. s. w

Reformirter Katechismus herausgegeben von Ehrw. Hermann.

Der neue, Americanische Landwirthschafts-Calender. Auf das Jahr . . 1820.

* Der Readinger Adler.

Reading. H. B. Sage.
* Der Weltbote.

Shellsburg, Bedford Co. Friederich Goeb.
Der Somerseter Calender auf das Jahr 1820.

York. Andreas Billmeyer.
* Der Wahre Republikaner.

Druckort unbekannt.
Herr, J. Eine Kurze und Apostolische Antwort von mir, Johannes Herr, auf den Brief von Abraham Reincke, Prediger zu Litiz, an mich geschrieben im Juli 1819. 16mo. 70 S.

1820.

Allentown. Heinrich Ebner.
Christlicher Unterricht der Religion. In Fragen und Antworten. 12mo. 57 S.

In diesem deutschen Alphabet, Viel guter Lehr geschrieben steht. Folioblatt.

Schwenkfeld, Caspar v. Offing. Von der himmlischen Arzeney, Oder daß Jesus Christus der wahre Arzt und der arme sündhafte Mensch der Patient, Verwundete oder Kranke sey. 8vo. 102 S.

Von dreierlei Leben der Menschen. 8vo. 134 S.

Verhandlungen der Deutsch=Evangelisch=Lutherischen Synode von Penn= sylvanien. Gehalten in der Stadt Lancaster in der Trinitatis Woche 1820. 12mo. 28 S.

Allentown. Georg Hancke.
Der Neue Allentauner Calender. Auf das Jahr . . 1821.

Allentown. Joseph Ehrenfried.
* Der Friedensbothe und Lecha County Anzeiger.

Allentown. Carl L. Hütter.
Tagebuch des Senats der Republik Pennsylvanien. 1819—1820.

* Der Unabhängige Republikaner und Lecha County Freiheits=Freund.
In November of this year George Hanke became the proprietor.

Baltimore. Schäffer u. Maund.
Amerikanischer Stadt und Land Calender. Auf das Jahr 1821.
The publishers announce in their almanac that the issue of the forthcoming volume on Luther's Life has been delayed by other work.

Der Volksfreund und Baltimore Calender. Auf das Jahr 1821.

Carlisle. H. W. Petersen.
Tagebuch des ein und dreißigsten Hauses der Repräsentanten des Staates Pennsylvanien.

Chambersburg. F. W. Schöpflin.
* Der Redliche Registrator.

Doylestown, Bucks Co. Simeon Siegfried.
According to W. W. H. Davis' History of Bucks County, p. 816, the first German paper in Bucks County was published in 1820. It was short-lived and its name has not been ascertained. The *Readinger Adler* of February 18, 1817 quotes a *Doylestown Zeitung*.

Easton. Christian Jacob Hütter.
Der Northampton Bauern Calender auf das Jahr 1821.
* Der Northampton Correspondent.

Ephrata. Jof. Bauman.
Francke, A. H. Der sichere Himmelsweg oder Anleitung zum Christen= thum. 12mo. 36 S.

Sangmeister, Ezechiel. Mystische Theologie. Dritter Theil. An= hang: Kurze Lebensbeschreibung des sel. Ez. Sangmeisters. Erste Auflage.

Germantown. M. Billmeyer.

Deutsches Buchstabir- und Lesebuch zum Gebrauch deutscher Schulen. 16mo. 128 S.

Die Kleine Geistliche Harfe. (Mennonitisches Gesangbuch.)

Das Neue Testament. Neunte Auflage.

Der Hoch-Deutsche Americanische Calender. Auf das Jahr Christi 1821.

Hägerstadt. J. Gruber u. D. May.

Helffenstein, Samuel. Predigt gehalten vor der General-Synode der Deutschen Reformirten Kirche von N. A. 8vo. 14 S.

Thiede, Joh. Fr. Tägliche Unterhaltungen mit Gott in den Abend-stunden. Erster Theil. Americanische Ausgabe. 12mo. 301 S.

Der Volksfreund und Hägerstauner Calender. Auf das Jahr . . 1821.

Hanover, York Co. D. P. Lange.

* Die Hanover Gazette.

Harrisburg. John S. Wiestling.

Gall, H. L. L. Gut gemeinter Rath an meine deutschen Landsleute.

Gall, after whom a method of improving wine has been called (Gallisiren) came to Pennsylvania in 1819 and stayed about a year. He was much interested in land associations for settlements, the field of his efforts being mainly Harrisburg. After his return to Germany he wrote a book on America. See *Deutscher Pionier*, vol 13, p. 41—56.

An die freyen Leute von Pennsylvanien. 16mo. 11 S.

Thatsachen und Beweiße, beziehend auf Joseph Hiester und William Findlay. Dem Volke von Pennsylvanien zur Ueberlegung übergeben. 16mo. 32 S.

Harrisburg. Gleim u. Wiestling.

* Härrisburger Morgenröthe.

Lancaster. William Albrecht.

Der Gemeinnützige Landwirthschafts Calender. Auf das Jahr 1821.

* Der Americanische Staatsbothe.

Lancaster. Johann Bär.

Unpartheyisches Gesangbuch, gesammelt auf Begehren der Brüderschaft der Mennonisten Gemeinen. Dritte verbesserte Auflage. 12mo. 76 S. 472 S. u. Reg.

Mennonite hymn-book.

Mühlenberg, H. A. Bußtagspredigt am 20. August 1820.

* Der Volksfreund.

* Deutsches Wochenblatt für Belehrung und Unterhaltung. Herausgegeben von Wilhelm Braun.

The paper was published at Braun's expense and lasted only two months.

Lancaſter, Ohio.

* Der Ohio Abler.

Libanon. Joſeph Hartman.

* Der Unpartheyiſche Berichter.

Philadelphia. Conrad Zentler.

Americaniſcher Stadt und Land Calender auf das 1821ſte Jahr Chriſti. 4to. 36 S.

Philadelphia. Gedruckt von Michael Billmeyer in Germantown.

* Plitt. Amerikaniſche Anſichten von dem Gottesdienſt und andere Eigenheiten der Deutſchen. Der Mosheimiſchen Geſellſchaft in Philadelphia zugeeignet und monatlich herausgegeben von Paſtor Plitt.

The first number appeared in January 1820. The Monthly was ably edited and brought articles of permanent interest, but does not appear to have been sufficiently supported.

Reading. C. A. Bruckmann.

Im Namen der allerheiligſten Dreyfaltigkeit. Das gülbene A. B. C. für Jedermann, der gern mit Ehren wollt beſtahn.

Rinaldo Rinaldini, der Räuberhauptmann. Eine romantiſche Geſchichte unſeres Jahrhunderts. Erſte Amerikaniſche Auflage. 12mo. 331 S.

* Der Readinger Poſtbothe.

Reading. Johann Ritter & Comp.

Der Neue Americaniſche Landwirthſchafts-Calender. Auf das Jahr . . 1821.

The astronomical data of the Reading and other almanacs were at this period attended to by *Carl Friedrich Egelmann* who was schoolmaster at the so called *Spiessen Kirche* in Alsace township, Berks Co. He also printed copperplate *Vorschriften* or writing models for his school and general use.

* Der Readinger Abler.

Reading. Charles M'Williams.

Stilling, Heinrich Jung. Die sieben letzten Poſaunen oder Wehen. 12mo. 142 S.

Reading. Heinrich B. Sage.

Der Weg zum Glück, oder Leben und Meynungen des Dr. Benjamin Fränklin. Von ihm ſelbſt geſchrieben. 16mo. 128 S.

Hohermann, Dr. J. Chriſtliches Gebetbüchlein. 16mo. 168 S.

* Der Weltbote.

Reading.

Das Universal=Traumbuch oder der vollständige Traum=Ausleger aller Arten von Träumen u. s. w. Aus dem englischen übersetzt. 16mo. 142 S.

Shellsburg, Bedford Co. Friederich Goeb.

Der Somerseter Calender auf das Jahr 1821.

York. Andreas Billmeyer.

* Der Wahre Republikaner.

1821.

Allentown. Henrich Ebner.

Henrich Stillings Alter, von ihm selbst beschrieben. 12mo. 94 S.

Habermann, Dr. Johann. Christliches Gebät=Büchlein. Wie auch Doctor Neumanns Kern aller Gebäter u. s. w. 16mo. 160 S.

Allentown. Joseph Ehrenfried.

* Der Friedensbothe und Lecha County Anzeiger.

In June 1821 Heinrich Ebner & Co. (Friederich G. Rütger) succeeded J. Ehrenfried as publishers of the *Friedensbote*.

Allentown. Georg Hande.

Der Neue Allentauner Calender. Auf das Jahr . . 1822.

* Der Unabhängige Republikaner und Lecha County Freyheits=Freund.

Baltimore. Johann T. Hanzsche.

Der Amerikanische Teutsche Hausfreund und Baltimore Calender. Auf das Jahr . . 1822. Zum erstenmal herausgegeben.

Canton, Stark Co., O. Eduard Schäffer.

* Der Westliche Beobachter und Stark und Wayne County Anzeiger.

See *Deutsche Pionier*, vol. 16, p. 219.

Carlisle. H. W. Peterson.

Tagebuch des Senats der Republik Pennsylvanien. 1820 — 1821.

Chambersburg. F. W. Schöpflin.

* Der Redliche Registrator.

Easton. Chr. Jac. Hütter.

Der Psalter. Neue nach der jetzigen Ortographie verbesserte Auflage. 16mo. 266 S.

* Der Northampton Correspondent.

With the number issued November 21. the name of the publishing firm changed to Heinrich und Wilhelm Hütter.

Eaſton. H. u. W. Hütter.

Der Northampton Bauern Calender auf das Jahr 1822.

Friedrich Stadt, Md. M. Bartgis.

Hoch Deutſches Reformirtes A. B. C. Buch.

Germantown. M. Billmeyer.

Der Hoch=Deutſche Americaniſche Calender. Auf das Jahr Chriſti 1822.

Hägerstaun, Md. Gruber u. May.

Der Volksfreund und Hägerstauner Calender. Auf . . 1822.

Hanover, York Co. D. P. Lange.

* Die Hanover Gazette.

Harrisburg. Gleim u. Wiestling.

* Die Harrisburger Morgenröthe.

Harrisburg. John Wyeth.

Die Franklin Harmonie und leichter Unterricht in der Vocal=Muſik.
    Queer=Folio. xii, 144 S.

Lancaſter. Johann Bär.

Das Neue Teſtament. 8vo. 515 S.

* Der Volksfreund.

Lancaſter. William Albrecht.

Der Gemeinnütige Landwirthſchafts=Calender. Auf das Jahr 1822.

* Der Americaniſche Staatsbote.

Lancaſter, Ohio.

* Der Ohio Adler.

Libanon. Joseph Hartmann.

* Der Unpartheyiſche Berichter.

Philadelphia. Conrad Zentler.

Americaniſcher Stadt und Land Calender auf das 1822ſte Jahr Chriſti.

Reading. C. A. Bruckman.

Tagebuch des zweiunddreißigſten Hauſes der Repräſentanten der Republik
    Pennſylvanien.

* Der Readinger Poſtbothe.

Reading. Johann Ritter & Comp.

Der Schul=Pſalter. Zweite Auflage.

Verhandlungen der Deutſch=Evangeliſch=Lutheriſchen Synode von Penn=
    ſylvanien, gehalten in Chambersburg 1821. 12mo. 27 S.

Der Neue, Americanische Landwirthschafts=Calender. Auf das Jahr . .
1822.
* Der Readinger Adler.

Reading. Henrich B. Sage.
Haupt=Inhalt der Christlichen Lehre. Nebst einer kurzgefaßten Kirchen=
Geschichte. Fünfte verbesserte Auflage. 16mo. 51 S.
* Der Weltbote.

Shellsburg, Bedford Co. Friedrich Goeb.
Somerseter Calender auf das Jahr 1822.

York. Andreas Billmeyer.
* Der Wahre Republikaner.

1822.

Allentown. H. Ebner u. Comp.
Erbauliches Gebät=Buch und Unterhaltungen mit Gott zur Beförderung
der Häuslichen Gottesverehrung für Christen aller Benennungen.
12mo. xvi, 396 u. 202 S.
Der Neue Pennsylvanische Stadt und Land Calender. Auf das Jahr
1823. Zum erstenmal herausgegeben.
* Der Friedensbothe und Lecha County Anzeiger.

Allentaun. Georg Hancke.
Der Neue Allentauner Calender. Auf das Jahr 1823.
* Der Unabhängige Republikaner und Lecha County Freyheits=Freund.

Baltimore. Johann T. Hanzsche.
Der Americanische Teutsche Hausfreund und Baltimore Calender. Auf
das Jahr . . 1823.
* Marylandische Teutsche Zeitung.
    Mentioned in *Reading Adler* of March 12.

Canton, Stark Co., O. Eduard Schäffer.
* Der Westliche Beobachter.

Chambersburg. F. W. Schöpflin.
* Der Redliche Registrator.

Easton. Christian J. Hütter.
Tagebuch des drei und dreißigsten Hauses der Repräsentanten der Republik
Pennsylvanien.

Easton. H. u. W. Hütter.

Der Northampton Bauern Calender auf das Jahr 1823.

* Der Northampton Correspondent.

Ephrata. Joseph Baumann.

(Böhm). Ein Systematischer Auszug aus des Gottseligen und Hoch=
erleuchteten deutschen Theosophi Jacob Böhmens
Sämmtlichen Schriften u. s. w. Erste Auflage. Erster Theil.
12mo. 395 S.

Germantown. M. Billmeyer.

Erbauliche Lieder=Sammlung, zum Gottesdienstlichen gebrauch in den
Vereinigten Evangelisch=Lutherischen Gemeinen in Pennsylvanien 2c.
16mo. 627 S. u. Reg. Kurze Andachten einer Gottsuchenden Seele
2c. 23 S.

Das Neue Testament unsers Herrn und Heilandes Jesu-Christi. Neunte
Auflage. 12mo. 537 S. u. Reg.

Der Hoch=Deutsche Americanische Calender. Auf das Jahr Christi 1823.

Hanover, York Co. D. P. Lange.

* Die Hanover Gazette.

Hägerstaun. J. Gruber u. D. May.

Der neue Nord=Americanische Stadt und Land Calender. Auf das Jahr
. . 1823.

Gruber and May published also an English almanac "in the German
style".

Harrisburg. J. S. Wiestling.

Schabalie, Joh. Philipp. Die Wandlende Seele. 12mo. 454 S.

* Die Harrisburger Morgenröthe.

Harrisburg. (?) Henry C. Martthen.

Tagebuch des Senats der Republik Pennsylvanien. 1821—1822.

Harrisburg. William White u. Co.

* Der Unabhängige Beobachter.

According to Dr. Wm. H. Egle (Hist. of Dauphin and Lebanon Counties)
William White issued the first number of this paper May 22, 1822 and
continued it with varying success eight or ten years. Among its editors are
mentioned Rev. Dr. E. W. Hutter and Capt. Jacob Baab.

Lancaster. Johann Bär.

Felbinger, Jeremias. Christliches Hand=Büchlein. Mack, Alex.
Rechte und Ordnungen des Hauses Gottes. Gruber, E. L. Grund=
forschende Fragen, nebst Antworten von einem Aufrichtigen Mitglied
der Gemeinde zu Wittgenstein (Alexander Mack.) 12mo. 128 S.,
99 S., 40 S.

See 1774.

Das letzte Bekenntniß von John Lechler.

* Der Volksfreund.

Lancaster. William Albrecht.

Der Gemeinnützige Landwirthschafts=Calender. Auf das Jahr 1823.

* Der Americanische Staatsbothe.

Lancaster, Ohio.

* Der Ohio Adler.

Libanon. Joseph Hartmann.

* Der Unpartheyische Berichter.

Philadelphia. Conrad Zentler.

Gesänge bei der Antrittsrede des Ehrw. C. R. Demme. 12mo. 8 S.

Rev. C. R. Deme (1785—1863) was minister of Zion's Congregation in Philadelphia from 1822—1859.

Americanischer Stadt und Land Calender auf das 1823ste Jahr Christi.

Reading. Carl A. Bruckman.

Goßler, J. C. Lebensgeschichte Napoleon Bonaparte's, des Ersten Kaisers der Franzosen. Vier Theile in einem Bande. Mit Kupfern. Gedruckt auf Kosten des Verfassers.

* Der Reabinger Postbothe.

Reading. Carl A. Bruckmann für M'Williams u. Comp.

Gott ist die reinste Liebe oder Morgen= und Abend=Opfer Bestehend in Auszügen aus Witschels und Eckartshausens Gebätbüchern. 12mo. 300 S.

Recommended by Lutheran and Reformed ministers of Pennsylvania. Witschel's prayers are in verse, those of Eckertshausen in prose.

Reading. Joh. Ritter & Co.

Charfreytags=Gedanken, Oder, Das Leiden Christi in Reimen gesetzt.

Lied eines Lehrers an seine Confirmanten, Oder Denkringlein.

Der Neue, Americanische Landwirthschafts=Calender. Auf das Jahr 1823.

* Der Reabinger Adler.

Reading. Heinrich B. Sage.

Das Herz des Menschen, ein Tempel Gottes oder eine Werkstätte Satans. In zehn Figuren sinnbildlich dargestellt. (Nachdruck). 12mo. 48 S.

* Der Weltbote.

Gudhus, who came to America in 1822 reports (*Meine Auswanderung*, II, p. 86) that there are two papers published in Reading the *Adler*, by *Ritter* and the *Weltbote*, by *Sage*. If this information is reliable Bruckman's Postbote had ceased to appear.

Reading. Auf Kosten des Verfaßers.

Gock, Carl. Die Vertheidigung der Freyen Kirche in Nord-Amerika. 12mo. 120 S.

    Against the establishment of theological seminaries.

Gock, Carl. Politische Ansicht und Fortsetzung der Vertheidigung der Freyen Kirche in Nord-Amerika. 12mo. 119 S.

Schellsburg, Bedford Co. Friedrich Goeb.

Der Westliche Menschenfreund und Schellsburger Calender auf das Jahr . . 1823. Unter diesem Titel zum ersten überhaupt aber zum siebentenmal herausgegeben.

York. Andreas Billmeyer.

* Der Wahre Republikaner.

Ohne Druckort.

Epistel und Weißagung Von Gott gesandt an die Gemeine und Einwohner in Amerika. Geschrieben in der Aufsicht Gottes 1794 durch den Trieb seines Geistes, nun aber neulich abgeschrieben im Jahre 1817. 8vo. 68 S.

1823.

Allentown. H. Ebner u. Comp.

Kurzer Inbegriff der Christlichen Lehre. 16mo. 26 S.

Milton, J. und F. Schwalbe. Neue Englische Sprachlehre oder gründliche Anweisung, die Englische Sprache auf eine neue Methode in kurzer Zeit ohne Lehrer zu lernen. 12mo. 188 S.

Der Neue Pennsylvanische Stadt und Land Calender. Auf das Jahr 1824.

* Der Friedensbothe und Lecha County Anzeiger.

Allentaun. Georg Hancke.

Tagebuch des Senats der Republik Pennsylvanien. 1822—1823.

Der Neue Allentauner Calender. Auf das Jahr 1824. Zum fünftenmal herausgegeben.

* Der Unabhängige Republikaner und Lecha County Freyheits-Freund.

Baltimore. Johann T. Hanzsche.

Das Buch Sirach in Deutscher und Englischer Sprache.

Der Amerikanische Teutsche Hausfreund und Baltimore Calender. Auf das Jahr . . 1824.

* Maryländische Teutsche Zeitung.

Canton, Stark County, O. Eduard Schäffer.

* Der Westliche Beobachter.

Chambersburg. F. W. Schöpflin.

Ribble, Samuel. Des Advocaten bester Rath „Halte dich frey vom Gesetz" oder der Rathgeber des Landmanns.

* Der Redliche Registrator.

Easton. Heinrich u. Wilhelm Hütter.

* Der Northampton Correspondent.

Tagebuch des vier und dreißigsten Hauses der Repräsentanten der Republik Pennsylvanien.

Der Northampton Bauern Calender auf das Jahr 1824. Zum sechsten mal herausgegeben.

Easton. Heinrich Held.

* Der Republicanische Bauer. Wöchentlich (Freitags) herausgegeben.

Germantown. M. Billmeyer.

Der Hoch=Deutsche Americanische Calender. Auf das Jahr Christi 1824.

Hägerstaun. J. Gruber u. D. May.

Der neue Nord=Americanische Stadt und Land Calender. Auf das Jahr . . 1824.

Hanover, York Co. D. P. Lange.

* Die Hanover Gazette.

Harrisburg. J. S. Wiestling.

* Die Harrisburger Morgenröthe.

Harrisburg. William White u. Co.

* Der Unabhängige Beobachter.

Lancaster. William Albrecht.

Der Gemeinnützige Landwirthschafts Calender. Auf das Jahr 1824.

* Der Americanische Staatsbothe.

Lancaster. Johann Bär.

Geistliches Blumen=Gärtlein inniger Seelen u. s. w. 16mo. 522 S.

* Der Volksfreund.

Lancaster, Ohio.

* Der Ohio Adler.

Libanon. Joseph Hartmann.

* Der Unpartheyische Berichter.

Orwigsburg, Pa. Heinrich Riehm.

* Die Freiheitspresse.

Philadelphia. Conrad Zentler.

Kaufmann, Peter. Betrachtung über den Menschen. 12mo. 244 S.

Zentler, Conrad. Eine Sammlung von Gesprächen und Redensarten in Deutsch und Englisch. 12mo. 228 S.

Americanischer Stadt und Land Calender auf das 1824ste Jahr Christi.

Philadelphia.

Das letzte Bekenntniß von Wm. Groß, welcher am 7ten März zu Philadelphia sein Leben am Galgen endete.

Advertised in the *Reading Adler*.

Reading. Carl A. Bruckman,

Goßler, J. C. Carl Gocks Verläumbungen oder die Rechtfertigung der hoch=deutschen Lutherischen und Reformirten Synoden von Nord=America. 12mo. 160 S.

A reply to Gock's Vertheidigung der freyen Kirche. See p. 218.

Eylert, Theodor. Schullehrer in Tulpehacon Township. Die Finsterniß in der Freyen Kirche von Amerika. 12mo. 36 S.

Die Constitution der Vereinigten Staaten von America mit ihren Verbesserungen und die der Republik Pennsylvanien, u. s. w. 12mo. 156 S.

* Der Readinger Postbothe.

Was perhaps published a few years longer.

Reading. Johann Ritter u. Comp.

Der Kleine Reformirte Katechismus.

Der Neue, Americanische Landwirthschafts Calender. Auf das Jahr 1824. Von Carl Friedrich Egelmann.

* Der Readinger Adler.

York, Pa. Heinrich C. Neinstadt.

Woltersdorf, E. G. Sämmtliche Lieder oder Evangelische Psalmen, welche bisher sowohl einzeln, als auch in kleinen Sammlungen herausgekommen, zum Theil aber noch ungedruckt geblieben und nun auf Begehren in eine vollständige Sammlung gebracht sind. Erste Americanische Auflage. 12mo. 452 S.

Ernst Gottlieb Woltersdorf was a minister in Bunzlau, Bohemia.

York. Andreas Billmeyer.

* Der Wahre Republikaner.

1824.

Allentaun. Heinrich Ebner u. Comp.

Der Neue Pennsylvanische Stadt= und Land=Calender. Auf das Jahr 1825.

* Der Friedensbothe und Lecha County Anzeiger.

Allentaun. Carl L. Hütter.

* Der Unabhängige Republikaner und Lecha County Freyheits=Freund.

George Hancke died in February and Carl L. Hütter resumed the management of the paper in June.

Baltimore. Johann T. Hanzsche.

Der Amerikanische Teutsche Hausfreund und Baltimore Calender. Auf das Jahr . . 1805.

* Maryländische Teutsche Zeitung.

Carlisle. Heinrich E. Marthens.

Das Pennsylvanische Deutsche Buchstabir und Lesebuch. 12mo. 130 S.

Carlisle. Moser u. Peters.

Das Neue Testament. Mit 12 Bildern. 511 S.

Chambersburg. F. W. Schöpflin.

* Der Redliche Registrator.

Easton. H. Held.

Der Mitleidige Samariter. Eine Beschreibung von der Mode, auf welche eine Arzeney zusammengesetzt und gebraucht werden muß um die Würkungen eines Wüthenden Hundsbisses oder die Hydrophobia Einhalt zu thun. 12mo. 25 S.

The cure of hydrophobia described here is the one recommended and applied by Wm. Stoy, who came to America 1752 and combined preaching with the practice of medicine.

* Der Republikanische Bauer.

Easton. H. u. W. Hütter.

Tagebuch des fünf und dreißigsten Hauses der Repräsentanten der Republik Pennsylvanien.

William Turners Wörterbuch der Englischen und deutschen Sprache.

Announced in Reading Adler.

Der Northampton Bauern Calender auf das Jahr 1825.

* Der Northampton Correspondent.

Ephrata. Joseph Bauman.

Der Zweyte Theil des systematischen Auszuges aus des gottseligen und hocherleuchteten deutschen Theosophen Jacob Böhmens sämmtlichen Schriften. 12mo. 267 S.

Germantown. M. Billmeyer.

Der Hoch=Deutsche Americanische Calender. Auf das Jahr Christi 1825.
36 S.

Hägerstaun. J. Gruber u. D. May.

Der neue Nord=Americanische Stadt uud Land Calender. Auf das Jahr
. . 1825.

Hanover, York Co. D. P. Lange.

* Die Hanover Gazette.

Hanover, York Co. Joseph Schmuck u. Dr. Peter Müller.

* Das Hanover Intelligenzblatt.

Harrisburg. C. Gleim.

Tagebuch des Senats der Republik Pennsylvanien. 1823—1824.

Harrisburg. Wilhelm Wheit.

Wißler, Johann. Das Hoch=Deutsche Pennsylvanische A. B. C.=
und Buchstabir=Büchlein. 16mo. 67 S.

Das Kleine Davidische Psalterspiel.

* Der Unabhängige Beobachter.

Harrisburg. J. S. Wiestling.

* Die Harrisburger Morgenröthe.

Lancaster. William Albrecht.

Der Gemeinnützige Landwirthschafts Calender auf das Jahr 1825. 36 S.

* Der Americanische Staatsbothe.

Lancaster. Johann Bär.

* Der Volksfreund.

Lancaster.

Schmidt. Daniel. Das Allgemeine A. B. C. Buchstabir= und
Lesebuch. Illustrirt. Erste Auflage. 12mo. 96 S.

Lancaster, Ohio.

* Der Ohio Adler.

Libanon. Joseph Hartmann.

* Der Unpartheyische Berichter.

Orwigsburg, Berks Co., Pa. Heinrich Riehm.

* Die Freyheitspresse.

Philadelphia. Conrad Zentler.

Betrachtung über den Menschen. 12mo. 244 S.

Americanischer Stadt und Land Calender auf das 1825ste Jahr Christi.

Reading. Johann Ritter.

Villee, H. W. Der Bauer als Landmesser oder die Practische Feld=
messerkunst. 12mo. 155 S.

> A treatise on Plain and Solid Geometry and Surveying. The author
> lived at Spang's Iron Works, Oley, Berks Co. The book contains a list of
> subscribers.

Der Neue, Americanische Landwirthschafts=Calender. Auf das Jahr . .
1825.

Karte von Berks County, angefertigt vom verstorbenen Heinrich Reichert.

Reading. Johann Schneider.

* Der Readinger Adler.

> Karl A. Kessler, Ritter's partner died in October 1823.

Reading u. Philadelphia. J. E. Goßler.

Readinger Magazin für Freunde der deutschen Literatur in Amerika.
Eine Monatsschrift, enthaltend: Aufsätze aus dem Gebiet der Religion,
Natur, Kunst, Laune und Phantasie. Herausgegeben von J. E.
Goßler, Reading und Philadelphia. (Beim Schlusse der letzten
Nummer heißt es: Mit diesem Hefte endigt der erste Jahrgang des
Readinger Magazins, das unter verändertem Titel in Philadelphia
fortgesetzt worden wird.) 8vo. 297 S.   G. S.

York. Andreas Billmeyer.

* Der Wahre Republikaner.

York.

* Die York Gazette.

> Mentioned in the *Reading Adler* July 13th.

Druckort unbekannt.

Das Bekenntniß von B. Stewart am 4. Februar 1824 in Harrisburg
hingerichtet.

1825.

Allentaun. Heinrich Ebner.

Der Neue Pennsylvanische Stadt= und Land=Calender. Auf das Jahr
1826.

* Der Friedensbothe und Lecha County Anzeiger.

Allentown. Carl. L. Hütter.

* Der Unabhängige Republikaner und Lecha County Freyheits=Freund.

Baltimore. Johann T. Hanzsche.

Der Amerikanische Teutsche Hausfreund und Baltimore Calender. Auf
das Jahr . . 1826.

* Märyländische Teutsche Zeitung.

Canton, O. Heinrich Kurtz.

* Der Friedensbote von Concordia. Fortsetzung des Wiedergefundenen
Paradieses der Menschen.

See Pittsburg *infra.*

Canton, Stark Co. Eduard Schäffer.

* Der Westliche Beobachter.

Carlisle. Moses u. Peters.

Mayer, Ludwig. Eintritts Rede gehalten in Gegenwart der Verwalter
über die Deutsche Reformirte Theologische Schulanstalt in Carlisle,
Pa. wie auch der Facultät und der Verwalter der Dickinson hohen
Schule daselbst. Von Ludwig Mayer, Professor in besagter Anstalt.
8vo. 16 S.

> In 1824 the Synod of the Reformed Church convened at Bedford, Pa.,
> sanctioned an arrangement with the trustees of Dickinson College in Carlisle
> for the establishment of a Theological Seminary in Carlisle. The College
> was to furnish suitable rooms for the use of the Seminary and in return to
> receive the services of the Professor of Theology of the Seminary as teacher
> of History and German Literature in the College. Rev. L. Meyer was
> elected to fill both chairs. The arrangement proved unsatisfactory and in
> 1829 the Seminary was removed to York.

Stark, Joh. Fr. Tägliches Hand=Buch in guten und bösen Tagen.
Mit fünf Bildern. 8vo. 382 S.

—— —— Tägliches Gebet=Büchlein für Schwangere, Gebärende und
Sechswöchnerinnen. 8vo. 88 S.

Carlisle. H. E. Marthen.

Tagebuch des Senats der Republik Pennsylvanien. 1824—1825.

Chambersburg, Pa. F. W. Schöpflin.

* Der Redliche Registrator.

Easton. H. u. W. Hütter.

Tagebuch des sechs und dreißigsten Hauses der Repräsentanten der Republik
Pennsylvanien.

Der Northampton Bauern Calender auf das Jahr 1826.

* Der Northampton Correspondent.

Ephrata. Joseph Bauman.

Sangmeister, E. Das Leben und der Wandel des in Gott ruhenden
und seligen Bruders Ezechiel Sangmeisters. Von ihm selbst beschrieben in sechs Theilen. Erster Theil. 8vo. 96 S.

Sangmeister, E. Dieses Folgende ist der zweite Theil und der
Anfang meiner armen Lebensbeschreibung. Zweiter Theil. 8vo.
158 S.

Henry Sangmeister (he called himself brother Ezechiel upon entering the Ephrata cloister) was born in Hornberg, Prussia, 1724 and came to America in 1743. After sowing his wild oats he felt conscience-stricken and was induced to join the Ephrata brethren in 1748. Much disgusted with his experience he secretly left his refuge in company of his friend Anton Höllenthal and settled in the Shenandoah valley, where other non-descripts of both sexes associated with him. He revisited Ephrata several times and finally came back to stay in 1764. He died about 1785 and left concealed behind the wainscoting of his room an autobiography which was accidentally discovered in 1825. About one half of it was printed by J. Bauman in four parts, published in 1825—1827. The rest Bauman offered to print if a sufficient number of subscribers were found to cover him against loss. The book is very scarce. It has been said that nearly all copies were designedly destroyed on account of the scandalous charges made against Conrad Beissel and other inmates of the cloister.

Landis, David. Das Güldene A. B. C. für Jedermann, der gern mit Ehren wollt bestahn. 12mo. 250 S.

D. Landis was a Dunker who differed from his brethren in holding peculiar mystical views on abstruse subjects of religion, which he illustrates by charts. Verses beginning with the successive letters of the alphabet and arranged in two sets, contain precepts on Christian duty and life. The prose is mainly made up of controversial correspondence.

Ein neu Trauer-Lied Wie man vernommen, Von einem Menschen der nach seinem Tod ist wiederkommen. Gedruckt für Jacob Schweitzer bey J. Bauman in Ephrata. 16mo. 8 S.

Dell, Wm. Das reine und Lautere Evangelium. 24mo. 82 S.

Germantown. M. Billmeyer.
Der Hoch-Deutsche Americanische Calender. Auf das Jahr Christi 1825. 36 S.

The Christian's Duty, in a Series of Hymns collected from various authors. Fourth Edition.

Dunker hymn-book.

Hägerstaun. J. Gruber & D. May.
Der neue Nord-Americanische Stadt und Land Calender. Auf das Jahr . .. 1826.

Hanover, York Co. D. P. Lange.
* Die Hanover Gazette.

Hanover, York Co. Joseph Schmuck u. Dr. Peter Müller.
* Das Hanover Intelligenzblatt.

According to information from A. L. Fisher, Esq. in York, this paper was removed to Adams County.

Harrisburg. J. S. Wiestling.
* Härrisburger Morgenröthe.

Harrisburg. William White u. Co.
* Der Unabhängige Beobachter.

Lancaſter. William Albrecht.

Der Gemeinnützige Landwirthſchafts=Calender. Auf das Jahr 1826.
36 S.

* Der Americaniſche Staatsbothe.

Lancaſter. Johann Bär.

Der Kleine Catechismus des ſel. Dr. Martin Luthers, u. ſ. w. 16mo.
122 S.

Weitenkampf, Joh. Fr. Vernünftige Troſtgründe bey den Trau=
rigen Schickſalen der Menſchen. 12mo. 221 S. u. Regiſter.
>Reprint. The original appeared in Germany 1758.

* Der Volksfreund.

Lancaſter, Ohio.

* Der Ohio Adler.

Libanon. Joseph Hartman.

* Der Unpartheyiſche Berichter.

Orwigsburg, Berks Co., Pa. H. Riehm.

* Die Freiheitspreſſe.

Philadelphia. Johann Georg Ritter.

Bedenklichkeiten über den Plan zur Vereinigung der deutſchen Ev.=Lutheri=
ſchen Gemeinen in und bey Philadelphia. Auf Koſten der Geſell=
ſchaft zur Beförderung des Deutſchen Gottesdienſtes gedruckt
und den Gliedern der Evangeliſch=Lutheriſchen deutſchen St. Michaelis=
und Zions=Gemeinde zur Einſicht und Warnung übergeben. 8vo.
20 S.

Demme, C. R. Die letzte Ehre des chriſtlichen Predigers zur Gedächt=
niß=Feier des Paſtors J. H. C. Helmuth. 12mo. 23 S.
>Rev. J. H. C. Helmuth, b. 1745, came 1769 to America and accepted
a call to the Lutheran church in Lancaster. In 1779 he became Pastor of
Zion's Church in Philadelphia, which office he filled 40 years. He died
February 5th 1825.

* Amerikaniſcher Correſpondent für das In= und Ausland. (11 x 9.)
Motto: O Freyheit: erkämpft mit dem Schwerte des Ruhms, wer
bein ſich nicht freut, von hinnen mit bem!
>Johann Georg Ritter was born 1772 in Schwäbish Gmünd, Würtemberg.
At the death of his father, a bookseller and printer, in 1795, he undertook
the management of the inherited business, which he pushed with much
energy. He published a large number of books, also artistic works and a
periodical (*National Chronik der Deutschen*) which was suppressed by Napoleon.
After 33 years of active life in business, dissatisfaction with the political
condition of Germany induced him to emigrate to America. In 1825 he
arrived in Philadelphia with a complete printer's outfit and large stock of
books. He established himself 263 (O. N.) N. Second Street, as printer,
bookseller and importer of books. He died April 26, 1840. An interesting

sketch of his life by Mr. H. A. Rattermann will be found in the *Deutsche Pionier*, xiv, p. 468—474.

The *Americanische Correspondent*, published twice a week, was at the beginning edited by Dr. Wm. Schmidt and subsequently by Mr. J. C. Gossler. With it begins the revival of the German newspaper press in Philadelphia which, it would appear, had been dormant for about ten years.

Philadelphia. Conrad Zentler.

Americanifcher Stadt und Land Calender auf das 1826ste Jahr Chrifti.

Pittsburg. F. J. Cope u. Comp.

* Das Wiedergefundene Paradies. Kein Gedicht. Eine Zeitfchrift für Chriften aller Benennungen. Herausgegeben von Heinrich Kurtz, Prediger. 12mo. 216 S.

A religious monthly devoted to the improvement of man and society. The editor, a Dunker, proposed to establish a German colony on the basis of Christianity, absolute equality of all members and communism. An outline of a constitution for such a "Christian Industrial Society" to be called Concordia, was published 1826 in the March number of his Monthly.

Reading. Johann Ritter.

Der Neue Americanifche Landwirthfchafts=Calender. Auf das Jahr . . 1826.

Reading. Johann Schneider.

* Der Reabinger Adler.

Sumnytown, Montg. Co. C. Royer.

* Der Advocat und Montgomery County Anzeiger.

York.

* Die York Gazette.

York. Andreas Billmeyer.

* Der Wahre Republifaner.

1826.

Allentown. Henrich Ebner & Comp.

Probft, Joh. Aug. Die Wiedervereinigung der Lutheraner und Reformirten. Mit einer Vorrede von Joh. Conrad Jäger, Ev. Pred. zu Allentown. 12mo. xix, 172 S.

Der Neue Pennfylvanifche Stadt= und Land=Calender. Auf das Jahr . . 1827.

* Der Friedensbothe und Lecha County Anzeiger.

Allentown. Carl L. Hütter.

* Der Unabhängige Republifaner und Lecha County Freyheits=Freund.

Baltimore. Johann T. Hanzsche.

Der Amerikanische Teutsche Hausfreund und Baltimore Calender. Auf das Jahr . . 1827.

* Märylänbische Teutsche Zeitung.

Cambridge, Mass. Hillard u. Metcalf.

(Follen, C.) Deutsches Lesebuch für Anfänger. 12mo. 252 S.

Charles Follen, b. at Giessen 1796, like his brothers an enthusiastic exponent of liberal principles and on that account persecuted, arrived in America 1824, received 1825 an appointment as Professor of German in Harvard University, became afterwards Unitarian minister, and lost his life on the Sound steamer Lexington which was burned February 13, 1840.

Canton, Ohio. Eduard Schäffer.

* Der Westliche Beobachter.

During this year Schäffer moved to Germantown, Ohio, where he resumed for a short time printing and publishing. After his departure from Canton Johann Sala procured a press and types and revived the *Westliche Beobachter*. (From information of Mr. Rattermann).

Carlisle. Moser u. Peters.

Das gemeinnützige Haus=Arzeneybuch. Aus den nützlichsten Schriften zusammen gestellt von Daniel Schmidt. 12mo. 164. S. u. Reg.

Das Neue Testament. Sechste mit Stereotypen gedruckte Auflage. 12mo. 211 S.

Carlisle. H. C. Marthen.

Tagebuch des Senats der Republik Pennsylvanien. 1825—1826.

Chambersburg. Heinrich Ruby.

* Der Redliche Registrator.

(Richard, History of Franklin County.)

Cincinnati, Ohio.

* Die Ohio Chronik.

Mentioned in G. Körner's *Deutsches Element*, p. 182, as the first German paper of Cincinnati. It did not last long.

Easton. Heinrich Held.

(Reich, Joh. Chr. Fr.) Beschäftigung des Herzens mit Gott in den Morgen= und Abendstunden. 12mo. 251 S.

A reprint.

Easton. Heinrich u. Wilhelm Hütter.

* Der Northampton Correspondent.

Easton. Hütter u. Müller.

Tagebuch des sieben und dreißigsten Hauses der Repräsentanten der Republik Pennsylvanien.

Ephrata. Joseph Baumann.

Sangmeister, E. Dieses Folgende ist der dritte Theil meiner armen und elenden Lebensbeschreibung. 8vo. 88 S.

  See 1825.

Germantown. M. Billmeyer.

Der Kleine Katechismus u. s. w. Elfte Auflage. 16mo. 127 S.

Erbauliche Lieder=Sammlung, zum Gottesdienstlichen Gebrauch in den Ev.=Lutherischen Gemeinen in Pennsylvanien und benachbarten Staaten. Achte Auflage. 12mo. 463 S., Reg. u. Anhang.

Der Hoch=Deutsche Americanische Calender. Auf das Jahr Christi 1827.

Germantaun, Ohio. Eduard Schäffer.

* Die National=Zeitung der Deutschen.

  Mr. Rattermann of Cincinnati transcribes the following passage from the *Westliche Beobachter* of November 15, 1826: Wir haben die erste Nummer einer deutschen Zeitung empfangen, betitelt: „Die National Zeitung der Deutschen", herausgegeben von Herrn Eduard Schäffer, zu Germantaun, Montgomery County, Ohio. Sein Ansehn ist respectable und wir wünschen dem Herausgeber die beste Unterstützung in diesem schwierigen Geschäft.

Hägerstaun. J. Gruber u. D. May.

Volksfreund und Hägerstauner Calender. Auf das Jahr . . 1827.

Hanover, York Co. D. P. Lange.

* Die Hanover Gazette.

Harrisburg. J. S. Wiestling.

* Die Harrisburger Morgenröthe.

Harrisburg. W. Wheit u. Co.

Büchlein des Hans Frumann, welcher von Himmel und Hölle zeuget, und die Gotteslästerer vor der heißen Hölle treulich warnet. 16mo. 45 S.   H. S.

  Other editions of this book were noticed under the years 1803 and 1815.

Hübner, Johann. Zweymal zwey und funfzig auserlesene Biblische Historien aus dem Alten und Neuen Testamente, versehen mit 104 Kupferstichen. Erste Americanische Auflage. 12mo. 335 S. u. Register.

  Contains a list of subscribers.

* Der Unabhängige Beobachter.

Lancaster. William Albrecht.

Der Gemeinnützige Landwirthschafts Calender. Auf das Jahr 1827.

Lancaſter. Baab u. Billee.

* Der Lancaſter Adler.

> There was a proposal printed in 1826, signed by Friedrich List, for the publication of a German Monthly to be called: Der Lancaſter Adler. F. List, the famous advocate of protection and of railroads, was at that time in America and it would, therefore, be of much interest to have more light shed on the origin of the Lancaſter Adler, which, by the way, supported the Democratic party.

Lancaſter. Johann Bär.

Der Pſalter des Königs und Propheten Davids. 16mo. 252 S.

* Der Volksfreund.

Lancaſter. Joſeph Ehrenfried.

* Der Chriſtliche Hausfreund. 4to. 208 S.   G. S.

> The first number of this short lived Monthly appeared April 1, 1826. the last March 1, 1827.

Lancaſter, Ohio.

* Der Ohio Adler.

Libanon, Pa. Joſeph Hartmann.

* Pennſylvaniſcher Beobachter. Ein republikaniſches Volksblatt der Bürger von Libanon= und den benachbarten Counties. (18 x 11).

> A continuation of the *Unpartheyiſche Berichter* and hence counted as the 19th Jahrgang.

Oeconomy, Beaver County, Pa.

Krauſe, K. H. Lehrbuch der deutſchen Sprache für Schulen. Erſter Theil. Sprachunterricht über einfache Sätze. Erſte Amerikaniſche Auflage. 12mo. 78 S.

Orwigsburg, Berks Co. H. Riehm.

* Die Freiheitspreſſe.

Osnaburgh, O. Heinrich Kurtz.

Die Kleine Liederſammlung der Kinder Gottes. 24mo. 206 S.

> Collection of Hymns, principally for Dunkers.

Philadelphia. Johann Georg Ritter.

Abhandlung über die Rechenkunſt oder Practiſche Arithmetik. Geſamelt, überſetzt und herausgegeben von Enos Benner. 12mo. vi, 162 S.

Das Neue Teſtament u. ſ. w. Mit ſtehenden Lettern. 12mo. 304 S.

> Probably printed in Germany.

* Amerikaniſcher Correſpondent für das In= und Ausland.

> The paper had regular subscribers in New York.

Philadelphia. **Conrad Zentler.**

A Catalogue of the books belonging to the Incorporated German
  Society. 12mo. 28 pp.   G. S.

> The Library of the German Society was instituted in 1817.

Americanischer Stadt und Land Calender auf das 1827ste Jahr Christi.

Philadelphia.

Karsten, J. H. M. D.   Von der Nothwendigkeit geschickter Hebammen.

Nöthige Aufklärung in Betreff der Röbelsheim'schen und Streit'schen
  Legate, deren Nutzanwendung bisher, nach dem Willen der sel. Stifter
  zum Besten deutscher Lutherischen Gemeinen in Pennsylvanien, der
  Corporation der deutschen Lutherischen St. Michaelis= und Zions=
  Gemeine zu Philadelphia übertragen gewesen; deren Vertheilung
  jedoch einige Glieder der Ehrw. Luth. Synode von Pennsylvanien
  sich, obwohl vergeblich, bemüht haben, in ihre Hände zu bekommen.
  12mo. 16 S.

Pittsburg.

* Stern des Westens.

> G. Körner in *Das Deutsche Element in den Ver. Staaten*, p. 45, states, that
> this paper was published 1826—1829 and supported A. Jackson.

Pittsburg.   F. J. Cope.

* Das Wiedergefundene Paradies, herausgegeben von Heinrich Kurtz,
  Prediger.

> See 1825. Said to have been continued in Canton, Ohio, under the title:
> Der Friedensbote.

Reading.   Johann Ritter.

Der Neue, Americanische Landwirthschafts=Calender. Auf das Jahr . .
  1827.

Reading.   Johann Schneider.

* Der Reabinger Adler.

Reading.   Jeremiah Schneider u. Samuel Myers.

* Der Reabinger Democrat.

> The first number of this paper was issued October 4, 1826. It was
> published for several years by Schneider and Myers and then passed into
> the hands of Daniel Rhoads who conducted it till 1833.

Reading.

Gulbin, J. C.   Betrachtungen und Gebete. 8vo. 320 S.

York, York Co.

* Die York Gazette.

York.   Andreas Billmeyer.

* Der Wahre Republikaner.

1827.

Allentown. Heinrich Ebner.

Goßner, Joh. Der Weg zur Seligkeit.

Loosungen und Lehrterte der Brüdergemeinde.

Der Neue Pennsylvanische Stadt und Land Calender. Auf das Jahr
1828.

* Der Friedensbothe und Lecha County Anzeiger.

Allentown. Carl L. Hütter.

* Der Unabhängige Republikaner und Lecha County Freyheits=Freund.

Allentown. John D. Roney.

* Der Lecha Patriot.

Baltimore. Johann T. Hanzsche.

Der Americanische Teutsche Hausfreund und Baltimore Calender. Auf
das Jahr . . 1828.

* Märyländische Teutsche Zeitung.

Canton, Stark Co., O. Johann Sala.

* Der Westliche Beobachter.

Carlisle.

* Magazin der beutsch=reformirten Kirche, herausgegeben von Dr. L.
Mayer. Erstes Heft. November 1827.

Chambersburg. Timotheus Evans.

The Economy of Human Life.—Haushaltungskunst des Menschlichen
Lebens. Englisch und Deutsch. 12mo. 264 S.

Chambersburg. Heinrich Ruby.

* Der Redliche Registrator. (?)

Doylestown, Bucks Co. Manassah K. Snyder.

* Bucks County Expreß und Allgemeiner Anzeiger.

> Mr. Snyder who had been at work in the office of the *Reading Adler* was
> urged to establish a German paper in Doylestown. He bought a complete
> outfit of materials for a printing office and commenced the publication of
> the *Bucks County Express* July 4, 1827. Two years later he became also
> the proprietor of the *Democrat and Farmers Gazette.* (Davis, History of
> Bucks Co., p. 817.)

Easton. H. Held.

Kurtz, H. Gott ist die Liebe, eine Predigt.

Easton. Heinrich u. Wilhelm Hütter.

Verhandlungen der deutschen Evangel. Lutherischen Synode von Penn=
sylvanien, gehalten zu Easton 1827. 12mo. 20 S.

* Der Northampton Correspondent.

Easton. Hütter u. Müller.

Tagebuch des acht und dreißigsten Hauses der Repräsentanten der Republik Pennsylvanien.

Easton. Jacob Weygandt, Jr. u. Samuel Innes.

* Republicanische Presse.

First number issued February 15th.

Ephrata. Jos. Bauman.

Die Kleine Lieder Sammlung oder Auszug aus dem Psalterspiel der Kinder Zions. 24mo. 216 S.

Sangmeister, E. Folgendes ist der Vierte Theil von meinem armen Lebens=Lauf. Nimmt seinen Anfang im Jahr 1766. 8vo. 72 S.

At the close of this part the publisher announces that no more of Sangmeister's Life will be printed unless subscriptions warrant the issue of the remainder, about one half of the whole. The unpublished part of the manuscript appears to have been destroyed.

Germantown. M. Billmeyer.

Der Hoch=Deutsche Americanische Calender. Auf das Jahr Christi 1828.

Germantown, Ohio. Eduard Schäffer.

* Die National=Zeitung der Deutschen.

Hägerstaun. J. Gruber u. D. May.

Volksfreund und Hägerstauner Calender. Auf das Jahr 1828.

Hanover, York Co. D. P. Lange.

* Die Hanover Gazette.

Harrisburg. Wm. Boyer u. J. Baab.

Arndt, Johann. Wahres Christenthum. Mit 63 schönen sinn= bildlichen Stichen. Samt den Parabies=Gärtlein.

* Harrisburger Morgenröthe und Dauphin und Cumberland Counties Anzeiger.

After November 3d the name of Wm. Boyer is omitted.

Harrisburg. Moser u. Peters.

Kirchen=Ordnung der Reformirten Kirche in den Ver. Staaten von N. A. durch eine von der Synode dazu bestimmten Committee aufgesucht und zur Annehmung vorzuschlagen. 12mo. 30 S.

Harrisburg. Wm. White u. Co.

* Der Unabhängige Beobachter.

Wm. White died October 30, 1827. His name appears to have been continued in the firm.

Harrisburg. Johann S. Wiestling.

Thornton J. Die Buße, erklärt und anbefohlen. Ein ernstlicher Ruf an das Gewissen eines jeden Menschen. 12mo. 256 S.

Lancaster. William Albrecht.

Der Gemeinnützige Landwirthschafts=Calender. Auf das Jahr 1828.

Lancaster. Johann Bär.

Herr, Johannes. Erläuterungs=Spiegel, Oder Eine gründliche Erklärung von der Bergpredigt unseres Herrn Jesu Christi. 12mo. 394 S.

* Der Volkfreund.

Lancaster.

Grosch, David. Der Lebenslauf von T. Jefferson und J. Adams.

Dated: Earl Township, probably and printed in Lancaster.

* Der Lancaster Adler.

Lancaster, Ohio.

* Der Ohio Adler.

Libanon, Pa. Joseph Hartmann.

* Pennsylvanischer Beobachter.

Kurzgefaßter Bericht des Mordes, Verhörs und Betragens des James Quinn u. s. w., hingerichtet für die Ermordung seiner Gattin Babby Quinn.

Libanon. Johann u. Joseph Miller.

* Der Libanon Demokrat.

An Anti-Masonic paper.

Oekonomie, Beaver County im Staat Pennsylvanien.

Harmonisches Gesangbuch, theils von andern Authoren, theils neu verfaßt. Zum Gebrauch für Singen und Musik für Alte und Junge. Nach Geschmack und Umständen zu wählen gewidmet. 12mo. 403 S. u. Reg.

This songbook printed for Rapp's colony at Economy, Beaver County, Pa., is quite rare and curious. The style of the hymns is sentimental, florid and tinged with mysticism. The allegorical "Sophia" is addressed with all the warmth of a lover. Not a few hymns of Ephrata origin have found admission. The appendix contains songs dwelling on the beauties of nature, the seasons, friendship etc. This cannot be the same hymnbook which the Duke of Saxe-Weimar alludes to in his *Journey through North America*, vol. II, p. 111, for he visited Economy in May 1826, while the *Harmonische Gesangbuch* did not appear till 1827. What the Duke says of the offensive features of some of the hymns applies also to those published in the later book.

Orwigsburg.

* Die Freiheitspresse.

Philadelphia. Johann Georg Ritter.

* Amerikanischer Correspondent für das In= und Ausland.
> See 1825.

Philadelphia. Conrad Zentler.

Zuschrift der Verwalter der Bibelgesellschaft von Philadelphia an die Einwohner des Staates Pennsylvanien. 16 S.

Americanischer Stadt und Land Calender auf das 1828ste Jahr Christi.

Pittsburg.

* Stern des Westens.

Pottstown. U. F. Schrader.

* Montgomery County Adler. Erster Jahrgang.

Reading. Johann Ritter & Comp.

Der Neue Americanische Landwirthschafts=Calender. Auf das Jahr . . 1828.

* Der Readinger Adler.
> Johann Ritter associated himself in the beginning of the year with a son of Carl Kessler, who had formerly been Ritter's partner.

Reading. G. Adolf Sage.

Gemeinschaftliches Gesangbuch zum Gebrauch der Lutherischen und Refor= mirten Gemeinden in Nord=America. Aufs neue durchgesehen. 12mo. 344 S. u. Reg.
> Identical with the Baltimore edition of 1817.

Reading. Schneider u. Meyers.

Habermanns Christliches Gebetbüchlein. 16mo. 157 S.

Tagebuch des Senats der Republik Pennsylvanien. 1826—1827.

* Der Readinger Democrat.

Shellsburg. Friederich Goeb.

Eine Sammlung von Neuen Recepten und bewährten Curen für Menschen und Vieh. 12mo. 40 S.

Somerset.

* Der Republikaner.
> Mentioned in the *Reading Adler* of December 4th.

York, York Co.

* Die York Gazette.

York. Andreas Billmeyer.

* Der Wahre Republikaner.

1828.

Allentown. Henrich Ebner u. Comp.

Probst, Johann August. Die Wiedervereinigung der Lutherischen und Reformirten. Ein faßliches Lesebuch. 12mo. 172 S,

Der Neue Pennsylvanische Stadt- und Land-Calender. Auf das Jahr . . 1829.

* Der Friedensbothe und Lecha County Anzeiger.

Allentown. Carl L. Hütter.

* Der Unabhängige Republikaner und Lecha County Freyheits-Freund.

Allentown. John D. Roney.

* Der Lecha Patriot.

Baltimore. Johann T. Hanzsche.

Kurzgefaßte Anweisung über die Anlegung von Weinbergen; die Behandlung des Mostes und des Weines und andere dahin gehörigen Gegenständen mit besonderer Rücksicht auf die V. St. Von einem praktischen teutschen Weingärtner.

Der Amerikanische Teutsche Hausfreund und Baltimore Calender. Auf das Jahr . . 1829.

* Märyländische Teutsche Zeitung.

> Number 361 of January 30, 1828, is in possession of a son of the publisher. How much longer the paper was issued, has not been ascertained.

Canton, Ohio. Johann Sola u. Salomon Sala.

* Der Westliche Beobachter.

Carlisle.

* Magazin der deutsch-reformirten Kirche, herausgegeben von Dr. L. Mayer.

> Was removed to York in 1829.

Chambersburg. Heinrich Ruby.

* Der Redliche Registrator. (?)

Doylestown, Bucks County. Mannasseh H. Snyder.

* Bucks County Expreß und Allgemeiner Anzeiger.

Easton. Heinrich u. Wilhelm Hütter.

* Der Northampton Correspondent.

Easton. Jacob Weygandt, Jr. u. Samuel Innes.

* Republicanische Presse.

Ephrata. Joseph Bauman.

Der Sichere Himmels-Weg oder Anleitung zum Christenthum. Von August Hermann Francke, ehemaligem Prediger in Halle. Dritte Amerikanische Auflage. Zum drittenmal befördert von Jacob Schweizer. 12mo. 36 S.

Germania.

Gemeinschaftliches Gesangbuch zum Gottesdienstlichen Gebrauch der Lutherischen und Reformirten Gemeinden in Nord-Amerika. 12mo. 364 S.

Title from Zahm's Catalogue.

Germantown. M. Billmeyer.

Das neue und verbesserte Gesangbuch, u. s. w. für die Ev. Reformirten Gemeinen in den Ver. Staaten von America. 6te Auflage. 16mo. 95 u. 422 S. nebst Reg.

Edition in small size and small print. See 1799.

Der Hoch-Deutsche Americanische Calender. Auf das Jahr Christi 1829.

Germantown, Ohio. Eduard Schäffer.

* Die National-Zeitung der Deutschen.

Greensburg, Westmoreland Co. F. A. Cope.

* Der Stern des Westens.

"At one time there were two newspapers published in the German language in Greensburg, one was published by F. A. Cope about 1828 in connection with the Gazette. This was subsequently published by John Armbrust. It was called in German *The Star of the West.* The other was published by Jacob G. Stark in connection with the Argus." History of Westmoreland County. See Pittsburg 1825 and 1826.

Hägerstaun, Md. J. Gruber u. D. May.

Volksfreund und Hägerstauner Calender. Auf das Jahr . . 1829.

Hanover, York Co. D. P. Lange.

* Die Hanover Gazette.

Harrisburg. Jacob Baab.

Ettinger, Adam. Der König-Saul. 8vo. 75 S.

Bunyan, Johann. Eines Christen Reise nach der seligen Ewigkeit. 12mo. 158 S.

* Harrisburger Morgenröthe und Dauphin und Cumberland Counties Anzeiger.

Harrisburg. J. S. Wiestling.

Doddrige, D. Philipp. Anfang und Fortgang Wahrer Gottselig-keit in der menschlichen Seele. 8vo. 392 S. u. Reg.

* Der Unabhängige Beobachter.

Harrisburg. Wm. Wheit.

Franke, A. H. Der sichere Himmelsweg oder Einleitung zum Christen-thum. Zweite Americanische Auflage, befördert von Jacob Schweitzer.

Harrisburg. Gustav S. Peters.

Lochman, Johann Georg. Hinterlaſſene Predigten von Johann Georg Lochman. Zum Druck befördert von Auguſt H. Lochman A. M. 12mo. 332 S.

> Geo. Lochman, b. in Philadelphia 1773, received a University scholarship from the German Society and his preparation for the Lutheran pulpit from Rev. Dr. Helmuth. He accepted a call to Lebanon in 1794 and to Harrisburg in 1815. Died July 10, 1826.

Lancaſter. William Albrecht.

Der Gemeinnützige Landwirthſchafts=Calender. Auf das Jahr 1829.

Lancaſter. Joh. Bär.

Bunyan, Joh. Der Himmliſche Wandersmann oder eine Beſchreibung vom Menſchen, der in Himmel kommt. 16mo. 68 S.

Guion, J. M. B. de la Mothe. Die Heilige Liebe Gottes und die Unheilige Naturliebe nach ihren unterſchiedenen Wirkungen. Mit Kupferſtichen. Ueberſetzt aus dem Franzöſiſchen von G. T. St. (Terſteegen). 12mo. 360 S.

> A reprint of Tersteegen's translation which appeared 1751 in Mühlheim.

* Der Volksfreund.

Lancaſter. Benjamin Grimler.

* Der Wahre Americaner.

> According to History of Lancaster County, p. 502, the publication of this paper was resumed in 1828.

Lancaſter. H. W. Villee.

Fiſk, F. Die Vergnügungen der Sünde. Rede gehalten im Capitol zu Waſhington. 8vo. 18 S.

Poetiſcher Himmelsweg, zuſammen getragen von Daniel Hertz. 12mo. 295 S.

* Der Lancaſter Adler.

Lancaſter, Ohio.

* Der Ohio Adler.

Libanon. Johann u. Joſeph Miller.

* Der Libanon Demokrat.

Libanon, Pa. Joſeph Hartmann.

* Pennſylvaniſcher Beobachter.

Libanon. Jacob Stöver.

Tagebuch des Senats der Republik Pennſylvanien. 1827—1828.

Philadelphia. Kimber u. Sharpleß.

Biblia, das iſt: die ganze Heilige Schrift des Alten und Neuen Teſtaments. 4to. 932 S.

Philadelphia. Georg W. Mentz.

Die Bibel oder die ganze Heilige Schrift alten und neuen Testaments. Nach Dr. Martin Luther's Uebersetzung. Stereotypirt von J. Howe, Philadelphia. 8vo. 828 u. 269 S.

Bachmair, J. J. A Complete German Grammar containing the theory of the language through all the parts of speech. 12mo. 144 pp.

Philadelphia. J. G. Ritter.

Das Neue Testament u. s. w. Neue Auflage. 12mo. 541 S.

> Probably printed in Germany, but not the same book as the edition of 1826.

* Amerikanischer Correspondent für das In= und Ausland.

> See 1825.

Philadelphia. Conrad Zentler.

Americanischer Stadt und Land Calender auf das 1829ste Jahr Christi.

Philadelphia. (Laodicea.)

Der Schlüssel zur Offenbahrung von Jesus Christus selbst aufgeschlossen und entsiegelt. Philadelphia, d. 12. August 1825. Laodiceae, gedruckt im Jahr Christi 1828. 12mo. 54 S.

> It is possible that the word "Philadelphia" on the title page is used in its mystic sense. But the book was unquestionably printed in Pennsylvania.

Pittsburg, Pa. G. Dietz.

* Pittsburger Beobachter.

Pottstown, Montgomery Co., Pa. Slemmer u. Benner.

* Der Bauern=Freund. Jahrgang 1.

> The first number appeared August 6th.

Princeton, N. J. D. A. Borrenstein.

Das Neue Testament unseres Herrn und Heilands Jesu Christi. 8vo. 269 S.

> Printed from stereotype plates made by J. Howe in Philadelphia. No German printing establishment appears to have existed in New Jersey at that time.

Reading. Johann Ritter u. Comp.

Handbuch für Deutsche; Formen zu Handschriften u. s. w. Nebst allerley Formen der englischen Sprache, Interessen=Tabellen u. s. w. Zweyte verbesserte Auflage. 12mo. 108 S.

Das Neue Testament.

Der Schulpsalter. Vierte Auflage.

Der Neue, Americanische Landwirthschafts=Calender. Auf das Jahr . . 1829.

* Der Readinger Adler.

Reading. Heinrich B. Sage.

Fischer, Gust. Aug. Adolph, Arzt. Eine Rede von dem Daseyn eines Gottes, des Urhebers des Weltalls. 12mo. vii u. 57 S.

The preface is dated from Landesburg, Perry County 1822.

Reading. G. Adolph Sage.

Recht, J. S. Der verbesserte praktische Weinbau in Gärten und vorzüglich auf Weinbergen. Mit einer Anweisung den Wein ohne Presse zu keltern. Mit 2 Kupfertafeln. Den amerikanischen Weinbauern gewidmet von Heinrich B. Sage. 12mo. 84 S.

The editor (H. B. Sage) who on a journey through Germany had become acquainted with the author, strongly recommends the introduction of viniculture in America.

Reading. Schneider u. Myers.

Tagebuch des nenn und dreißigsten Hauses der Repräsentanten der Republik Pennsylvanien.

* Der Reabinger Democrat.

Somerset, Someset Co.

*Der Republikaner.

Waterloo. *William Child.*

Erlaeuterung der Frey-Maurerey wie beschrieben von Capt. William Morgan nebst einem Schluessel zu den Geheimnissen des hoehern Ordens. Von einem Frey-Maurer. 8vo. 96 S.

Translated from the English. The Anti-Mason wave reached also the German population.

York, York Co. Andreas Billmeyer.

* Der Wahre Republikaner.

York, York Co. Samuel Wagner.

* Der Republikanische Herald.

York, York Co.

* Die York Gazette.

* Die Evangelische Zeitung. Herausgegeben von Ehrw. J. H. Dreyer.

Druckort ungenannt.

Eine Geschichte der That-Sachen und Umstände, die Entführung und vermuthete Ermordung des William Morgan betreffend. 12mo. 80 S.

1829.

Allentown. Heinrich Ebner u. Comp.

Nützliche und erbauliche Anrede an die Jugend von der Wahren Buße vom seligmachenden Glauben u. s. w. Zum drittenmal herausgegeben. 12mo. 96 S.

Der Neue Pennſylvaniſche Stadt= und Land=Calender. Auf das Jahr
1830.

* Der Friedensbothe und Lecha County Anzeiger.

Allentown. Carl L. Hütter.

* Der Unabhängige Republikaner und Lecha County Freyheits=Freund.

Allentaun. John D. Roney,
(ober Alexander Miller.)

* Der Lecha Patriot.

Baltimore. Johann T. Hanzſche.

Der Amerikaniſche Teutſche Hausfreund und Baltimore Calender. Auf
das Jahr . . 1830.

* Maryländiſche Teutſche Zeitung.

Canton, Ohio. Johann Sala.

* Der Weſtliche Beobachter.

During 1829 the name of this paper was changed to *Vaterlandsfreund und
Geist der Zeit.* (H. A. Rattermann).

Chambersburg. Heinrich Ruby.

* Der Redliche Regiſtrator. (?)

Ruby and Hartney started in August 1829 a new paper by the name:

* Chambersburg Correſpondent und Allgemeiner Volksberichter der Deut=
ſchen in Franklin und benachbarten Counties.

Doylestown, Pa. Manaſſeh H. Snyder.

* Bucks County Expreß und Allgemeiner Anzeiger.

Easton. Heinrich u. Wilhelm Hütter.

* Der Northampton Correſpondent.

Easton. Jacob Weygandt, Jr. u. Samuel Innes.

* Republicaniſche Preſſe.

Germania.

Das Kleine Davidiſche Pſalterſpiel. Fünfte verbeſſerte Auflage. 8vo.
510 S.

Die Kleine Harfe. 48 S.

Germantown. M. Billmeyer.

Erbauliche Liederſammlung zum Gottesdienſtlichen Gebrauch in den
Vereinigten Evangeliſch=Lutheriſchen Gemeinen in Pennſylvanien und
den benachbarten Staaten. Die Siebente Auflage. 12mo. 626 S.
. u. Regiſter.

Der Hoch=Deutſche Americaniſche Calender. Auf das Jahr Chriſti 1830.

Germantown, O. Eduard Schäffer.

* Die National=Zeitung der Deutschen.

    See 1827.

Hägerstaun, Md. J. Gruber u. D. May.

Der Volksfreund und Hägerstauner Calender. Auf das Jahr . . 1830.

Hanover, York Co. D. P. Lange.

* Die Hanover Gazette.

Harrisburg. Jacob Baab.

Habermanns Christliches Gebetbüchlein. 16mo. 153 S.

Tagebuch des vierzigsten Hauses der Repräsentanten der Republik Penn= sylvanien.

* Harrisburger Morgenröthe und Dauphin und Cumberland Counties Anzeiger.

Harrisburg. Wm. White u. Co.

* Der Unabhängige Beobachter.

    Wm. White died October 30, 1827.

Kutztown, Pa.

* Kutztauner Herold.

Lancaster. William Albrecht.

Der Gemeinnützige Landwirthschafts Calender. Auf das Jahr 1830.

Lancaster. Johann Bär.

Unpartheyisches Gesang=Buch, Enthaltend Geistreiche Lieder und Psalmen zum allgemeinen Gebrauch des Wahren Gottesdienstes. 4te Auflage. 12mo. 483 S. u. Reg.

    Mennonite Hymnbook.

* Der Volksfreund.

Lancaster. L. Grimler.

* Der Wahre Amerikaner.

Lancaster. H. W. Villee.

Die deutsche Theologie, ein edles Büchlein vom rechten Vorstande, mit D. Luther's und Arnd's Vorreden. 12mo. 159 S.

Schmidt, Daniel. Gemeinnütziges Haus=Arzneybuch. Aus nützli= chen Schriften zusammengetragen. 2te Auflage. 12mo. 192 S.

* Der Lancaster Adler.

Lancaster, Ohio.

* Der Ohio Adler.

Libanon.

Reformirtes Gesangbuch, oder: Ein Auszug von 270 Lieder aus dem Reformirten Gesangbuch u. s. w. Erste Auflage. 24mo. 416 S.

Libanon, Pa. Joseph Hartmann.
* Pennsylvanischer Beobachter.

Libanon. Johann u. Joseph Miller.
* Der Libanon Demokrat.

Libanon. Jacob Stöver.
Tagebuch des Senats der Republik Pennsylvanien. 1828—1829.

Marietta, Lancaster Co. Penna. G. Grosch u. G. Meyers.
* Der Fröhliche Bothschafter und Vertheidiger der allgemeinen, oder Univer=
sal=Erlösung. Erster Band. 8vo. 192 S.

A German Monthly advocating the doctrine of the Universalists. The first number appeared in May 1829.

Neu=Berlin, Union Co., Pa. Joseph Miller.
* Anti=Freymaurer Advocat, und Freund des Freyen Volkes.

Pennsylvanien. Gedruckt für den Verfaßer.
Jörres, Ludwig. Die Freymaurerey, oder Offenbarung aller Geheim=
nisse, Ceremonien, Eides = Formeln, Handgriffe und Sinnbilder der
drei ersten Grade. Nach Morgan und andere Schriftstellern, u. s. w.
12mo. 164 S.

Philadelphia. Goßler u. Blumer.
* Amerikanischer Correspondent für das In= und Ausland. 5ter Jahrgang.

Evangelisches Magazin der Hochdeutschen Reformirten Kirche in den Ver=
Staaten von N. A. Herausgegeben von Ehrw. Samuel Helffenstein.
Erster Band. 290 S.

Philadelphia. Conrad Zentler.
Der Calender Eines Christen für das Jahr 1830. Herausgegeben von
dem Pennsylvanischen Zweig der Americanischen Tractat=Gesellschaft
und zu haben in der Niederlage an der Ecke der Vierten und Archstraße.

Americanischer Stadt und Land Calender auf das 1830ste Jahr Christi.

Pittsburg, Pa. G. Dietz.
* Pittsburger Beobachter.

Reading. Johann R. Christian.
* Der Pennsylvanische Anti=Freymaurer Calender. Für das Jahr unseres
Herrn und Heilandes 1830. 8vo. 48 S.

Reading. Joh. Ritter & Co.
Der Neue, Americanische Landwirthschafts=Calender. Auf das Jahr . .
1830.

* Der Readinger Adler.

Reading. [Jeremiah Schneider u. Samuel Myers.]

* Der Reabinger Democrat.

Somerset.

* Der Republikaner.

Sumnytown, Montgomery Co., Pa. Enos Benner.

* Der Bauern Freund.

> E. Benner bought the interest which Slemmer had in the *Bauernfreund* (started 1828 in Pottstown) and removed it to Sumnytown.

York, York Co. Samuel Wagner.

* Der Republikanische Herald.

York, York Co.

* Die York Gazette.

Die Evangelische Zeitung. Herausgegeben von Ehrw. J. H. Dreyer.

Druckort unbekannt.

Das Leben und letzte Bekenntniß von Georg Swearing, hingerichtet den 2. October 1829.

1830.

Allentown. Heinrich Ebner.

Der Neue Pennsylvanische Stadt= und Land=Calender. Auf das Jahr . . 1831.

* Der Friedensbothe und Lecha County Anzeiger.

Allentown. Carl L. Hütter.

* Der Unabhängige Republikaner und Lecha County Freyheits=Freund.

Allentown. Alexander Miller.

* Der Lecha Patriot. (?)

Baltimore. Johann T. Hanzsche.

Der Amerikanische Teutsche Hausfreund und Baltimore Calender. Auf das Jahr . . 1831.

Canton, Ohio. Johann Sala u. Solomon Sala.

* Vaterlandsfreund und Geist der Zeit.

Chambersburg. Ruby u. Hartney.

* Chambersburg Correspondent und Allgemeiner Volksberichter der Deut= schen von Franklin und den benachbarten Counties. Erster Jahrgang.

Cincinnati. Robinſon u. Fairbank.

Rupp, Daniel J. Geſchichte der Martyrer nach dem ſehr ausführ= lichen Original des Ehrw. Joh. Fox und Anderer. 8vo. 2 Theile. 266 u. 288 S.

Mr. Daniel I. Rupp, the father of Pennsylvania Local History, was born July 10, 1803 in Cumberland County, Pa., and died in Philadelphia May 31, 1883. His grandfather immigrated in 1751. While the bulk of his writings was done in English, Mr. Rupp occasionally brought out books in German.

Doyleſtown. Manaſſeh H. Snyder.

* Bucks County Expreß und Allgemeiner Anzeiger.

Eaſton. Chriſtian J. Hütter.

Tagebuch des Senats der Republik Pennſylvanien. 1829—1830.

Eaſton. Heinrich u. Wilhelm Hütter.

* Der Northampton Correſpondent.

Eaſton. Jacob Weygandt u. Samuel Innes.

* Republicaniſche Preſſe.

Was discontinued with the issue of February 5th.

Ephrata. Joſeph Baumann.

Ein Angriff auf das Afterreden oder die Verläumbung. 12mo. 44 S.

Germantown. M. Billmeyer.

Der Hoch=Deutſche Americaniſche Calender. Auf das Jahr Chriſti 1831.

Germantaun, O. Eduard Schäffer.

* Die National=Zeitung der Deutſchen.

Gettysburg. H. C. Neinſtedt.

Das Evangeliſche Magazin der Evangeliſch=Lutheriſchen Kirche in den Ver. St. von N. A.

Hägerſtaun. J. Gruber.

Der neue Nord=Americaniſche Stadt und Land Calender. Auf das Jahr . . 1831.

Hanover, York Co. D. P. Lange.

* Die Hanover Gazette.

Harrisburg. Jacob Baab.

Bericht der Committee über Mittel und Wege betreffend die Finanzen der Republik. 8vo. 12 S.

Eine Sammlung von Geiſtlichen, Lieblichen Liedern zum Gebrauch des Oeffentlichen und privat wahren Gottesdienſtes. 16mo. 366 S.

Tagebuch des ein und vierzigſten Hauſes der Repräſentanten der Republik Pennſylvanien.

Harrisburg. Gustav S. Peters.

Der Kleine Kempis oder kurze Sprüche und Gebätlein. 16mo. 256 S.

Das Neue Testament. Zehnte mit Stereotypen gedruckte Auflage. Mit 12 Bildern geziert. 12mo. 511 S.

Lindl, Ignaz. Der Kern des Christenthums. 16mo. 58 S.

Harrisburg. Joh. Weinbrenner.

Mead, M. Der entdeckte Beinahe Christ, oder der geprüfte und verworfene Bekenner. 12mo. 153 S.

Harrisburg. J. S. Wiestling.

* Die Harrisburger Morgenröthe.

Harrisburg. William White u. Co.

* Der Unabhängige Beobachter.

Harrisburg. J. u. F. Wyeth.

Das Neue Testament. 24mo. 472 S.

Lancaster. William Albrecht.

Der Gemeinnützige Landwirthschafts Calender. Auf das Jahr 1831.

Lancaster. Johann Bär.

Wynantz, W. Predigten über höchst wichtige Gegenstände des Christenthums. Antwort auf einige Fragen, oder Anweisung über die Meidung der Abfälligen, von Menno Simon. 12mo. 297 S.
Translated from the Dutch by David Zug, Mifflin Co., Pa.

Das Apokryphische Neue Testament. Eine Sammlung aller Evangelien, Episteln und anderer Schriften, welche in den ersten vier Jahrhunderten Jesu Christo, Seinen Aposteln und deren Gefährten zugeschrieben wurden und in dem eigentlichen Neuen Testament nicht enthalten sind. Erste Amerikanische Auflage. 12mo. 484 S.

* Der Volksfreund.

Lancaster. C. Grimler.

* Der Wahre Amerikaner.

Lancaster.

* Der Lancaster Adler.

Lancaster, Ohio.

* Der Ohio Adler.

Libanon. Joseph Hartmann.

Poetischer Himmels-Weg, oder Kleine, geistliche Lieder-Sammlung. Zusammengetragen von Daniel Hertz, Reformirter Prediger des Evangeliums in Lancaster County. 16mo. 286 S.

* Pennsylvanischer Beobachter.
The name of the paper was changed in 1837 to Der Wahre Demokrat.

Libanon. Gideon Schmidt und C. u. J. Licht.

Tersteegen, G. Kleine Perlenschnur für die Kleinen nur. 16mo. 322 S.

Libanon. Johann u. Joseph Miller.

* Der Libanon Demokrat.

Marietta, Lancaster Co., Penna. G. Grosch u. G. Meyers.

* Der Fröhliche Botschafter und Vertheidiger der allgemeinen, oder Universal Erlösung. Zweyter Band. 8vo. 192 S.

Neu-Berlin, Union Co. Joseph Miller.

Der Verborgene Arzt oder Nützliche Hausfreund; Ein neues System der Arzeney-Kunst. 12mo. 179 S.

Orwigsburg, Berks Co. Thoma u. May.

Stürr, John. (Organist und Schullehrer an der Zionskirche in in Windsor Taunship, Berks County). Ueber den Zustand der Seele nach dem Tode bis zur Auferweckung ihres Körpers. 16mo.

Philadelphia. Goßler u. Blumer.

Wilmsen, F. P. Der Deutsche Kinderfreund, ein Lesebuch für Volksschulen. Erste americanische Auflage nach der sechzigsten europäischen. Vermehrt mit geographischen Zusätzen und einer kurzen deutschen Sprachlehre für americanisch deutsche Volksschulen. Gedruckt auf Veranstaltung einer Committee der St. Michaelis u. Zions-Gemeinde. 12mo. 320 S.

Evangelisches Magazin der Hochdeutschen Reformirten Kirche. Hrsg. von Ehrw. Samuel Helffenstein.

* Philadelphischer Correspondent und allgemeiner Deutscher Anzeiger.

The paper appeared, like its predecessors semi-weekly. It was printed, but not owned by A. A. Blumer.

Philadelphia. G. W. Mentz.

Das Neue Testament. Stereotypirt.

Philadelphia. Mentz u. Rovoudt.

Das Kleine Davidische Psalterspiel der Kinder Zions.

Philadelphia. Conrad Zentler.

Americanischer Stadt und Land Calender auf das 1831ste Jahr Christi.

Der Calender eines Christen. Für das Jahr 1831.

Pittsburg, Pa. G. Dietz.

* Pittsburger Beobachter.

Reading.   Johann Ritter u. Comp.

Walz, E. L.   Lutherischer Prediger in Hamburg, Berks County. Voll=
ständige Erklärung des Calenders mit einem fastlichen Unterricht über
die Himmelskörper. 12mo. 315 S.

Der Neue, Americanische Landwirthschafts Calender. Auf das Jahr
1831. Von Carl Friedrich Egelmann.

* Der Reabinger Adler.

Reading.   Schneider u. Myers.

* Reabinger Democrat und Anti=Freimaurer Herold.

Selins Grove.   Amos Stroh.

Mead, Matthew.   Der Beinahe ein Christ entdeckt: Oder: Der
irrige Religions=Bekenner geprüft und verworfen. Aus dem Engli=
schen übersetzt von Daniel Weiser. 8vo. xxxvi, 192 S.

Somerset.

* Somerset Republicaner.   (?)

Sumnytown, Montgomery Co.   Enos Benner.

Erläuterung für Caspar Schwenkfeld und die Zugethane seiner Lehre.
Zweyte Auflage. 12mo. 507 S.

* Der Bauern=Freund.

The paper was published in Sumnytown till 1858, when Mr. A. Kneule
bought it. He removed it to Pennsburg where he still edits it, being
probably the oldest German publisher living.

York, York Co.

* Die York Gazette.

* Magazin der deutsch=reformirten Kirche.

York, York Co.   Samuel Wagner.

* Der Republikanische Herold.

Druckort unbekannt.

Wilhelm zur Megede.   Sammlung vorzüglicher Stücke aus den
beliebtesten neueren deutschen Dichtern.

Recommended by H. A. Muhlenberg in the *Reading Adler* of July 27th.

ADDENDA.

P. 6. The second title on p. 6 was taken from the *Chronicon Ephratense*, p. 35, which appears to assign the publication of the book to the year 1728. After a part of the present volume had gone through the press, the writer discovered a copy (the only one so far known to exist) in the collection of Mr Henry Heilman in Lebanon. The book turns out to be a Franklin print of 1730, similar in appearance to the *Göttliche Liebes und Lobesgethöne* of the same year. Its correct title is as follows:

Mystische und sehr geheyme Sprueche, welche in der Himlischen
    schule des heiligen geistes erlernet. Und dan folgens, einige
    Poetische Gedichte. Auffgesetzt den liebhabern und schülern
    der Göttlichen und Himmlischen weiszheit zum dienst. Vor
    die säu dieser welt aber, haben wir keine speise, werden ihnen
    auch wohl ein verschlossener garden und versiegelter brunnen
    bleiben. Philadelphia. Gedruckt bey Benjamin Franklin,
    1730. 12mo. 32 pp.

The *Mystische und sehr geheyme Sprüche* count up to 99 and fill p. 3—p. 14.

The collection of Mr. Heilman also contains a set of small paste board cards with lines of religious poetry printed on one side. They fit in a case after the manner of *Der Frommen Lotterie*, first issued by Christopher Saur in 1744, but are smaller than the latter. The import and tone of the poetry leave no doubt that they are of Ephrata origin.

P. 168.
Reading. Gottlob Jungmann. 1806.
Ein Ausführlicher Bericht von Capitain Gere, welcher den Schooner Little
Pätty befehligte, der am 21. August, zur See scheuterte. Nebst einem
Anhang einer überaus Sanberbaren Erscheinung, welche sich am letzten
31. July, in Nord-Carolina zugetragen hat. 12mo. 18 S.

P. 187.
Baltimore. Gedruckt für Fielbing Lucas, Jr. 1813.
Das Neue Testament unsers Herrn und Heilandes Jesu Christi nach der
Deutschen Uebersetzung D. Martin Luthers. 12mo. 587 S. u. Reg.

Allentown, Pa. Christian J. Hütter, 1810. Carl L. Hütter, 1811—1828. Joseph Ehrenfried, 1812—1816: Heinrich Ebner & Co., 1817—1830. Georg Hancke, 1820—1823. John D. Roney, 1827—1828.

Baltimore, Md. Samuel Saur, 1795—1808 (?). George Keating, 1796. Christian Cleim, 1808—1809. Magill & Cleim, 1810—1811. Wm. Warner, 1814—1818. Schäffer & Maund, 1816—1820. Johann T. Hanzsche, 1821—1830.

Cambridge, Mass. Hillard & Metcalf, 1826.

Canton, Ohio. E. Schäffer, 1821—1826. Heinrich Kurtz, 1825. Johann & Solomon Sala, 1827—1830.

Carlisle, Pa. Friedrich Sanno, 1808—1813. H. W. Petersen, 1820—1821. Moser & Peters, 1824—1826. Heinrich E. Marthens, 1822—1826.

Chambersburg, Pa. Johann Herschberger, 1809—1813. Friedrich Wilhelm Schöpflin, 1813—1826. Heinrich Ruby, 1826—1828. Timotheus Evans, 1827. Ruby & Hartney, 1829—1830.

Chesnuthill, Phila. Nicholas Hasselbach, 1763. Samuel Saur, 1790—1794.

Cincinnati, O. Office of Liberty Hall, 1807. Publishers of the *Ohio Chronik*, 1826. Robinson & Fairbank, 1830.

Doylestown, Pa. Simeon Siegfried, 1820. Manasseh H. Snyder, 1827—1830.

Easton, Pa. Jacob Weygandt, 1793—1809. Christian J. Hütter, 1802—1830. J. Weygand & Sohn, 1798—1804. Samuel Longcope, 1804. Heinrich & Wilhelm Hütter, 1821—1830. H. Held, 1823—1827. Jacob Weygandt, Jr. & Samuel Innes, 1828—1830.

---

* The dates of this summary agree with those of the foregoing bibliographical record, and may, upon fuller information, require in many instances a correction of the time limits.

Ephrata, Lancaster Co., Pa. Brüderschaft, 1745—1786. J. Georg Zeissiger, 1763. A. C. Reben. 1771. Ephrata, (without printer's name) 1786—1793. Solomon Meyer, 1794—1797. Joseph Bauman, 1800—1830. Bauman & Cleim, 1804. Jacob Ruth, 1811—1812. Jacob Pfauz, 1817.

Friedensthal, near Bethlehem, Pa. Johann Brandmüller, 1763—1767.

· **Friedrichstadt, (Frederick) Md.** Matthias Bärtgis, 1779— 1809. C. T. Melsheimer, 1811. M. Bärtgis. 1821.

˙ **Germantown, Phila.** Christoph Saur, I., 1738—1756. Christoph Saur, II., 1756—1777. Christoph Saur & Sohn, 1776. Christoph Saur, Jr., III., 1776. Christoph & Peter Saur, 1777 —1778. Leibert & Billmeyer, 1784—1787. Michael Billmeyer, 1787—1814. Peter Leibert, (Leibert & Sohn) 1788—1796. Michael Billmeyer, 1819—1830.

Germantown, Ohio. Eduard Schäffer, 1826—1830

Gettysburg, Pa. H. C. Neinstedt, 1830.

Hagerstown, Md. Johann Gruber, 1795—1810. Jacob D. Dietrich, 1806. Gruber & May, 1811—1830.

Halifax, N. S. Anton Henrich, 1787—1790.

Hamburg, Berks Co., Pa. 1810.

Hanover, York Co., Pa. H. Willcocks, 1793. Stellingius & Lepper, 1797—1805. Lange & Stark, 1805—1815. D. P. Lange, 1816—1830. Joseph Schmuck & Dr. Peter Müller, 1824 —1825.

Harrisburg, Pa. Benjamin Mayer & Conrad Fahnestock, 1794—1799. (?) Benjamin Mayer, 1800—1809. Gleim & Wiestling, 1811—1820. J. S. Wiestling, 1820—1830. John Wyeth, 1821—1830. Wm. White & Comp., 1822—1830. C. Gleim, 1824. Wm. Boyer & J. Baab, 1827. J. Baab, 1827—1830. Moses & Peters, 1827. Gustav S. Peters, 1829—1830.

Harrisonburg, Va. Laurentz R. Wartmann, 1816—1818.

Kutztown, Pa. Publisher of the *Herold*, 1829.

Lancaster, Pa. H. Müller & S. Holland, 1752. S. Holland, 1753. Francis Bailey, 1774—1784. Matthias Bärtgis, 1776—1777. Theophilus Cossart, 1778—1782. Jacob Bailey, 1784—1790. Stiemer, Albrecht & Lahn, 1787. Albrecht & Lahn, 1787—1790. Albrecht & Comp. 1790—1799. Wm. & Robert Dickson, 1796. Christian Jacob Hütter, 1799—1802. Johann Albrecht, 1800—1806. Georg & Peter Albrecht,

1806—1808. Heinrich & Benjamin Grimler, 1804—1814. Hamilton, Albrecht & Ehrenfried, 1809. Hamilton & Ehrenfried, 1808—1810. W. Hamilton & Comp., 1810—1817. Johann Ehrenfried, 1810—1817. Anton Albrecht, 1800—1819. Benjamin Grimler, 1815—1830. S. Kling & J. Bär, 1817. Johann Bär, 1818—1830. William Albrecht, 1820—1830. Baab & Villee, 1826—1830. Joseph Ehrenfried, 1826—1827. H. W. Villee, 1829.

Lancaster, Ohio. Carpenter & Green, and their successors, 1807—1830. Eduard Schäffer, 1816.

Lebanon, Pa. Jocob Schnee, 1799—1816. Jacob Stöver, 1809—1829. H. B. Sage, 1809—1810. Joseph Hartmann, 1816—1830. Johann & Joseph Miller, 1827—1830.

Marietta, Lancaster Co., Pa. G. Grosch & G. Meyers, 1829.

Neu Berlin, Union Co., Pa. Solomon Miller & H. Niebel,. 1818. Joseph Miller, 1829—1830.

Neu Market, Va. Ambrosius & Solomon Henkel, 1808—1819.

New York. (?) E. Schäffer, 1819.

Norristown, Pa. David Sower, 1807—1812.

Oeconomie, Beaver Co., Pa. 1826—1827.

Orwigsburg, Pa. Heinrich Riehm, 1823—1827. Thoma & May, 1830.

Osnaburgh, Ohio. Heinrich Kurtz, 1826.

Philadelphia. Andrew Bradford, 1728—1742. Benjamin Franklin, 1730—1742, 1751—1752. Isaias Warner, 1742. I. Warner & Cornelia Bradford, 1743. Joseph Crellius, 1743—1746. Gotthard Armbrüster, 1747—1748. Johann Böhm, 1748. Franklin & Böhm, 1749—1751. Anton Armbrüster, 1753—1755. B. Franklin & A. Armbrüster, 1755—1757. A. Armbrüster, 1758. P. Miller & L. Weiss, (Miller & Comp. Teutsche Buchdruckerei) 1759—1762. Henrich Miller, 1760—1779. A. Armbrüster & Nicholas Hasselbach, 1762. A. Armbrüster, 1763—1767. Melchior Steiner & Carl Cist, 1776—1781. Christoph (III.) & Peter Saur, 1777—1778. Johann Dunlap, 1778—1783. Carl Cist, 1781—1805. Melchior Steiner 1781—1791. Joseph Crukshank, 1782. Klein & Reynolds, 1784. Jacob Zeller, 1791. Steiner & Kämmerer, 1792—1797. Wm. Woodhouse, 1792. Samuel Saur, 1794. Heinrich Kämmerer, 1796. Neal & Kämmerer, 1796. Heinrich & J. R. Kämmerer, 1797—1798. Heinrich Schweitzer, 1798—1810. Joseph R.

Kämmerer & G. Helmbold, Jr., 1799. Helmboldt & Geyer,
1800—1803. Johann Geyer, 1804—1811. Carl Cist's Wittwe,
1805—1806. Conrad Zentler, 1807—1830. Joseph Forster,
1805—1806. Johnson & Warner, 1809. Jacob Meyer, 1810—
1812. Zentler & Blake, 1813. Georg & Daniel Billmeyer, 1814
—1818. James Stackhouse, 1814. Kimber & Sharpless, 1816—
1828. Georg W. Mentz, 1813—1830. Philipp Hagel, 1818—
1819. Johann Georg Ritter, 1825—1828. Gossler & Blumer,
1829—1830. Mentz & Rovoudt, 1830.

Pittsburg, Pa. F. J. Cope, 1825—1826. Publishers of *Stern
des Westens*, 1826—1828. G. Dietz, 1828—1830.

Pottstown, Pa. U. F. Schrader, 1827. Slemmer & Benner,
1828.

Princeton, N. J. D. A. Borrenstein, 1828. (Probably a
bookdealer, who had his name put on the title page of a New
Testament stereotyped in Philadelphia.)

Reading, Pa. Johnson, Barton & Jungmann, 1789. Barton
& Jungmann, 1790—1792. Jungmann & Gruber, 1793—1796.
Schneider & Comp., 1796—1802. Gottlob Jungmann & Comp.,
1797—1803. Schneider & Ritter, 1802—1804. Johann Ritter &
Comp., 1804—1830. Jungmann & Bruckmann, 1804. Gottlob
Jungmann, 1805—1807. Gottlob & J. E. Jungmann, 1808—1816.
H. B. Sage, 1810—1828. C. A. Bruckmann, 1816—1823.
Charles M'Williams, 1820. Johann Schneider, 1824—1826.
Jeremiah Schneider & Samuel Myers, 1826—1830. G. A Sage,
1827—1828. Johann R. Christian, 1829.

Reading & Philadelphia. J. E. Gossler, 1824.

Schellsburg, Bedford Co., Pa. Friedrich Goeb, 1814—1827.

Selins Grove, Pa. Amos Stroh, 1830.

Somerset, Somerset Co., Pa. Friedrich Goeb, 1806—1817.
Publishers of the *Republikaner*, 1827—1830.

Staunton, Va. Eagle Office, 1808.

Sumnytown, Montgomery Co., Pa. C. Royer, 1825. Enos
Benner, 1829—1830.

Waterloo, Pa. William Child, 1828.

Winchester, Va. Jacob D. Dietrichs, 1805.

York, Pa. Solomon Meyer, 1796—1803. Andreas Billmeyer, 1799-1828. Christian Schlichting, 1803-1804. Schlichting & Billmeyer, 1805—1806. Heinrich C. Neinstedt, 1823.
William Wagner, 1828—1830. C. Cline, 1804. Moyer & Atkin-
son, 1804.

Places of German Printing arranged in the order of first issues. *

1728 Philadelphia, Pa.	1809 Norristown, Pa.
1738 Germantown, (Philad'a).	1810 Allentown, Pa.
1745 Ephrata, Pa.	1810 Hamburg, Pa.
1752 Lancaster, Pa.	1811 New Market, Va.
1763 Chestnuthill, (Phila., Pa.)	1814 Schellsburg, Pa.
1763 Friedensthal, near Beth-	1816 Harrisonburg, Va.
lehem, Pa.	1818 Neu Berlin, Pa.
1776 Frederick City, Md.	1819 New York, N. Y.
1787 Halifax, N. S.	1820 Doylestown, Pa.
1789 Reading, Pa.	1821 Canton, O.
1793 Easton, Pa.	1823 Orwigsburg, Pa.
1793 Hanover, York Co., Pa.	1825 Pittsburg, Pa.
1794 Harrisburg, Pa.	1825 Sumnytown, Pa.
1795 Baltimore, Md.	1825 Cambridge, Mass.
1795 Hagerstown, Md.	1826 Germantown, O.
1796 York, Pa.	1826 Oeconomie, Beaver, Co., Pa.
1799 Lebanon, Pa.	1826 Osnaburgh, O.
1805 Winchester, Va.	1827 Pottstown, Pa.
1806 Somerset, Pa.	1828 Waterloo, Pa.
1807 Cincinnati, O.	1828 Princeton, N. J.
1807 Lancaster, O.	1829 Kutztown, Pa.
1808 Carlisle, Pa.	1829 Marietta, Pa.
1808 Staunton, Va.	1830 Selins Grove, Pa.
1809 Chambersburg, Pa.	1830 Gettysburg, Pa.

* Further information may lead to some changes of the order here given.